It wasn't immediately obvious that anything was wrong.

The door was ajar and he knew before he entered what he would find inside. . . . Someone had systematically gone through the cages, removed the animals, slit their throats with a razor, and dumped the bleeding bodies in the corner. Monkeys, ferrets, guinea pigs, white mice . . .

He closed the door and leaned against it for a moment. Somebody other than himself had known that French had isolated the agent; somebody other than himself had known that French had inoculated the animals. Hanson? But Hanson would hardly have destroyed the laboratory. It had to have been somebody else.

But who?

THE NIGHTMARE FACTOR

*Thomas N. Scortia
and
Frank M. Robinson*

BANTAM BOOKS
TORONTO · NEW YORK · LONDON

THE NIGHTMARE FACTOR

*A Bantam Book | published by arrangement with
Doubleday & Company, Inc.*

PRINTING HISTORY

*Doubleday edition published February 1978
2nd printing .... February 1978
Bantam edition | January 1979*

*Bantam Books are published by Bantam Books, Inc. Its trade-
mark, consisting of the words "Bantam Books" and the por-
trayal of a bantam, is Registered in U.S. Patent and Trademark
Office and in other countries. Marca Registrada. Bantam
Books, Inc., 666 Fifth Avenue, New York, New York 10019.*

PRINTED IN THE UNITED STATES OF AMERICA

For WALT LIEBSCHER,
a long-time friend and faithful reader—
of which there can never be too many.

THE
NIGHTMARE
FACTOR

1

IT WAS THE kind of November night that Sergeant Frank Borelli liked best—a wet one. Not only was the rain good for the farmers, it chased the muggers off the street and kept the pimps and hookers penned up in their hotel rooms.

He thought about the evening ahead with pleasure, shifting to a more comfortable position so his belly could push back against his seat belt. A night like tonight, he wouldn't even bitch about being CSTF—Crime Specific Task Force. Unlike other patrols, they weren't restricted to any one district; they could roam the city at will. *Well, rank has its privileges,* he thought.

The rain was sheeting so heavily now that their headlights penetrated it by little more than a man's length. The traffic, lighter than usual, moved at a crawl. Later in the evening, he promised himself, they'd patrol in the avenues and spend a few minutes watching the breakers pound seal rock just below the Cliff House. Come midnight, he'd let Kolbaum talk him into taking their dinner break at Hamburger Mary's in the Mission. There was a good barbecue rib and chicken spot in the Fillmore, but the silent resentment of the blacks always ruined his appetite.

He concentrated on the radio for a minute. Nothing but collisions. Things were relatively quiet now. The Sixth Street on-ramp swam into view and he nudged Kolbaum in the ribs. "Take the freeway over to Eighteenth, and we'll give the district the once-over and then hit the avenues."

1

Kolbaum was reluctant. "Nothing's going on in the avenues, Sergeant."

Borelli half-smiled. He couldn't think of a better reason for going there. Aloud he said, "On a rainy night, burglaries go up, Kolbaum. And they don't hit the factories out here, they hit the homes." He squinted at the oncoming traffic on the far side of the freeway, the headlights watery blurs in the darkness. Damn few people would be out tonight; if you lived at the bottom of a hill, your car would be up to its hubcaps in water runoff. It was definitely going to be a slow evening and about time, too. Last week had really been a pisser: three family fights, one knifing, and the old guy from Iowa who decided fifty bucks was too much to pay for one last fling. They got the pimp who shot him, but who would've thought an old man could bleed so much. . . .

He glanced over at Kolbaum, staring out at the gray slick in front of the windshield. It was hard for him to like Kolbaum. A year out of the Academy, new wife, new baby, crisp new uniform without a patch or darned spot, and no sense whatsoever. He'd have to bail Kolbaum out of a tight one some night, and the thought alone was enough to make him resentful. Never buy trouble. That was the one thing his old man had managed to teach him and it was the one thing he couldn't seem to get through Kolbaum's thick head. A smart cop handled trouble when it came to him; he didn't go looking for it.

"Something's up ahead."

Borelli blinked. A van was pulled over on the shoulder, but the driver hadn't set out any flares or lanterns. He leaned forward to peer through the downpour. Big van, pale blue, with two figures in white squatting by the left rear double wheel.

Jesus, what a night to have to change a flat. . . . Kolbaum parked two car lengths behind, cut the ignition, and started buttoning his slicker.

"Just give 'em the flares," Borelli grumbled. "We're not mechanics." He climbed out of the car, pulling the slicker tight around his neck so the rain wouldn't run down his back. Kolbaum brought up the rear. In the glare of their headlights, Borelli could make out the lettering: MEMORIAL BLOOD BANK OF SAN FRANCISCO on the back and sides of the van.

Kolbaum lit two flares and dropped them to block the outer lane, then two more closer to the rear of the van. "You guys want us to call for some help?" he asked.

It was the cheerfulness that got to Borelli. Where the hell did the kid get it anyway? He walked over, his hands jammed into the wet interior of the slicker's pockets. The man sweating over the lug nuts was older, dark-haired, and thin-faced, the type who ought to be working out of a Tenderloin hotel. The younger man beside him was light-haired with a wispy blond mustache. He looked up nervously as Borelli approached. There was something about the way the blond stared at him that triggered a warning bell in Borelli's mind. The man looked scared.

The van itself was perched precariously on a badly seated bumper jack, its shaft bowing dangerously. Borelli squatted down by the man changing the wheel. "Your jack's gonna go any minute. It could drop a ton of van on your hand." No answer. Borelli continued sarcastically: "Ever seen somebody get hit by a jack when it flipped loose?"

For the first time the man glanced up at Borelli. He looked annoyed. "No sweat."

Borelli straightened up. "Let it down, Mac, and we'll call a truck."

The younger man nervously plucked at his sleeve. "We can't spare the time, Officer—we're overdue right now."

Kolbaum unlimbered his flashlight. "Here, let me give you some light."

Borelli was disgusted. They had given him a goddamned Boy Scout for a partner; now they'd be there all night. He dropped back and beamed his own flashlight in one of the windows of the van. There wasn't much to see: two couches, some metal shelving, what looked like a small refrigerator and a number of waxed cardboard cartons, their sides marked with a red cross and dotted with beads of moisture. He'd given blood several times before and knew the boxes contained tightly sealed plastic bags filled with blood and packed in ice.

, The blond had followed him. "No dope." He forced a smile. "Just blood."

"Yeah," Borelli grunted. The man gave him the creeps. He started walking back to the patrol car and Kolbaum shouted, "I'll be through in a minute."

Borelli glanced back. "You're the one who volunteered, take your time. I'm just gonna run a ten twenty-eight." Then he noticed the look on the blond's face and added: "It's routine." But he should've kept his mouth shut, he thought.

Five minutes later, he wasn't so sure. The van was legitimate enough but the blood bank said it was two hours overdue. The tire might have held them up that long but he had the feeling the real answer might not be so simple. They were on the freeway going where? Daly City? South San Francisco? The blood bank was the other way. Something was definitely not kosher. Borelli started to sweat. He couldn't just get out and walk over with his pistol drawn; Kolbaum was between the two of them.

He got out of the car and shouted casually: "Hey, Marty—Flaherty wants to talk to you." It wasn't very clever and it didn't work. The dark-haired man glanced up, then suddenly knocked Kolbaum sprawling and bolted for the front of the van. The blond raced around to the back and climbed in while Borelli swore and tried to work his pistol free from the slicker. Then the engine roared into life and the van surged forward. The jack shot from beneath it, the shaft arrowing straight for Borelli.

Borelli dropped to the pavement and heard the jack strike the highway behind him. Kolbaum scrambled to his feet and ran toward him. They leaped into the patrol car and Kolbaum started the motor. Borelli flipped on the siren and grabbed the microphone from the dash to call in. Fifty feet ahead, the van suddenly made a U-turn and started back toward the on-ramp, against traffic. Borelli cursed silently. Kolbaum braked and muscled the wheel to follow. They missed one pair of oncoming headlights and by the time they straightened out, the van was half a block ahead, almost lost in the darkness and driving gusts of rain. Borelli saw only one oncoming set of headlights and breathed a silent thanks. The van was staying far to the right.

"They didn't have time to tighten the bolts," Kolbaum said tensely. "Look." Ahead of them the van was swaying badly, the outer left wheel wobbling.

"What the hell!" Borelli's jaw went slack. The van had rounded a curve to the right and for a moment the rear doors flapped open. In their headlights the blond man in the back of the van was slashing at the cardboard boxes with a knife. Jets of blood spurted from the wounded cartons, staining his lab coat and the walls of the van. Then the wind caught the doors and slammed them shut again, but a stream of red still trickled from under the door.

"We can't block him!" Kolbaum shouted. "The damn van's too heavy!" Then: "Where the hell's he going?" The van raced up a darkened cut-off to the right.

"That's no exit!" Borelli yelled. A moment later metal screeched against the side of the patrol car; then their wheels were spitting gravel. Three hundred feet ahead of them, the van abruptly vanished.

"Hit the brakes," Borelli screamed. "Hit the brakes!"

Kolbaum jammed on the brakes and twisted the wheel at the same time. The patrol car skidded sideways, turned a quarter circle, hit the guard rail, and slid to a stop, still pointing in the same direction.

Five feet in front, the freeway disappeared in the darkness.

Kolbaum was shaking. "I forgot."

"So did they." Ahead the freeway stopped in mid-air, just where the anti-Embarcadero Freeway referendum had left it years before. The van had crashed through the barrier at Sixth that blocked the southern lanes of the Embarcadero Freeway, which stopped abruptly at Third Street. Borelli found his flashlight on the floor and got out. For once the rain felt good on his sweaty face. He walked to the edge and looked over. The van had landed upright in the parking lot across Third Street. The roof was crumpled and Borelli guessed it had turned over at least once. Two wheels had been torn off and lay another fifty feet away.

Kolbaum looked down, then turned and started running back. "We can cross over just past Fifth." Borelli jogged after him, swearing. They could have driven back to the Mariposa off-ramp and taken the northern lanes back in less time than they could run it and with less effort. . . .

There was no sign of life in the van when they got there. "You cover," Borelli panted. Kolbaum dropped back and Borelli ducked low. He sidled up to the front of the van, listened, and then pulled open the driver's door. The light from his flashlight showed the steering wheel half-buried in the driver's chest. He stared for a moment, then, with revolver still drawn, walked around to the back. The rear doors were badly dented. He holstered his gun and tugged on one of the handles with both hands. The door came open with a screech. The blond tumbled limply out. There probably wasn't much point in calling an ambulance, Borelli thought. From the kid's twisted position, he guessed that the man's spine had probably been snapped in the crash.

Borelli knelt down to feel the pulse, then straightened up and swept the sprawled body with his flashlight. He caught his breath. The man's lab coat and pants were soaked with blood, his hair and mustache were thick with it. The swirling rain started to smear the red that covered the figure and Borelli flashed the light into the van's interior.

Blood was still trickling out and puddling on the asphalt. All of the cartons had been broken and slashed. Punctured plastic bags of blood were strewn along the floor or hanging limply from the metal shelves.

Behind him, Kolbaum said "Beat it!" in a faint voice. Borelli turned to see a rib-thin dog lapping at one of the watery pools of blood. Kolbaum was leaning against the side of the van, watching the dog. He started to gag.

Borelli felt disgusted. He turned back to the van, ignoring the unmistakable sounds that Kolbaum was now making. He stepped into the rear and poked at some of the bloody cartons with his flashlight. Why the hell had the blond been dumping the blood? And where the hell had they thought they were going when they took the cut-off? To East Bay? They couldn't have known the freeway system very well.

The rain was stronger now, lashing at Borelli's face and seeping down the inside of his slicker. He started to shiver.

2

"WE'RE HERE," the little man at the lectern said, "to talk about the last days of the last victim in the longest war in the history of the human race."

The speaker paused, and the rustling and coughing that had filled the auditorium abruptly stilled. Doohan smiled to himself. Espinosa was the most adept practitioner of the dramatic pause that he had ever met and Doohan had the scars to prove it. Five years before he had fallen prey to one of those pregnant pauses and had spent the next two years trudging around the backwaters of India and Bangladesh because of it.

He fumbled in his pocket for his briar pipe, then reluctantly put it back, even though he could see the pale tracery of smoke drifting over the back rows. One of the reporters, probably. Yanks. No respect for their own rules. The spicy smell of pipe smoke continued to tickle his nose and he thought sheepishly: Sour grapes. He'd give his bloody soul for some tobacco right now.

"Millions have died in that war," the little man continued in a dry, dramatic voice. "More millions than died in all the wars ever fought—victims of an enemy they couldn't even see." Pause. "Smallpox." Pause. "Ramses V suffered from it more than a thousand years before the birth of Christ. Its final victim died November eighth of last year. His name was Aklilou Imru, a herdsman in the Ogaden desert in the province of Bale, Ethiopia. He had never married and he left no heirs. He was thirty-nine years old." Pause. "Between those two dates, and those two people, lies a graveyard more populous than your present United States."

Doohan glanced around the room again. There were probably five hundred seats in the auditorium and every one of them was filled. Every public health official and hospital executive in the Bay Area must be there and all of them were hypnotized by Espinosa. Even Woodruff, who had clasped his hands behind his head, ready for his first lecture hall snooze since medical school, was fascinated.

Doohan listened with admiration as Espinosa launched into the history of the smallpox program. Dr. Raphael Espinosa, one of the most remarkable men he had ever known. The man who had talked him into volunteering for the smallpox program in the first place. He had never regretted it, though Bangladesh had proved more of a cultural shock than he had expected. Not much like Scotland, he mused, or Wales, where he'd practiced. Images now crowded his mind . . . ferrying supplies to the island of Bhola just after the monsoons, arguing with tea-stall owners to keep records of suspected smallpox victims, insisting that natives show their "tika"—their vaccination scar, nailing up posters that promised 250-*taka* rewards to those who reported a smallpox case, comforting the mother with the three-year-old girl on whose hands and face the pustules were so close together they almost touched . . . the stench, the flies, the mud and the dust. . . . When he closed his eyes, he could smell it and taste it all over again.

"Impressive speaker," Woodruff whispered.

Doohan blinked. He felt vaguely guilty; Espinosa was near the end of his speech and he had missed at least half of it.

"With the death of Imru, and when appropriate prophylactic measures were taken within his village and the last of those exposed had been inoculated, smallpox ended its centuries-long reign of terror among humanity. Except for isolated cultures in our laboratories, the smallpox virus is now extinct."

There was a scattering of applause, which quickly died.

"There is, however," Espinosa continued, "a dramatic difference between the demise of the smallpox virus and that of the Passenger Pigeon and the Great Auk." His bright, intense eyes swept the tier of seats in front of him. "This marks the first time in biological history that one species has deliberately waged genocidal warfare against another—and won a complete victory. As a physician, of course, I'm delighted." His face became grim. "But as a philosopher, I'm appalled."

During the short silence that followed, Espinosa closed the folder in front of him and sat down. The applause started then, those in the front rows standing for an ovation. Then the entire auditorium was on its feet. Espinosa stood up, bowed slightly, and once again sat down.

"How did you meet him?" Woodruff asked.

Doohan stretched. "Mutual friends in England. He was a regional director for the World Health Organization, I had a struggling local practice in Wales. Too struggling and too local, and too much paperwork from National Health; smallpox and Bangladesh made a sort of idealistic sense and I volunteered." Doohan shrugged. "It wasn't a bad go, actually. I was in a funk after Elizabeth died and I wanted to get away. And Espinosa is a very persuasive man." People were leaving the lecture hall now, the usual knot of well-wishers and reporters clustering around Espinosa on the podium. "Care to have an early dinner with us? I'm sure he'd like to meet our rat man."

Woodruff shook his head. "Sorry, it's tempting, but Heather and I have tickets for the theater and she'd never forgive me if I didn't take her." He smiled slyly. "Besides, I'd just get in the way of a lot of old-times talk."

"I'll tell him you're a devil with the rats," Doohan muttered.

Woodruff left, and Doohan walked down the aisle toward the podium. Close up, Raphael Espinosa looked surprisingly athletic despite his small frame and sixty-odd years. His skin was dark olive, contrasting with the white of a full mane of hair. His speech, in talking to the battery of reporters who barred Doohan's way, was as clipped as his mustache.

"Now that WHO has wiped out smallpox, what's the next target, Doctor?"

"It's not that easy. Smallpox is unique among the diseases, it's transmitted directly from human to human. There is no vector, no middleman, so to speak. Cure the human carriers and you kill the disease."

"What about malaria or bubonic plague?"

Espinosa shook his head impatiently, his white hair flying. "No, no, no—to eradicate those, you would have to destroy the middleman, the reservoir. You would have to kill every Anopheles mosquito, every rat and plague flea. It's quite impossible."

"What about swine flu?"

A shadow passed over Espinosa's face. "We've had only one isolated outbreak so far—and a suspect one at that." He hesitated. "Tell me how it's transmitted and perhaps I can answer your question." He spotted Doohan in the corner of the crowd and started to edge through the reporters. "I'm sorry, gentlemen, that's all for now; I really have nothing more to say." He left the reporters trailing in his wake and then had embraced Doohan and was pumping his hand. "So very, very good to see you, Calvin." He glanced around, suddenly puzzled. "I thought you were with a friend."

"Alex Woodruff, an old classmate—our local lab man on the rat project. I asked him to dinner, but he couldn't make it."

Espinosa looked thoughtful. "For tonight, perhaps, it's just as well." Then anxiously: "But you still can?"

Doohan nodded. "You're planning something."

"Perhaps."

"Let me cancel a GO game and I'll be right with you."

Doohan found a phone in the corridor outside the lecture hall. When he came back, Espinosa noticed the worried look on his face and frowned. "Something wrong?"

"Dr. Benoit's not feeling well—said he thought it was the flu. Asked me if I could pop around later."

Espinosa slipped into his topcoat. "I would like to meet your Dr. Benoit some day; in your letters he sounds very interesting. I used to play Gobang; it's an English version more popular in the last century than this one. Like GO, it takes a lot of skill." He smiled. "And a lot of patience. Do you win very often, Calvin?"

Doohan laughed. "I win my share." He stepped out in the street and hailed a cab, still thinking of Benoit. A thin, pale man whose skin was almost translucent and whose health had always seemed frail. Like most medical men, he never really took care of himself. And his voice had sounded tinny and strained with a slight rasp in it. Come over after dinner, he had said, even if it was late. There was something he wanted to talk about.

It had sounded important.

Dinner at La Mère Duquesne was very French and so was the byplay between Madame Duquesne, the owner, and Espinosa. "You come too rarely, *monsieur le docteur*," she protested to Doohan, as she showed them to their table. Espinosa guessed at her southern French origins immediately and said something in French that first brought a gasp and then a quick trill of laughter from her. When Doohan asked for a translation, Espinosa only smiled and refused to comment.

Espinosa spoke rarely during the dinner, concentrating intently on the food. "Eating is the second most important thing we do, Calvin—we don't pay it the attention it deserves." Over coffee and brandy, he sat back in his chair and looked at Doohan thoughtfully.

"Do you have many friends here in America, Calvin?"

Doohan looked down at his coffee and smiled. "Are you playing father?"

"I don't think we ever get so old that we can't use one," Espinosa said kindly. He suddenly looked contrite. "I do not mean to pry."

"I have a few friends. Dr. Benoit perhaps is the

closest. We play GO a lot. He talks politics, I listen."

"And women?"

"Not many."

"The memory of Elizabeth is still too strong?"

"Probably. I haven't found any woman who could match her."

"And you haven't spent much time looking," Espinosa said shrewdly. He shook his head. "Her accident left too deep a scar." He held up his hand. "I know, I know. Now I'll ask you about your work and then—to business."

"Work." Doohan shrugged. "Counting fleas on rats isn't my idea of an exciting job."

"Your Dr. Woodruff is a help?"

"When it comes to animals, one of the best lab men around." He glanced sharply at Espinosa. "We're talking business now, aren't we?"

"Perhaps." Espinosa motioned to the waiter to bring more coffee. "What did you think of the speech?" He chuckled. "'I'm like a politician—that's 'the speech.'"

Doohan hesitated. "That was quite an ending."

Espinosa looked pleased. "Very effective, no? It's not original with me—I forget who said it first but I share his sentiments completely."

Doohan studied him for a moment. "You're not really appalled at the eradication of smallpox."

"I was being playful," Espinosa admitted. "But there are so many things inimical to mankind in their wild state—where do you draw the line? We save the wolf and slaughter the smallpox virus. The only ones left now are behind the glass walls of a viral zoo."

Doohan smiled. "I can't believe you would prefer seeing smallpox loose in the world."

"Nor would I." He was watching Doohan intently and Doohan felt uneasy. "It's a question for the philosophers to play with and I'm not enough of one—or perhaps too much of one, I'm not sure. But what I want to talk about is molecular biology—you're familiar with the recent research?"

"The recombinant DNA work?"

Espinosa nodded. "That's right. Our genetic research where we take the very stuff of heredity and
in the test tube shatter it to bits and then remold.
Where by altering the gene and reintroducing it into a
carrier cell, we can literally tailor new forms of life."

Doohan was puzzled. "That frightens you?"

"I'm a cautious man. There is always the possibility
we may modify a bacillus in such a way that it becomes deadly to man, that we may accidentally release a disease of devastating proportions for which
there is no cure—create a man-made illness for which
there is no natural immunity."

Doohan concentrated on the brandy in his glass.
He didn't look up. "Everything we do in science has a
measurable risk. I think it can be reduced to one that's
acceptable."

Espinosa frowned, choosing his words carefully. "It's
not so much what *we* may do in high containment
laboratories, Calvin. Genetic research is a game at
which almost anybody can play. You've worked in
primitive societies; you know the level of technology. How many native technicians would realize that
cellulose nitrate test tubes can turn into high explo-
sives when sterilized in an autoclave? Or that the
rotors in a laboratory centrifuge are subject to metal
fatigue? Or that merely lifting the lid off a Petri dish
can create a highly infectious aerosol of the agent
inside?"

Doohan felt his rebuttal die on his lips. Instead, he
said: "You have something in mind?"

"WHO has called for international controls on ex-
periments in genetic engineering." There was a tinge
of pride in Espinosa's voice. "They would like me to
chair a watchdog committee. And I would like you to
work with me."

Doohan felt his face go stiff. "I'm sorry, Raphael—I
can't."

He toyed with his coffee during a long moment of
silence and finally Espinosa said: "I take it you have
a different view?"

"All right." Doohan looked up at Espinosa defiantly.
"I guess if I'm an expert on anything, I'm an expert

on smallpox. I spent two years fighting it. Two years pulling leeches off my legs, breathing dust in outdoor temperatures as high as 120, and watching people die in some of the most horrible ways imaginable." He drained his brandy. "I'm not a philosopher at all, Raphael, I'm a country doctor and a nuts-and-bolts lab man. How can I reject a future in which it might be possible to build in natural immunities to small-pox, even plague? I can count fleas on rats until the day I die and it won't eliminate plague but the labora-tory approach might do it in a relatively few years. We could eliminate hemophilia, Tay-Sachs disease, sickle-cell anemia. We could tailor plants to produce oil, to bear fruit in desert regions, to modify the tissue and blood of animals so we're no longer dependent on human beings for blood transfusions or even trans-plant parts." He hesitated, shaking his head in puz-zlement. "I've followed the research for a long time and with a great deal of hope. For me, personally, it gives those two years meaning. And you would like to call a halt."

Espinosa half-smiled. "I didn't know you were capa-ble of such passion, Calvin." His face grew serious. "I'm hardly against any of those. I just think we should proceed with caution. There's a difference be-tween the gods and men, Calvin. If you're not sure what it is, I would suggest you read your morning paper."

"You keep treating it as a matter of morality," Doo-han said bitterly.

"Perhaps it is."

Doohan leaned forward, not trying to hide the sar-casm in his voice. "Where's the morality in a child scarred by smallpox, in a mother blinded by the black-fly disease? The morality is simple, Doctor. Human suffering is immoral; human disease is immoral. You were back in headquarters reading the reports. I was in the villages. If you had been with me, maybe we would think the same." He felt faintly flushed. The brandy, he thought. He hadn't drunk in months and he had had one brandy too many.

"You spent two years there," Espinosa said in a

brittle voice. "I spent six, before you ever arrived."
He looked at Doohan sadly. "I'm glad you believe in
something, Calvin. A doctor has to. But I think what
I believe in more than anything else is the fallibility of
human nature. Are you familiar with Erwin Chargaff?
He provided the evidence for the Watson-Crick model of the DNA structure. He once said he was almost
congenitally opposed to improving the human lot because it began with the do-gooders and ended with
the exterminators. Perhaps all the things you say can
be done, perhaps the doctor as such will become ob-
solete, perhaps someday a gene mechanic will make
a snip here and a clip there and eliminate Tay-Sachs
or sickle-cell anemia. I'm not sure they'll stop there."

Doohan could feel his resentment fading. "And if
they don't?"

"I don't think we're ready to play God, I don't
think we're ready for the . . . responsibility. We should
remember the verse in Omar Khayyam: '. . . the first
Morning of Creation wrote what the Last Dawn of
Reckoning shall read.'"

Doohan said faintly, "I'm sorry, Raphael." He
shrugged. "But I can't help what I believe."

Espinosa reached over and tapped Doohan on the
chest. "Never apologize for your beliefs, Calvin. But
God help us all if one of our captive diseases escapes
in some far future when all natural immunity has been
lost. Or if we make a mistake in our gene tailoring or
if one of us is not as noble and selfless as the rest of
us. It's the bomb builders who worry me, the nuclear
weapons men who keep piling overkill on top of
senseless overkill. These men will see nothing but a
new way to kill in this technology and kill with a subtlety that may not even be detectable."

"There's nothing very subtle about an epidemic, especially one spread by the military."

"No, I'm not talking about anything that crude,"
Espinosa said. "Etzioni has suggested, for instance,
that a warring nation might secretly change the genetic makeup of an enemy so that carbon dioxide
would be poisonous to the next generation."

"That's madness," Doohan protested.

Espinosa swirled the remaining drops of his brandy in his glass and held it up to the light. "Madness?" he said. "Perhaps, but I see through a glass darkly—and I do not like what I see."

He signaled the waiter for the check. "I'll miss working with you. I respect your abilities more than you might think." He suddenly smiled and there was a faint twinkle in his eye. "Still friends, Calvin?"

After Espinosa had left, Doohan chatted for a moment with Madame Duquesne, then searched out the telephone. The talk with Espinosa had left him both depressed and tired and he decided to cancel out on Benoit. Akira, Benoit's houseboy, answered. He sounded upset.

"Dr. Doohan, I've been trying to call you." There was a breathless excitement and something close to fear in his voice. "The ambulance has come and taken Dr. Benoit away."

For a moment, Doohan couldn't adjust. "He said it wasn't serious."

"Oh yes, he did, sir—but it became much worse during the evening."

"Where did they take him, Akira?"

"The ambulance man said St. Joseph's Hospital."

"Thanks—I'll ring you back."

Doohan started to drop in another dime, then hesitated. The admissions clerk wouldn't tell him anything over the phone, and the resident would probably be too busy to talk. He pocketed the dime, stepped out on Geary, and hailed a cab. At the hospital, he identified himself at the admissions desk and said: "I understand Dr. Benoit was brought in earlier?"

The clerk riffled through the cards in her Rolodex. "Dr. Hugh Benoit? He's up in Intensive Care."

"Who's the resident on duty?"

"Dr. Mittleman." She hesitated. "He's very busy. . . ."

"He's up in Intensive Care, too?"

She nodded. Doohan turned and hurried to the elevator. It was somehow comforting to be back in

the practical halls of a hospital. Espinosa's philoso-
phizing had been very heady and very depressing.
He could handle this at least. . . . Probably a matter
of relative competence, he thought wryly. And then
his thoughts switched to Benoit. It must have come
on fast . . .

Dr. Mittleman was a young man, thin to the point
of emaciation. He was stripping off his gloves and
mask when he came out to see Doohan. "My God,
you would think this was a Friday night. . . ." He
looked at Doohan with interest. "I saw you at UC
Medical this afternoon—you know Dr. Espinosa?"

"Worked under him on the smallpox campaign,"
Doohan said hurriedly. "What's the problem with Dr.
Benoit?"

Mittleman looked grave. "They brought him in
three hours ago and we've had him under continuous
monitoring. Damnedest thing I've ever seen. General
pulmonary inflammation and pronounced tachycardia.
He's cyanotic, which is understandable. There's so
much exudate he isn't getting enough oxygen."

"Which lung is involved?"

"Both of them—very rapid fluid buildup."

"What's the prognosis?"

"Hard to say. Sputum smears are negative. Frankly, it looks like a viral pneumonia. Only—"

"Only what?"

A shrug. "Only both lungs are involved and the
speed of onset was pretty dramatic. We put him on a
positive pressure respirator half an hour ago."

It didn't make medical sense, Doohan thought. "Is
there anything more that can be done?"

Mittleman was already preoccupied with the problems of another patient, talking hurriedly to a nurse
hovering at his side. "Pray, I guess."

Doohan took the elevator back to the lobby and
called a cab. Benoit was in his sixties and had never
been in the best of health, but still . . . such a rapid
build-up and with a general pulmonary involvement
and no detectable bacteria in the sputum. A viral
pneumonia was a logical diagnosis.

But this fast?

He spotted the cab and ducked out of the lobby to climb in. San Francisco was a port town, he thought. You had to expect that every mutant bug from the Orient would show up here first.

3

To THE YOUNG man, the living room is impressive. It is easily twenty feet by thirty feet with two-story ceilings. Through one glass wall, he can see the entire sweep of the Bay framed by the delicate tracery of the Golden Gate Bridge. From his vantage point he can see the blue-black of the Pacific and the nearer shore where waves foam about the jagged rocks.

The young man is standing near the Spanish grill-work that opens onto the formal dining area and absently watching a distant freighter slip over the thin edge of the horizon. He isn't concerned with the view, however. He is listening to the slight rustle as the pages of his report are turned. The middle-aged man reading it is heavy-set and dark with the shoulders and arms of a wrestler. Thick lips and dark brows stretch the full width of his face without interruption above a lean nose and delicately flared nostrils.

The rustling stops, and the older man gets up from his chair and walks over to the window. He is wearing a Hawaiian shirt that is tight around his chest and arms; his baggy slacks don't quite hide the start of a paunch. The younger man automatically measures himself against the older, as he does at every meeting, and once again finds himself lacking. Not yet, he thinks. And then: Perhaps never.

The older man turns and stares at him. "We should have anticipated such problems in advance."

"There was no way to foresee that kind of accident," the younger man says sullenly.

Now it's the older man's turn to measure him. His

voice is unforgiving, filled with contempt. "When you lost the blood, you lost the data. And because of that, we've lost valuable time setting up a duplicate situation."

The younger man now realizes his mistake in being defensive and licks his lips nervously. "We can deduce some of the results even without the data. We constructed a model of the problem and ran a prognosis on the data spread and . . ."

The older man throws the report on a nearby table and walks across the room to the wet bar. His voice is heavy and there is menace in it. "Computer models. Don't bullshit me."

"Yes, sir," the young man says quietly. The older man keeps harping on the accident—an accident that happened a year ago. To remind him that he hadn't covered all possibilities? He doesn't need reminding —this time, everything will be taken care of.

"Do you like martinis?" the older man suddenly asks, his voice gentle. The young man is suddenly wary—waiting. "Of course you do. I almost forgot our last meeting."

The older man explores the bottles behind the bar. He takes a cut-glass decanter from the top shelf and begins the ritual of measuring gin and a touch of vermouth over ice cubes. "My man in Europe sends me a special gin made from a Far East juniper berry, called habhel. I first ran across it in Hong Kong several years ago." He pours the mixture into two frosted glasses and smiles bleakly. "It's one of my few indulgences."

For the first time, the young man is surprised. He sips at his drink and glances around the room at the framed Miro above the fireplace, the brilliant Chagall on another wall, the deep Persian rug, obviously woven especially to fill the immense space. Yet the gin is the indulgence. The magnificent room with the sun streaming through the far windows is merely an apartment, the Miro and Chagall merely decoration. He wonders about the mind of the man behind the bar.

The young man studies the older, wondering if there is any human being whom the older man cherishes as much as he cherishes his special gin.

It's not just that he is cold, *the younger man decides*. It's that he doesn't think as other men do. He doesn't have the mind of a man who stays at home, who farms or runs the store. He has the mind of a nomad. A Hun.

4

DOOHAN AROSE WITH a headache and a jittery brandy stomach. He was still sleepy and feeling a bit ill when he parked in the Civic Center parking lot and walked the two blocks to 101 Grove. The Public Health Department had given WHO a small office on the administrative floor; it contained the essentials of Doohan's new trade: a desk, chair, filing cabinet, and telephone.

Doohan hated all of them, especially the telephone.

Ordinarily he'd stop in one of the laboratories upstairs and cadge a cup of coffee along with the latest gossip, then go back to his office with the nauseous pale green walls to read the latest set of rat statistics from the port of Long Beach or Oakland.

This morning he couldn't stand the thought of either coffee or making small talk. He spent half an hour scanning the reports and making notations for a geographical survey. Finally he gave it up as a bad job, leaned back in his chair, and closed his eyes. Was it only the brandy that had made him flare up at Espinosa like that? Or was it because Espinosa had deliberately reminded him of Elizabeth? He could have refused the job offer with good grace. The old man was certainly entitled to his views. . . .

He meditated for a few minutes, concentrating on the mumble of traffic outside and the even whisper of his own breathing. Then he gradually became aware of doors slamming in the corridor, the shrill chatter of telephones ringing, the sounds of people talking and desks being shifted.

What the devil was going on?

He opened his office door and bumped into Anna Goldstein, an assistant director in the Bureau of Infectious Diseases, half-running down the hall. A plump, energetic woman with a taste for knit dresses, she had always reminded him of a younger Golda Meir. She clutched his arm, her fingers digging into muscle. "Nobody remembered to tell you, did they? Damn! Calvin, we could use your help." She didn't wait for an answer but continued down the corridor; Doohan had to half-jog to keep up with her.

In the health department conference room, Anna plopped down by a desk in the corner and mopped at the perspiration that beaded her faint mustache. Her two assistants and a girl in a white smock were manning telephones. One of the upstairs lab assistants, Doohan thought with surprise, crossing the class barrier. At the other end of the room, a maintenance man was tacking up a huge map of California and the surrounding states. More lab people were crowding in now.

"What's happening, Anna?"

She ignored the question and pulled another Kleenex from her pocket. "Calder's out with a hernia operation and won't be back until Monday," she complained. Calder was the head of the department. "So for the moment at least, I'm it. As if I didn't have enough to do, my God . . ." She pushed a loose strand of hair away from her eyes; her normally smooth face was now creased with worry lines. "I'm sure it would have come over my desk, but if it did, I have no recollection of it—and neither State nor the CDC has issued one."

Doohan had forgotten his headache. "Issued what?"

"A flu bulletin. Has WHO reported any new influenza strains in the Far East?"

"I would have told you—you'd get them next."

"Could you double-check with Washington and Geneva? We need to know as soon as possible."

"Be glad to help. How about telling me what's going on?"

People were still pushing into the room and she

lowered her voice. "The reports started coming in late yesterday afternoon—three pneumonia cases from San Francisco General, a few more from Mount Zion and Children's. By evening we had a dozen, all tremendously virulent, all tremendously invasive—they wouldn't have been reported otherwise. So far we're unable to find any bacterial pathogen; we think it's viral. It resembles influenza in its early stages but the condition develops rapidly, usually within forty-eight hours, into a full-blown pneumonia. And it's no ordinary one."

"Symptoms?"

"Dry throat, rasping cough, chills, vomiting and diarrhea, a temperature that can go as high as 107. And it's fast, Calvin, very fast. Flu's a presumptive diagnosis; I've never seen anything like it."

Doohan reviewed the symptoms in his mind. "Swine flu?"

"Maybe—the National Institute of Health predicted it."

"Did you inform the CDC?"

"An hour ago; State last night. They'll get back to me."

"How many cases?"

She took a breath. "Fourteen as of last night. I haven't counted yet this morning; the reports are still coming in."

The girl in the lab smock at a nearby desk looked up from her phone. "State Health reports a case in Tahoe, two in Crescent City, and one unconfirmed in Eugene, Oregon." She handed over a slip of paper.

Anna studied the note for a minute, then crumpled it up. "I wish Calder were here," she muttered, then glanced at Doohan with a wry smile. "It's not a sexist thing, Calvin; it's the responsibility. If it's a new form of swine flu, we're in trouble. The public more or less shunned the inoculations in seventy-six and the disease could spread faster than the ability of people to develop antibodies, even if they were inoculated today."

Three more desks were now occupied with lab assistants taking phone calls; silent spectators lined the back of the room. Doohan turned to look at the map. There were a lot more than fourteen pins in it. Most of them were blue, about a third red. "How many fatalities?"

"Seven as of last night."

He counted. "Make it nine. Anna, is there anything I can do?"

"You can get on the horn to Washington and check out any new flu strains." She drummed her fingers on the desk top, thinking. "Calvin, if it's as bad as I think it's going to be, we'll need all the help we can get. The workers won't be a problem—I can hit Personnel with a request for temporary transfers; I can tap sixty inspectors from Environmental Health and maybe seventy public health nurses. But we need more chiefs. The state has six epidemiologists up north; the city has one, but even in ordinary weeks, we could use six."

Doohan had been studying the map. It was too early to tell but it looked as though there might be a pattern; he'd have to get a breakdown of the city cases. "Common source?"

She shrugged. "Who knows? We haven't had the time or the manpower to take complete histories. That's one of the things you can help us with."

"Be glad to, Anna." Anything but go over rat statistics, he thought. And it was at least a faint flashback to the work in Bangladesh.

"You're a godsend, Calvin," she said, getting up from the desk. "Between you and a pot of hot coffee, I'll make it through the day yet."

One of her assistants on the phone suddenly waved at her, and Anna hurried over to take the call. Doohan started to leave to lock up his office, then abruptly remembered Benoit and dialed St. Joseph's.

The resident was properly sympathetic. Dr. Doohan was a friend? He was sorry, genuinely sorry, everything possible had been done. . . . Cardiac failure officially at five thirty-seven. The pleural cavity was filled with fluid effusion before he died.

Doohan hung up the receiver and stood there for a long moment, thinking of nothing at all. Then he walked over to the map, picked up a red pin, and stuck it next to the small clot of blue and red that marked San Francisco.

"Make it ten," he said quietly to the man at the map.

By five o'clock there were thirty-three cases and twelve deaths, and pins sprouted as far south as San Diego and as far east as Phoenix. Doohan was hoarse from talking on the phone and desperately wanted a hot meal and a cup of coffee and definitely a soak in a steaming tub of hot water.

One more set of relatives to talk to and he would have a fairly accurate sampling. Odd how many people had no idea where their parents had spent the weekend or how many wives merely reported their husbands had been on a business trip and no, they didn't know the details. San Francisco, sin city of the West, Doohan thought cynically.

He dialed the last number and introduced himself, sympathized for a few minutes and finally got a chance to ask his sample questions. When he hung up, he riffled quickly through his notes, feeling a growing sense of excitement. One mention here, another, then half a dozen . . .

Anna nodded when he walked in, motioning him to sit down. She was hunched over the phone but noticed Doohan's excitement and hastily finished the call. "You've got something?"

"Common source—almost definitely."

"San Francisco?"

"Hotel Cordoba. Last weekend, a convention of the Veterans of American Wars. When family members knew definitely where the victim had been, it was always the convention."

"What about the women?"

"Same thing. A few members of the auxiliary services, the rest were wives of members."

She drummed her fingers on the desk. "I'll notify the CDC again. They'll have to send in teams to help us check out all the victims—names and addresses, movements, who else was exposed, arrival dates, where did they eat, the sexuals. . . . We can use all the manpower we can get. My God, how many were at that convention?"

"I haven't had a chance to check it."

"It sounds like a replay of the Legionnaires' Disease, but if it is, the CDC should be able to verify that in a hurry. Anything specific about the convention or the hotel?"

"We'd have to go to an in-depth questionnaire, Anna." She nodded. "And we'll need a team of investigative epidemiologists to go over the hotel."

"The Environmental Health Services can help out with that; they've got the sanitation and food inspectors." She sighed and leaned back in her chair, her face somber. "You did very well, Calvin. You also look like hell. You didn't eat today, did you?"

"No, and you probably didn't either."

"Wrong—I sent out. Cream cheese and date nut bread and don't nag me about my diet, not on a day like today."

Doohan hesitated at the door. "I knew one of the red pins—Dr. Hugh Benoit. I'm going to check out his home and see if his houseboy has contacted any relatives."

"Of course." Then, seriously: "You don't work for us, Calvin, but we need all the time you can give us."

Her face looked puffy and pale beneath its sparse make-up. "Time," she mused. "We never have enough of it, do we? And it's our biggest enemy on this, Calvin. The veterans who attended that convention are like stones dropped in a pond—and we're trying to stop the spread of the ripples. A week from now, we might as well forget any effort at containment. Whatever it is, most of the continent will have been exposed to it."

She yawned and Doohan wondered if she had been to bed at all the previous night. "I wouldn't admit it to anybody else, Calvin," she said quietly, "but I think I'm scared stiff."

5

BENOIT HAD LIVED IN the Diamond Heights section of San Francisco, a development thick with apartment houses and condominiums that overlooked the rest of the city. Doohan couldn't think of another city that offered quite such a view. He parked in the Carnelian Way turnaround and then took a moment to stare at the city below. It was dusk and the last rays of the sun were gilding the towers of the financial district and the cables of the Bay Bridge. It was a far cry from the packing crate slums of Dacca and Bombay, a far cry from the heat and filth and the running sores of smallpox.

The golden city, he thought, alive with pretty girls and healthy youngsters. And then the one image of India that he had never been able to shake floated into mind. A gaunt mother holding her son and casually pulling a tapeworm from his raw bottom. In a few seconds she had pulled out several feet of white, wriggling parasite which she casually discarded in the street, unaware that the head remained attached in the child's gut and eventually would regenerate itself completely.

Was it better to live one's life at half potential with a thin, white snake coiled within you, sucking at your guts—or end it by drowning in one's own body fluids rising in response to some complex, not-quite-alive thing called a virus? There was one thing they both had in common: A life was cut short. A brilliant man like Benoit was denied his final years and a native who might have been another Gandhi would live his life at half-throttle, a starved caricature of his fellow men.

It seemed as though he had devoted all of his life to fighting disease, Doohan thought calmly, for perhaps the first time that day. He did it because it gave life meaning, because it made him feel good about himself, because he was serving Humanity.

He was also doing it because he personally hated the wriggly white parasite that sucked the life from its three-year-old host, because he detested the microscopic thing that opened sores by the hundreds on the bodies of the poor and the unfortunate, because he hated losing a friend to something that wasn't quite alive but certainly wasn't dead, either.

He took one last look at the gold-tipped towers below, then turned to the condominium behind him and rang the doorbell. The lights were on upstairs, but there wasn't any answer. He rang again and finally tried the door. It swung open and he stepped inside. There was the sound of water running upstairs and then it cut off. Akira hadn't heard him because he had been taking a shower, Doohan thought.

He jogged up the stairs to the bedroom he knew belonged to the houseboy. A rock record was on, and Doohan paused. Akira usually listened to the Japanese records that Benoit picked up at the Trade Center, almost all of them classical *koto* music. He pushed the door open. Akira had slipped into a pair of jockey shorts and was toweling his shoulders and chest; he was still singing in slightly nasal but otherwise perfect English.

"Ah." Akira had spotted Doohan in the mirror over the bureau and froze. "I did not hear you, Doohan, *san*," he said in confusion.

"You heard about Dr. Benoit?"

"Yes-s-s, it is a tragedy." His eyes were frightened but alert—and the sibilance was overdone.

Something flickered behind Akira's eyes that jarred Doohan, and then it was gone, the face once more that of an amiable Japanese houseboy in his late teens. Akira finished toweling himself.

Doohan glanced around the room. On the bed

was a canvas and leather suitcase half-filled with clothing. Next to it was the ivory-inlaid GO board that normally rested on a table in the living room, along with a portable overseas shortwave radio that Doohan knew cost close to a thousand dollars. Benoit had liked to listen to the world, as he called it. It kept him up-to-date on what was happening, more up-to-date than any television news program or newspaper.

"Going someplace?" Doohan asked.

Again something flickered in Akira's eyes. "You know what the doctor died from? I don't either but I don't want to stay here and catch the same thing."

"If you were going to catch it, you would've come down with it by now," Doohan lied. He pointed to the bed. "The radio and the GO board, they're worth a lot of money."

Akira became poker-faced; he continued dressing. "It is not important what they're worth. Doctor promised them to me in case something ever happened to him. I was with him for three years."

"I'm sure he made a will," Doohan said slowly. "But taking them before the will's probated is stealing."

Akira looked at him insolently. "Perhaps there are things you might want." He sauntered over to the bed and dumped the clothing out of the suitcase. "I will stay. His heirs would appreciate that, wouldn't they?"

Benoit and he had once discussed his will, Doohan remembered. Everything went to his maiden sister, even the GO board; he had taught her how to play years ago and she'd become a fan.

"Have you notified any of his friends?"

"You are his best friend. The others will call once they read about it."

"How about his relatives?"

Akira was slicking down his long black hair in the mirror. "Doctor never talked about them."

"He had a sister," Doohan persisted. "An unmarried sister." His voice was harder now and Akira's bravado became uncertain.

"Yes, she called sometimes. She lives in St. Louis."

Doohan walked back downstairs and started going

through the drawers in the modular teak desk. In the second one on the left he found a small phone book bound in red Cordovan leather. Under the B's, Doohan found an entry for a Celeste Benoit. The address was in Webster Groves, one of the better suburbs of St. Louis. A frail, precise voice finally answered after four rings: "Yes, this is Celeste Benoit."

She took the news calmly. She was certainly sorry, but she hadn't seen her brother in years and they had grown somewhat apart. She was the only relative; yes, she would be glad to fly out and tend to the details. And yes, she would prefer the houseboy stay on, at least until she arrived.

Akira was somewhat uncertain. "I don't want to work for a woman."

Doohan shrugged. "You can leave then; there's nothing legally holding you." He glanced around the room with its exquisite furnishings and valuable prints hanging on the walls, then noted that Akira had replaced the GO board. "You'd be leaving all this behind, of course."

Akira frowned, then bowed slightly "I would be honored to stay, sir." The face was servant-blank, the sibilance just right. "She will be grateful, I think."

Doohan looked at him with contempt, then walked to the window and pulled the wide drapes. It was dark out now and the lights of the Trans-America building and the Montgomery Street high-rises seemed distant and unreal. How many evenings had they sat just inside the huge sliding glass doors and played GO while the sun painted the city a dazzling gold? And Benoit himself, crusty and argumentative, convinced that the world was "going to hell in a handbasket" and how the United States had failed to pick up all the pieces, as he put it, when it was the only country that had the atomic bomb. Somebody was going to run things, why shouldn't it have been the United States? But he had been a charming conversationalist with all that, one who had been able to draw Doohan out about the smallpox campaign and who listened with quiet attention while Doohan relived his life in India and Bangladesh.

He would miss him, Doohan thought. Quite as much as if Benoit had been a part of his own family.

He could hear Akira back upstairs, unpacking, and he quickly decided against saying good-by. Akira would stay now until the sister showed up. What happened after that was up to her.

Outside, he had just started to get into his car when a voice said tentatively: "Dr. Benoit?"

A battered Volkswagen had driven up. The driver alighted and approached him as he fumbled for the keys to his Chevelle. "I'm sorry," Doohan said harshly, "Dr. Benoit died early this morning."

The man was under the street light now. A tall man, perhaps six feet, but he was fat and looked shorter than he was. He was wearing a brown tweed suit that hung badly on him, its narrow lapels betraying its age. His eyes blinked uncertainly behind heavy glasses. "How strange," he said at last. "They must have died within hours of each other."

Doohan got the rest of the way out of his car. "Who died?"

"I'm sorry," the fat man said, extending a pudgy hand. "I'm Paul French."

"Doohan, Calvin Doohan."

"I couldn't see you in the dark," French apologized. "I only met Dr. Benoit once." Then: "It was my brother. He and Dr. Benoit were friends. Before he died, he asked me to stop over and give Dr. Benoit a note and some personal mementos. I don't think he knew Dr. Benoit was sick, too. . . ." His voice trailed off. "What happened?"

"Viral pneumonia."

French pursed his lips thoughtfully. "Odd. I mean coincidental." He pulled at his chin for a moment.

"Viral pneumonia, too?"

"That was the diagnosis. From the first respiratory symptoms to death . . . It was all very rapid."

"You're a medical man?"

"Me?" French seemed surprised. "No. Roy was the M.D. in the family; I'm just a clinical biochemist, the black sheep." He laughed self-consciously. "The natural defensiveness of the so-called pure scientist.

I split my time between UC Berkeley and the State Department of Health."

French was hardly his idea of a clinical biochemist, Doohan thought. He was about to tell French of the other deaths reported to Public Health, then changed his mind. "Your brother—when was the last time he and Benoit saw each other?" Roy French had been one of the red pins, too. If there had been close contact with Benoit, or vice versa . . .

"A month or more ago—that was the impression I got."

Doohan stepped closer, close enough to make out French's rumpled shirt and stained green tie. "Was he a member of the Veterans of American Wars?"

"He had been in the Army but I really couldn't tell you what groups he belonged to." French sounded embarrassed. "We never really got along." There was a note of regret in his voice.

Doohan turned to get in his car. "I'm sorry about your brother." Behind him, French repeated: "We weren't very close."

He'd have to get back to Public Health, Doohan thought as he started up the car. He'd been away too long as it was. He drove down Portola, the lights of the city gradually swelling before him, thinking of French and his brother and the odd coincidence. What was it French had said?

That he didn't know if his brother was a member of the VAW or not. There was some doubt there. But Benoit definitely wasn't. The previous weekend, he had played GO with Benoit. If Benoit had been at the convention, he had never mentioned it. It could be that the deaths of both French and Benoit were ordinary background noise. A certain number of viral pneumonia cases occurred all the time.

But it had been far from an ordinary pneumonia and there had been a link between French and Benoit. Somehow, there must also be a link between the two of them and the convention.

Back at the Public Health Department, the lights were burning and the doctors and lab assistants were scurrying in and out of the front door, their faces grim. Doohan headed for the conference room. The pins on the map had multiplied.

"It isn't looking very good, is it?" Anna's face was haggard, the ever-present circles under her eyes now deeply etched.

"How many cases?"

"Forty-five, counting the other states. Twenty-nine in the city alone, sixteen fatalities." She paused. "More than five hundred people attended that convention," she added grimly.

That made five hundred probables then, Doohan thought. Plus whoever *they* infected. He hadn't considered that personal possibility before. Both he and Akira had been close to Benoit during the last week.

"The same symptoms in all cases?"

She nodded. "Yes. Same rapid progress, involvement of both lungs. Some instances of the infection spreading to the pleural cavity; although most of the fatalities occurred before the infection became widespread. Half the cases are on respirators and they're all in isolation. By morning, there'll be a run on the beds in the intensive-care wards in the city."

She took a phone call and when she returned, Doohan asked: "Any success in identifying it?"

"We've got sputum and bronchoscope fluid samples from most of them as well as sera. We've been running cultures on them: Microbiology has had some incubating for forty-eight hours now; no obvious colonies on the Petri dishes, though."

Doohan frowned. "It progresses too rapidly for most bacteria."

"I know. I'm sure it's viral, so is the lab."

"Any success in surveying hospitals and private practices?"

She waved at the operators manning the phones. "We're trying to identify every case—do you realize how many private practices there are in the city and East Bay, including the osteopaths?"

"What's CDC doing?"

"A number of teams from Atlanta will be flying in tomorrow; some field operatives are already en route.

They're operating on the assumption that it may be swine flu."

"Think they're right?"

She signed something on a clipboard that an assistant shoved at her and turned back to Doohan. "I rather doubt it. I think at least a part of CDC also has its doubts. They told us to be very careful in handling any cultures or tissue samples, just in case it was a repeat of the Legionnaires' Disease." She was lost in thought for a moment. "The thing that really puzzles me is that we've had no second-generation patients. We've quarantined what families we could and started to trace the movements of contacts." She shook her head. "Do you realize how many people that is when you've got five hundred possible victims? But we haven't found any infection chain as yet."

"What if the incubation period is unusually long? Say ten or fifteen days?"

He could sense the shudder. "Then we'll have our hands full." She glanced around, then drew him over to the far side of the room. "The newspapers have guessed that something is up; we've warned everybody against talking to them, but it's only a matter of time. It's bad enough as is; we don't need a panic situation." She seemed moody for a moment, then made up her mind to something. "Calvin, could you help us?"

He felt a little put off. "I thought I was."

"I mean more or less on an official basis. We need somebody to correlate the case histories, somebody to act as a go-between with the CDC investigative teams and our own, somebody who can see the patterns, who's used to handling people—both the patients and the professionals. Ordinarily I'd be doing a lot of that, but I'm swamped—and you've got more experience than anybody else. Would you handle it until Calder comes back?"

He half-smiled. "It's better than rats."

Somebody called for her across the room and she walked away, favoring a slight limp that Doohan had never noticed before. She was getting tired and she didn't have enough energy left to hide the faint pains of early arthritis. She called back over her shoulder: "I have to get hold of State Health; I don't know who'll be there tonight."

Doohan suddenly remembered French and said, "I met a clinical biochemist who works there, a Paul French. He said his brother was a friend of Benoit's; we met at the house."

She turned back. "Paul French? He's the man I want to contact. He's more than a clinical biochemist; he's in charge of one of their virology labs. I know—his suit is ten years old, his socks don't match, and his shoes flap when he walks. But he's the best there is. Try and get hold of him and bring him up to date."

Doohan walked down the hall to his office, lit his pipe, and reached for the phone directory. He should have asked Anna for the number. But chances were that French wouldn't be in his laboratory at this hour.

Then he remembered; he reached in his pocket and pulled out Benoit's address book. During the conversation with Akira, after he phoned St. Louis, he had absently put it in his pocket. He opened it up, started to thumb it, then turned back to the inside cover. Written on the inside were the names and phone numbers of Roy French, an R. Guitterez, and himself. All of them were underlined. Fellow GO players? he wondered.

He turned to the F's, found Paul French's phone number, and started dialing.

6

DR. PAUL FRENCH jockeyed his Volkswagen into what must have been the last parking space in Pacific Heights. His paunch rubbed against the steering wheel, eroding still further the black plastic cover already worn thin from years of abrasion by his belt buckle. He accepted the shredded plastic with resignation, acknowledging that it was in keeping with the dents and faded paint of the rest of the car. Selma had wanted to get rid of it years ago, but it had suited him, much as his worn but comfortable shoes or his faintly baggy pants suited him. He supposed that was why he had decided to buy Isaac a new Pinto for graduation: as atonement for having kept the Beetle for so long against Selma's wishes.

Selma had never really nagged him about the car, she had never really nagged him about anything. But if she had, he would have given in. Eventually.

He walked to the crest of the hill where his brother's house overlooked the Bay. It resembled for all the world an Italian villa baking in the afternoon sun. The façade was of white limestone with an elaborate stone balustrade running the length of the porch that looked out over a small lawn precisely manicured, with potted citrus trees clipped into leafy spheres. The perfect home for a successful internist and his society wife, he thought wryly.

Gladys had dismissed the maid for the day, saying she was going to stay at her sister's; there were too many ghosts in the house now that Roy was gone. He found the key in the mailbox where Gladys had promised she would put it and walked in. A shaggy floktati rug covered the center section of the hall, its bleached white mat showing not a trace of dust, as though it had been freshly laundered. It was typical of Roy, French thought: Buy two at a time so one was always at the cleaner's while the other graced the entranceway.

He walked down the hall to the study, glancing in the rooms along the way. They were all very formal, very rich, with the sun slanting through the curtains to paint the settling dust. But it wasn't a warm house, certainly not a friendly house, not at all like the home the two brothers had known as children. For a moment he grew nostalgic. He had always been the partygoer, the dater, the happy-go-lucky one. Roy had remained on the sidelines, thin-lipped and disapproving, studious and secretive. From as early as he could remember, they hadn't gotten along. His father had accused him of being overbearing and something of a bully. Roy, he had called a snitch. After he left home, Roy became even more reserved and austere. He married Gladys with the same practical sense that dictated every other decision in his life: After all, she was both wealthy and decorative. Their marriage was one for which they both had rehearsed since childhood.

The heavy damask draperies in the study were drawn, filling the room with shadows. French turned on the floor lamp by the Herman Miller chair and glanced around, blinking. For a moment he wondered what was out of place; then he realized that nothing was—and that was what was wrong. At home, Roy had been an altogether different person than he was in his office. He grew excited over books and ideas. On those rare occasions when Paul visited him, they always wound up in the study. There Roy would speak more and more rapidly, plucking volumes from his shelves and literally throwing them at Paul to make a point. Before the evening ended, stacks of journals would litter the floor. Dressed in a worn cardigan and slacks, he would punch out his ideas at a machine-gun clip, but always talking at Paul, never with him. He was, Paul remembered, a man of strong opinions who used his books as weapons to back up his arguments, striding up and down, so carried away he would dribble ashes on the rosewood desk top and the woven Irish rug. Gladys had hated the study. It represented the one aspect of Roy's character that she had never succeeded in changing.

Until now, that was. When had he seen it last? French thought. Two years ago? The books were now aligned with almost military precision, and on the desk, the roll blotter, letter knife, and paperclip container stood in an orderly row. The usual clutter was gone.

The books drew him, and French walked over and ran his finger along the top of several. Dust. The standard medical editions and Roy's collection of books about world history and politics. No fiction. Roy had always been big on politics; at one time a hawk on Vietnam and a member of the Committee to Impeach Earl Warren. There were a lot of new books on the shelves now: pop sociology and a number of "cocktail table" volumes, laid flat. French picked one out; the pages had never been cut and now, Paul thought sadly, Roy would never read it.

He sat down at the desk and started to go through the drawers. Half a dozen Christmas cards in the top drawer, a desk organizer with a tray holding accounts to be paid, a ring of keys, each one labeled. Paul found one for the safe deposit box; the will and house deed would be there. There was also a spare set of car keys, an extra for the front door. . . .

He made a few notes, then glanced again at the books shelved on the wall in front of him. The new books, the neatness . . . Gladys had won out after all, he thought. And that implied an aspect of his brother's personality that he had never suspected, the ability to change. Or worse, to be beaten.

And then it hit him. How little he had known his brother and how completely they had, without ever putting it into words, despised each other.

7

WHEN DOOHAN arrived on Monday morning, he found police posted at both the main and emergency room entrances to 101 Grove. A small knot of men were arguing with the policeman who barred their way. Doohan felt uneasy. Reporters, he thought, there to flesh out the rumors. One of them looked familiar.

"Look, guys, I've got my orders, only authorized persons allowed—"

"It's a public building, we've got—"

"You've got nothing, buster, only those on official business . . ."

Doohan walked up and identified himself; the officer checked him off on a clipboard and waved him in. Suddenly a young reporter, smelling of aftershave and coffee, shouldered past the policeman to confront Doohan. "Maloney, medical reporter for the *Chron*, Doctor. I met you at a rat abatement conference two months ago. Is WHO involved in this?"

"I'm sorry; no comment," Doohan said brusquely.

Maloney held his ground as other reporters edged up the stairs. Out in the street, a television crew with a shotgun mike zoomed in. "What's the story, Doctor? Just what the hell is the Veterans' Disease?"

Doohan blinked. "Veterans' Disease?"

"Only the veterans who attended the VAW convention last week have come down with it, right?"

"You know as much as I do."

"You're with WHO's plague study, Doctor. Is it plague?"

"We've ruled out plague," Doohan said sarcastically. "But we haven't completely ruled out swine flu."

41

He immediately wished he had stuck to "no comment."

"I've talked with five different doctors since last night," Maloney said intensely. "They claim it doesn't fit the pattern of swine flu. Just how infectious is it?"

"I have no idea," Doohan said, trying to push past the man.

Maloney frowned. "Then you don't know what it is?"

"I didn't say that."

"Then what is it?"

Doohan turned to face the reporters. "Any news release will have to come from Public Health; I'm just an observer here." He pushed past Maloney and entered the building.

He had made a mistake, he realized. Maloney would interpret his refusal to answer as meaning the disease was unknown—and that in turn would force the Health Department to issue a statement. He was angry at the reporter but even angrier with himself for falling into the trap.

He dropped his briefcase in his office and hung up his coat. Then he noticed Anna's memo on his desk asking to see him immediately. More bad news, he thought, feeling the tension grow in his stomach.

Anna wasn't alone. "Calvin, this is Dr. Suzanne Synge. Dr. Calvin Doohan. Dr. Synge is a field investigator for the CDC; she flew up from Los Angeles this morning." Anna was using her formal voice which meant that she neither approved nor disapproved of Dr. Synge.

Doohan's first impression was of a tall woman, perhaps in her mid-thirties, who obviously scorned makeup. The eyebrows were too thick, the lips and cheeks too pale. She had a slender, almost athletic build, and wore a brown tweed suit and "sensible" shoes. Her face, except for high cheekbones, was a shade too full for the rest of her; he had expected it to be almost gaunt. She had brown hair, worn in a short, no-nonsense style, and sharp gray eyes set in a serious face. For some reason, Doohan couldn't imagine her laughing.

Then he had second thoughts. No ordinary tweed suit could ever be called chic and yet hers certainly was. From London, he speculated, and very expensive. And no woman who was basically "plain" could ever look that striking without make-up. With a little rouge and lipstick she would be—what was the word, handsome? And she was probably closer to her late twenties than her mid-thirties. The only false note was an obvious effort to project a professional image; that was what had probably set Anna's teeth on edge. With Anna, it was natural; her sense of professionalism had developed right along with her chewed fingernails and her rapidly graying hair.

"Dr. Synge is liaison from the CDC; so I imagine you'll see a lot of each other." Anna's voice was brisk and Doohan guessed correctly that the mental coin had come down tails. For whatever reason, Anna Goldstein didn't much care for Dr. Suzanne Synge. Anna glanced at her watch, then up at Doohan. "I've got to call the coroner. Would you show Dr. Synge around?"

It was going to be too busy a morning to play tour guide, Doohan thought, then mentally shrugged. Anna was right; they were going to see a lot of each other.

In the corridor, Suzanne said: "You're Scottish, aren't you?"

"My name gave me away?"

She chilled. "Sorry. It's the way you roll your R's." Then, crisply: "How bad is it?"

"Forty-five victims statewide as of last night; sixteen fatalities in the city alone." She showed no reaction. Poker-face, he thought.

"The field teams from Atlanta should arrive this afternoon," she said.

"I know, we got a TWX last night. All the living arrangements have been made, cots in the corridors and all that." What the devil was coming over him? Then they were in the quiet bedlam of the conference room and all thoughts of apology vanished. The room looked more like a secretarial bullpen than ever; several additional desks had been moved in and a dozen clerks and lab assistants were talking quietly into telephones and making entries on large tabulated sheets.

Doohan studied the map board in front. The number of pins had grown enormously. There was a running tabulation below the board that now read: CONFIRMED CASES: 58. FATALITIES: 28. That was a mortality rate of more than 48 per cent, he thought, appalled. He glanced at Suzanne; her face was pale.

"The distribution of cases is limited to the western coastal states, primarily California; the majority are from the Bay Area."

She nodded. "Any similarities among the victims? Traits they share in common?"

"Older than average. All the confirmed cases are men and women in their fifties and sixties."

"No one younger?"

He hesitated. "We had three cases in their twenties, but they're suspect. They don't show the identical symptomology; generally the pneumonia proceeds more slowly and is confined to one lobe of the lungs. They could be what you'd call background noise."

"Laboratory findings?"

He reached in his pocket for his pipe and tobacco pouch, then changed his mind. The room was crowded and he was bound to offend someone. "High temperatures," he said, "together with rapid pulse and respiration and low blood pressure; low red and white count. There's distinct cyanosis with skin pallor and clamminess. The whole picture suggests impending respiratory shock."

It was her turn to study the map. "Have you identified any common source? The Bay Area seems to be the focus."

"The Hotel Cordoba on Geary. Almost all of the victims are veterans who attended a VAW convention there last weekend. Most of the women are wives who stayed in the same hotel."

"The hotel was the first to report it, then?"

Doohan shook his head. "The last scheduled function was the banquet Saturday night. Most of the veterans had left by Sunday afternoon. Referrals started to come from family doctors."

"You said 'almost' all the victims."

"The three young men who didn't quite fit the picture to begin with. And two doctors, one a friend of mine, Dr. Hugh Benoit, and the other the brother of Dr. Paul French who runs the virology lab for State."

"Hardly background noise then."

"The kids, yes. Roy French and Hugh Benoit, not bloody likely. They knew each other. The logical assumption is that one of them contacted the disease through a carrier and passed it on to the other." He didn't say it had been a month since French and Benoit had seen each other. And then he wondered if that were really true; it was, after all, only hearsay evidence.

"How many attended the convention?"

"Slightly more than five hundred."

She thought about it for a moment. "Then the number of second-generation victims could be enormous. Everybody they've come into contact with since they've left: their families, the other people on the plane, people in restaurants—"

Doohan interrupted. "The number *could* be enormous but so far there have been no second-generation cases with the possible exception of the two I've mentioned. It has all the earmarks of a highly infectious disease—or a toxin."

Ten o'clock in the morning and already he felt as though he could use a drink.

Doohan felt a tug on his sleeve. "Dr. Doohan?"

Paul French was standing beside him, blinking through thick lenses and looking as rumpled as a pile of dirty laundry. He wore a wrinkled suit, a shirt whose collar had lost one of its buttons, and a frayed and suspiciously stained green tie. Doohan was suddenly glad to see the doctor; there were some growing suspicions that perhaps French could confirm.

"Dr. Paul French, Suzanne Synge."

"Dr. Synge," she corrected with no apparent trace of irritation.

Doohan reddened and wondered if it had been intentional; he honestly didn't know. "Dr. French is with the State Health Department; he's the chief of the virology lab in Berkeley."

She inspected French for a moment and Doohan thought he saw a glint of amusement in her gray eyes. "I understand State and the CDC will be setting up parallel facilities."

French cleared his throat, obviously a little uncertain about Dr. Synge's position. "For most tests. We don't want to run the risk that the bug, whatever it is, might not survive the time of transit. We want to get a cross section of the specimens into culture within one to two hours after they've been obtained from the patient."

She looked skeptical. "There'll be a lot of tissue specimens. Can State handle them?"

French hesitated. "Anything . . . but the most exotic. We have a number of negative pressure chambers and a medium containment facility that we built for a recombinant DNA program." He plucked at his tie, suddenly self-conscious under Suzanne's stare. "It's unlikely that we'll use it for that—too much political hassle."

"There are three different labs concerned," Suzanne said, frowning. "Is there a job breakdown?"

"They all overlap to some extent." Again, French was reviewing in his mind exactly what each of the labs did. Despite the way French dressed, he was a precise man, Doohan thought. "The city can handle most of the tissue samples in their microbiology lab upstairs. They can also handle some viruses but I imagine our labs and the CDC will get the bulk of them."

They moved without comment to a small table where somebody had installed the thirty-five-cup coffee brewer from the lab upstairs. Suzanne took hers black. He knew it automatically and gave her the cup without even asking; French loaded his with both sugar and powdered cream.

"And there's no possibility of its being swine flu?" Suzanne persisted.

Doohan shook his head. "I don't think it's swine flu nor do I think it's any mutant of that strain."

"What about the A-Victoria or any of the other strains?"

"No, no, Doctor," French interrupted. "We're quite certain that it's an unknown virus." French sounded like a professor reprimanding a student; Doohan suddenly felt himself warming toward the fat man.

"You should have had time to culture for bacterial agents," Suzanne said defensively.

French stared at her over the top of his thick lenses; he looked genuinely surprised that she should even ask. "Doctor, have you ever seen a bacterial infection that moves as fast as this one?"

"No," she admitted.

"We've had plates on some cultures for two days now and there are absolutely no signs of abnormal growth."

"What about the rickettsiae?"

French sipped noisily at his cup of coffee and Doohan found himself waiting in suspense for the first drops to hit French's shirt. "The rickettsiae don't fit the pattern, not even the more obscure ones. It might be some sort of supervirulent psittacosis, but I don't think that even the great-grandfather of parrot fever bugs could do this. But we are checking out the pigeons around the hotel and trying to discover if any of the veterans brought pets along."

"I can't imagine anybody checking into a hotel with a birdcage." Suzanne had made a bad joke to recover, Doohan thought. There was a trace of a smile on her face but it looked oddly out of place, the first awkward thing about her that he had noticed.

French started to pour himself another cup of coffee, then suddenly nodded at the map in front of the room. The totals had changed again. CONFIRMED CASES: 62. FATALITIES: 34.

"It's like the scoreboard at a football game," French said thoughtfully. "And we're the losing team."

"It's frightening," Suzanne said in a tight voice. "That's a mortality rate of fifty-eight per cent. It's going up."

"Up from forty-eight per cent when we came in," Doohan said.

"We should be able to get some clues from the blood sera antibodies of those who recover." She sounded oddly desperate.

Doohan couldn't help himself. "Dr. Synge," he interrupted bluntly, "there are only two categories of victims in this disease: the sick and the dead. So far there have been no recoveries."

8

THEY MET again in Doohan's office for lunch, a round of sandwiches and more coffee that tasted faintly of plastic and chemicals. Nobody had much to say, and Doohan suspected that the mounting figures of disease victims had depressed all of them. Time was of tremendous importance, he thought, feeling frustrated. The work was slow and painstaking; there were no short cuts. Yet, there was nothing they could afford to overlook.

Once again he caught himself watching French with a certain morbid fascination. The doctor had ordered a hamburger and liberally dosed it with catsup and mustard. Now he was eating around the edges, catching the drippings a fraction of a second before they ran off the edges of the bun and landed on his tie.

He realized that he was staring and turned his attention to Suzanne. She had surprised him. An admirably organized mind with a ready grasp of the logistics between the Bay Area and Atlanta. She had already arranged for two courier pickups of tissue samples a day—a non-stop Delta flight around noon and another at ten in the evening—with an armed escort to the airport and an armed pickup in Atlanta. The tissue specimens were to be packed in maximum-security dry-iced containers.

It also seemed to him that she had gotten progressively more tense and nervous.

She took a bite of tuna salad and set it aside. "Dr. French mentioned they were checking out the birds around the hotel. Why just the birds at that hotel? And why has the disease been almost exclusively restricted to the veterans? Why none of the hotel employees?"

"My dear Doctor," French said, his mouth full, "once we know the answers to those questions, we may know a great deal indeed."

"And the age-distribution curve," she continued. "Only those past fifty."

"We haven't checked out everybody," Doohan warned. "That may not hold up."

"But it certainly looks that way. Your disease seems to be oddly selective." There was something about the way she said "your disease" that annoyed Doohan.

Anna suddenly stuck her head in the door. "Mail, Calvin—the top bulletin is from the Department of Agriculture; Haitian goatskins are showing anthrax again. If you've got any hippie friends, better let them know." She then gave him the afternoon *Examiner*. "We made the front page—bound to happen sooner or later, I guess. And Calder will be out for another week; he won't be here to take any of the heat."

She disappeared and Doohan opened the paper. The headline read: SWINE FLU OUTBREAK IN BAY AREA?

"What a bloody mess!" He quickly scanned the article, then passed the paper to Suzanne. The article itself was fairly accurate; as always, the headlines were more damaging than the story. The reporter concluded that this was an outbreak of the long-awaited swine flu and reviewed the first appearance of the disease at a New Jersey army post. There were quotes from the mayor, a no-comment-at-this-time from Anna, and assurances from somebody in Washington that stocks of swine flu vaccine were adequate and that authorities were considering reinstituting the inoculation program abandoned in 1976.

"How many people were involved in the New Jersey outbreak?" Suzanne asked.

"Just a handful," French replied. "And only one fatality."

"I wonder what the papers will say," Doohan speculated, "when they find out it's all a good deal more serious than swine flu?"

"Miltrait will have some ideas," French said, finally dabbing at the inevitable spot on his tie.

"Miltrait?"

French looked surprised. "I thought you had met him. Gordon Miltrait, head of the team from the CDC."

Doohan was interested. "What sort of chap is he?"

"Seems competent." Pause. "But I think he's frightened." He glanced at his watch. "I've got to get back to Berkeley." A thoughtful nod at Suzanne. "Nice to have met you, Doctor. Call me if there are any scheduling problems."

Doohan said, "I'd like to talk to you later; I'll try to drive over."

"Any time. What about?"

"No second-generation infections," Doohan said quietly. "Without them all of this could be just a drill."

French looked thoughtful. "Come over when you get the time."

French left and Doohan was suddenly acutely aware that he and Suzanne were alone. He felt uneasy around her and knew that she sensed it and probably resented it. He thumped the newspaper on the desk. "That'll blow over in a few days."

"You really think so?" There was a certain distance in her voice. "Probably the worst disease of all is panic. It'll be bad enough if people think it's swine flu. If they think it's something worse, it could be disastrous. I imagine several conventions will cancel the moment the news gets out. They did in Philadelphia several years ago."

"I recall the incident," Doohan said.

"You can expect a number of countries to embargo shipments from San Francisco and Oakland," she continued coolly.

Her somewhat supercilious attitude had bothered him all morning. She had a good mind but she was too bloody conscious of it. "You know a great deal about probabilities, Doctor," he said.

Her gray eyes were frosty. "So should you. It's WHO that sets the international health regulations regarding travel and shipments between countries."

There was challenge in her voice. Doohan was about to rise to it, when somebody said, "There you are, Dr. Synge. I've been looking for you."

The man in the doorway was small, almost skeletal, dressed in black, with thinning brown hair combed straight back and a nervous tic in his cheek. A cigarette with an inch-long ash dangled unnoticed from his mouth. Doohan glanced at his hands; the index and forefinger were heavily stained. A two-fisted smoker, he thought. Cancer at fifty-five by all odds.

"I've checked your courier schedule, Dr. Synge. It seems fine to me. Wilcox will handle press relations; I want you to coordinate the sampling and autopsy programs." He noticed Doohan for the first time and stared at him suspiciously.

Suzanne came to the rescue. "Dr. Miltrait, Dr. Calvin Doohan."

The small black eyes were unimpressed. "Doohan? You're with the WHO people, isn't that right? Good to have a contact with Geneva." He turned back to Suzanne. "There's a story in the afternoon paper; somebody talked. Goldstein can't control her own people apparently. I'll have Wilcox put something out." Almost as an afterthought, he said: "We'll be based at Laguna Honda hospital. It's too crowded here. I understand they have a lab we can use." He glanced at Doohan. "I think it might be wise if you transferred there, too; at least for the duration. Goldstein says you're working as liaison."

Then he was gone, two assistants trailing after him like dogs on a leash.

"Steinmetz, without the handicap of being human," Suzanne said after he left. "But he's a first-class administrator."

Doohan said: "We're not getting along, are we?"

She stiffened. "No, we're not. It's . . . been a strain for me."

"Your first outbreak of this kind?"

"It's been chilling," she said quietly. "I've always dealt with people before. Today it's been nothing but facts, figures, and symptoms. Nobody dies, it's just that a blue pin is replaced by a red." She looked at him, still distant. "It doesn't seem to affect you at all."

"Two years with smallpox in India and Bangladesh," Doohan said. "You get used to a lot. We didn't have time for a bedside manner."

"Nobody told me," she said simply. "I just thought you were callous."

Doohan was surprised how easy it was to feel sympathetic toward her. "If you're going to be worth a damn, you *have* to divorce yourself from the idea that you're dealing with people. They *have* to become just statistics, sources of data. Once you acknowledge their humanity, you lose all usefulness to them. If you and the other professionals here panic, become too concerned with the value of the individual, then every effort at containment can be endangered. Did you ever read *Arrowsmith?*"

"A long time ago. When I was a freshman in college."

"The hero of the book had discovered a bacteriophage and was running a controlled experiment in the middle of an epidemic, giving only half the patients the 'phage. Then he couldn't stand the suffering of the other half; so he gave the 'phage to everyone, ruining the experiment. He lost his control group. He couldn't say 'These people had the serum and survived, these did not and died,' thus proving that the serum was effective. In the end, the results were so muddled no member of the medical community would believe the 'phage was worth a damn. Thousands of people who might have been saved in other epidemics by his discovery died, simply because he had weakened."

He brought himself up short. "Sorry, I didn't mean to preach."

"You didn't. And you're right, of course." She smiled

and this time it didn't look forced. "Thank you, Calvin Doohan."

Doohan wadded up his sandwich wrapper and coffee cup and dropped them in the wastepaper basket. "They're taking patient interviews at San Francisco General. Come along, if you like." He hesitated. "In fact, I insist. If you're going to help code the results, you ought to know the conditions under which the questioning is held."

"The interviews are difficult?"

"I would say so. It's not easy to get information out of a dying man." He slipped into his coat and picked up his briefcase. "After that, we'll see what the investigators are doing at the hotel."

9

HERMAN ROSENBERG was over six feet tall and weighed more than 220 pounds, with the heavily muscled shoulders of a laborer. He was fifty-nine years old but, except for his sun-weathered face, looked ten years younger. It was the musculature that did it, Doohan decided. He was thick in the middle with the thickness that came even to trained athletes when they hit their fifties, but his arms were huge, the biceps large and well-defined. There were few traces of gray in his predominantly black hair, though it was thinning a little on top. Despite his size, he nevertheless struck Doohan as fragile. There was a waxiness about his face and a heaviness in his breathing that Doohan knew only too well; he had heard it often enough in the past.

He glanced again at the medical history. Rosenberg had worked as a plumbing contractor and probably did most of the heaving and hauling himself; that accounted for the rugged constitution and the fact that he had fought the disease longer than any other patient. Now he lay in a bed that seemed too small for his body, his chest laboring. His head was restrained with a strap to keep him from thrashing in his sleep and dislodging the nasotracheal tube that fed into his left nostril. The other end was attached to a respirator nearby that forced oxygen-rich air into his lungs; the machine's soft mutter sounded funereal to Doohan.

Rosenberg was sleeping and the elderly duty nurse frowned at Doohan and Suzanne when they spoke above a whisper.

"How long has he been on the respirator?" Doohan asked.

"Ten hours." She looked worried. "It's the last respirator we've got. If another patient comes in, I don't know what we'll do."

Doohan glanced at the cardiac monitor. The alpha pulse was strong but the tau pulse, the resting phase, was attenuated and in some cycles nonexistent. There was no sign of the fibrillation that the attending physician had noted earlier on the chart. Even so, the resting pulse was high. Doohan timed the monitor with his watch. One hundred five beats a minute; high, but not dangerous.

Rosenberg now stirred and opened his eyes. On the monitor, the pulse rate suddenly increased and showed the first signs of instability.

"Mr. Rosenberg," the nurse said, "can you understand me?" She used the same tone of voice that adults reserve for the senile and the partially deaf. There was a faint nod from the man on the bed. "These people are from the Public Health Service. They want to talk to you."

Rosenberg stirred, moved his lips slightly, then gave it up and closed his eyes again. Doohan motioned for the nurse's stethoscope and moved it over the gray hair on Rosenberg's chest, listening to the anterior pleural cavity. He could hear little in either the left or right cavity, but in the anterior part the bubbling overtones of the *râles* were ominous.

He handed the stethoscope to Suzanne. She listened a moment. "He must be down to about twenty per cent of his vital capacity." She examined his nails and Doohan noted the ashen blue of the nail beds. Rosenberg's lips showed the same cyanotic color, a sure indication he wasn't getting enough oxygen, even with the assistance of the respirator.

Doohan pulled back the sheet and felt along the abdomen, probing and tapping. The lymph nodes under the arms were badly swollen. Rosenberg began to shiver and Doohan replaced the blanket.

"Mr. Rosenberg," the nurse repeated loudly, "your wife is outside. Do you want to see her?" The man shook his head slowly, the pulse trace on the monitor suddenly jumping in frequency. He was angry, Doohan thought, surprised.

"No," Rosenberg whispered faintly.

Doohan examined the chart again. It listed all the symptoms he'd become accustomed to seeing with the Veterans' Disease. (The name was going to stick, he realized—the power of the press.) A very high leucocyte count, depleted hemoglobin levels, and a swollen spleen that was working overtime.

"Mr. Rosenberg," Doohan asked, "do you feel up to answering some questions?"

Rosenberg lay there for a long moment, then whispered, "Yes."

"Five minutes," the nurse said, leaving. "No more."

Doohan took his time with the questions, making sure Rosenberg understood them. Yes, Rosenberg had attended most of the convention; he lived in the Sunset but had doubled up with a widower friend at the convention for the duration. Had he attended the parties in the hospitality suites? The eyes opened slightly, the voice was faint. "I . . . boozed it up . . . a lot." Had he eaten in the hotel coffee shop? Sometimes, mostly breakfast. He couldn't remember all the places he ate dinner . . .

Yes, he had gone to several meetings in the convention auditorium. They were pretty dull. Most of the time he had socialized in the hallways and at the bar, that's what a convention was for. No, he didn't recall anything unusual about the food or the drinks. Birds? Rosenberg's mind wandered. A lot of pigeons in Union Square . . . and the old lady who had a pet toucan; he'd seen it through an open door one day when he was walking down a hall.

Doohan hesitated at the next one, then realized he had to ask it. Had he slept with any prostitutes? A flutter on the monitor and the whisper of a smile from Rosenberg. "A real . . . show. Nice . . . girl." No, it hadn't been a street pickup; she was working the inside of the hotel.

The responses were getting weaker now and Doohan bent closer to listen. What did Rosenberg think

caused his illness? A slow shake of the head. "Don't
. . . know." The ghost of a smile again. "Something . . .
I . . . ate."

Suzanne suddenly said: "Did you take your wife?"
There was a pronounced reaction on the monitor. "Are
you separated?" Nod. Increased pulse rate, ragged
now.

The responses were feeble. Doohan started to turn
away, then noticed that Rosenberg was trying to say
something. He bent low over the bed. "Tuck . . . me
in."

Doohan rearranged the blanket slightly, then
touched Suzanne on the arm and motioned toward
the door. "He's getting tired." Outside, they stripped
off their protective masks and gowns in silence and
dropped them in a nearby hamper.

The duty nurse strode in, her face grim. "I was
watching on the cardiac monitor; I told you not to
tire him." She disappeared into the room and Doohan
and Suzanne walked down to the small waiting room
opposite the nurse's station. A woman was sitting in a
rattan chair by one of the windows, idly twisting her
handkerchief while she stared at the trees outside.

"Mrs. Rosenberg?" Suzanne asked.

The woman glanced at them with no interest.
"That's right." She was at least fifteen years younger
than her husband, Doohan realized. Conventionally
pretty, with hair dyed an unreal red and bright
clothing designed to show off a too-lush figure. A woman who must have had tremendous sensual beauty in
her early twenties and who had lost almost all of it by
her late thirties. Close up, her perfume was overwhelming. Doohan noted clinically that her face
looked flushed, her lips dry and chapped.

Suzanne pulled over another rattan chair. "You and
Mr. Rosenberg are separated?"

"We have been for several months now." Her voice
was pleasant and husky and Doohan revised an initial
estimate. "I live in Santa Clara now."

"But you went to the convention with him?"

For a moment she looked nostalgic. "It was nice of
him to ask. We had gone to the one the year before

and had a ball." Her lips thinned. "This one sure wasn't. Herman and I started fighting almost immediately. After the banquet, he started to drink. That's what broke up the marriage; he'd drink and get abusive. So I left. I haven't seen him since. Until today, that is." She mopped at her forehead with the twist of handkerchief and Doohan wondered if she were feeling well.

"What room did the two of you have in the hotel?" Suzanne asked.

She looked surprised. "I didn't stay in the hotel. Herman shared a room at the hotel with a friend. He got me one at the Travelodge; the hotel was all booked up. I think it was a last-minute thing for him. Maybe he wanted to see me again to try and patch things up, I don't know. It sure didn't work out that way. I came in Saturday morning, he started drinking Saturday afternoon in spite of all his promises, and I left right after the banquet on Sunday."

There was a sudden flurry of activity at the nurse's station and a moment later two doctors came running down the hall and ran into Rosenberg's room. A team of nurses followed.

Doohan walked over to the glass enclosure. "What happened?"

The nurse watching the monitors murmured: "Cardiac arrest."

Mrs. Rosenberg had half-risen from her chair. "What's that mean—'cardiac arrest'?"

"They're doing everything they can," Doohan said.

They sat in silence for half an hour. Mrs. Rosenberg had leaned back in her chair and closed her eyes. Her face showed a distinct flush now and she would dab at it every now and then with the handkerchief. Doohan found himself watching her intently, something ticking in the back of his mind.

Then the doctor was standing there telling them the same things he must have told the bereaved a dozen times before. It was always the same and it was always new, Doohan thought. There was no such thing as getting used to it.

"I'm sorry, Mrs. Rosenberg, we tried everything we

could. His lungs were completely filled. He couldn't possibly have survived."

Mrs. Rosenberg nodded, dabbed at her face once more and started to get up from her chair. She swayed uncertainly for a moment, said pathetically, "I don't feel very well," and abruptly crumpled to the floor.

The doctor turned to the nurse's station. "Stretcher!" Doohan knelt down next to Mrs. Rosenberg. Her breathing was labored. He put his hand on her forehead. A hundred and two, at least.

"She's pretty sick."

"I can guess why," the doctor said curtly.

Two orderlies were hurrying down the hall with a stretcher.

"Same thing as her husband?"

"That's what it looks like to me."

The orderlies rolled her gently on the stretcher and left, the doctor following them. Doohan watched them go down the corridor and then Suzanne said, "She didn't stay at the hotel."

"Not overnight," Doohan said. "In fact, she wasn't there very long at all and my guess is she really didn't go to many of the functions or the parties."

"Then she could be the first of our second-generation victims."

Doohan walked over to the nurse's station to call Anna. "If she is, then she won't be the last." He asked to use the phone, and as he dialed, he thought with regret of Mrs. Rosenberg's illness.

He had been building a theory and her sickness might come very close to ruining it.

10

THE HOTEL CORDOBA reminded Doohan of the Strand Palace, just off Trafalgar Square, a few blocks from London's theater district. The Cordoba was on Geary, several blocks west of the Geary and Curran theaters that made up San Francisco's own theatrical area. Like the Strand Palace, it had once boasted an elegance that made it one of the most exclusive hotels in the city. But that was years ago. The exclusive hotels now were the Fairmont, the Mark Hopkins, and the Stanford Court—San Francisco's equivalent of Claridge's, the Connaught, and the Savoy.

The lobby was small, the palms well tended, and the carpet by the front desk well worn. Doohan glanced around the almost empty lobby and noted evidence of an aborted renovation that had probably been started the year before. You rarely saw the type of elaborate scrollwork that decorated the base of the mezzanine balcony. It had obviously been stripped to the plaster and wood base and lovingly repainted a beige with gold highlights in the medallions of the scrolls.

"It's growing old gracefully," Suzanne said.

"But you'd hate to live here."

"I'd hate to *die* here," she corrected.

They were almost to the desk when the CDC man intercepted them, flipped open his wallet to show his temporary Department of Health ID, and said, "Gifford, Public Health. I'm sorry, you folks can't register here. Department of Health regulations."

A young desk clerk hastily materialized from the inner office. "It's only temporary," he said smoothly.

"I can recommend the Raphael or the Lombard. The next time you're in San Francisco, please stop back. We'll be able to serve you then." A winning smile from a young man who believed most of life's problems could be solved by winning smiles, Doohan thought. San Francisco was plagued with them.

He introduced himself and Suzanne. Gifford nodded, said: "The EIS team is working the kitchen; the city's Environmental Health Services is checking out the HVAC system and the rooms and hallways."

The desk clerk shook his head in disgust. "You know, you people are ruining a fine hotel. Three conventions have canceled. We've lost ten permanent residents and we have no new guests." He turned to Gifford. "One of your men has impounded Mrs. Ferguson's pet toucan," he said seriously.

Gifford winced. "I told her it was just for testing and observation. I'll talk with her again if you think it'll help."

"It shouldn't take long to inspect the hotel," Suzanne said.

The desk clerk was stiff. "Reputations make or break hotels, Dr. Synge. And right now the Cordoba has a reputation as a pesthouse. If all I had to go on was what I had heard and read, I wouldn't register here—and neither would you. The hotel has always been a marginal one; this will kill it."

It was like closing down a tea stall in Bangladesh to fumigate it, Doohan thought. "We don't have any choice; we'll be out as soon as possible."

The clerk shrugged. "Take your time; the damage is done."

Gifford headed for the coffee shop, Doohan and Suzanne following.

"What's been the procedure so far?" Doohan asked.

"We've got a floor plan of the hotel and marked all the rooms where the veterans stayed—personal rooms and public as well. There may be a link with the HVAC system, we're checking it."

"Did you get a complete registration list?"

Gifford nodded. "One from the manager and another from the convention chairman. We're starting to trace movements now and believe me, that's going to be a bitch. Most of them drove up, about a third flew in."

"What about fellow plane passengers?"

"The airlines are tracing them. The police taxi detail is talking with the local cab drivers who worked the hotel."

The sign on the coffee shop door read CLOSED. Gifford pushed through. Inside, several men were vacuuming sections of the wallpaper near the dining area and periodically taking small plastic bags from the vacuum cleaners which they sealed and labeled. "We're checking the wallpaper and the draperies— you can get Valley Fever from the fungus in dry dust. A possibility, though it's a faint one."

In the kitchen, two men were going through the food stores, taking samples from every container and bin. "What about room service?" Suzanne asked.

"We've got samples of tap water, samples of ice water, even one of the pitchers they served the ice water in. Some of the hospitality suite punch was stored in the icebox and we've got a sample of that."

Doohan was looking around the kitchen. It was small but well laid out, divided into a grill area and a more elaborate cooking section. "The kitchen serves both the coffee shop and the small restaurant upstairs," Gifford explained. "Some things we'd like to check, but it's impossible. How often, for instance, were the refrigerators opened so we can get some idea of the actual temperatures inside, not the ones they were set at. And the same thing with the steam tables."

"It seems a small kitchen to serve a banquet for five hundred," Doohan said.

"A small kitchen, well organized, can serve an amazing amount of food. The main crunch comes in the help. You have to have more waiters, more busboys, bring in extra bartenders, some more kitchen help. It's a strain, but you can do it."

Doohan made a mental note to check out the catering director. "What about the mop closets?"

"The chemistry division is checking out all the insecticides and cleaners. Toxicology will double-check."

"Any wine or liquor served?"

"We've got samples, though we haven't a complete check on what the veterans brought in with them, outside of the fact that it was a lot. Some cigarette companies were handing out samples and we managed to get a few packs of those too."

"What about prostitutes?" Suzanne asked. "We talked with one man who had met a prostitute here."

Gifford looked surprised. "Probably an amateur. Professionals stick to a few of the Tenderloin hotels and this is hardly one of them. But the average age is getting up there. If they had been younger, we would have expected more sexuals."

"You've checked the bottled water on the floors?" Doohan asked.

Gifford nodded. "Also the hotel's main water system, including the water softener and filtrations units."

They followed Gifford through the kitchen and down to the basement. Two men were working on an air-conditioning unit while another team was disassembling a boiler. "This particular boiler serves the floors that were used by the conventioneers. They were blocking rooms, by the way, so the veterans were restricted to a relatively few floors. Too many permanent guests to scatter them around the hotel."

Doohan knelt down by the men working on the boiler. The firebox was an older model with a cast-iron flame spreader and a series of multiple jets beneath it. The flame spreader had cracked near one of its mounts and somebody had used heavy-gauge wire to anchor it to its support instead of welding it back.

"Hand me the wire cutters, will you?" He tugged for a moment, then snipped and came up with a piece of wire lodged in the jaws. Gifford looked at him questioningly. "When you test for heavy metals, see if it has any nickel in it. If I remember my chemistry, nickel reacts with carbon monoxide at a fairly low temperature to produce nickel carbonyl. It can be damnably toxic."

Back in the lobby, Gifford carefully placed the wire

in another plastic envelope, labeled it, and dropped it in one of a number of wooden boxes stacked against the lobby wall. All of them were partially filled with plastic envelopes, sealed and labeled, or with plastic canisters, also labeled.

"There's only one thing wrong," Gifford said sadly. "It will take us weeks to go through this stuff and sort out all the false leads. And I have a feeling we don't have that much time."

"That's right," Doohan agreed, "we probably don't." He glanced around the empty lobby again, then asked, "Where's the main conference room?"

"There's a small auditorium on the mezzanine. It's where most of the meetings were held."

In the auditorium, Doohan moved a folding chair beneath one of the air-conditioning ducts and sat down, apparently lost in thought. Suzanne watched him curiously for a while, then finally said: "What *are* you thinking?"

"I'm imagining I'm a conventioneer," Doohan said slowly. "Breathing in . . . something . . . from the air duct above my head. Whatever it is, there's no cure for it. In a week, I'll be dead."

"You're being morbid. Besides, not every conventioneer came down with it, which would seem to eliminate its being airborne."

"None of the hotel staff came down with it either," Doohan said. "That bothers me a lot."

Suzanne shivered. "I could use some coffee."

Doohan smiled. "So could I. But not here."

In the Pam Pam across the street, Suzanne leaned against the back of the booth and sighed. Doohan glanced at her sympathetically. "Tired?"

"Bushed. Probably a little jet lag. I'll be a lot more tired before it's all over." Pause. "You must have gotten pretty tired in India at times."

"Bangladesh. Most of the time."

Curiously. "What was it like?"

"Hard, frustrating. Sickening. The refugee situation made it difficult. You'd think an area would be cleared of smallpox and then it would pop up again." The images started to crowd in once more. "And it was hot. My God, it was hot—I lost thirty pounds in the first ninety days. And it was difficult getting around. Traveling by trains was out. It was standing room only and, believe me, you didn't want to stand on those trains."

"How did you get around?"

"Any way I could—motorcycle, rickshaw, oxcart, bicycle, you name it. You didn't travel much after dark; the bugs would eat you alive. We'd cover thirty to forty outbreaks a week, and after a while, you felt you were vaccinating people in your sleep."

"What did you get out of it?" she asked suddenly. There was an intensity in her voice and he glanced up at her. He couldn't read her expression. "They certainly didn't pay you much."

He thought for a minute before answering. "Did you ever see a three-year-old child with smallpox—a full-blown, fully developed, shrieking case of smallpox? You can't see the skin for the sores, literally. And the victims carry the scars all their lives; you wind up with skin that looks like the craters of the moon. Every time you see yourself in a mirror, you're reminded of the torment you went through."

"You're telling me why you did it," she said gently. "Not what you got out of it."

Doohan felt uneasy. "It sounds idealistic when I say it now, but it was very real to me then," he said slowly. "I guess it still is. What you get is . . . a tremendous feeling of accomplishment. You feel good about yourself. You're spending every day saving other people's lives. Sometimes I felt guilty about it because it's such a sense of . . . power."

"Every doctor feels that way at times."

Doohan felt contemptuous. "No, they don't. There aren't that many people who are sick over here, not really sick, not by comparison. It's day after day, treating them by the hundreds . . . It's like you're playing God. You lose one or two, you lose a dozen, but when you win, you win big. You hate to lose; *I* hate to lose, I'm a terrible loser. But then you find the source of infection and you stamp it out and the people line up by the hundreds to be saved and you're . . . God."

There was a thoughtful look on her face. "How did you feel about Herman Rosenberg today?"

"I hated to lose him," Doohan said softly. "I hated to lose Benoit. All those people who died because of this—whatever it is—I hated to lose all of them. I want desperately to find out what did it. I *will* find out. But I want to find out more than just what did it, I want to *beat* what did it."

He was moody for a moment. "I sound manic, don't I? I am. I feel pretty deeply about what I do. There's a family side to it, too. My father died in the Welsh coal fields after we moved from Aberdeen—black lung disease that clogged his alveoli with dirty tar. My mother died of diphtheria. Diphtheria, mind you, in an age when it had become one of the rarest of all diseases, because she had never been vaccinated, never had the opportunity to get vaccinated. . . ."

She had deliberately drawn him out, he thought, and he had been carried away. Well, whether she liked it or not, she now had an idea of what motivated him. "Please, for ten minutes, let's not talk about disease."

She had made notes earlier and now lifted her briefcase to the table to slip her notebook inside. A rich-looking leather case, Doohan thought, with "SP" embossed in delicate script on the side. He watched her hands as she worked the latches. They were perfectly groomed hands, long and tapering with professionally shaped nails. Expensive hands. Like faces and figures, they had cost time and money to keep in that condition. They must be a point of vanity with her, he thought; they didn't go with her "no-nonsense" image.

"Are you married?" He pointed at the initials on the briefcase.

"In a sense." She hesitated, not looking directly at him. "I wouldn't call it a successful marriage."

"That's an expensive case."

Her face was carefully blank. "He has his faults, but

I can't claim that lack of generosity is one of them. What about yourself? You wear a ring but you've never mentioned your wife."

"Beth died in an accident back home several years ago."

"While you were away?"

He nodded. "I should have been there. I wasn't."

"I'm sorry."

"It happens." He lapsed into silence for a long moment, thinking he hadn't talked so much in years. Bangladesh . . . He toyed with his cooling cup of coffee, the images flooding in again.

"The ten minutes are up, aren't they?" Suzanne said.

He blinked, shaking the mood. "They went fast, didn't they?" He hunched over the table. "Consider the extreme selectivity of the disease, the high fatality rate, the rapidity of onset. We may be dealing with something that had been introduced into the environment for a period of time and then withdrawn."

"You mean some kind of poison?" she said tentatively.

He reached in his pocket for his wallet. "It's an idea. If I could only think of a motive for somebody wanting to murder a hotel full of aging war veterans."

As they were leaving, Suzanne said: "You've heard of the meeting tonight?"

Anna had mentioned something, but he couldn't recall it. "No, I haven't."

"Rumors are that we're going to meet the Army representative who's working with Dr. Miltrait."

Doohan laughed. "The Army? I wondered how long it would be before the bloody military stepped in."

11

MAJOR LAWRENCE HANSON teetered back in the wooden chair and waited patiently for Dr. Miltrait to finish reading the letter. The meeting would start fairly soon and he didn't want to hold Miltrait up. As far as the meeting went, he was there only to observe, to be introduced briefly since his presence couldn't exactly be hidden, and to keep a low profile from then on. As far as Miltrait went, it was crucial that the man understood just what was at stake.

Brilliant man, Hanson thought; at least, that's what the dossier said. He watched Miltrait's eyes dart nervously over the page, the ash on his cigarette growing longer and longer. He wasn't reading it, Hanson decided; he was analyzing it and that meant trouble. He glanced at the clock on the wall. A quarter to seven. They were due in the auditorium in fifteen minutes.

Miltrait finally looked up. "You can't exactly keep this a secret, you know. I can't prevent people from talking."

You could try, Hanson thought to himself. Aloud, he said: "I'm not trying to be secretive about my presence, but I hardly intend to seek publicity. It wouldn't help to have my name in the papers." Miltrait looked as if he were about to say something; Hanson decided to keep him off balance. Christ, he hated dealing with civilians. Who was the idiot who said that war should be left in the hands of the civilians? Wars were made by the civilians to begin with. "We had hoped we could keep the whole outbreak under wraps for another forty-eight hours."

The cigarette jiggled and another half inch of ash cascaded over Miltrait's trousers. "With almost every isolation ward in the city filled? The public health people are part of the community. They go home at the end of the day. They talk with their wives; they talk with their friends. You want to impose a news blackout? You might as well paper the city with headlines six feet high."

"A news blackout would be stupid," Hanson agreed easily. "But it might be a good idea if all press releases were cleared through me from now on."

Miltrait shrugged. He couldn't care less about press relations, Hanson thought. What annoyed him was the piece of paper he was holding that said Major Lawrence Hanson was to be advised of all information obtained by the CDC in regard to the so-called "Veterans' Disease" and also advised of all decisions made. In effect, Miltrait was ordered to defer all such decisions to the Chemical Corps field representative, namely Major Hanson.

"We've maintained a liaison with the CDC headquarters in Atlanta for four years," Hanson continued smoothly. "We're lost among the thousands down there, so you were probably never aware of us. But we're there, Doctor."

"A tribute to national paranoia," Miltrait said curtly. "Will you be disappointed if we find out it's a bacterium after all?"

"I'd be very happy," Hanson said. He was half ashamed that there was a part of him that delighted in bearding Miltrait. It wasn't Miltrait's fault that he resembled one of Hanson's old instructors at the Point. "Doctor, your outbreak is not only curious, it's frightening. Primarily men and women in their fifties plus, the great majority of them veterans. The disease is tremendously virulent and invasive and if it continues to spread, the Army may become actively involved if only for reasons of civil disorder. Ever since swine flu showed up at Fort Dix a few years back, we get jumpy when there's an outbreak like this that we can't identify."

Miltrait was not impressed. "I'll post this on my bulletin board." He stood up and brushed off his pants. "Major, the only serious germ warfare attacks against the United States were made by the United States. I'm old enough to remember the simulated tests against San Francisco in the fifties and the fact that one man died because of them. *Serratia Marcescens,* as I recall."

Hanson's eyes narrowed slightly. "If you're aware of that, then you're also aware that all offensive bacterial warfare research was discontinued years ago."

"So they say." Miltrait took a file folder of paper out of his briefcase. "We've got a serious outbreak; my people are overburdened, and I personally don't like the idea of the Army looking over my shoulder. Any contact you have with my teams will come directly through me."

"My own people have been instructed on that," Hanson said.

"That's something else I don't like. How many people are you bringing in? The letter doesn't specify and you haven't told me."

Hanson sighed. "I've been assigned some toxicology experts and a biologist, some lab technicians and some clerical help. And some security people, but they're hardly going to interfere with the technical end." Time for the iron hand, he thought. He let his voice harden. "The situation here may or may not develop into something of military significance. I'm to make my own judgments and report back."

Miltrait glanced at the wall clock. "I understand you perfectly, Major. Let's go; I don't suppose anybody will leave before we get there. People know you're here; so you might as well come along and be introduced."

There were times when he wished he were back in Vietnam, Hanson thought. Commanding the troops of a Smoke Generator Company was a neat and uncomplicated existence; it was far removed from the endless conferences and reports and temporary assignments that had become his life since his transfer to Washington. Perhaps he was just getting older; maybe that was it. Regression. He preferred to command

troops and fight battles than to read endless studies of
new defensive agents or protective clothing and to
worry constantly about the public-relations image of
the corps.

The atmosphere in the auditorium was one of sub-
dued expectation. They were curious about him, Hanson thought, and he couldn't blame them. Once on
stage, he took a seat at the far left and waited while
Miltrait talked to two assistants who had been waiting
for him.

Most of the people in the audience knew the others
on stage, but they didn't know him and they stared in
curiosity. Hanson leaned back in his chair, crossed his
legs and returned the inspection. A bright, alert
group, he thought, and let his eyes rove. They stopped
when they came to a tall blonde in the next to the
rear row. Severely tailored suit, slender, glasses. He
had met her someplace, he thought, and then the
tumblers started falling into position. Dr. Suzanne
Synge, early thirties, undergraduate from Columbia,
doctorate at Boston Medical College, internship at
County Hospital in Chicago . . . And six weeks at the
Chemical Center in Anniston, Alabama, attending a
series of seminars on the containment of a biological
attack. A good mind . . .

Miltrait had finished his whispered conference and
one of the men was helping him set up a large chart-
card display. Miltrait adjusted his lapel mike and
turned to the audience.

"Before we get started"—a pause to clear his throat
—"I want to call your attention to the draft of the
Morbidity and Mortality Report we'll be circulating
tomorrow morning. We have had seventy-one confirmed cases and a fatality rate approaching seventy
per cent." He waited until the wave of whispering had
subsided. "I would like Dr. Marshall here to review
the symptomology . . ."

Hanson's attention drifted back to Dr. Synge. Next
to her was a lean man with reddish hair, smoking a
pipe. The photographs flicked through his mind again

and he quickly settled on one. Dr. Calvin Doohan, the field representative for WHO. To be handled with kid gloves . . . and watched very closely. It was to be remembered at all times that Doohan was a foreign national and did not have security clearance.

And then he realized with something of a shock that Doohan was inspecting him as closely as he was inspecting Doohan. Their eyes met for a moment and he thought that Doohan half-smiled. Was he that obvious? Hanson wondered uneasily. Did he look that much the military man, even in mufti?

". . . and no second-generation infections of which we're aware. Any questions?"

A man in a lab smock in the front row raised a hand. "Isn't it possible we're dealing with an organism that has an unusually long incubation period? It could be something like hepatitis-B with an incubation period of six months."

"I don't think so," Miltrait said dryly. "Our best guess on the source of the infection is the VAW convention that ended ten days ago. That's the only common contact in the recent past among all the known cases."

Miltrait was about to continue when a young man stood up and said, "Doctor, has there been any evidence of a toxin?"

"We'll get into that in the course of this briefing," Miltrait said, irritated.

"But a toxin is a possibility, isn't it?" the young man persisted.

Miltrait stared at him nearsightedly. "I don't believe I know you; would you identify yourself, please?"

There was a stir in the audience now. Hanson was suddenly alert, knowing instinctively what was going to happen next.

"And I notice that Major Hanson of the Army Chemical Corps is on the platform. Does this mean the outbreak has military implications?"

Hanson got to his feet and borrowed Miltrait's lapel mike. "What it means," he said easily, "is that the Army has some of the best toxicologists in the field. We're here to assist the CDC in every way possible." He gave the mike back to Miltrait and sat down. He was still tense.

The young man was shouting now. "Isn't it true you testified before the congressional subcommittee investigating the accidental release of nerve gases in Utah several years ago?"

Hanson stood up again; he didn't bother with the microphone. "I'll have to ask you to identify yourself, sir."

"You're not answering my question! Why does the Chemical Corps have a representative here? Is this a simple outbreak of disease, as the public has been told, or is this a military attack against the United States?"

"I gather you're a member of the press," Hanson said coolly. "The alternative press, perhaps?" Laughter. "But others in the room may have wondered, so I'll answer your question now rather than later in the discussion—and then I'll have to ask you to leave. This is a closed meeting."

"Answer my question!" the young man shrilled.

"I'll be glad to. Yes, it's possible that a toxin of some kind is involved. The Chemical Corps routinely maintains liaison with the CDC and in situations such as this they routinely call on us. There is no other reason for our presence here. I have no reason to believe that the Veterans' Disease represents a military excursion nor are we conducting any investigation on that basis."

"Have you seen yesterday's *Pravda*, Major?"

"You haven't identified yourself yet," Hanson said calmly.

"I'm from the Berkeley *Shaft* and I want to know if you've seen yesterday's *Pravda!*"

Two men were moving in from the rear of the auditorium now. Hanson stalled. "Perhaps you can tell me what it said?" Not much laughter now. The audience was uneasy.

The young man suddenly spotted the two others working their way toward him. He started waving a paper. "The Russians have accused the United States of using the veterans' convention for a field test of a biological weapon!" He was trapped in the aisle now. Another ten seconds.

"As most of the audience knows," Hanson said, "all offensive biological weapon research ended in the United States in 1969 by executive order."

"Bullshit!" the young man shouted. "That's bullshit! You can't tell me we're letting such a weapon go to the enemy by default!"

They had him then. One of Hanson's men clamped the reporter's arms behind his back; the other grabbed his feet as the young man started kicking to get away.

"Neither you nor your goons—!"

Hanson said, "Don't hurt him!" a moment too late. There was the soft thud of a fist hitting flesh and the young man suddenly sagged, blood trickling from his mouth and down his shirt. The audience watched in stunned silence and then the three men were out of the auditorium.

Hanson sat back down. It was Miltrait's show, let him try and salvage it. Miltrait started to speak, and then several people were on their feet shouting questions and a moment later the room was in uproar with Miltrait gaveling for order and yelling for quiet.

Hanson folded his arms, stretched out his legs, and gloomily watched the audience while Miltrait rapped for order. There was no way on God's green earth that he could now convince the Department of Health and the CDC teams that the investigation was other than a military one. Some things would be easier now; it wouldn't be necessary to handle anybody, including Miltrait, with kid gloves.

But he would still have preferred it the other way.

12

"AFTER THAT, I think I need a drink," Doohan said. "What about you?"

"I think I need a good night's sleep more."

"Very sensible attitude," Doohan murmured. "I mean, it goes with the shoes and the suit." He threw up his hands before she could respond. "You're right, you're absolutely right. We've been burning the candle at both ends and tomorrow comes too soon and all that rot."

"If I didn't know you better, I would think you were charming," she said. "Where to?"

In the car, he said: "What about the lobby of the Hyatt Regency? They make a great Ramos fizz."

"Love to—I've never seen it."

Ten minutes later, he had parked outside of 101 Grove. Suzanne looked at him questioningly. "Guilty conscience?"

"Self-protection. I couldn't enjoy a night out if I thought I was needed here." He was back in five minutes.

"Do they need us?"

"Anna said to enjoy ourselves."

"Then why the frown?"

He was silent for a moment. Then: "Reflex action; there's really nothing to frown about." He sensed that she was going to accuse him of holding something back; then she had changed her mind and relaxed. It was just as well, he thought. They really couldn't be sure of it until morning anyway.

In the hotel, Doohan watched with amusement as Suzanne craned her head back to take in the full expanse of the enormous lobby that extended skyward for seventeen floors, the balconylike halls jutting out over the lobby floor all the way up to the skylight in the form of an inverted "V." Trees in huge tubs lined one side, while the center of the lobby was dominated by a four-story-high sculpture of anodized aluminum tubing looking for all the world like an enormous blowup of the Wool Institute symbol. Beneath the sculpture was a reflecting pool with sheets of water cascading over its sides.

"Originally they were going to hang the sculpture from the ceiling rather than set it on risers. Then somebody pointed out that in an earthquake it might act like a pendulum and knock out the side walls."

She looked skeptical. "Is that true?"

"I have no idea—but I think it makes a splendid story."

He found an empty table in the conversation pit just beyond the sculpture and motioned to the waitress. The first night out in . . . how long? He placed their orders, watched the tourists for a moment, then said: "Hanson's explanation won't wash, you know."

"That he's here as an observer, or just to supervise an army toxicologist or two? That was for the newspapers." She tapped a cigarette on the back of her hand and lit it, ignoring his hasty fumble with a pack of matches.

"The newspapers won't buy it either," he said. A girl at the next table caught his eye; she was very young, very pretty, and had a light, musical laugh that momentarily reminded him of Elizabeth. Beth had been about that age when they first met—and laughed in much the same way. "He's going to make it very difficult for me, you know."

Suzanne was watching the elevators, outlined with lights, climb toward the skylight far above. "How do you mean?"

"A lot of countries want detailed information about the outbreak and they're expecting me, as the representative of WHO, to supply it. Tomorrow I'm going to have to tell them that the American military is involved."

"I keep forgetting—"

"—that I'm not an American national." Even the way the girl held her head, just *so*, reminded him of Beth.

"You think you'll have trouble getting information from our good Major Hanson?"

"I doubt that the major will extend himself very far out of courtesy." He thought about it for a moment. "If the United States restricts information, it will worry the health departments of other countries overseas. They'll probably increase travel and import restrictions, and you can hardly blame them. National boundaries are only lines drawn on maps. Animals can't read the signposts and the winds are remarkably unprejudiced. The smallpox virus certainly never paid much attention to borders. A full-fledged epidemic of some unknown disease in the United States and it's only a matter of days before it shows up somewhere else."

"We live in a dangerous world," Suzanne said slowly. "You can hardly blame Washington for being concerned. We still don't know much about the disease."

"Hanson's much more than just an observer," Doohan said with conviction.

"You don't like him, do you?"

He shrugged. "I'm prejudiced against the military; they're in a different business than I am. They take lives; I save lives." He toyed with his drink for a moment. "You read the lives of military men and once they're retired, they all hate war. But why did they join in the first place? And why do they never quit before it's time to draw a juicy pension."

"They're necessary," Suzanne said quietly.

"We hire the wolves to protect the lambs from other wolves?"

"You're an innocent, Calvin." He started to protest and she smiled. "You're classifying everything in terms of black and white. I thought that was an American trait, that Europeans were more worldly, more sophisticated." She patted his hand. "It's a deadly world, Calvin, and it's filled with violent people. The bar-

barians were never defeated, you know—and now they're within the city's gates."

She wasn't teasing him so much as probing him, Doohan thought. "Do you think the underground reporter was right?"

She looked surprised. "About the disease being a military weapon? Good heavens, no. The government has tested the spread of bacterial weapons in the past but I can hardly believe it would test an actual weapon, discounting the basic immorality. There's always the risk it would result in a massive pandemic. And I rather doubt it's an enemy attack or even a test. The United States has the largest medical infrastructure in the world. We're automatically the best equipped when it comes to defense. If another country challenged us in that field, it would be no contest at all."

The girl at the next table rose to leave; Doohan watched her all the way. She even walked like Elizabeth. "What do you think will happen?"

"I think by tomorrow we'll know. The chances are very good that we'll have a terrifying epidemic on our hands."

Suzanne couldn't forget 101 Grove either, he thought. "And when it's over?"

"We'll take the sera we've collected, seal it up in our vaults in Atlanta and wait for the next outbreak in the hope we can identify the bug. But it will end and we may be no wiser. The only thing we'll know for sure is that there's some new bug in the world and it's deadly and we don't know how to handle it."

"And you?"

"I'll go back to Los Angeles. Or perhaps I'll take a job in Atlanta. They've offered me one in the epidemiology section. I'll find a quiet bachelor girl's pad and try to get my head together, as they say. Maybe I'll even get a cat."

"Was it that bad?"

She studied the elevators in the distance. "Maybe not as bad as all that. Maybe worse."

"How long were you married?"

"An eternity. And a day." She laughed. "It's much

the same thing. Part of it was very satisfying. The sense-of-belonging part. My husband was a very strong man, a man of substance, I guess you'd call him. People admired him; they looked up to him. It was marvelous, basking in his reflected glory."

"Until you realized it was only reflected?"

She looked down at her drink. "I was never the old-fashioned sort of wife. I wasn't even your stylish, modern wife who can fill her day with social events and do-gooder causes and all the other trivia. I wanted a life of my own and Arnold wouldn't allow that. In his own mind, I suppose, he thought he owned me."

"Why did you marry him?"

Her eyes were suddenly cool and appraising. "He bought me with roses and theater tickets and a feeling of financial security. I discovered I liked money; my family was very poor and it took every cent I could scrape up to get through school."

Doohan felt embarrassed. Listening to Suzanne was like watching somebody take off their clothes in public. "Didn't you ever love him?"

She downed the rest of her drink in one gulp. She smiled but her gray eyes were icy with contempt and he realized that part of her had suddenly become completely inaccessible to him.

"Love? No, not ever. But that's not surprising; I don't think I've ever known what the word means. When we're younger, we have fantasies about what love is. Then we spend the rest of our lives discovering that no two people share the same fantasy."

She looked at him quizzically. "Calvin, do you want to go to bed with me?"

There was no way he could have seen it coming, Doohan thought. "That's not why I asked you out."

"Do you?"

He had a flash of the girl sitting at the next table who had reminded him so much of Elizabeth. "I don't think so. Not tonight at any rate."

"But perhaps later? At your time and your convenience?"

He reddened, feeling immensely foolish. "It's just that circumstances aren't right."

"But there will be some other time. When circumstances include flowers and dinner and the theater?"

"There's something wrong with that?"

She stared at him for a moment, then rose from the table without replying. She walked briskly up the steps of the conversation pit and headed for the escalators. Doohan hurried after her. A knot of tourists delayed him at the pool and he didn't catch up to her until she had reached the street.

"I've nothing in common with your ex-husband," he said angrily. "I wish you would remember that."

She glared at him coldly for a moment longer, then sighed and gave it up. "All right, Calvin, I'll try and remember that. But no promises."

Once in the car, he could sense her beginning to thaw. He suddenly felt a deep empathy for her. Strange woman, he thought. It was the first time in his life he found himself torn between two conflicting desires: to kiss her and to hit her, very hard.

And then he found himself thinking about 101 Grove Street and the situation map and the totals of the dying and the dead and what they might be tomorrow.

He was startled when Suzanne suddenly curled up against his side. He had momentarily forgotten her.

13

REPORTERS AND TV crews were still besieging the Department of Health the next morning. Doohan checked in with the guard on duty, then hurried to the conference room to check the situation map. There were now seventy-three cases; fifty-five of them fatalities. An increase of six in the number of fatalities, but only two in the number of additional cases.

Anna was on the phone when he walked into her office. He took a seat and waited patiently for her to finish. "You noticed?" she said when she was through.

"It's leveling off."

"Only two cases in the last twelve hours and I don't think there'll be any more after today. Miltrait will probably make an announcement this afternoon." She lifted a cup of hot coffee and blew on it. "You could cut the sense of relief around here with a dull knife."

"And the fatalities?"

She looked glum. "We're approaching a hundred per cent. All of those who have it will probably die of it. Don't ask me what it is; nobody has any idea, including the CDC. I'm just grateful that it seems to be dying out; another day of this and the whole city would probably be in a panic."

Doohan picked up his briefcase. Anna frowned. "Calvin—the army toxicologists are working out of Laguna Honda where we have the toxicology lab. Miltrait and Hanson have set up offices there as well; it's not as crowded as it is here. They want you as WHO liaison to work there, too."

"I'm not so sure I like that," Doohan said slowly. "I'm not assigned to them."

"You are now; Hanson got Espinosa's approval early this morning." She reached for the phone again. "Miltrait is all right; he's an odd duck but he comes with good recommendations. I don't know a thing about Hanson. My guess is that he doesn't consider you a friendly and wants to keep an eye on you." She started dialing, looking at him over the top of her glasses. "Good luck. The rats and I will miss you."

At Laguna Honda, two blue-uniformed security guards were posted on the floor housing the CDC offices; both carried side arms. They checked his identification with studied courtesy before letting him on the floor. Lean, young guards with bleak eyes and a professional air, Doohan thought. Most civilian security services used older men, usually retired policemen with fallen arches and attitudes to match. Civilian guards? he wondered. Not bloody likely. The Army was starting to take over.

What did Major Hanson know, he speculated, that he, Calvin Doohan, did not?

He found Miltrait in a large office with a situation map duplicating the one at 101 Grove. "Come on in, Doohan." The little man waved at the map. "Just two cases since last night; it's winding down."

"Any second-generation infections?"

"Only Mrs. Rosenberg, and I'm not sure she qualifies. Goddamnit, Doohan, that's what bothers me. As virulent as the primary infection is, it doesn't seem to be transmitted." He shook his head in frustration. "All our plates in Atlanta have proved negative. Which means it's either a toxin or a completely new viral strain."

"That seems to rule out a bacteriumlike agent such as the Legionnaires' Disease."

"Not likely. But we'll find out eventually. We've got two thousand cultures going in Atlanta and French has several hundred going over in Berkeley." He paused in irritation. "Do you know what a problem it is getting fertile eggs from antibiotic-free flocks when you start this broad a screening program?" Doohan looked sympathetic. "We'll be spending the next six months trying to find out what it was. Don't fool yourself; if it happened once, it can happen again. Damned world's filling up with bugs we don't know anything about."

Doohan waited for an opening, then asked: "Will I be briefed by your office?"

Miltrait suddenly looked uneasy. "Your briefings will come from Major Hanson." He read the expression on Doohan's face. "I don't have anything to say about that, Doohan. He's a military man and I appreciate the antagonism that most civilians feel toward the military. But both Major Hanson and his people have proved to be a great help."

"People?"

"He's brought in a team of army toxicologists from Toole, Utah. Give the boys from Dugway Proving Grounds their due; they know their poisons." He looked faintly embarrassed. "Hanson's office is on the right, Doohan—next one down."

Hanson was still in mufti but he wore his suit like a disguise. Even though he was sitting down, Doohan guessed him to be a tall, spare man. Early thirties, thin, carefully trimmed mustache, none of the puffiness about the jowls that some peacetime civilian officers acquire. Doohan made another guess, then: To Hanson, the United States wasn't at peace. A career man, narrow-minded and righteous, undoubtedly incorruptible. The worst kind, Doohan thought; you could never outmaneuver them.

Hanson was as professionally smooth as he had been at the meeting. "Since Grove Street is so overcrowded, Doctor, I thought it would be more practical if you moved down here for the duration. I've already put you down to receive the daily M&M report."

Doohan thought he could detect the standard contempt of the military for the civilian, then wondered if it was just a reflection of his own prejudice. "I've promised WHO a complete report every day," Doohan said casually. "I imagine I'll check out Grove Street once a day too."

Hanson studied him for a moment and Doohan got the impression he was being weighed and found wanting. "I'm not so sure that's wise, Doctor. They're working under a lot of pressure over there and I have a feeling frequent visits would only slow down their work." He held up a hand. "More importantly, a good deal of what you might hear would be speculative and unevaluated data. We've already had a problem with misinformation reaching the press."

"I'm not the press," Doohan said calmly.

Hanson stood up and paced to the window for a moment. His guess had been right, Doohan thought. Tall. Angular. A handsome DeGaulle. "Then I'll have to be blunt, Doctor. This is a sensitive internal situation and I'd appreciate it if you would limit your reports to material in the daily M and M plus whatever briefings you get from this office." A pause, his face carefully deferential: "If that's all right with you?"

"Of course," Doohan said sarcastically. "I'll send you a courtesy copy of my reports."

"I was about to request one," Hanson murmured.

"Am I allowed to ask questions?" Hanson nodded. "Is there any indication it's a toxin?"

Hanson stood up, his face still bland and affable. "That's one of the assumptions we're working on. Nice meeting you, Doctor. Your office is further down the hall. And by the way, shipping is first floor, rear. You'll find Dr. Synge down there."

It was a subtle warning of some kind, Doohan thought. There was nothing he could read in Hanson's face, but he knew the major was an antagonist. And he hadn't the slightest idea why.

In the shipping area, packing crates were stacked against both walls; bags of excelsior and polyurethane packing mats spilled from several open cardboard containers. Against another wall were several large freezers; one was open and Doohan could see blocks of dry ice stacked inside. Several lab men were busy packing and labeling plastic containers, then sealing them into fiber cartons for shipment. Some of the cartons were being packed with dry ice from the freezer.

Suzanne was standing by a pallet of crates, checking off items in the shipment. "You're setting up a production line," Doohan said.

She glanced up. "Blood samples, sputum samples,

feces, urine samples, tissue samples from autopsies—
and the samples from the hotel. You name it." She
started checking off another crate.

"I stopped over at Grove Street; it's starting to level
off. Nobody knows why; nobody knows the cause
either."

"I haven't been told anything," she said. There was
an odd inflection in her voice and Doohan glanced at
her sharply.

"What do you mean?"

"I don't think it's a good idea that you drop around,"
she said in a low voice. "They don't particularly trust
you."

"I think we ought to have dinner tonight and talk
about it."

"With flowers and wine?"

"We could skip the flowers and pick up some Guin-
ness."

She hesitated, vaguely troubled. "Let's see what it
looks like at six o'clock. If there are no rush shipments
to go out and I can't be useful elsewhere—maybe. I'll
call you."

He went back upstairs to the cubbyhole he had
been assigned for an office, lost in thought. Last night,
he had almost resolved to forget Suzanne. This morning, he had ignored his resolution. But she still wasn't
the sort of woman who attracted him, he thought, and
then immediately wondered if that were true. Elizabeth and Suzanne were somewhat alike in tempera-
ment—perhaps very much alike—though there the
similarity ended. Elizabeth had been smaller, more
petite, certainly more . . . girlish, if that were the
word. Suzanne was older, more mature.

But then, so was he. In his mind, Elizabeth would
never age a day from that spring morning in Aberdeen.
But he was five years older now, and would be another day older come morning, and two days older
come the next.

He looked around the office, then walked to the
window and stared down at the world below. Hanson
had isolated him. He had been pulled from the Department of Health at Grove Street, and ten to one

that facility was under a tight security blanket now too. Anna had probably been forbidden to give him any information, and Suzanne had gotten the message. He could sit in his office and stare at the walls and once a day read the Mortality and Morbidity report and be briefed by Hanson who would tell him absolutely nothing at all of what was happening.

Whatever it was, it concerned WHO and the rest of the world as much as it concerned the United States. And he wasn't going to sit in Coventry rewriting Hanson's press releases.

No second-generation infections, he thought—with the possible exception of Mrs. Rosenberg. And all the victims had attended the VAW convention. Excluding, of course, Drs. Hugh Benoit and Roy French.

It was Paul French that he had to see next.

Security guards hadn't been stationed yet at the virology labs on Berkeley Way. Doohan took the elevator up to French's floor and pushed through the door marked AUTHORIZED PERSONNEL ONLY. He blinked at the brightness inside. The lab windows faced directly into the early afternoon sun and the sunlight was reflected from rows of stainless steel laboratory benches. Each of the long benches held Plexiglas glove boxes with individual gloves; with them, a technician could manipulate the contents of the box without coming into direct contact with the glovebox air.

The bench along the far wall held what looked like glove boxes filled with racks of yellow-white eggs two-thirds immersed in temperature-controlled water. Incubators, Doohan thought. They held the eggs inoculated with extracts made from the hundreds of tissue samples and environmental samples gathered by the city health people and CDC technicians.

Huddled around one of the Plexiglas enclosures were two men and a woman. The man standing up was as broad in the hips as he was in the shoulders and wearing a lab coat considerably more rumpled and worn than those of the others. He looked up as Doohan walked over, his face breaking into a wide smile.

"I tried calling several times," Doohan said.

"Probably knocked the phone off the hook in my office," French said. "I've done it before—a good Freudian psychiatrist would say I'm trying to wrap myself up in the womb of my work."

Doohan grinned and watched the two assistants for a moment. The husky young man with his hands in the glove box was working on a rack of eggs. He had ear-length hair and a shaggy beard and wore Levi's under his white lab coat. As Doohan watched, he took an egg from which a tiny section of shell had been removed, produced a plastic syringe from a sealed sterilized envelope, filled it from a sample vial, and carefully injected a drop of material from the container onto the yolk sac of the egg. The girl sitting next to him sealed the egg with paraffin, labeled it with a crayon, and set it in a half-filled rack. The young man now pulled his hands out of the glove box; the gloves remained inside. Negative pressure, Doohan thought; otherwise they would have popped out like so many balloons. The young man looked like an amiable football player, fair-skinned, with a scattering of freckles and dark reddish-brown hair.

"This is Darryl Anderson, one of my harried assistants," French said as Doohan shook hands. "He'd be less harried if he shaved more often."

The young man groaned. "One of the qualifications for working here is the ability to put up with puns like that."

French's eyes danced. "It's not a sin to commit a pun; it's just a sin to perpetuate one—and I've forgotten who said that. The lovely scientist to your right is Celia Kovacs." The girl looked up and nodded. A chubby, serious face, hiding behind heavy horn-rimmed glasses.

Doohan pointed at the eggs. "Some of Miltrait's work?"

"God, yes," French said. "All of this is. Thank heavens we're doing mostly tissue sections."

"They've not given you sera and the like?"

"No, they're flying that to Atlanta, along with duplicates of the tissue sections they're sending me now—

lungs, kidneys, spleen, liver—all the tissue sections from the autopsies. We macerate them in a blender, do an aqueous extract, and inoculate the eggs."

"Anything so far?"

French laughed. "We haven't killed an embryo yet except with bad lab techniques. A few airborne yeasts. Nothing else. Nothing on the plates, either." He nodded at a commercial incubator sitting in the corner. "I need a full-time dishwasher just to wash the Petri dishes and slant cultures. Nothing comes out. A few mold colonies, some gram-positive stuff but nothing significant. We've just about abandoned culturing for bacteria."

He turned and waddled up the aisle, just clearing the benches on either side. "Come on—I've got a hot plate in my office. It's strictly illegal to have anything to eat in the lab, but I'll be damned if I'll do without my coffee."

French's office was a small room next to the laboratory, made to look even smaller by a huge old oak desk almost buried under stacks of the *Journal of Biochemistry* and the *Journal of the American Chemical Society*. Some copies had ragged paper markers sticking out, others were stacked in toppling heaps with loose papers and ancient manila folders sandwiched in between the journals. The piles of magazines and the spare chair were covered with a film of dust. Doohan hesitated, and French said, "Here, let me clean that." He grabbed several Chemwipe tissues from a nearby box and ran them over the seat of the chair.

"Housekeeping was never one of my strong points—another difference between Roy and myself; he was a regular Tidy Tom." French sobered for a moment. "You know, I keep remembering little things about Roy but I don't feel much there. We weren't friendly as kids and as adults, even less so." He smiled a little sadly. "The only thing I feel is guilt that I don't feel anything."

He started making coffee at a porcelain-topped table near the windows. The pot was an Erlenmeyer flask with a fritted-glass filter holding an accordion-fold filter paper. He measured coffee into the filter cone, pouring water into it from a beaker steaming on a nearby hot plate. When it had dripped through, he poured a cup for Doohan and himself, then eased into a battered oak swivel chair in front of the desk.

"They've been trying to get this chair and desk away from me ever since I moved in here; they want to replace it with a lot of chrome and plastic crap. Fat chance. It's the only chair I ever found that fits my fanny." He gingerly tasted the coffee, then swiveled to face Doohan. "I understand they moved you to Laguna Honda?"

"This morning," Doohan said. The coffee was searingly strong and left an astringent taste in the back of his mouth.

"It's the military mind. Ever since Hanson started bringing in his own men, the whole operation has been changing color."

"Does that mean anything to you?" Doohan asked.

"That they're frightened." French's shrewd eyes studied Doohan for a moment. "You said the other day you wanted to talk to me about something."

"No second generation infections. It's happened before." Doohan blew on his coffee. "We were wrapping things up in Bangladesh when you had the Legionnaires' Disease in Philadelphia. That was a veterans' convention as well, and there were no second-generation victims there either. A friend of mine wrote me about it. He said the year before they had a Eucharistic Congress at the same hotel and there had been an outbreak there too."

French looked thoughtful. "It couldn't be the same as this; it wasn't anywhere near as virulent."

"That's right, but the military were into that one also —and they ran scared. My friend was with public health and he said the Chemical Corps had a whole platoon of toxicologists and biological warfare people looking over the CDC's shoulders."

French chose his words carefully. "You have to be careful what you think or it becomes a paranoid's world. They finally isolated the etiological agent for the Philadelphia disease. It was a new, bacteriumlike organism, a slow-growing one, it's true, but definitely identified as the cause."

Doohan held out his cup for a refill. "And they had the sera stored in their Atlanta banks from a similar outbreak several years before in Pontiac, Michigan. And the yolk-sac isolates from Philadelphia gave the same fluorescent antibody reaction to sera from both Philadelphia and Pontiac. They don't know what it is or where it came from but they had seen it once before and so therefore it was a known agent. Rare and difficult to identify—but 'known.'"

"All right," French said. "So perhaps Philadelphia and Pontiac have had simple outbreaks of a new organism. It's the sort of thing we should become accustomed to seeing with more frequent air travel. But eventually they'll find out what it is here, just as they did in Philadelphia."

"What they claimed they found in Philadelphia," Doohan said, "was an organism that was too slow-growing to appear on agar cultures and very late in appearing in eggs. It was an organism that was apparently non-infective and yet managed to cause a mini-epidemic before it subsided. I'm not so sure I believe all of that. I don't think you do either. Not there. Not here."

"This isn't the same disease as the one in Philadelphia," French argued. "The symptomology is different in a number of ways and the mortality rate is one hell of a lot higher. There were people who survived in Philadelphia. So far, there haven't been any who have survived here."

"And that seems rather improbable," Doohan said. "Man has been around for a long time; it shouldn't be quite that easy to kill him off."

French studied him for a moment. "All right, Calvin —what are you thinking?"

"Do you grant my reasoning so far?"

"You've got an argument."

Doohan now ticked off the facts on his fingers. "The disease was restricted to the hotel; it was restricted to the veterans; it's apparently a hundred per cent fatal;

and we've got nothing on the plates—granted it may be too soon for something to show up. If it wasn't for Mrs. Rosenberg and your brother and Benoit, I'd think it might be a toxin; perhaps in all three cities, that maybe some terrorist group is killing selected segments of the population and the government wants to hush it up for fear of panic."

French stared at him, then shook his head. "I thought only Americans believed in conspiracies. I can't take that seriously, Calvin. You're playing Devil's Advocate, aren't you?"

Doohan nodded. "That's right. The Army is here in force and has let everybody know they're working on the assumption that it's a toxin. But if you believe that, then you have to come to the same conclusion that it's an individual, somebody who's completely crackers. Either that or it's some off-the-wall terrorist group and that's why the government wants to keep it quiet. I think it's what they want us to believe."

French was staring out the windows, deep in thought. He finally looked back at Doohan, shrugged and said: "I don't know what to think; ask me again tomorrow." He leaned over the desk to turn on the lamp and Doohan realized the afternoon shadows had lengthened the room. "There's something concerning my brother that I thought you ought to see; I was going to call you about it . . ." He pulled open one of the desk drawers, took out a pamphlet and tossed it over to Doohan. "I found this among Roy's papers."

Doohan held the pamphlet under the light. It was the program booklet for the veterans' convention. He glanced quickly through it. A typical convention booklet, trivial and uninteresting except to those attending the convention. It listed the various meetings, the keynote speech, the major get-together with the no-host bar, hints of numerous parties for this and that division, the banquet Saturday night, and the farewell brunch Sunday.

"It wasn't the sort of thing Roy would do," French said, puzzled. "It wasn't a matter of patriotism—he was as jingoistic as the best of them—but he probably would have been contemptuous of the VAW as a 'do-gooder' activity."

Doohan was confused. "What are you talking about?"

French took the booklet and turned to the last page, then handed it back to Doohan, a stubby forefinger marking a passage. "Right there at the bottom."

The last paragraph was titled VAW BLOOD PROGRAM and was an appeal for donors, with the days and hours that a bloodmobile would be outside the hotel. There were instructions on who could donate and finally a list of the physicians in attendance and the VAW's thanks for their volunteering.

"That's the connection," French said. "It's one I never would have thought of."

Doohan read rapidly through the paragraph and then caught his breath.

The first name on the list of attending physicians was that of Dr. Roy J. French.

14

Doohan picked up Suzanne at her Union Street apartment on Russian Hill precisely at seven. As he pulled up to the curb, he could see through the glass doors that she was waiting in the vestibule. Before he could set the transmission to "park" and get out of the car, she was halfway across the street.

"No chivalry, Calvin." She slipped into the seat beside him and sighed. "God, I like a man who's prompt."

"Aren't you even going to say 'Good evening'?"

"Good evening," she said crisply. "I'm glad you asked me out. It's been one hell of a day." He glanced sideways at her, noting how fresh she looked, not at all like a woman who'd had a bad day. "Sorry," she said, "you probably don't like women who swear."

"You're mistaking a slight accent for a natural reserve," he said loftily. He smiled in the darkness. "I'm really not that way at all." He turned right on Van Ness and a few blocks later onto Lombard Street.

"You're taking the bridge," Suzanne said, puzzled. "Where are we going?"

"Sausalito—a Basque restaurant called Guernica." The bridge was gray with fog and he slowed down; in his rear-view mirror he could see the lights of San Francisco gradually disappear in the growing darkness.

"You never came back this afternoon."

"I went to Berkeley to see French; spent more time than I thought."

"I think the major missed you."

So Hanson was keeping tabs on him, Doohan

thought. "It's the nationalistic mind—he doesn't trust me. No military man quite trusts anyone whose loyalties aren't clearly defined."

"And yours aren't?"

"I think they are. I passionately believe in what I'm doing—WHO is the most important social experiment in the world today. It menaces no one, challenges no sovereignty, and works for the good of all without regard for national boundaries."

"None of that would endear you to Hanson. You're also a British subject."

Doohan laughed. "Funny—if you're British, you're a subject; if you're an American, you're a citizen. The Revolutionary War in one sentence." He took the Sausalito turnoff and followed the winding road into town, passing Sally Stanford's Valhalla and the town square, Suzanne eyeing the shops as they passed. A mile past the main shopping district, he pulled up in front of the low, white building that housed Guernica. Inside, it was dark and candlelit. A reproduction of Picasso's "Guernica" graced the side wall. The maître d', a young man in a flowing Basque smock, showed them to a booth whose upper panels were stained-glass windows salvaged from ancient Victorians.

They ordered drinks and Suzanne admired the decor. "It's very nice," she said approvingly.

Doohan half-rose from his seat. "There's a Kentucky Fried down the road," he said semi-seriously. "If this is too—"

She laughed. "Stop it Calvin; you win, you win! Did I really sound that bad?"

"Almost." He lit a match to inspect the menu. "What happened at Pentagon West after I left—everybody get along without me?"

She sobered. "A security man has been appointed— somebody named Roberts. And lock files have been brought in; all files now have to be locked up before we go home. And nothing's done without Major Hanson's approval. Even Dr. Miltrait toes the party line."

"Any more victims?"

"One—the 'unofficial' word is that the outbreak is over. It's been leaked that patients who have recovered have been sent home and those still in the hospital will be discharged as soon as possible. By week's end, it will be on the back pages."

Doohan was startled. "There have been recoveries?"

She shook her head. "No, and no patients have been sent home. You said it earlier; the mortality rate will probably wind up at a hundred per cent. There won't be any survivors." She sounded depressed. "The few patients still in the hospitals are under security guard so they can't talk to reporters. It's not . . . quite that blatant, of course."

"That's Hanson's idea, isn't it? Along with the security guards who are fresh out of the Military Police Academy." Why was Hanson trying to manage the news? he wondered. What was he afraid of? "Anything more on Mrs. Rosenberg?"

Suzanne's voice was strained. "She . . . wasn't as strong as her husband."

Leona Rosenberg had been more than just a name or a statistic to her, Doohan thought. Suzanne had met and talked with her, if only for a short time. He covered her hand with his and squeezed slightly. "It'll be over soon."

She shook her head, trying to throw off the mood. "I'm afraid not for some time. There are still a lot of veterans we have to follow up whom we haven't contacted yet. And we have to run the questionnaires through a computer, try and determine if there is any single item that is common to all cases, or perhaps a group of items. You know the routine."

"That won't take a full staff."

"I'm to be one of the chosen." She toyed with her drink for a moment. "You've heard about our crank letter?" Doohan shook his head. "It was on the evening news; I thought you might get a kick out of it."

Doohan was wary. "Why should I get a kick out of it?"

She studied him from behind her drink. "Because the writer claims he poisoned the veterans with nickel carbonyl; he sounded very knowledgeable. I remember you suggested the same thing when we went through the hotel."

For a moment, Doohan thought she might be ragging him. "That was just a wild hunch after seeing the repairs on the furnace grate."

"Hanson's taking it seriously. He's authorized a news release on it." She was questioning now. "Could it happen like that?"

"It's possible. A number of heavy metals could give the same symptomology. But it's not very likely. Poisonous gases aren't selective. Nobody else in the hotel came down with it. None of the other guests, none of the help. It may be a possibility, but it's got to be a remote one."

Doohan finished his drink and ordered another round. They sat in silence. "We're not doing very good at leaving the office behind, are we?" Suzanne asked.

"Ask me a question about something else," Doohan said, smiling crookedly. "Anything else."

"You moved to Wales when you were very young; did you like Wales?"

"Some of it."

"Tell me about it."

"I guess you could say there are spots as beautiful as any you'd find here or in Europe. And then there are the dirty little coal towns that thread through the countryside. They're worse than your coal towns in West Virginia; you're coughing your lungs out before you're fifty, and the women have turned into crones by their forties." He had never talked about it before but then, he had never found anybody to listen to it before either. "My father died spitting up bloody coal tar. I buried my mother at the age of forty-three; she looked seventy. I'd be working in the mines right now if I hadn't won a scholarship."

"It was a simple question," she said defensively.

"But the wrong one."

"It's the past. You can walk away from the past."

He shook his head in frustration. "Suzanne, the past is the one thing you can never walk away from. You carry it around with you, like the albatross around the Ancient Mariner's neck. It's all sorted and filed and just waiting there. Press the right button and you have instant replay."

"Is there a safe subject, Calvin? We can't seem to talk about much of anything." There was a note of pleading in her voice.

Doohan suddenly grinned. " 'It's been one hell of a day,' to quote a lady I know. How about brightening the evening and spending the night with me?"

"The whole night?" she said sarcastically.

"It's not safe to go home alone at three in the morning." He suddenly plucked the bud out of the small vase on the table and laid it next to her champagne cocktail. "Dinner with wine and roses," he mocked.

"Followed, as usual, by a proposition." For a moment she tried to be angry, then burst out laughing. "You promised me you wouldn't do it."

"I lied," he grinned. "Besides, you asked me first."

Afterward, they lay awake in the darkness, the sheets clinging to their damp bodies. Doohan was conscious of the small but definite distance separating them. It hadn't been at all like that with . . . Elizabeth, Doohan thought. He and Elizabeth had clung to each other like children, the orgasm almost unnoticed as they ran their fingers over each other's flesh and hugged each other for what seemed hours. With Suzanne, it had been a tremendous burst of hunger and passion and when it was over, it was like the ocean tide receding at a beach and leaving the bed empty of emotion.

She was smoking a cigarette, the tip a glowing ember in the darkness. The smoke made him think of his pipe and he suddenly wanted it badly, but the idea of lying naked in bed with his briar was too bizarre an image for him. He wondered if she expected him to make conversation. Finally, he reached over and took the cigarette from her, inhaled deeply, and then handed it back.

He had never made love quite that violently, he thought. He hadn't expected it would be like this from watching her during the day. A very controlled woman when she was at work, her emotions always on a leash.

But it hadn't really been love-making, he decided; it had been a frenzy of lust. And in spite of his attempts to lead her slowly to a satisfying climax, she had been very much the aggressor.

"You're a very gentle man, Calvin," she said quietly. "I'm not used to that."

"Was he so violent?" he asked, and then mentally kicked himself for asking.

"Arnold?" She lifted herself up on one elbow. "No, he was very cold and clinical. It was like pushing a series of buttons, each one designed for a specific reaction. You could have timed him with a stopwatch. So many minutes for foreplay, so many minutes for primary sex, so many minutes to orgasm. He was . . . is . . . a very disciplined man."

"You make it sound like two robots coupling."

"That's close."

He was about to ask another question when the phone rang. He glanced in annoyance at the digital clock on the bureau. It was still early, eleven-thirty. "You better answer that," she said distantly. There was certainly no mood to break, Doohan thought. He lifted the receiver and spoke for a minute, then set it back on its cradle. "Why do they always ask if they're interrupting something when they call late at night?"

She laughed lightly. "It seems like a reasonable thing to ask."

He sensed the unasked question and said, "It was Paul. He wanted to know if I had heard of Hanson's press release about the nickel carbonyl; he'll be running some heavy metal tests in the morning."

"Does he think that's what it is?"

"I don't believe so." And then he remembered what he had meant to tell her earlier. "Paul's brother, Roy. He was at the convention after all. He worked on a blood donor drive."

She didn't say anything and he started to drift off to sleep when he sensed that she was lying closer now, her body touching his. He could feel her fingers glide lightly over the hair on his stomach and he started to rouse to her caress. In his mind's eye, he could see her once again, naked in the dim illumination from the night light. She had been . . . stunning, far more stunning than a woman doctor had any right to be.

He turned to her once more, ignoring that small part of his mind that wondered if this was really what he wanted to do.

15

CARL ROSTOV, the Director of Operations at the San Francisco Memorial Blood Bank, was a small, pudgy man who blinked rapidly as he talked. Doohan found himself fascinated by the blink and guessed from the enlarged irises that Rostov wore contact lenses with an extreme correction.

"Ordinarily, I'd refuse your request." Blink. "Our records are confidential." Rostov pursed his lips, studied Doohan's identification a moment longer; then, just before Doohan started to protest, he smiled graciously and said, "But if we can help WHO in any way ..."

Doohan forced himself to return the smile. "We'd appreciate it very much."

French, sitting next to him, shifted uncomfortably in a plastic captain's chair that looked as if it were about to collapse under his weight. "I'm surprised that my brother was one of the physicians with the blood-mobile. I didn't think it was his type of cause."

Rostov frowned. "He wasn't one of our regulars. We have our own physicians and we have a group of doctors who are very good about volunteering. Frankly, we'd asked him to volunteer before, but he turned us down. But he asked for the VAW convention specifically, right out of the blue; he said he had friends at the convention." He blinked a few more times, looking vaguely froglike. "We were very glad to have his help. We're always short of personnel and conventions that sponsor blood drives are a major source of supply for us. The VAW conventions are particularly good."

"You said he usually turned you down," Doohan interrupted. "Why did you ask him to volunteer in the first place?"

Blink. "He worked with us once before as a volunteer. Naturally, those are the ones we ask first. We—"

"When?"

Rostov gaped for a moment, then frowned. "I'll have to check." He walked to a file cabinet in the corner and returned with another folder. "Let's see . . . the Elks; they held a convention a year ago at the Royalty Hotel."

"May I see that?"

Rostov's frown grew deeper. He hesitated, then handed the folder to Doohan. Pinned to the cover was a mass of data sheets and a short list of attending physicians. Roy French was one of four. Doohan pointed to another sheet in the folder. "Is this the list of donors?"

"That's right."

There were actually four lists representing the four days of the convention. Each name was followed by a code number and address. It had been a big turnout, Doohan thought; probably as high as the VAW drive. He looked up from the list. "There's something the donor fills out, isn't there?"

Rostov sat back and steepled his fingers. "We have a standard receipt and a personal history form"—he fished a form-carbon manifold out of his desk and gave it to Doohan—"like this. You can keep it if you wish."

Doohan flipped through it. There were four sheets with carbons sandwiched in between. The top one was white, followed by yellow, pink, and gold. There were spaces for the donor's name, address, and signature as well as "blood number" and "transfusion date." Stapled to the manifold was a history card with room for the donor to fill in his personal history, a section for blood pressure and other data from the physician, and a section for the laboratory report. The blood number on the history card was keyed to a similar number on the receipt.

"The pink copy of the receipt," Rostov droned, "is always attached to the sample and we keep very close watch on the blood numbers. If there's any confusion, we don't try and use the blood as whole blood but fractionate it for plasma and gamma globulin, that sort of thing."

Doohan studied the form for a minute. There was nothing here, he thought. It was going to prove a dead end. All they had were names and numbers. But Roy French had died of the Veterans' Disease, and Roy French, in an action totally unlike him, had volunteered to help with the donor program. Not once, but twice. He glanced back at Rostov. "Could I see some forms that have been filled out? I think it would give me a better feel for what Dr. French was doing."

Rostov was hesitant. "They contain confidential information, Doctor. There are lab tests for VD, for instance, and the answers to the medical history questions are certainly confidential."

Doohan let a note of insistence creep into his voice. "It could be important."

Rostov sighed. "All right, read me off five of the donor numbers and I'll have my secretary pull the records."

When they came out, Doohan read them carefully. They weren't of much help, exactly as he had expected. Then he stopped and fanned the cards quickly. "Something's wrong; there's no laboratory data on any of these cards."

"That's impossible." Doohan handed over the cards and Rostov quickly thumbed through them. He suddenly looked uneasy. "Which sheet did you get these numbers from?"

"The top one." Doohan gave it to him.

"The last day of the Elks convention," Rostov mused. He moved his lips slightly and Doohan guessed he was swearing to himself. "There won't be any data on the cards from the last day," he said in a tight voice.

"Why not?"

"Tragic thing, really," Rostov said quietly. "The

newspapers made quite a story of it at the time. We still don't understand it." He was silent for a long moment.

"It may be important," Doohan prompted.

"There's not much to tell. The last day's collection of blood was destroyed in an accident. The driver lost his way in the dark and went off the end of an incompleted section of the Embarcadero Freeway."

French whistled. "How did that happen?"

"We never found out the full story. The bloodmobile was being chased by a police car. The police said later the driver was speeding. He took the wrong exchange and . . ." Rostov made falling motions with his hands. "Both the driver and his attendant were killed."

Doohan looked back at the donor lists in his hands. There was something there, screaming at him, but he couldn't see what it was. The list of doctors, the forms the donors had filled out, the lists of donors themselves . . .

Then a name suddenly jumped out at him. Herman Rosenberg, Plumber. The same name, the same address, the same occupation, the same age. "May I see the list of donors from the veterans' convention?"

Rostov was starting to look put upon. "I suppose so."

Doohan quickly scanned it. Sure enough, the Rosenberg who had given blood Thursday at the VAW convention was the same Rosenberg who had given blood the year before for the Elks. "Could I use your desk for a moment?" Doohan sat down with the two folders in front of him and started to compare names between the two lists.

French circled around the desk to peer over his shoulder. "You're on to something," he accused.

"There are fifteen names common to both lists," Doohan said grimly.

Rostov was puzzled. "That's not at all unusual. These people are joiners; if they belong to one fraternal organization, they very likely belong to another. There's a great deal of cross-over between the veterans' group and the others."

"Do you get many repeat donors?"

"Almost all our donors are repeat donors. They

come into town for a convention, the group has a blood drive and they contribute. They do it almost every time; it becomes a habit."

"I wonder if I could impose on you for something else." Doohan smiled as ingratiatingly as he could.

Rostov looked reluctant. "It all depends; I'm really quite busy—"

"You've got more than ninety donors from the veterans' convention. Could you have somebody work up a sheet with their names and lab data on them—blood type, Rh factor, antibody count, that sort of thing? Nothing confidential, of course. It would help a lot."

"I can give you Xeroxes of the work sheets from the convention," Rostov suggested hopefully.

"That's fine." A few minutes later, Rostov's secretary brought out the sheets and slid them into an envelope for Doohan. "You've been very helpful," Doohan said.

Rostov managed a wry smile. "I only wish it had been for a good cause." He shook his head ruefully. "When we heard of the disease at the convention, we had to dump the blood. A terrible thing . . ."

It hadn't occurred to Doohan. "I'm sorry."

"It was a great deal of work for nothing," the pudgy little man said sadly.

In the car, Doohan gave French the list of overlap donors, those who had contributed blood at both conventions. "Recognize any of the names?"

French mumbled aloud. "Rosenberg . . . Kemp . . . Greenhorn . . . Martell—they're all names on samples in my lab, people who died of the Veterans' Disease."

"Any conclusions?"

French was hesitant. "It would seem that almost everybody who gave blood at both conventions died. But a lot more people died than gave blood at both the VAW and Elks meetings. My guess is that probably all those who attended both conventions, whether they gave blood or not, were victims." He glanced at Doohan. "That's what you're thinking, isn't it?"

Doohan nodded. "First, to become a victim, you probably had to attend both conventions. If you attended only one or the other, you were safe. The two conventions were radically different; so we can assume that nobody had it in for veterans as such. Two, there was a bloodmobile at each convention. Not especially significant at the moment since many people died who didn't give blood. Three, Roy was one of the attending physicians at both conventions. It's reasonable to assume that he had the same thing in common with those who gave blood at both conventions and which made them victims. Fourth, the blood from the Elks' convention was lost under peculiar circumstances. I have no idea what to make of that or even if it's connected in any way."

French looked unhappy. "There's a possible explanation—that the bloodmobile was the source of the infection. That somehow the donors were infected in the process and managed to infect the others. And I suppose if that's true, it's possible Roy had something to do with it."

Doohan shook his head. "Not very likely. None of the donors got sick at the first convention and only some of the donors got sick at the second. And there are still the questions of why no second-generation infections and why it was restricted only to veterans. What did they have in common that excluded passers-by, casual visitors, other guests in the hotel, and even the help?"

"It was just a thought." French sounded relieved

"The sticky part," Doohan said, "is that we're morally bound to turn the information over to Miltrait and Hanson. This is obviously something they don't know about yet."

French smiled thinly. "Major Hanson won't appreciate it when we tell him."

Doohan started the car and pulled out into the traffic. "I don't think you should come along, Paul. Hanson wouldn't understand your poking around outside the laboratory. You have freedom of movement now; you won't have if he thinks you're interfering."

French looked at him, curious. "What are you going to do, Calvin? I mean after you tell Hanson about this?"

"What am I going to do?" Doohan asked grimly.

"I'm going to do what WHO is paying me to do—find out all I can. It's top priority to them now; they consider it vitally important."

"And you want me to help you?"

Doohan realized he had taken it for granted. "Won't you?"

French looked out the window at the traffic. "I hadn't really thought about it, Calvin."

16

THERE WERE TWO additional guards on the floor at Laguna Honda Hospital, and Doohan had to show his credentials to both of them. He found Hanson with his shirt sleeves rolled up and his collar open, looking as tired and sweaty as if he had been there all night. He glanced up, startled, when Doohan walked in. "Goddamnit, where the hell's the girl?" He stalked to the door, looked around the outer office for his secretary, then turned to face Doohan. "Something I can do for you, Doctor?"

Doohan explained briefly what he had discovered at the blood bank. "Everybody didn't give blood, of course, but my guess is that everybody who sickened and later died attended both of the conventions."

Hanson listened without expression, then flipped the intercom switch on his desk. "Roberts, contact the manager of the Royalty Hotel. Tell him we want his registry for last year." He glanced at Doohan. "What was the date of the Elks' convention?"

"October seventh to the eleventh."

"Ten seven to ten eleven, Roberts. Compare the registration list for the Elks' convention with our Veterans' Disease victims list. Take it over the phone and let me know the overlap. And don't take all day."

He switched off the intercom, leaned back in his chair and closed his eyes. Hanson was exhausted, Doohan thought clinically. His eyes were puffy, the rest of his face gray and strained. The ashtray on the desk in front of him was piled high with cigarette butts that dribbled in a trail to the wastebasket at the side.

"You know what you'll find," Doohan said.

"Yes, Doctor," Hanson sighed, "I know what we'll find. It doesn't take too many coincidences to make a point. What we'll discover is that everyone on the victim list also attended the Elks' convention of a year ago. Right? I'm just not certain where that leaves us."

"Both conventions had blood-donor programs," Doohan suggested. "The bloodmobile at the last day of the Elks' convention was wrecked, apparently because the personnel feared they were going to be stopped and searched."

Hanson opened his eyes. "Do you have an explanation for that?" Doohan shook his head. "Neither do I." Hanson made some notes on a scratch pad, then stared curiously at Doohan. "Tell me, Doctor, why are you playing Sherlock Holmes?"

Doohan felt a surge of anger. "Because I thought the information about the convention overlap might be important."

"Oh, I'm sure it is, Doctor; I'm sure it is. But I think I would have preferred that you come to us with the basic information first. We would have been much more thorough with the followup at the blood bank, for one thing."

"I don't think your men could have done any better."

Hanson yawned and rubbed his eyes. "That's not even debatable," he said. "Look, Doctor, let's be honest with each other. You really don't trust us to give you the information you want and, to be perfectly frank, we're not too sure just how far you can be trusted or where your sympathies lie."

"You must have checked me out by now," Doohan said coldly. "You must know there's no reason for suspicion."

"No? Doctor, at this moment I'm suspicious of everyone. I'm paid for my attitude and my attitude is a suspicious one. If it *can* happen, it will happen, and that's as basic a tenet of belief with me as believing the sun will rise tomorrow morning." He suddenly slapped the desk with his hand. "What the hell do you think is going on here? This is no classroom exercise in the containment of a disease. That course is being taught next door by Dr. Miltrait. I deal in possibilities, and what's possible is that there may be a good deal more at stake than the lives of a few hundred veterans. I'll admit the present tragedy, Doctor, but I can't dwell upon it. What I'm concerned with is the internal integrity of the United States. I'm being asked to believe that seventy-five veterans have caught a mysterious disease which is a hundred per cent fatal. What the government is paying me for is *not* to believe that, and I don't."

"You think it's a biological warfare agent?"

Hanson looked grim. "I didn't say that, Doctor, and I can't prove it. But if it is, whoever's spreading it will have observers on the spot to report on the results of their field test, and to check out our ability to contain it. As far as I know, that observer could just as easily be Dr. Calvin Doohan as anybody else."

Doohan shrugged. "If that's what you want to believe, I guess I can't dissuade you."

"You don't like military men very much, do you?"

"What do you expect me to say, Major? You're in a different business than I am."

Hanson got up and walked over to the window. He adjusted the venetian blinds until the sunlight streaked his face with harsh, cold lines.

"I've been a soldier all my life, Doctor. My father was regular Air Force; I was an air-force brat. It's the only life I've ever known, the only life I've ever wanted to know. I knew since I was a child that I would go to one of the Academies. I considered it then, and I consider it now, the most honorable and also the most misunderstood of all the professions. And with the kind of civilian attitude we've had in this country since 'Nam, it's a thankless one. It's trite to say it, but somebody has to fight this country's wars, and they have to be ready to do it *now*. We'll never again have the time to train an army from scratch." He stood there for a moment squinting into the sunlight. "Nobody ever gets as far as the last verse of the national anthem but there's a line in it about free men standing 'between one's lov'd home and the war's desolation.' Do you think that's so dishonorable?"

He turned around, half-smiling. "Sounds corny, doesn't it? But make no mistake, Doctor. I have a very clear image of duty and what comprises it and there's nothing I won't do to carry it out."

"It seems to me that one of the defenses the Nazis put forth at Nuremberg was that they were just carrying out orders," Doohan said bitterly.

"Doohan, you're what we call in this country a 'smart ass.'" Hanson's voice was ice. "As contradictory as it sounds, there's a moral law that's binding on all men, even in war, Doctor. We hanged the Nazis because they broke that law."

"You're right. It sounds contradictory," Doohan said softly. "But I wonder if I'll ever see the day when Major Lawrence Hanson stands before some tribunal and says, 'But I was only following orders.'"

"That'll be a frosty morning in hell," Hanson half-whispered, staring at Doohan with contempt. "That's something you're never going to hear me say."

The door behind Doohan opened and a voice said, "Major, we checked the names—"

A young man in sports blazer and slacks stood in the doorway. He had stopped in midsentence, eyeing Doohan with suspicion. Doohan stared back. Blond, muscular, a boyish face only slightly marred by the tight lines in the cheeks and around the eyes. Hard, Doohan thought. The type who would have followed orders at My Lai. Or Buchenwald. That one swift glance and Doohan knew he had been analyzed and assessed. An odd choice for Hanson's assistant. Or maybe not.

Hanson said impatiently, "Go ahead, Roberts."

"The manager of the Royalty read off his list for the Elks' convention. Every name on our victims' list was on it with the exception of one."

"What about the Rosenbergs?"

"Both the husband and wife were at the Royalty a year ago."

"Who's the exception?"

Roberts glanced at the list in his hand. "A woman named Guitterez. She and her husband attended the veterans' convention but not the Elks. She died; so far, her husband has shown no signs of the disease."

"That's enough," Hanson said abruptly. "Thanks, Roberts." The young man shot a final glance at Doohan and withdrew. Hanson rubbed his eyes. "Doctor, I'm damn tired and maybe I've let more of myself show than I should have. I appreciate what you've done for us. In spite of our differences of opinion, I really do appreciate it. You understand, of course, that what we've said here will have to remain confidential. Until you get a release from me, please don't put it in your reports to WHO."

"I can't do that," Doohan said in a low voice. "I work for WHO, and what's happening here is just as important to WHO as it is to the United States. Disease doesn't recognize national borders. If the Veterans' Disease proves contagious in the long run, the rest of the world has a right to know about it."

Hanson sighed. "Maybe it has a right to know about it in the long run, but right now it concerns the security of the United States."

"You should have been with me in Bangladesh," Doohan said bitterly. "Have you ever seen what smallpox does to its victims?"

Hanson studied him for a long moment. "Your tour in Bangladesh meant a lot to you, didn't it, Doctor? Well, it doesn't mean a damn thing to me and I'm not going to feel guilty about the starving Bengalis. Smallpox doesn't exist any more; this does." He picked up a sheaf of papers from his desk and started reading through them. "We don't have anything more to discuss, Doctor," he said distantly.

He had been dismissed, Doohan thought; at the moment, he no longer even existed as far as Hanson was concerned. He got as far as the door, then turned back in anger. "I think we do have something—"

Hanson suddenly stood up, shoving over the chair behind him. He balled his fist and brought it down hard on the desk, knocking the ashtray off the top and spilling cigarette butts on the floor. His eyes were blazing. "Goddamnit, Doohan!" He fought for a moment to regain control. When he did, his voice was shaking. "We're tight for space here, Doctor; I think you ought to make other office arrangements."

"I'll talk with Dr. Miltrait," Doohan said coldly.

"You'll find he's full up. And I think the same might be true at 101 Grove."

They stared at each other for a long moment; then Doohan turned and slammed out the door. He had been quarantined, he thought. First, Hanson had pulled him out of the Department of Health where he had contacts, and now he had been chucked out of his office here. He was completely isolated from any further information about the Veterans' Disease. Except . . . except, he corrected himself, except possibly for French and Suzanne.

And there was something else, he thought. He was naïve—Hanson had proved that to him—and he was getting in above his head in a type of situation he had never been in before.

And he wasn't at all sure he could handle it.

17

DOOHAN PARKED HIS car in the Civic Center lot, then walked over to the nearby plaza and sat on a bench to wait. Suzanne had agreed, reluctantly, to meet him for lunch. There had been a great deal to do and she felt guilty about taking the time. . . . But of course she would meet him.

He would be using her, he thought, staring down glumly at the bricks of the plaza. And she would know it. But he had to keep abreast of what Hanson was doing and she was the only source he had. The real difficulty was that not only Suzanne would know his motivation but so would Hanson—if not immediately, then relatively soon.

And he was also assuming that she would agree to help him simply for the asking.

"If you're thinking of suicide, the bridge is that way." She looked a little less the no-nonsense type today. The severe suit was gone and so were the flat heels. She looked tall and willowy, her light brown hair framed against the wide brim of her hat. More the model than ever, he thought. She could be as stunning with clothes as without.

"Do I look that low?"

"Like somebody who had just had a long talk with Major Lawrence Hanson. And that isn't prior knowledge; that's a shrewd guess."

"Well, you're absolutely right."

She cocked her head. "I take it back. You don't look like a potential suicide—more like one of those foreign waifs in World War II who used to panhandle by singing 'No mama, no papa, no Uncle Sam.' "

"I didn't know you went that far back."

"Hardly. My father told me." She sat down next to him. "What happened?"

"You going to buy me lunch?"

She snapped her fingers. "Darn, I knew there'd be a catch. Fortunately, Dr. Miltrait has been bragging about his favorite Italian restaurant and it's only a block away. Promise you'll buy the drinks and not order more than three dollars' worth of food and the lunch is on me."

In the restaurant, she glanced around at the faded decor and shook her head. "Don't blame me; blame Miltrait." They ordered, and she said, "I suppose you've seen the afternoon papers?"

"Not yet," he said, fishing for his pipe.

"They released the contents of our crank letter. Our unknown assassin claims he mixed nickel carbonyl with dry ice and left it in an alcove just off the main meeting hall. Presumably the contents evaporated while the conventioneers were listening to the keynote speech. Miltrait has told reporters they've found nickel in the tissues of the disease victims and that this may be the actual explanation."

"I don't believe it," Doohan said flatly.

She wrapped some linguine around her fork. "The question is: Will the man in the street buy it? The CDC has been severely criticized for not coming up with an answer, you know. We even caught it on the floor of the Senate yesterday during a debate on an HEW appropriation."

"It should get the wolves off your back, at least temporarily—but eventually the explanation will make you look silly."

"I don't think so. The public's memory is pretty short."

Doohan felt mildly irritated. "It's a foolish explanation because it's so implausible, even to a layman. If it was in the air, why did only the veterans come down with it? None of the help, none of the other guests were affected. The hotel meeting room certainly wasn't airproof. Frankly, the theory seems like the least likely of all the possible explanations."

"Argue that with Major Hanson; he ordered the press release. Maybe you were right all along; perhaps the nickel carbonyl did come from the repaired grating in the furnace room. That unit served the two floors that most of the conventioneers were on; it would explain why only the veterans came down with the disease."

Doohan shook his head. "It's got the same basic fault as the other one. And any explanation that doesn't explain everything is no good." He took a bite of his cannelloni. It was remarkably good; Miltrait knew his restaurants after all. "There are two things I can't explain. One is the Rosenbergs. She didn't stay at the Hotel Cordoba and she was at the convention itself for what amounts to a day and a half."

"We haven't established how long an exposure you might need," Suzanne said. "That is, if it's airborne."

"And what about Guitterez?" Doohan asked. "His wife died of it; he escaped unscathed. And neither attended the earlier convention at the Royalty; they're the only ones who didn't."

"You're forgetting somebody."

"Who?"

"Your friend, Dr. Hugh Benoit."

He *had* forgotten Benoit, Doohan thought. And Hugh had attended neither convention nor had he been associated with the bloodmobile. "Background noises. The same symptoms, but it could have been something else entirely."

"And Dr. French?"

He felt unhappy. So there was more than one exception.

She toyed with a forkful of linguine a moment. "What happened with you and Hanson?"

"Major Hanson doesn't care for dedicated Scottish doctors, especially curious ones." He told her of the Elks' convention.

"Hmmm." She thought about it, then shook her head. "You're assuming the significant factor is that those who come down with the disease attended both conventions. Maybe the important thing is that they were just members of both organizations. Those who attended the Elks' convention could very easily have had other contacts in the past year; they move in the same social circles. You've established two points of contact, the Elks' convention and the veterans' convention. But there could have been a third contact."

"It would make sense if they were all local, but some came from as far away as Nevada and Oregon." The waiter cleared the table and Doohan ordered coffee. "What do you know about Guitterez?"

"He's a Latin. Which might be significant." Doohan looked at her quizzically. "He might be Cuban," she explained.

Doohan smiled wryly. "I forgot. All Americans think the Castro regime is a threat to their security; you've developed a national fixation."

"I might agree with you," she said calmly, "if it weren't for one thing. Several years ago, in the middle of all the hassle about the covert actions of the CIA, one of the two-day sensations was the accusation that the CIA had plotted to release African swine fever in Cuba to kill Cuban pigs. The accusation was never verified; nevertheless, there was a swine fever epidemic during that period that practically eliminated pork from the Cuban table for a number of months. The story is that the Cubans were preparing to mount a counteroffensive to spread hoof-and-mouth disease among the cattle herds in Texas."

"That's insanity."

"Apparently somebody else thought so too, probably their Russian advisers. The Cubans didn't go through with it and no one really knows if we actually spread the swine fever or if it was accidentally imported."

After lunch, they walked back to Suzanne's car. "I'm stuffed," she said. "The linguine was as filling as a five-course banquet."

Something ticked in the back of Doohan's mind then. "I've been wondering about Mrs. Rosenberg," he said suddenly.

"That was ... tragic."

Doohan grabbed her arm. "She didn't stay at the hotel; yet she came down with the disease. In fact, she was at the convention for only a day and a half

and, if you eliminate the time she spent in the Travelodge, it wasn't even that much."

"I don't see what you're driving at," Suzanne said.
"We have no idea what the exposure time might be."

And then Doohan had it. "The exposure time was
about thirty seconds."

Suzanne stopped. "You shouldn't drink at lunch."

"I'm serious. What's the one thing she had in common with the rest of the conventioneers—and remember, she wasn't there early enough to have been at the
keynote speech. In fact, what did they all have in
common?"

Suzanne looked puzzled. "What are you driving
at?"

"She attended the banquet," Doohan said. "So did
most of the conventioneers. And I'll bet those who got
sick also attended the banquet at the Elks' convention. It wasn't something they breathed. It was something that they ate—the one thing that might separate
them from the other guests in the hotel and the hotel
personnel."

Suzanne smiled slightly and shook her head. "Forget
it. That was one of the first things we checked. It was
strictly a rubber chicken banquet. They had their
choice of roast sirloin of beef, turkey, or filet of sole
along with mashed potatoes, green peas, a salad, and
spumoni for desert. For a convention banquet, not bad
at all. They still had quick-frozen leftovers of the beef
and turkey and some of the other banquet food; we
checked it all out."

"But you still didn't know what you were looking
for," he insisted.

"Well, if we *do* identify a bug or a virus, we have
stored samples of all the food in Atlanta. We'll be able
to pin it down quickly enough."

The thought struck him then. "You can't," he said.
"All you have are samples of the food that *wasn't*
eaten; you don't have samples of the food that was."

They reached her car and she turned to face him
shielding her eyes from the sun. "They're pretty
thorough in Atlanta. If there's anything to find, sooner
or later they'll find it."

Doohan wasn't entirely convinced. "If you say so. What about the help?"

"None of them got sick, remember?"

"But you don't know if there was anybody who worked both conventions?"

She shook her head. "Calvin, we didn't know about both conventions until today. But according to your theory, if somebody had, they would have gotten sick, right?" She touched his face lightly, then fished in her handbag for a card. "We've been forced to get unlisted phone numbers as a precautionary measure." She smiled. "I rarely get to bed before twelve and I'm never upset if a good friend calls or even drops in unexpectedly. And I consider you a good friend, Calvin." She got in her car and rolled down the window to lean out. "Calvin, Hanson's deadly serious about this. He doesn't want any interference of any kind and he'll go to great lengths to stop it."

"I'm serious too. What I might find out is important to a lot of people."

There was something in her face that he couldn't quite read. "Be careful."

"I was going to ask you to help me," he said. "You're the only source of information I have. I'm not sure I can rely on Paul."

She looked uncertain. "I don't think you can find out much on your own. Not many people are going to co-operate once Hanson passes the word. And in the last analysis, I don't think I could be of much help to you. They don't tell me that much as it is."

It had been his best chance, he thought, but he couldn't blame her. "You're probably right. You'd compromise yourself even if you were seen with me."

"You're determined?" she asked. Doohan nodded. She made up her mind then. "I don't work for Major Hanson," she muttered. "I'll do what I can."

Then she was gone and for once the image of Elizabeth didn't blot out the picture of Suzanne. He shook his head, remembering her invitation. The woman wasn't supposed to make the move, he thought. But that was the double standard and it was a different world from the one he had been brought up in. His ego appreciated the implied compliment. She was eager to continue what they had started the previous night and she wasn't going to give him much choice in the matter.

So much for machismo, he thought.

He got in his car, but before he started it, he thought once again of her warning. Hanson was serious, he would do anything to prevent interference. Which merely underlined his own assessment of Hanson.

Once more, he had the feeling he was getting in over his head.

18

RENÉ KOENIG WAS the third man whom Doohan interviewed at the Royalty Hotel the next morning. The manager had referred him to the catering director who in turn had referred him to Koenig, the headwaiter. It was Koenig who kept the work assignment sheets for both the day-to-day running of the kitchen and also for special events such as banquets.

"Yes, of course I have the records." His voice still carried the trace of an accent. "The IRS requires that you keep them for seven years. You didn't know that?" He was a tall, spare man in his fifties with great reserve and poise and Doohan guessed he was French or Swiss and that his family had been in the hotel business for generations. In his mind's eye, Doohan could see him presiding over the Royalty dining room, snapping his fingers to catch the attention of the lesser mortals who worked for him.

Koenig led the way to his office, a room that was as impeccably neat and tidy as his kitchen. He thumbed the folders in a filing cabinet, then lifted one out. "We had 460 guests for the banquet at the Elks' convention, which means we asked Local 2 to supply about thirty waiters and . . . wait, here they are." He took a pair of glasses from his pocket and slipped them on, then removed a sheet of paper from the folder. "Actually, twenty-eight waiters—you figure one for every fifteen guests, five busboys, four bartenders, and four extra kitchen help including two utility men."

He looked over the top of his glasses at Doohan. "It's quite complicated putting on a banquet. With multiple entrees, the guests have to indicate a choice

121

seventy-two hours in advance and then you still have to prepare a few more for those who change their minds and the last-minute additions. Then you have to draw up a seating chart so the waiter knows how many of each entree goes to each table. You have to make sure the housemen set up the tables correctly—"

"Was all the food prepared here?" Doohan asked.

Koenig's attitude chilled. "Of course, it was all prepared here—even the Chicken Kiev. I understand some hotels bring in frozen entrees. Not the Royalty. Never."

There was a vast difference between the Royalty and the Cordoba, Doohan decided, and part of the difference was named René Koenig. "Can I see the list?" Koenig slid it across the polished surface of his desk. Doohan took out the list he had obtained from the Cordoba and compared the two; they weren't in alphabetical order and it took a moment. There was no duplication at all, he thought, disappointed. Then he went back again and stopped. He was wrong; one of the waiters had worked both the Royalty and the Cordoba for the conventions.

He pointed at the name with his finger. "Richard Miller. Do you know anything about him?"

Koenig nodded. "The first time they work here, we have them fill out a form for the IRS—social security number, address, that kind of information." He reached for a different file drawer, searched for a moment, then pulled out a card for Doohan. "I can't say whether that's his current address or not." He looked enigmatic. "He only worked here once."

"May I use your phone?" Koenig nodded, picked up the file folders and put them back in the cabinet. Doohan dialed, got a referral to a new number—Miller had moved, as Koenig had suggested—dialed the number, and waited. On the ninth ring, just before he was about to hang up, a sleepy voice answered. Doohan explained who he was and what he wanted.

"Look, I don't know anything about the disease." Pause. "Yes, I worked the banquet." A sigh. "What time is it? My God . . ." Doohan asked where they could meet and the voice woke up slightly. "At Home Cafe, first block off Castro below Market. I look like everybody else except I'll be wearing a T-shirt that says 'Keep on Truckin'.'"

Doohan hung up and turned to Koenig. "Do you know where the At Home Cafe is?"

Koenig didn't change expression. "I have no idea," he murmured. "I can't imagine ever wanting to go there."

Doohan left his car in a bank parking lot across the street. Most of the pedestrians were men in their twenties and thirties, the majority in Levi's and checkered shirts with rolled-up sleeves. It was like a western movie, he thought, with a hundred mustachioed villains crowding the sidewalk. Few of the men looked like laborers but all the Levi's were well worn; and from some of the bare skin showing through some of the worn spots, it was obvious that underwear was *déclassé*.

The cafe was crowded when he walked in, the long counter almost entirely occupied by young men wearing the same Levi's uniform he had noticed on the street. The two women at the counter were both dressed in what he had come to know as a "funky" style. The taller and thinner of the two wore large Carmen Miranda earrings and clutched her coffee cup with a hand on which sparkled four elaborate rings, one for each finger.

The waitress, a large, friendly woman wearing a name tag that read "Bessie," bustled over. "There's a booth toward the back," she said helpfully.

"I'm looking for a Richard Miller," Doohan said.

"Dick Miller? Last booth, the skinny dude with the T-shirt."

Doohan couldn't tell how old he was from a distance. Anywhere from his middle twenties to his middle thirties; that anonymous age which meant you were holding up very well or were spending a great deal of time making sure it looked that way. It was more difficult for a man than a woman, he thought.

Miller saw him coming and stood up, a tanned, slender man with sandy hair, wearing the ubiquitous skin-tight Levi's and a wide black belt heavy with rectangular chrome studs. The promised T-shirt was slightly soiled and featured the cartoon figure of a young man with outsize shoes bending way back and strutting over the inscription, "Keep on Truckin'."

For a moment, Doohan didn't know what to make of him. In London, there would be no doubt that he was a renter, but then almost everybody on Castro Street looked like a renter. "Mr. Miller? Dr. Calvin Doohan."

Miller shook hands and motioned Doohan to sit down. Doohan found himself staring at Miller with almost a clinical fascination. It was a warm day and their section of the restaurant was even hotter because of the open grill on the other side of the counter. But on the seat next to Miller was a well-worn black leather cyclist's jacket with a snap-down collar and zippered sleeves. And on the table was a jaunty black leather German field cap with a small Luftwaffe eagle and wreath-enclosed swastika.

Miller himself had a lean-jawed muscular look with a heavy chest and biceps that suggested that he spent a great deal of time in the gym. His hair was short, not quite a crew cut, and he had a bushy but neatly trimmed mustache and a small gold stud in his left ear.

Bessie hurried over with a menu and said, "Can I take your order?"

"Just coffee for me." Doohan gestured to Miller. "Put his on my bill."

Bessie winked. "See, Dick, what'd I tell you? I told you he'd be good people."

"Hey, thanks a lot." Miller inspected the menu with pleasure. "Gimme the New York steak with fries, coffee, and a slice of banana cream pie." He settled back in the booth and inspected Doohan with a frank curiosity that was uncomfortable. "I don't know what I can tell you in payment for the steak," he said at last. "I already told the others everything I know. They took samples . . ." He rolled his eyes. "I couldn't *believe* what they wanted samples of."

"They're pretty serious," Doohan said. He fished out his pipe and lit it. "You worked the Elks' convention a year ago?"

Miller looked surprised. "Now that they didn't ask me." He motioned to Bessie for another cup of coffee. "I work a lot of the conventions. It's only part time and it keeps me going until I get my head together." He noticed Doohan's blank expression. "You got an accent—English? What I mean is, I drift around a lot; I hang out a lot; but when I need bread, this does it. I just go down to the union hall. No regular hours to bug me and enough money to get by. If I need more, I can always pick up a steady gig at one of the restaurants."

Doohan glanced around the cafe. In this area, not working more than you had to was probably a way of life. Where would they be ten years from now? he wondered. And then: Where would everybody be? "The Elks' convention," he prompted.

Miller's eyes had wandered over to the line of stools in front of the counter. For a moment he locked eyes with a young man dressed much like himself. He glanced back at Doohan and nodded. "Yeah, I worked it. Royalty Hotel, strictly Class A."

"Did you eat at either of the conventions?"

Another nod. "You show up an hour before work and get your station and they usually give you something to eat then too. Some hotels will ask that you eat before you come to work; the class ones feed you and usually they give you the same thing they're serving. I guess they figure that way you won't cop a bite off some guest's plate."

Bessie appeared with a platter and set it down before Miller. It held a surprisingly large cut of steak flanked by an enormous pile of french fries. A smaller dish held a limp-looking salad. Miller cut into the steak with relish. "You get tired of banquet food after a while; everything's usually cooked to hell and then warmed up. Besides, I got to watch the belly." He patted his stomach, flexing the abdominal muscles beneath the worn T-shirt. "Nobody loves a fat man." He pushed the salad across the table. "You want my salad? Rabbit food . . ."

"You didn't sneak even a bite at the convention?"

"Not me, man. Maybe somebody else did; I don't know."

"How about the cooks?"

"It'd be a pretty lousy cook that didn't sample his own food."

This lead was slipping away, too, Doohan thought in desperation. There was only one more point that he could double-check. "Did anybody besides you work both conventions?"

Miller didn't even hesitate. "Sure, old Ced Laval, the *garde-manger*, the cook who handles all the salads, all the cold dishes."

Doohan stared. "The work assignment sheets didn't indicate anybody else but you had worked both of them."

"I don't care what the sheets said. Laval was at the last one and I sure as hell remember him from the Elks. I was taking in a tray of salads and some bastard bumped me by the door and I lost the whole tray." He shook his head, laughing. "I honest-to-God thought old Laval was going to kill me."

Doohan frowned. "I can't understand why the assignment sheet didn't show him—"

"Look, he usually works at the Royalty; he's one of the best *garde-mangers* in town. The regular at the Cordoba was sick and the head chef called in Laval at the last minute. They probably settled it between them rather than make up a work chit. Maybe Laval just traded a shift."

Miller finished and stood up, wiping his mouth. Doohan picked up the check, slipping a dollar bill under his cup for Bessie. "See you," Miller said in a distant voice. At the counter, he slipped with practiced ease onto the vacant stool next to the young man he had eyed earlier.

Young love, Doohan thought cynically. He paid his bill and pocketed the change, accidentally jiggling the arm of the tall, beringed girl he had noticed earlier. "Pardon me . . ."

"That's all right, honey." The voice was husky, and for the first time Doohan realized she had the start of a five o'clock shadow.

19

IT'S LATE AFTERNOON and the young man stands at the window of the living room, staring out past the Golden Gate to the edge of the ocean. The sun is just touching the water, a slightly flattened, orange-hued globe that reminds him of sunsets back in the Midwest. A low-hanging mist reflects a blood-red color that dazzles his eyes.

But he really doesn't notice the racing colors that streak across the distant ripples of the ocean. He's worried. He's tried to stay on top of the situation, but now it's deteriorating rapidly.

And he knows very well who will be blamed.

He turns as the older man enters, his face a study in contained fury. His eyes are cold and distant. The younger man feels as if the older really doesn't see him, or if he does, that he sees something distasteful and tolerates it only because it's useful.

"Are you sure that Doohan is everything he claims to be?"

"We've checked him out thoroughly," the young man says. "There's no solid basis for believing he's anything other than what he appears."

"He's too curious," the older man says.

The young man nods. "He's too friendly with French. And he—"

Dryly. "I know, I read your report. For once, you could have spared me the details."

"There are ways of handling him."

"Just watch him. For now."

The young man is surprised. It's not the way he would have done it. There's more than Doohan's *friendliness with French, a great deal more. Doohan is dangerous and you don't tolerate danger. The older man shouldn't. And he himself won't. He would swing from a rope just as quickly as the others.*

"The situation with Laval . . ."

"Cedric? What does he want?"

"More money."

"What for? We've given him plenty." The older man stalks over to the bar. "A silly question, I suppose. Laval's turned out to be an odd combination—an altruist and a blackmailer."

"I wouldn't say that," the young man objects.

"No? What the hell would you call it?"

"I think it's conscience money," the young man says.

The older man thinks about it for a moment, then says: "It's his conscience. Not mine."

20

DOOHAN MADE IT over to Berkeley and French's lab by midafternoon. French was in his office, pacing back and forth before the big windows that looked out on Berkeley Way. He grunted when Doohan came in and pointed to the coffeepot. "Help yourself; it's one day old and twice as strong."

Doohan poured himself a cup and sat down. The fat man was angry at something and he had an idea just what it was. "I read in the papers that it was heavy-metal poisoning—nickel carbonyl."

"That's bullshit," French said curtly. "There was hardly any nickel at all in the initial samples the CDC sent, not a hundredth part per million. That is, there wasn't any until yesterday."

"Yesterday?"

French stopped in front of one of the windows, his hands clasped behind his back. "They sent me some samples with a request I run them for nickel. It was there all right—about two hundred parts per million based on fluid content. There were only traces before; this time the samples were almost drowning in it." He walked back to the coffee pot and poured himself a cup, slopping sugar into the cup so part of it spilled on the table. "Goddamnit, that makes me mad—the nerve of those bureaucratic bastards using me for a patsy."

"I don't follow you," Doohan said, frowning.

"Somebody had doused the samples with nickel chloride," French said with disgust.

"A practical joker?"

"Not a chance—not unless you think Major Lawrence Hanson is capable of practical jokes, and I must admit he never struck me as the type." He started pacing again. "They want something to back up their news story; so I'm the fall guy. They certainly didn't doctor the samples they sent to Atlanta." He turned to face Doohan. "You know what they want, Calvin? The virus has run its course; all its victims have died. Seventy-five contracted it; seventy-five died of it. The major now advances a theory as to why. I unwittingly confirm it; the major is commended; the public forgets about it. Finis. Except Hanson keeps doing whatever he's doing—under cover."

Doohan felt himself grow angry. The CDC was having enough difficulty culturing an organism, if it was an organism. But to deliberately compromise specimens . . .

"They won't get away with it," French continued coldly. "The major isn't the only one who can call a press conference. Give me time to do a few more tests and I'll blow the whistle on him; Washington will have his head on a platter."

"Hanson's tough," Doohan warned. "Don't do anything rash."

"The rashest thing I could do is not to do anything at all," French said slowly. "It's my reputation that's on the line." He finished his coffee, then settled into his swivel chair with a sigh. "We ran neutron activations on a number of tissue extracts; no significant amounts of nickel, but there was something else. Would you believe vanadium?"

"Vanadium?"

French nodded. "We checked the spectra on a number of samples and then ran some tests on water extracts. Organic vanadium compounds are highly colored; there's no way you can miss them."

"Enough vanadium to cause heavy metal poisoning?"

French threw up his hands. "I don't know. I have to do some more tests, but it's possible."

Doohan frowned. "How the devil did they get vanadium in their systems?"

"Your guess is as good as mine. Maybe our letter-writing friend made a mistake and it was a vanadium compound he put in with the dry ice instead of nickel carbonyl. An inventive assassin but a lousy chemist. Anyway, I've started a number of cultures with varying levels of vanadium salts."

"You suspect something," Doohan accused.

French shook his head. "Calvin, the difference between you and me is that you're inherently suspicious and I'm not. In that respect, I rather think you and Hanson have a lot in common—and forgive me for saying it. So I find vanadium, and like a good practical scientist, I start some cultures to see what will happen. If we see any growth in the chorioallantoic membrane of the egg or in the embryo, then we've got the start of an answer."

"Have you told Atlanta?"

French looked uneasy. "Not yet. Grant me a scientist's conceit; I would rather report to Atlanta with a complete wrap-up. Maybe I'll submit it in the same report with some choice comments about specimens that contain nickel chloride." He hesitated. "I don't dare be wrong on the vanadium." He walked back to the windows. "I understand you've been rather busy since Hanson kicked you out."

Doohan grinned. "Suzanne's been talking."

"She's the soul of discretion; nevertheless, it's the male of the species who dissembles, not the female. But I wasn't talking about Suzanne."

Doohan shook his head. "No progress. I checked out the staff who worked the banquets at both conventions. There were only two overlaps; neither one of them so much as caught a cold."

French was curious. "Who were they?"

"Richard Miller, a waiter. And the salad chef, a Cedric Laval."

"I don't remember the complete menu," French said offhand. "What kind of a salad did they serve at the Cordoba? Not one with a lot of vinegar, I'll bet; it'd be too acid."

"It was a tossed green salad with a special dressing at both conventions," Doohan said slowly. "Laval is famous for his dressings; the one he used both times was a Thousand Island variation."

They were both staring at each other now. "A colored dressing," French mused. "But of course, neither of them was allowed to eat anything. So we can't prove much."

Doohan shook his head. "Miller said they were fed an hour before they served the banquet in both hotels."

"But they didn't get sick," French said.

"Miller probably didn't eat the salad," Doohan said, remembering. "He considers it 'rabbit food.' "

French started to unbutton his lab smock. "Leaving only our Mr. Laval, the salad chef, who knew better than to eat his own creations. Do you know where this Laval lives?"

"I could probably get it."

French pointed at his desk and started to put on his coat. "The phone's right over there."

"Paul." Doohan paused. "If you get involved, it could be embarrassing to you."

French laughed. "It's much more embarrassing to me right now. If we leave it up to Hanson, then we're going to have to believe that noxious vapors did everybody in. And I haven't believed in the vapors since I gave up reading English mystery stories."

The apartment house on Noriega was a three-story building covered with stucco and painted a pastel blue. Doohan guessed it had been considered quite stylish when it had been built. It was going to seed now, the windows betraying several layers of paint and the small lawn in front leprous with two bald spots. The double doorway was draped with two single strings of Christmas lights and sported a cardboard cut-out of Santa Claus to one side.

He pressed the button opposite Laval's name, and a moment later the speaker above the board crackled and a woman's voice said, "Yeah?"

"Is Mr. Laval home?"

"I can't hear you," the small, tinny voice complained. Doohan repeated it. Petulantly: "Never mind." The buzzer sounded and Doohan tried the door, which opened under his push. French followed him in and they walked up the carpeted stairway to the third floor. At the top of the staircase, Doohan gave French a moment to catch his breath and then walked down to 3-D. He rang the bell and waited. From somewhere inside, they heard movement, then the clatter of something falling. Finally, the door opened and the puffy, slightly pudgy face of a woman of about thirty peered out at them. An aging baby's face, Doohan thought.

"Mrs. Laval?"

"That's right." Her hair was tangled in some plastic curlers and her eyes were bloodshot. From what Doohan could see, she was wearing a dirty, flowered robe with a cigarette burn in one lapel.

Doohan introduced himself and French. "It's very important I speak with your husband."

"He ain't here." Suddenly she sniffed. "Oh, Christ, my omelet." She disappeared, leaving the door ajar. Doohan looked at French, shrugged, and pushed open the door. They walked in, French closing the door behind them. For the type of house, the living room was surprisingly well furnished, with a nineteen-inch color TV in one corner and a selection of costly hi-fi components in the other. A Betamax videotape machine sat on a table next to the TV set; while nearby a cocktail table of glass and chrome held two alabaster eggs, a bouquet of dried flowers and two large crystal ashtrays piled high with lipstick-smeared butts. A haze of smoke and the smell of burned grease hovered in the room. From the kitchen, there was the clatter of a pan and the sound of running water followed by a sizzle.

The woman they had seen at the door was standing at the sink, scrubbing a pan. On the cutting board beside her was an old-fashioned glass, half filled with ice and whiskey.

"Mrs. Laval?"

"Jenny." An accusing glance. "Look what you made me do. I burned the hell out of my eggs."

"Sorry," Doohan said softly. There were eggshells on

the counter, plus an open can of mushrooms and a bottle of ketchup that had been tipped over and was now bleeding red on the masonite counter top. There had to be a small television set somewhere. There was, sitting on the table in the breakfast nook.

Jenny finished with the pan and lit a cigarette. "Pops usually does the cooking; I'm all thumbs in the kitchen."

"Pops?"

"My husband." She brushed aside a strand of over-bleached, cornstalk hair. She was, Doohan thought, somewhat defiant-looking. "If you're wondering why I'm eating breakfast at three in the afternoon, I slept in. Pops lets me sleep as long as I want." She picked up her drink and poked at it with a forefinger, then handed it to French. "Be a good guy and get some ice. You two want a drink?"

"It's a little early for us," Doohan said. Behind him, he could hear French swearing at the refrigerator. The ice-cube trays were probably frozen in.

"Straight arrow, huh? Never too early for this girl; Pops says I thrive on the stuff."

"Is your husband around? We'd like to talk to him."

"So would I. He took off yesterday evening and he hasn't been home since." She sat down in a kitchen chair and pulled her robe tight around her. Doohan could see a hint of wariness in her eyes. It had finally occurred to her that he and French were official. "Goddamnit, I hate to sleep alone. It's cold at night, but with Pops in bed, it's like having your own heater."

"Do you have any idea when he'll be back?"

"It better be soon; he's working the evening shift." She bit her lip. "It's not like him, really not like him. He hasn't been himself lately at all."

"How so?" Doohan asked.

"He seems frightened all the time. And mad—like somebody had pulled a dirty deal on him." She thought for a moment. "And he's depressed. It's not like Pops to be depressed. You know, these people came around—" She looked at Doohan, vaguely re-membering the ID he had showed at the door. "You're from the same place, aren'tcha?"

"I think I'll have that drink," French said behind them. Doohan turned in surprise. French was holding a tray of cubes and a bottle and looking for all the world as if a heavy belt of whiskey at three in the afternoon was standard.

"Help yourself—glasses on the top shelf."

"Could we talk in the living room?" Doohan asked. Jenny shrugged and led the way. In the living room, she plopped down on the couch and snuffed out her cigarette in one of the overflowing ashtrays, knocking some of the butts onto the glass table top.

She noticed Doohan's reaction and looked embarrassed. "Look, I'm a slob," she admitted. "Pops always said I was a slob, but he didn't mind cleaning up after me. Three years we've been married and he still likes to clean up after me." She tried a tentative smile. "I guess he thinks I'm his little girl. He's a real sweetpants. Always buying stuff for me. He's gonna buy me a new car; don't ask me where he's gonna get the money. But God, he's nice to me—more'n I deserve." She looked at Doohan with a surprisingly open expression. "You know, he's twenty years older'n me but I really love that old jelly belly."

French now came out of the kitchen holding another drink. In his other hand, he carried a rumpled paper bag. Doohan sensed a vague excitement about the man. French gave the glass to Jenny. "I thought you might like another."

She drained the drink she was holding. "Now that's real nice." She was fishing in her pockets for cigarettes when the door buzzer sounded. "Get that for me, will you, honey?" she said, looking at Doohan. "Just buzz it, the damned speaker hasn't worked for a month."

Doohan found the buzzer and pushed it. He walked over to Jenny, taking a card from his wallet and writing his home number on it. "Will you have your husband call me when he returns? It's very important and it might be profitable."

"Money? He'll run all the way."

She walked them to the door, hanging tightly onto Doohan's arm for support. "Sorry I'm such a mess;

come around some time when I'm fixed up. Y'know, they still look at me when Pops and I walk into a bar."

She opened the door. A uniformed policeman stood on the other side, his hand just reaching for the bell. "Mrs. Laval?"

She leaned against the open door. "You've got it. Whatever it is, Officer, I didn't do it, and I've got two witnesses to prove it."

The policeman took off his cap and Doohan caught his breath; he could sense it coming. "Could you come downtown with me, ma'am?"

Her smile grew tremulous, then faded altogether. "Something's wrong." It was a statement, not a question.

The policeman looked uncomfortable. "I'm sorry, Mrs. Laval. We have to ask you to identify someone; he was carrying your husband's identification."

"Well, whyn'tcha ask him who he is?" She was sobering up fast and Doohan could see the fear start to grow in the back of her eyes. He suddenly wanted to get out of there; it was going to be embarrassing to watch.

"The Coast Guard found him in the Bay this morning."

"Pops?" She was completely sober now and it came out as a half scream. "My God, not Pops!"

"An accident?" Doohan asked.

"You family friends?" Doohan nodded. "Accident or probably suicide. The coroner said he had been drinking but outside of alcohol in the bloodstream, there wasn't a mark on him. You care to come down too?"

Doohan shook his head. "No, I don't think so." They left, leaving the policeman to console a quietly weeping Jenny Laval.

In the car, Doohan sagged back in his seat and sighed. "Well, that wraps that one up. One more dead end."

"I don't think so." French sounded oddly gleeful. "I think I got what we came for."

Doohan turned around. Under the circumstances, French's cheerfulness was almost black humor. "I don't follow you."

"Read this."

French handed him a curled piece of paper, faintly cold to the touch. It read, "Jenny: Special sample. Don't touch." The "Don't touch" was underlined three times with a marking pen.

Doohan looked at French questioningly and French pulled a pint jar out of the paper bag. The label read: MELROSE FOODS—MARKETING SAMPLE. The jar itself was half filled with a slightly bluish-tinged mayonnaise.

Doohan started to unscrew the cap and French grabbed his hand. "Uh-uh, better not."

"Why not?"

"What were you going to do, taste it?"

That was exactly what he had been about to do, Doohan realized. He suddenly felt cold.

"My guess," French said quietly, "is that it's loaded with vanadium. And just maybe—something else."

21

FRENCH, BLEARY-EYED AND unshaven, was sitting at his desk drinking black coffee when Doohan came in the following morning. "My God, Paul, you look as though you've been up all night."

"I have," French grunted. "You didn't think I was going to drop that stuff in the lab and go home for a good night's sleep, did you? I had Isaac run me over a couple of sandwiches and I slept on the couch here."

"Isaac?"

"My son, the light of my life—you haven't met him yet."

Doohan sat down and poured himself a cup of coffee. "What about the mayonnaise?"

"As I thought. It's high in vanadium."

"Tell me something, Paul." Doohan stared down at his coffee for a moment. "When we went to the Lavals', you knew what you were looking for, didn't you?"

French blinked, trying hard to wake up. "My line of thinking was the same as yours. The victims had to have attended both conventions. Which meant they had to come into contact with the same agent twice—or combination of agents. You now have a choice: The agent is airborne, transmitted through the skin by touch, or else it's in something that they ate."

He slumped in his chair and yawned. "If it had been airborne, other people would certainly have come down with it. After all, the two hotels are within blocks of each other. To be transmitted by touch was highly improbable. It had to be something they ingested. And there was only one time at each convention when large numbers of the conventioneers all had the same food—the banquet. When you mentioned Laval, it had to be him; he was in the position of access."

"And the lack of second-generation infections?"

French stared into space, thinking for a moment. "I think our bug needs trace vanadium to grow. We found ten successive autopsy liver sections with vanadium concentrations ranging from ten to fifty parts per million—enough to raise your eyebrows, but probably not enough to cause heavy-metal poisoning. The concentration of vanadium in the mayonnaise is far higher than that; the human body fluids greatly dilute it. My guess is that the vanadium is in the form of a chelate, sort of a buffered system; the more you dilute it, the more vanadium it releases so once in the body it hangs in around that ten-to-fifty parts range. Our bug is growing all right."

"And the mayonnaise—"

"I told you we found vanadium in the mayonnaise. We couldn't check it with a colorimetric sample until we ashed it, which means I'm right about the vanadium being bound with some organic molecule. Both the neutron activation and the spectrophotometer give the vanadium content of the mayonnaise nearly a tenth of a per cent."

Doohan stared at him blankly. "You still haven't told me why no second-generation infections."

"Sure I did, I just—" French laughed. "Okay, I'll try again. The veterans didn't die of heavy-metal poisoning, nickel carbonyl or, for that matter, vanadium. They died of a virus, a specially tailored virus that can grow only in a chemical environment that contains trace vanadium. Remove it from that environment and it dies. Ergo, no second-generation infections."

Doohan licked his lips. "If vanadium ions are the key to culturing the organism, if it needs vanadium to survive, then there's only one conclusion."

"That's right, Calvin. Our virus is artificial. Somebody made it." French watched his reaction, looking at Doohan curiously. "Calvin, unless I'm mistaken, you've suspected something was wrong right from the start. Now I tell you that you're absolutely right and you look unhappy. What's wrong?"

"No motivation," Doohan said slowly. "Why the devil would Laval want to feed it to a group of over-the-hill veterans? Or Elks, for that matter?"

French yawned. "Ask me again tomorrow, Calvin. Right now, I haven't the foggiest idea. In the meantime, let's check out what they're doing in the lab." He shot Doohan a serious look. "And then we've got something to discuss."

Doohan followed him down the hall and they entered the large lab where the inoculated eggs were incubating. Anderson was busy cutting out a small section of an egg and carefully removing the red mass that was the developing chick embryo. Only the embryo wasn't a healthy red now but a rather mottled color; it was obviously dead. The attached yolk sac he took out and deposited in a small glass container.

"We'll wash the yolk sac and macerate it," French explained. "We'll wind up with an aqueous solution and then we'll concentrate it by vacuum for transfer to a host animal. Some of the sample we'll lyophilize —freeze dry—and store as a reference source."

"What animals are you going to use?"

"Probably hamsters the first time around. We'll take an extract of the mayonnaise and inject it both nasally and peritoneally in a set of animals."

Anderson glanced up from his work. "Dr. French, there's been no pitting or growths in the egg membranes," he said, nettled. "The embryos just . . . died."

"That doesn't make sense," Doohan objected. "The virus should cause changes in the membranes."

"No, it makes sense," French said. "We just don't know exactly what kind of sense. It took more than one exposure to produce any symptoms of the disease; perhaps the first exposure sensitized and the second exposure killed, almost like developing an allergy. We'll have to cover our bets; we'll have to inject our animals with everything from the embryos to the allantoic fluid, along with trace vanadium."

"What are you doing with the mayonnaise?"

"Follow me; I'll show you."

At the far end of the room was a heavy oaken door with a massive cast-aluminum latch, designed to be opened with an elbow if one had both hands full. French opened it and pushed through the door. A wave of chill air blew out. Doohan closed the door behind them. The room was about eight by ten and contained a workbench; there was another door opposite the first. It must lead from the cold room to the sub-zero room, Doohan thought.

On a workbench a vacuum pump labored with a steady flutter. It was attached to a short-necked flask inside a glove box. The inside of the flask was coated with a frozen layer of liquid. French put his hands in the gloves and tapped at the flask; dry flakes peeled away from the inside surface. A simple freeze-drying process, Doohan thought.

"The mayonnaise extract," French explained. "The material we aren't using, I'll seal after drying in an ampoule; I don't want that stuff wandering around. Right now, it has to be some of the most dangerous material in the world."

"Will it survive the drying?"

"We're dealing with a virus; it will be just as active when it's rehydrated." Using the gloves, he detached the flask containing the dried material, then pulverized the substance inside the flask with a spatula. Finally, he transferred the now powdered contents to a glass tube with a drawn neck that acted as a funnel. He ignited the burner in the glove box and carefully melted the neck of the tube until it was sealed, pulling the funnel section away. He waited a moment until it had cooled, then placed it on a rack. He sealed the remainder in a second ampoule. Doohan noted the numbers etched on the sides of both tubes and automatically memorized them. French then covered the tubes with a layer of thick foil and turned on a battery of ultraviolet lamps in the box.

"We sterilize the whole interior of the glove box and then we'll have our little monster safely bottled where he can't get loose." He pulled his hands out of the gloves and walked to the opposite end of the cold room. Doohan had begun to shiver, but French showed no discomfort. He reached up on a shelf and took down the bottle which held the mayonnaise. "It's empty and clean—at least it's clean of what was in it." He moodily inspected the bottle, then turned to Doohan. "Calvin, we have some soul-searching to do."

Doohan shivered. "How about soul-searching in your office? I'm damned near freezing."

Back in the office, French turned on the hot plate. "You don't mind reheated coffee, do you?"

"If you're afraid of ruining it, you couldn't if you tried."

French turned the hot plate control to simmer, then sat down in his chair. His face was almost gray with fatigue. "Calvin, we've got a tiger by the tail."

"I'm well aware of that."

"Whatever was in that jar, it wasn't intended to fall into our hands. The problem is what do we do with it —it and the cultures we may develop from it."

Doohan was silent for a moment. "You're the one who's in the difficult position," he said at last. "I think my own responsibilities are pretty clear. I've given a sizable fraction of my life to an organization that works for the health of people, regardless of what particular flag they might be under. I think our virus is a threat to humanity, not just to governments."

"There's a lot we don't know," French said, frustrated. "We don't know who made it; we don't know how it was intended to be used; at the moment we don't even know much about it, aside from what I told you today."

Doohan made up his mind then. "We're assuming we have the same responsibilities and we don't. My responsibility is to notify the member nations of WHO as to what is going on. I guess your responsiblity is to wrap up your findings and present them to Major Lawrence Hanson."

French thought about it for a moment, then shook his head. "I might have agreed with you if Hanson hadn't tried to make me the cat's-paw with the nickel carbonyl explanation. Eventually they'll have to issue a disclaimer on that explanation and professionally, I'm set up to be the fall guy." He was half-talking to himself now, as if he were voicing some thoughts for the first time. "I think I ought to work on it a few more days, then take the complete results and go over Hanson's head directly to the CDC in Atlanta."

"Injured pride?"

"You mean do I want to show up Hanson? Of course I do." Now he looked uneasy. "And maybe there's something else. If we find out something vital here and I give it to Hanson, what assurance do I have that it will ever reach the CDC?"

It was a new thought to Doohan, a reminder that Hanson in turn had his own area of loyalties that just might not include the CDC.

French finished his coffee and stood up, yawning hugely. "Come back tomorrow, Calvin; I should know more by then." He was curled up on the office couch and snoring before Doohan got out the door.

Outside, Doohan sat in his car and stared blindly out at the city. They had a piece of the puzzle, but he had a hunch it was only a small piece. There was something they hadn't talked about, something he hadn't thought of, and something French might have avoided thinking of. The bloodmobile that had fled from the police. There was no explanation for it. Nor was there any explanation for Roy French's work with the other bloodmobile.

But then, he thought, he might be seeing shadows where none existed. There was certainly good reason for a bloodmobile to be present at both conventions. Paul had said it had been unlike his brother to contribute his time and labor to working with the blood drive, but Paul had never been close to his brother, particularly toward the last.

He turned on the ignition then and concentrated on the problem of slipping into the traffic pattern on the freeway. Still, there was something in the back of his mind. Something he had once read. Something about a German bacterial-warfare effort prior to World War II.

Then he wondered if he should go back to Laguna Honda and check the blood-donor records. There might have been something they had overlooked. It was worth a try, he decided.

22

MAJOR LAWRENCE HANSON was halfway through the door before he noticed that Miltrait wasn't alone. The CDC representative was in quiet conference with the head of one of his interrogation teams. The perpetual cigarette dangled from Miltrait's mouth, and the air in the office was hazy with smoke. Miltrait glanced up, nodded coldly, and quickly finished his conversation. The team head mumbled, "I'll get them right away." He gathered up his notes and left, shooting Hanson an enigmatic look as he went out. He wouldn't win any popularity contests with the troops, Hanson thought.

"Something I can do for you, Major?"

"If you have a moment, I'd like to talk to you," Hanson said affably.

"I'm at your command, Major," Miltrait said, a touch of irony in his voice. He leaned back in his chair and clasped his hands behind his head. "I was about to ring your office. My innate sense of fairness. I think you ought to know I've filed a formal complaint about interference on your part with the work here." Miltrait snuffed out his cigarette in the already overflowing ashtray on his desk and immediately lit another.

Hanson made himself at ease in a side chair near the desk. "I realize you haven't been happy under the setup." To himself he thought: *God, I'm tired of baby-sitting.*

"My personal happiness or unhappiness has nothing to do with it," Miltrait said coldly. "My professional happiness and reputation does. As far as I'm concerned, anything that compromises the credibility of the Center for Disease Control is a national disservice. I can't think of any national emergency so great that that would be justified."

"You have specific charges?"

"For openers, your press release about nickel carbonyl. It's at best a theory and hardly a sound one. You had that issued over my name." The little man was furious now and Hanson wondered idly if he were subject to high-blood pressure. "You slap a gag order on the rest of us and then you go ahead and issue bulletins in our names."

"Anything else?"

"Your bulletin that 'recovered victims' were being sent home but refusing to name names for fear it would 'turn into a media circus.'"

Hanson fought down an impulse to simply let it go; after today, it wouldn't matter a damn anyway. "You would have preferred panic?" He held up a hand before Miltrait could reply. "Doctor, you can file all the protests you wish but all that comes from Washington. If you doubt me, you're invited to check. *Anything* released without my authority is a violation of security."

"You think you can sit on this forever, Major? You couldn't get away with it in a totalitarian country and you certainly can't do it here. I should think the CIA experience would have taught you something." Hanson hesitated a moment before answering and Miltrait finished bitterly, "There's not much difference between the way we're operating now and the way we'd be operating in wartime."

Hanson could feel himself growing heated now. Why not take off the gloves? After today, Miltrait wouldn't be his responsibility anyway. "We've had seventy-five people come down with an as yet undetermined illness. All seventy-five died—no recoveries, no getting better and then having relapses, just a steady deterioration from beginning to end. We have every reason to believe that the victims became ill because of something that was deliberately fed to them.

There's no motivation we can think of; there's no indication why. That ought to suggest something to you, Doctor."

He looked at Miltrait curiously, puzzled and annoyed that the man couldn't see the obvious. "The fatality rate was an impossible one; it was far greater than that for the Legionnaires' Disease in Philadelphia and the pressure from both Congress and the media has been intense. We can't afford panic. Neither can we afford congressional hawks making assumptions as to just who the unknown enemy might be out there. So it's in this country's best interests that the story fade off the front pages. The government rightly thinks we'd be handicapped trying to do our job in the white light of publicity. So we gave a plausible explanation. If we had to, we'd produce the man who wrote that letter and set that pan of nickel carbonyl in the alcove. Then we'd see that he was shipped immediately to a sanitarium and that's the last anybody would ever hear of him. That's the way it has to be, Doctor."

Miltrait stood up, an aging little bantam rooster of a man. "I admire your subtlety, Major." He lit another cigarette. "You can also go to hell."

When his hand was on the doorknob, Hanson said sharply, "Dr. Miltrait." Miltrait turned. "What I originally stopped in to tell you was that the CDC's role in this operation is finished. So is that of the local Department of Health. The medical part of this operation is over. From now on, it's strictly a problem of national security."

Miltrait almost bit through his cigarette. "Whose medical opinion did you consult for that conclusion?"

"Does it matter? By tomorrow, the CDC teams will have been recalled to Atlanta. What little mop-up work remains here will be done by a very small team. We've asked certain of your team members to work with us for a week or two longer. Atlanta's cutting their orders now."

Miltrait looked calculating. "You'll be transferring your headquarters?"

"We'll be based at Endo-Syn Pharmaceuticals in Emeryville. They've done work for both HEW and the Department of Defense before and they have the facilities we'll need. And then we'll be completely out of the public eye. It will be easier to maintain security."

"There are a lot of loose ends to tie up. There are a lot of veterans we haven't followed up on."

Hanson drummed his fingers on the chair arm. The man was incredibly stupid or he just couldn't conceive of what was happening. "I don't think we're communicating very well, Doctor. If this were a natural disease, you'd be absolutely right. But there'll be no further victims. It doesn't spread; it's strictly self-limiting. Your own information indicates that beyond a shadow of a doubt. The point is, it's not a disease at all in the accepted sense. It was a small-scale military test, by what country or what organization, we haven't the foggiest idea. But it's no longer a medical problem; its a military one. Do you understand that?"

Miltrait thought for a moment, dropped his cigarette on the floor and scrubbed it out with his shoe. "Sometimes I think we're all captives of our occupations, Major. Good luck." He turned and slammed the door behind him, rattling the glass in its frame.

Hanson sat staring at the door, wondering if he should have treated Miltrait any differently. There had been a personality conflict right from the start and there had been no way to avoid it. Miltrait had been unable to help himself; he had resented the intrusion of the military and there was no way that could be smoothed over. And he, Hanson, had been given the final word and Miltrait couldn't stomach that. Pray to God that when Miltrait got back to Atlanta, they could somehow manage to shut him up.

And then he thought: *Miltrait was a narrow-minded little tyrant right from the start. What the hell am I feeling guilty about?*

He went back to his own office and buzzed for Roberts. "Get Dr. Gorshin down here and then ask that damned girl to make sure we're not disturbed."

Five minutes later, Gorshin and Roberts were sitting in front of his desk. Roberts, as usual, looked slightly apprehensive, Gorshin imperturbable. Hanson liked

Roberts; he felt a certain kinship toward him. *I must have been like that at his age.* Dr. Thomas Gorshin he liked a good deal less. A corpulent man with wattles and thinning gray hair, wearing Coke-bottle lenses and an air of authority that was almost palpable.

"General Varger called this morning," Hanson said without preamble. "The CDC is being relieved of its interest in the case and they'll be moving out tomorrow. So will the teams from the Department of Health. What's left of the operation, including our own offices will be shifted to Endo-Syn in Emeryville on Tuesday."

Roberts looked blank. "Endo-Syn?"

"An East Bay pharmaceutical house; it should be easier to maintain security there." Roberts still looked puzzled, and Hanson said, "In the eyes of Washington, this is no longer a civilian operation. Not hardly. Dr. Gorshin?"

Gorshin's voice was high and almost effeminate; a fifty-year old aging eunuch, Hanson thought. "The moment we verified that there were no second generation infections, it became highly probable that our disease was actually a military incursion of some kind. The conclusion is that it was a test with a virus of extremely high toxicity, and the test was made not once but twice. We haven't been able as yet to culture it."

Roberts frowned. "Twice?"

"From your bloodmobile data, it's possible that they tried a similar test at the Elks' convention at the Royalty Hotel a year ago," Gorshin said.

"With no result."

Gorshin shrugged. "A failed virus, probably one of extremely low virulence."

"Then why the overlap?"

A thoughtful pause. "We're working on that aspect."

Hanson felt a twinge of disbelief. Washington had touted Gorshin as unusually brilliant, a molecular biologist who was tops in his field. But the man had come up with remarkably few answers. He turned to Roberts. "How's French doing?"

Roberts hesitated. "From the activity, I would assume that Dr. French has made some progress.

We've had a man . . . ah . . . cultivate Celia Kovacs, one of the lab assistants. She's close-mouthed but she more or less confirms that they've made progress. French isn't reporting—at least not yet. My guess is that he wants to present a complete wrap-up, probably as a refutation of the nickel-carbonyl theory."

The real genius was the man they had chosen to provide their cover-up, Hanson thought. He shot another glance at Gorshin. It didn't take an expert to tell him that the nickel-carbonyl theory had been a mistake. Gorshin had suggested it as a plausible cover, though Hanson had had his doubts at the time. Now it looked as if French had been able to do what neither Atlanta nor Gorshin had been able to. But Gorshin had a reputation as being brilliant. . . .

"We could walk in and take it," Roberts suggested.

"And if French is in the middle of something, it'll never be finished. Not a bright idea, Roberts. What about Doohan?"

Roberts looked uneasy. "He's spent several nights with Dr. Synge. And he's also visited Dr. French in his laboratory a number of times."

Hanson cursed silently to himself. He had no idea what part Doohan played in all of this, but it wasn't that of an innocent bystander. It was reasonable to assume he knew whatever Dr. Synge knew and certainly was privy to French's own line of investigation. In short, he probably knew more than he, Hanson, knew. And Doohan was on record as wanting to tell all. "Get hold of State and see what it will take to revoke Doohan's visa. Set the wheels in motion and get back to me."

He thought then of cutting Dr. Synge from the list of personnel he was taking over to Endo-Syn. She had asked for the assignment, but it would be easy enough to bump her. Then he decided against it. As long as she was around, he would know where to find Doohan, if and when he wanted him.

He dismissed Roberts and Gorshin and walked over to the window to stare blindly out. It didn't make sense. There wasn't any doubt that the disease was a military thrust of some sort against the United States.

And yet he had been assigned Coxey's Army to find out exactly what it was and to contain it. He had asked the general for additional security men and lab personnel so that he would have more than a skeleton organization and he had been turned down; the various grades just weren't available. He had Roberts, he thought, and the relatively few men under him. Roberts was efficient but unimaginative. And Gorshin . . . he had no idea what went on behind those thick lenses. On balance, the man had made the right deductions so far, but they were still waiting for French to actually come up with what it was.

He looked out at the street below and smiled bleakly. His aces in the hole were the very men whom he didn't trust.

Dr. Paul French.

And, of course, Calvin Doohan.

23

ON HIS WAY to French's lab, Doohan parked his car
high in the Berkeley hills and got out to lean against
the hood and stare at the city below. It was an unusually clear day and he could see the university
campanile and, farther away, the Bay itself with the
towers of San Francisco in the distance. There was
just the faintest trace of fog to lend the distant towers
a fairyland touch and to partially obscure the Golden
Gate Bridge, a string sculpture in red. The wind rustling through the weeds at his feet drowned out the
muted drone of the city so far away.

Elizabeth would have liked living in the hills, he
thought. He wondered if Suzanne would and then
realized that in the last few days, the image of Elizabeth had faded even more ... *"but that was in another country; and besides, the wench is dead."* It
wasn't the right context but the feeling was there.
Suzanne was warm, witty, intelligent, and superb
sexually.

She was all of those things, he thought, and still he
was ... dissatisfied? Or did he distrust it because it was
too good to be true? There was a certain trade-off in
the world. Fantastically beautiful women made liai-
sons with the fantastically wealthy or the enormously creative. He hardly fit either category.

He wondered about it a moment longer, then shook
his head and got back into the car. French would still
be in his lab; it must be—he squinted at the sun—
around four o'clock. His wrist watch showed that he
was ten minutes off. How many watches had he lost

in Bangladesh, he thought, and been forced to rely
on sun observation? Ten? Fifteen? He glanced at the
city below for the last time, then started the engine
and drove down the winding road toward the city
and French's laboratory.

The friendly guard in the lobby, installed after the
student riots of the sixties and functioning more
as a source of information for visitors than as a guard,
was gone now, replaced by one of Hanson's superpro-
fessional rent-a-cops. On impulse, Doohan picked the
name of a doctor on another floor, signed in, and then
took the elevator to French's floor instead. By now,
Hanson must have issued orders that he wasn't to see
French.

When he stepped out of the elevator, another guard
met him with drawn gun. "I should have received a
call from downstairs clearing you," he said grimly. "I
didn't."

"I had several people to see," Doohan said casually.
"I can change my mind as to who I see first, can't I?
Check with Dr. French." The young guard quickly
searched him down, then called in from his makeshift
desk. A moment later, French came out to meet him.

"Everything's military now, Calvin; I feel as though
I'm under house arrest. Come on down to the animal
room; I was checking on a shipment." At the opposite
end of the hall from French's laboratory was a large,
gamy-smelling room filled with tier upon tier of wire
mesh and plastic cages. Some of them held individual
animals—rhesus monkeys or ferrets—while the smaller animals were held in communal cages. Close up,
the stench was pronounced.

Doohan took a moment to inspect one of the cages.
A watering bottle was fixed to the wire mesh wall
with a drinking tube curving inside; dishes to hold
pellet food were also attached to the wire mesh. The
floor of the room itself was of white poured plastic,
sloping toward a center drain so it could be hosed
down easily.

"I stopped over at Laguna Honda," Doohan said
casually.

French glanced up from the cage he was inspecting, surprised. "I thought you were *persona non grata* with Hanson."

"I didn't see him. I talked with one of the people who was coordinating clinical data." French put down the cage; Doohan had his undivided attention. "The blood types don't match," Doohan continued.

A blank stare. "I don't follow you."

"The hospital blood types on the victims don't match the blood types listed for them by the blood bank. One that I personally questioned, a Herman Rosenberg, was down for type O negative at the hospital; the blood bank had him listed as type O positive. Type O negative is one devil of a lot rarer."

"Clerical error?"

"In nine different cases? Hardly likely."

French picked up another cage and poked at the animal within. "You've got a theory, Calvin? You usually do."

"I think the blood was switched," Doohan said. "I don't think the blood that was turned over to the blood bank was the same blood that was collected at the convention. At least, not on the last day."

"What the hell would be the point of doing that?"

"I once read of the German biological warfare test in the Paris Métro in 1938. Did you ever hear about that?"

French shook his head. "In the Paris subway? No."

"The Germans spread a mild respiratory infection throughout all of the air intake of the subway. Then for several weeks following, they stationed agents at all the exits with counters, tallying the number of passengers with coughs and sniffles. The end results confirmed that biological warfare was feasible."

"So what's that got to do with the blood substitution?"

"A test is no good unless you can monitor the spread of the biological agent. That's why blood was collected at each convention; that's why Roy was working with them. You get a statistical sampling from the convention, analyze the blood for the presence of your agent and then you can project the effectiveness of the spread."

"And they couldn't afford to have the infected blood enter the blood program—"

"—so they switched it. Then they destroyed the blood they had collected."

From the look on his face, Doohan guessed that French didn't want to believe it. And he thought he knew why.

"That's a lot of blood; it would have been damned difficult to replace."

"Not really; there's been a black market in blood for years. And it would have affected only the blood they gave on Sunday, the morning after the Saturday night banquet. It wasn't much, maybe thirty pints."

"And the accident with the first bloodmobile?"

"When the police stopped them, they must have realized an investigation would reveal the switch. So they fled and tried to destroy the blood, and then they had the accident. The data they had were lost."

"So a year later they had to repeat the test?"

Doohan hesitated. "That's one scenario."

"There's more than one?"

"I think so, Paul. Look at it from another angle. If you were to devise a bacterial weapon, what would you try and design into it?"

French let a hamster nibble idly at his fingertip. "It should be something that's easy to spread and that is either fatal or disabling over the long run."

"And the safety of your own troops?"

"That's always been a problem. You wouldn't want your artificial epidemic getting out of hand and wiping out your own people. You'd probably have to inoculate all your people with an antitoxin right from the start."

"I think they did something else. I think they developed a bug that could grow only in the presence of a fairly rare material, one you could introduce into the body itself. Bug and environment in the same capsule, so to speak."

"The virus in the vanadium-mayonnaise."

"That's right. But it doesn't have to be mayonnaise;

it can be a thousand other things. If this were an American weapon, for example, you could use it to infect shipments of wheat abroad to Iron Curtain countries."

"It could work the other way too," French said dryly. "We import almost all our teas and coffee, a lot of specialty foods . . ."

There was a scramble in one of the cages and Doohan noticed one of the hamsters mounting another in frantic coitus. French grabbed at the cage, opened the door and started pulling the hamsters out. "Damn Anderson!" He finally gave it up in disgust. "Come on, I've still got some coffee on the hot plate."

On the way down the hall, French stopped in the lab where Anderson was working. "For God's sake, Darryl, you know you're supposed to keep hamsters segregated by sex. You've got them all in the same cage."

Anderson looked surprised. "I thought sure I had, Doctor."

"When you get a chance, go to the animal room and sort them out. In about two weeks, we're going to be up to our navels in hamsters."

In the office, French continued to complain. "Damn kid, he's too sloppy. No eye for details, no appreciation for the patience you need in experimental work. He screwed up a dozen times on the egg cultures."

Doohan turned on the hot plate and rinsed out two cups. "What about Celia?"

"Like a computer. If she gives you a result, you damned well can depend on it."

"Anything unusual in the animals you've injected so far?"

"No; but then we only saw the disease in those people who had been exposed to it twice."

Doohan measured out the coffee. "That's the other scenario, Paul. To sum it up: Somebody's succeeded in making a virus that cannot live without the presence of vanadium, so it's non-infectious, it can't start an uncontrollable epidemic. It's extremely effective —but it takes two exposures to kill. That means you could secretly infect an enemy population with your bug without any obvious symptoms. No one gets ill; the enemy has no idea he's harboring a deadly virus. Since second-generation infections are impossible, there's no way an enemy can pass it on—or pass it back. Now a war starts. A second exposure kills the enemy, but your own population is unaffected. You could use the agent right in the battle zone on your own men with complete immunity. It's like the magic bullet of folklore; it kills only the enemy but spares your friends."

French suddenly looked immensely depressed. "I think I need a drink on that one. Join me?" He took off his lab coat and fumbled behind the closet door for a brown tweed jacket with leather patches on the elbows.

"Why not? I've got to meet Suzanne at seven, but I could squeeze in one or two."

They found a bar and grill just off Shattuck, and French ordered a whiskey on the rocks with a roast beef and swiss cheese sandwich; Doohan had a scotch and water. French's face was a brown study. When their orders came, he gulped half his whiskey, then came out with what was on his mind. "You said the other day that we each had our responsibilities. I don't like Hanson; I think he used me. But I don't think I have the right to keep this from him either."

Doohan suddenly felt betrayed. "I thought you said you were going to withhold results until you had them pretty complete, then notify the CDC?"

French took another gulp of his whiskey and sagged back in his booth, a huge bear of a man looking rumpled and unhappy. "Your theories kind of change that, Calvin. But I'll notify the CDC, of course."

"Do you have any more tests to run?"

"A few."

"How long will they take?"

"One day, maybe two. No more."

Doohan swirled the ice cubes in his glass. "I'm flying to Washington tomorrow to see Espinosa. Why don't you hold off until I come back?"

French didn't meet Doohan's eyes. "It's a different

kind of ball game, Calvin. Hanson is interested in this thing from the military point of view and it looks as though he was right all along. It *is* a military problem. What kind of a citizen would I be if I held back information?"

"Twenty-four hours," Doohan urged desperately. "Just long enough for me to get the information to Espinosa. If you tell him your findings now, I'll be in protective custody within the hour."

French looked tormented. "I don't know, Calvin; I really don't know."

"Look at it from my point of view," Doohan argued. "Hanson wants to keep this under wraps, a hidden war that's fought completely out of sight. I have a larger loyalty. We're dealing with disease and epidemics, no matter how they're spread. Somebody is intent on using disease as a weapon—our virus may not be the only weapon in their arsenal. In a BW war, Paul, it'll be the young and the old and the poor who will die first."

French pushed the rest of his sandwich aside and picked up the bill. "Calvin." His expression was pained. "If you're right, then we Americans have experienced the tryout of a bacteriological weapon by an enemy. On our soil with our own countrymen as victims. What kind of a man would I be if I kept my mouth shut now?"

There were no more arguments, Doohan thought. French was in agony and he could only see the obvious side. He clapped the fat man on the shoulder in sympathy. "I'm sorry about Roy; I'm sorry he got involved."

French suddenly turned antagonistic. "You've been thinking about that all along, haven't you, Calvin? That because Roy had volunteered to work on the blood drive, that somehow he was involved, that somehow he was a traitor. I find it hard to believe. I find it even harder to believe that Roy would have handled something as dangerous as the virus and failed to take precautions against it. I didn't agree with him politically, but I know damned well he wouldn't have committed suicide. There were other doctors who worked both bloodmobiles, you know. As far as I'm concerned, Roy's as much a martyr as any of the veterans who died."

French got up and lurched away from the table. Doohan watched him go with sadness. In defending Roy, French had rediscovered his own feelings for him.

Outside, French was waiting for him, shamefaced. "I'm sorry, Calvin. But . . . Roy was my brother."

Doohan nodded. "I understand." Just before they parted, he added thoughtfully, "That mayonnaise was never supposed to fall into our hands, you know. Whoever made it is still out there and so far, they've killed seventy-five people. They know by now that we've got it and they'll do anything to get it back. They won't hesitate to kill you or me. Or Isaac."

"Isaac rates as one of the young who would die first?" French asked bitterly.

Doohan shook his head. "I didn't mean it that way, Paul."

"All right," French said thickly. "You've got your twenty-four hours. What the hell more do you want from me?"

24

Doohan crossed California to the Huntington Hotel, entered L'Étoile, and told the maître d' he would like reservations for two. Suzanne was waiting in the cocktail lounge, sitting on a couch at the far end, sipping a frosted daiquiri. She didn't see him at first, and he stood in the shadows by the wall, watching her for a moment. She seemed perfectly at ease, perfectly at home in the setting. Much more so than in a hospital, he thought, or a laboratory. Even if she were wearing her brown tweed suit and her "sensible" flats, she'd still look at home here. The plush surroundings, hardly your ordinary bar . . . a thickly carpeted floor, couches and groupings of easy chairs and a grand piano to the left with a young man in a tie and tails softly playing a Noel Coward song.

She noticed him then, and he walked over. The liveried waiter appeared at his elbow and he ordered his usual scotch and water.

"You're getting in deep, Calvin," she said lightly. "I have a habit of messing up the lives of the men I'm involved with."

"Are you warning me off?"

There was suddenly laughter in her eyes now and for a moment he thought she had been playing with him from the start. "I've been given orders to that effect."

"Hanson?"

"Of course. The good Major Hanson. He thinks I'm your pipeline into his operation and I think he would much rather it were vice versa."

"I'm about to be declared *persona non grata*," Doohan said.

"So I've heard," she said. "And speaking of gossip, I assume you know that the CDC and the Department of Health are out and what's left of the operation is to be transferred to Endo-Syn Pharmaceuticals in Emeryville."

He gaped. "They're not through with the investigation yet!"

"The major thinks they are," she said dryly.

"Are you going along?"

"I've been asked to." She toyed with her drink. "I don't know if I will."

"Personal reasons?"

"Perhaps." She began to hum lightly, following the melody from the piano. For the moment, he was distracted from the meaning of the move to Endo-Syn. She was a remarkably beautiful woman, he thought. Her high cheekbones and thin, aristocratic nose gave her the appearance of being unapproachable, an appearance contradicted by her full and sensuous mouth. Her breasts were small and firm and for an instant the image of her nude floated in his memory and he could feel the faint stirrings of desire.

She must have read his mind, for she looked up at him and laughed. "I have an idea," she said suddenly. "Why don't we eat at home? I have a couple of rock lobster tails crammed somewhere in the freezer and we can pop into the Safeway and pick up the extras. Lobster, a tossed salad and champagne. How does that strike you?"

"Give me time to make a phone call."

"You have to break another date?" Her voice was mocking.

"Plane reservations. I'm going to Washington tomorrow."

She looked concerned. "That's rather sudden."

"Business that can't wait. I'll be back in two days."

"You're sounding very mysterious," she accused.

"Of course," Doohan said promptly. "I can't let you know *everything* about me." He paid the bill and on the way out, dropped a dollar in the brandy snifter on the piano. The young man was lost in the melody; he didn't bother looking up.

In the supermarket, Suzanne bought butter at the dairy counter and two lemons in produce, along with butter, iceberg lettuce and romaine. "Do you like Thousand Island dressing?" she suddenly asked. Doohan nodded. "Good; I make my own from scratch; you'll love it."

It was automatic. She picked up a small jar of mayonnaise and he suddenly took it from her and inspected the label. "Très Fine." And at the bottom: "Packed by Melrose Food Company. Hayward, California." Doohan returned it to the shelf and reached for another brand.

Suzanne looked surprised. "What's wrong with Très Fine?"

"I got sick on it once," Doohan said, almost too casually. "One of those things."

She picked a different brand. "I didn't know you were that finicky. How do you feel about lobster and champagne?"

He laughed. *"Très fine!"*

Back in her apartment, he phoned the airlines while she got dinner. Then he had another thought and dialed French's home. A boy's voice answered and suggested he call the lab. Isaac, Doohan thought. He dialed once more, and French answered, sounding tired. "Paul, Calvin—you feeling all right?"

A slight hesitation, then: "Still in something of a funk. Sorry if I got upset today. Circumstances and all . . ." His voice trailed away.

"Look, I'll buy you a drink when I get back. . . . One thing: Could you check out the ownership of Melrose Foods while I'm in Washington?"

"Sure, sure, it shouldn't be much of a problem."

Doohan hung up and sensed somebody standing behind him. He whirled. Suzanne was leaning against the door of the bedroom, holding a chilled bottle of Mumm's in her hands. "You may as well pour the champagne now; dinner will be ready in fifteen minutes."

Later, they went to bed and made love. It began slowly as a gentle series of caresses, then rapidly escalated to a sort of hysterical coupling that was entirely new to him. Before, Suzanne had been a technician in her love-making, working precisely if somewhat coldly to build him to a peak and in turn controlling her own passions with an almost studied pacing. This time, her actions bordered on a frenzy and he found his own responses mirroring hers. It was a feral coupling with two rutting bodies driving against each other until he felt her repeatedly tense, retire, and then return to build to an even higher peak. There was something debauched and wholly exciting about it and when his body exploded, a wave of dizziness swept over him. He fell rather than lowered himself to the bed, for a moment frightened by the frantic beating of his own heart. It took measurable minutes for his heart to slow down and the intense migraine to fade.

She curled up to him, her head on her left arm and her hand playing gently with the hair of his head. He didn't feel drowsy so much as exhausted and . . . disturbed. Somewhere within his mind, he realized, there was an emotional niche that remained empty and unsatisfied. He explored it for a moment, wondering if there was some insecurity that required a final expression of love from her. Perhaps it was just habit, he thought. Elizabeth lying close to him and gentle with her reassurances of love. Perhaps it was the recognition that she was still married and the feeling of guilt that sprang from it.

And perhaps it was something that he didn't want to admit. That he liked her, that he admired her, that he was in many ways awed by her, but that he didn't love her. Not in the way that he had loved Elizabeth. Perhaps, he thought, it was because she didn't love him, that to her he was a new and somewhat different kind of animal and there wouldn't be too many more nights before she would lose interest.

Or he would.

"You seem as though you're a thousand miles away."

"I guess I am."

"Something bothering you?"

He found it hard to put into words. "Just wondering where we'll be a year from now."

"Perhaps in the same bed," she laughed. "Or a better one."

"Would you like that?"

"Calvin, I never make plans that far ahead, particularly when it comes to my emotional life. Marriage taught me the folly of that." She reached over and stroked his belly. "You're not worrying about making an honest woman of me?"

The banter in her voice annoyed him. "There are times when sex should be taken seriously."

She raised herself up on one elbow and he could sense her smiling in the dark. "Do you really think so? I think sex is one of the most comical activities of the human race."

He shook his head. "Not sex. What sex implies. That has to be taken seriously."

She suddenly sat up. "Look, Calvin, I enjoy your company, I enjoy you in bed. I'm really quite fond of you. I don't use the word 'love' because I'm not sure if it means the same to you as it does to me, and even if it does, if I'm really capable of it. The situation between us is completely satisfying to me at the moment. I will not, repeat, will not make a commitment beyond that."

"You're a very"—he searched for the right word and couldn't find it—"unusual woman."

"And you're a man who talks too much . . . and at the wrong time."

Then she was kissing him passionately and he was responding, pushing her back flat on the bed, his hands gripping her wrists and his knees holding her legs between them. He felt a surge of excitement, thinking that if he couldn't master her with words, he would do it with sheer strength. In the next few minutes, he felt all the brutal satisfaction of a rapist and when it was over, he realized that she had precipitated it, that far from being angry, she had thoroughly enjoyed it. She sank back on the pillow and even as he watched, she drifted off to sleep, her faint smile slowly erasing itself from her face.

He awoke quietly at five in the morning and dressed in silence; he had about two hours to shower, pack, and make it to the airport. At the door of the bedroom, he turned for a last look. The gray light from the window filtered in and blotted her face with harsh shadows. The sharpness of her nose and cheekbones made her seem somehow alien, a woman from another planet or another time and space.

He brushed the thought aside with a faint annoyance. She was real enough and earthy enough. And perhaps he should be grateful; she was teaching him not only what he was, but also what he was not.

He turned to go, wondering why he felt a vague sense of loss. She was, he thought, almost everything he had ever wanted in a woman.

Almost.

25

ESPINOSA WAS WAITING for him in the passenger lounge at Dulles International, a small, gray-haired figure almost lost in the crush. He smiled and held out his hand. "Calvin, it's good to see you! Bumpy ride?"

"Smooth all the way except over the Continental Divide—I always forget and it always scares the devil out of me."

"Have you had dinner yet?"

"I rode first class—I don't want to look at food for a week."

Espinosa guided him toward the baggage claim. "That's the way visitors usually arrive. Why don't we check you in at the Hilton, then we'll go over to my place. We can talk there, and if you get hungry, my man can make up something for you."

They stood in a small eddy at the baggage claim, staring at the bags traveling by on the carousel. "There's a lot we have to talk about," Doohan said grimly.

"Yes?"

"I'm afraid the genie is out of the bottle."

Espinosa's face was unreadable. "I thought as much from your telegram."

At his apartment, Espinosa lost himself in a black easy chair and Doohan sprawled on a couch facing an elaborate Chinese wall painting. The butler, a silent, dark-eyed Castilian of fifty, took their drink orders and disappeared into the kitchen.

When they arrived, Espinosa sipped his, then put it on the coffee table and leaned back to stare at

Doohan. "I gather you want to discuss the outbreak in San Francisco that they're calling the Veterans' Disease."

Doohan nodded. "It's not a disease," he said quietly. "At least it's not a disease in the sense of a natural outbreak. It's man-made, self-limiting, and a hundred per cent fatal."

Espinosa looked puzzled. "I thought I had read that survivors had been sent home."

Doohan shook his head. "There were no survivors. Of those who contacted it, all of them died. The press release was a government cover-up."

Espinosa's voice sounded bleak. "You better tell me more."

Doohan did so, outlining the progress of the disease, the accident with the bloodmobile and the death of Laval, what he and French had discovered, and, finally, his own suspicions as to the true nature of the disease. Espinosa let him proceed without interruption. When he had finished, the older man sat for a long moment, staring at the ceiling in thought.

"That explains the phone call I got today from the State Department."

Doohan looked surprised. "What was that about?"

"Your major wants to have your visa pulled. For 'interfering in the internal affairs of the United States.' If he wants to, he can make it stick. We'll fight it, of course." He clasped his hands behind his head. "You've put yourself in a rather uncomfortable position—and by extension, my entire department."

Doohan suddenly felt uncertain. "You resent that?"

"Of course not. What's happening in San Francisco is of vital interest to a good many more people than just Americans. You cannot have an epidemic in one part of the world without raising concerns about it in other parts. But your personal problem remains a problem and we still have to deal with it."

"I'm sorry if I've embarrassed you," Doohan said curtly.

Espinosa dismissed it with a wave of his hand. "Don't be so sensitive, Calvin. I'm not without my own champions in the American bureaucracy." He sounded worried. "What concerns me much more is that we are now facing a situation I've been dreading for years. I suppose it was inevitable. It's a sad burden that scientists carry, that their most cherished technologies become weapons of war." He paused. "We discussed that once, not too long ago as I recall."

Doohan winced. "You don't need to rub it in."

"I'm not. I asked for your viewpoint and I got it."

"I didn't think the remote possibility of an accident was worth a moratorium."

"What may be dangerous by accident," Espinosa continued wearily, "can be catastrophic by design. Biological warfare is extremely attractive to a nation —it takes a far greater degree of technological sophistication to join the atomic club. You've read the horror stories about India's 'nuclear engineers' using bamboo rods to fish around in the depths of their atomic reactors? Yet they exploded a crude bomb. That's all it takes to join the atomic club—explode a bomb and you jump several rungs on the ladder of national prestige, never mind that you have no rockets or missiles to deliver it."

He finished the wine and the Castilian appeared at his chair as if by magic. "Would you like to go out to eat, Calvin? An appetite is like lust, you cannot ignore it forever. No? José can make you a steak sandwich if you'd like."

"If it's no inconvenience . . ."

"None at all." José poured Espinosa another glass of sherry and vanished. Espinosa looked gloomy. "Biological warfare is forbidden by treaty, denied by all, and practiced covertly by almost everyone. The poorest countries in the world can afford the modest laboratories necessary. Your Veterans' Disease may very well be a field test of a very subtle weapon—but there doesn't have to be a major power behind it. It might be, say, Cuba or Algeria or even Uganda. Who knows? The tragedy is that the less technologically oriented countries are apt to overlook the luxuries of high-containment laboratories. From an ordinary laboratory, viruses, and bacteria could escape as easily as animals from an unguarded zoo."

Espinosa frowned in thought. "You're familiar with E. coli? It's the darling of the molecular biologists, but even they had second thoughts when it came to experimenting with it. Finally they developed a strain so crippled it cannot live outside the laboratory. But who is to say that someday it might not mutate and become something deadly and uncontrollable? Today your virus needs vanadium to live and grow; tomorrow, it may suddenly lose that dependency."

He drained his sherry and walked to the sideboard for more. "It was not so long ago that the Black Plague decimated Europe and killed off a third of the world's population; England alone required a hundred years to make good its population loss. I think perhaps the next time we may not be so lucky."

"We know now such a weapon exists and is being used," Doohan said. "What can we do about it?"

Espinosa sighed. "What do you want me to do, Calvin? Call a press conference tomorrow and reveal everything you've told me? The United States would deny it had ever happened and the other major powers would accuse me of slander. I would be expelled from this country as well as from WHO. But if I thought it would help, I would be more than willing to do it."

"Couldn't the Secretary-General of the UN do something?"

José came in with the sandwiches and Espinosa arranged a napkin neatly on his lap. "The Secretary-General's chief qualification for office is that he is a man who will offend no one. He also has his own small projects which he views as important to the peace of the world. He could, of course, make a formal statement in the assembly but that would probably succeed only in antagonizing everybody. . . ."

"What you're trying to tell me," Doohan said bitterly, "is that there's nothing we can do."

Espinosa wiped his mouth. "Not at all. I just wish to call your attention to the realities of the world. What you have come to me with is a theory. What I need is proof. With proof, we might find a patron nation—a sponsor as it were—Zaire or Kuwait or another small non-aligned nation that would be willing to raise the question on the floor. Without proof, it would be very difficult to convince them that it was to their political advantage to make such accusations in the General Assembly."

"I can provide a sample of the virus," Doohan said quietly. "And in a few days, possibly some laboratory animals sick with the disease."

Espinosa slowly put down his sandwich. "Calvin," he said quietly, "you realize you are now a marked man."

"Perhaps. But would my proof be believed?"

"To have a representative stand up and wave a vial of deadly virus on the floor of the Assembly? It would cause a sensation. Publicly, every nation in the world would deny it. Privately, they would probably all believe it."

Doohan shook his head. "To warn that such a weapon exists might result in belling the cat. I would hope that every nation would then try to find out who made it and what they intend to do with it. But we also run the risk that every country in the world would try to duplicate it."

"They're probably doing that this very moment," Espinosa said sadly. "But there's another risk that concerns me at the moment, Calvin, and that is the risk to you."

Taking a cab back to the Hilton, Doohan reviewed his conversation with Espinosa. Perhaps he had expected too much but even Espinosa had seemed caught in the molasses of international bureaucracy. How much autonomy did WHO really enjoy? he wondered. It didn't raise its own taxes, it depended for its existence on appropriations and contributions from member states. Espinosa had always walked a tightrope.

But Espinosa had a point, too. He needed proof. Without it, nothing was possible. With it, there were, at least possibilities.

At the hotel desk, there was a message from French

asking that he call. The number was French's lab. He glanced at his watch; it was a little after nine in the Bay Area. He took the elevator to his room, then dialed long distance. French was brief and to the point—and excited. The president and general manager of Melrose Foods was Ramon Guitterez. Doohan asked how the hamsters were coming along. French sounded disgusted. The hamsters were running a low-grade fever and most of the females were pregnant. There was no suggestion of anything as massive or as deadly as had infected the veterans. That wasn't surprising, Doohan thought. But if the hamsters were exposed again, the story might be completely different.

Just before he hung up, Doohan remembered Espinosa's warning and said: "Paul, take care of yourself. You realize that you're sitting on dynamite."

"I've got a well-padded fanny," French laughed, and cut the connection.

Doohan stared at the phone for a moment after French had hung up, imagining the huge man bustling about the lab and brewing some more coffee, or chewing on the end of his pencil as he tried to solve the mysteries posed by a hundred rotting eggs.

It had been a long time since he had really felt close to another man, Doohan thought.

He got up from the bed and walked to the window. In the distance, he could see the spotlighted Washington Monument and a little to one side the glow of lights that marked the Lincoln Memorial. Both men represented the best of the American character, he thought. Then he remembered that England had outlawed the slave trade thirty years before Lincoln had issued his Emancipation Proclamation. And England had done it as a matter of principle, Lincoln as a matter of political expedience.

England had its heroes, too, he thought, and abruptly felt homesick. In his mind's eye, he could see the hills of Scotland where he had been born and the blackened towns of Wales where he had grown up. There had been a lot of good mixed with all the agony and suddenly he wanted to see the hills and towns of his own country once again.

He thought of Espinosa then and the plan suddenly seemed shot full of holes. There was no guarantee of any kind and all the while, time would be slipping away. He had often bragged of having pledged a larger loyalty to WHO, but that didn't stop him from being a Scotsman and by extension, an Englishman.

Nationalism, he thought cynically. It was a disease you were born with. But it was one you couldn't shake. How many times had Hanson reminded him that he was a "foreign national"—meaning a national of England. He owed it something. And Britain still had a moral image and more clout in international affairs than any of the emerging "Third World" nations. He should have tried it before. . . .

He located the number under "Embassies" in the yellow pages. The night man was very London-British and thoroughly bored, even after Doohan had identified himself. Yes, he would have the ambassador's aide call first thing in the morning. And what should he say it was about?

Well, he would have preferred something a little more tangible, but if Dr. Doohan thought it was important . . .

26

FROM SOMEWHERE DOWN the street the sounds of "Adeste Fideles" drifted through the open window. It was one of Berkeley's better customs, French thought, staring at the phone. Student carolers. Odd that in the middle of the season dedicated to Peace on Earth, he and Doohan should be involved in such a horror. There was always something ironic about Christmastime, but this year the irony was so bitter he could taste it.

In the distance the carolers had now shifted to "Stille Nacht" and French smiled to himself. He had always preferred the original lyrics of the two carols. Young Isaac called him a purist, and occasionally a pedant, but they both knew the latter accusation wasn't justified. Perhaps he was a purist, he'd admit to that. But the songs seemed just right in their original languages: "Adeste Fideles" instead of "Oh, Come All Ye Faithful," and "Stille Nacht, Heilige Nacht" instead of "Silent Night, Holy Night." Probably for the same reason there really wasn't a popular opera written in English.

He felt a twinge of hunger and realized that except for a candy bar at four, he really hadn't eaten much since breakfast, and it was now ten past nine. There was that one place on Telegraph that he had gone to the week before and had a decent porterhouse steak and a baked potato. The restaurants were getting impossible, he thought—instant hamburgers or something called falafel served by waiters who thought that dirty hands somehow lent an Arabic touch.

Isaac would disapprove, he thought, getting his coat, but then Isaac was on a skiing trip and wouldn't be back until Christmas Eve. Isaac did the cooking at home and was forever metering out meals on a precise calorie-count basis, hoping to trim some of the mass from his father's bulk. Not for cosmetic reasons, he would insist. "I just want you to be around when I win the Nobel Prize," he would say. *Not unless you improve your math, Isaac,* French thought, and stepped out into the hall.

The lights were still on in the big lab. Probably Celia; she had been working late the past few nights so her projects would be in order before going on her Christmas vacation. If she were still there when he got back, French promised himself, he'd chase her out. She got as involved in her work as he did.

Once on the street, he hesitated, trying to remember where he had parked his car. Normally he would have left it in the underground garage but with most of the students away for the holidays, the streets were relatively deserted and he had left it a short way down on Walnut. There were only a few other cars on the street besides his VW; and he wouldn't have noticed the blue Oldsmobile at all if he hadn't spotted the glow of somebody's cigarette in the interior. Too cold a night to sit in your car and smoke, he thought.

He drove down to the restaurant on Telegraph and ordered the steak and a baked potato smothered in sour cream and bacon chips, all of it washed down by a good domestic Pinot Noir. It was a little after ten when he finished and paid his bill.

When he started the car and pulled away from the curb, he noted in the rear-view mirror another car turning on its lights. For a moment he thought it was the blue Oldsmobile he had seen earlier, but decided he was mistaken; with the glare of the lights, he couldn't tell anyway. But he was aware of it now, and as he drove back he noticed the other car following at half a block's distance. His parking space on Walnut was still open and he took it, observing when he got out that the other car was also jockeying into position half a block down. It *was* the blue Olds, he noted with a sudden touch of anxiety.

At the front steps, he suddenly stopped and turned. Half a block down Walnut, the tiny glow of a cigarette showed on the passenger's side of the Olds. An amateur, he thought with contempt. A professional would never have lit a cigarette. Certainly a pro wouldn't take the chance that his face might be identified in the glow.

The guards in the lobby had long gone for the night and he opened the door with his key and took the elevator up. Celia was working in the large lab, her hands buried in the glove box. "I thought you were going to Ohio for the holidays?"

She smiled. "Hi, Doctor. My plane takes off tomorrow morning and I wanted to finish some of the new cultures tonight."

"Tomorrow's Christmas Eve," he chided her. "You should be getting some rest for the trip."

"It's all right—I can sleep on the plane."

"Well, finish up and get the hell out of here," French growled. "I'll be getting the reputation of being a slave driver."

French walked into his office and threw open the window to let in some air. Just before he turned to click on the desk lamp, he heard a car door slam. He turned back to the window. Down Walnut, two men had gotten out of the Olds and were talking quietly together. One of them suddenly looked up at the window where French was standing and he hastily drew back into the room, then realized he wasn't backlighted and they probably couldn't see him. After a moment, he peered out again. The men had disappeared. Odd, he thought and started to walk away, then heard the muffled sound of the downstairs door being closed. The men had entered the building.

If they were Hanson's men, he thought slowly, they would of course tail him around town to see if he made any unusual contacts. So he was being watched; he had expected that. They would have followed him to the restaurant and they would have followed him back. But there wouldn't be any reason for their coming in the building.

For a moment he felt a touch of fear, then snorted. He was getting paranoid in his old age. So two of Hanson's men were coming upstairs to check up on him. He was working late at night. He wasn't alone; they were curious. Certainly that was nothing to panic about.

But why this time of night? The lab was completely buttoned up except for his floor. Even the guards had left, leaving only the one night watchman who made his rounds of the halls every hour. Of course, there was the nearby campus security office.

He lifted the phone and started to dial, then realized there was no dial tone. He pressed down on the cradle and started to dial again. Still no tone. He jiggled the cradle button for a few seconds, then slowly replaced the phone. It was out of order, he thought with a small chill of apprehension. Coincidence?

What if the men . . . weren't from Hanson? Of all the people working on the Veterans' Disease, only he had a viable sample of the virus. And only he had animals now obviously infected with the disease. What was it that Calvin had said? Whoever had created the virus had already killed seventy-five people.

He got to his feet, shaking slightly. There was the problem of Celia in the next room. She was in danger as well as he. And there was all the work he had done to date.

French walked quietly out into the hall and tried the elevator. But the button light didn't go on. Somebody must have gotten to the circuit-breaker box in the basement, as well as to the central switchboard. They would take care of the various alarms and communications first, then they would come up to see him. . . . He hastily walked to the end of the hallway and into the animal room. He poked around behind one of the benches and found the large carrying cage he was looking for. Around him, the hamsters began a sleepy squeaking and then the monkeys started to wake up and chitter back and forth.

French quickly opened up the hamster cages and began to transfer the animals to the larger cage. They were going to be crowded but there was no helping that. There was a cardboard carton in the back room that would just hold the cage and he slipped it inside, then hastily sealed the carton with paper tape from a nearby dispenser.

He carried the box into the main lab where Celia was still faithfully working at the glove box. "I told you I would chase you out if you were still here when I came back," he said. He tried to keep his voice light and humorous and knew he had failed miserably.

She blinked at him from behind her glasses. "Is something wrong? You look pale, Dr. French."

Damn the woman. "You're going home to Dayton tomorrow," he said. "You should get a good night's sleep."

She glanced around the lab, obviously reluctant to leave. "I only have a few more specimens to tend to, and then I thought I would clean up a little . . ."

"No, no," French said hastily. "I'll have the janitor do that." So little time, he thought, and so much to do. "Besides, I wanted you to do me a favor. Could you drop this box off at my house? You only live a few blocks away. It's some hamsters I promised Isaac as a Christmas present." She looked dubious and he knew the question would be why couldn't he do it himself. She would wonder at that, even if she wouldn't ask it. "I'll be here a little later than I thought and I'd like it safely in the garage before Isaac gets home from his skiing trip. Just leave it in the garage; the door is open."

She pulled her hands out of the glove box and slipped into her coat. "You sure you don't want me to clean up before I go?"

"No, no." He thrust the box at her, the sounds of frantic scurrying coming from inside as the animals were thrown off balance. He walked her into the hallway. "I'm afraid you'll have to take the stairs; the elevator isn't working."

So little time! he thought again. "You can handle that?"

"It's not too heavy." And then she had gotten to the landing, turned, and was lost to sight. French hurried back to the laboratory and lifted the latch of the outer cold room and went inside. Damn! He should have sent the two sealed ampoules of freeze-dried virus with her. He turned to the shelf behind him. The ampoules were in a rack with a number of other samples, each of them bearing an etched code number on the side. They would be safe enough, he thought. There was nothing about them to indicate that they were the virus samples. And there were at least two hundred other ampoules; the two would be lost in the forest of more routine samples.

There was one further thing he could do. He rescued the mayonnaise jar from where he had placed it on the shelf several days before. Then he opened one of the drawers in the bench before him and searched for the large tube of lanolin unguent that cold-room workers used to keep their hands from chapping. He unscrewed the lid of the empty mayonnaise jar and squeezed almost the entire tube of blue tinted unguent into it, tamping it down with a finger. In this light, the unguent looked enough like mayonnaise to fool amost anybody. And if they knew what they were looking for, they would hardly open the jar to sample the contents.

He put the now empty tube of unguent back in the drawer and replaced the mayonnaise jar on the shelf next to the racked samples. If they were looking for it, they couldn't miss it. Then he closed and latched the door and returned to his office. He tried the phone again in vain hopes. Still not working.

He had done as much as he could here, he thought. The next thing to do was to get out of the building. He walked back into the hallway and opened the door to the stairwell. Below, he could hear the sound of leather on concrete and a mumbled comment.

Too late, he thought. He was shaking more now

and his knees felt a little weak. He ran back to the office and glanced out the windows. The street was deserted; even the carolers had left. It would do no good to yell for help. As he looked, a single car drove up the street. Celia's Mustang, he thought. At least, she was out of it. They must have decided to let her go.

He was trapped in the building now; he couldn't leave. He wished desperately that he had kept a gun on the premises, then realized he didn't know how to use one anyway. There were no other weapons handy. . . .

Still . . . He opened his desk drawer and rummaged through it. An old X-acto knife, not much of a weapon but its razor-sharp triangular blade was capable of doing some damage as numerous generations of laboratory assistants had discovered. He gripped the metal handle of the knife and moved out into the hall. He couldn't wait for them in his office, he thought, and there was no place he could hide.

There were faint sounds coming from the big lab now, which meant they had left the stairwell. He had a sudden stirring of hope. If they weren't in the stairwell, he could get down it and out once outside.

Then he heard the sounds of shattering glassware. They were wrecking his equipment, he thought, the stuff he had wheedled out of the budget year after year. He was shaking with fury now, not fright. Who the hell did they think they were? He gripped the X-acto knife so hard that his fingers throbbed and turned toward the lab. There was more noise of breaking glassware; something heavy fell to the floor. They had probably overturned the incubator and hundreds of inoculated eggs were now ruined.

Damn them! Abruptly he pushed through the lab door and caught a glimpse of a balding man by the far desk. The man held a lab stool in his hand; he was smashing the other incubators and the egg cultures inside.

French charged forward. "God *damn* you!" he shouted.

Another man seemed to materialize directly before

him, holding something in his hands. It exploded and light flared before his eyes. French felt himself thrown backward, the X-acto knife flying from his hands. There was another explosion. He was suddenly sitting on the floor, leaning against one of the work benches. His shirt and trousers were growing damp and for a crazy moment he thought he had wet his pants.

Across the room, somebody was shouting: *"You idiot, what if we can't find it?"* Then somebody was standing over him. He felt something cold against his temple. There was a brief roaring sound and . . .

Nothing.

27

DOOHAN PACKED AND checked out of the Hilton early
the next morning, leaving his bag temporarily with
the bell captain. The morning was bitingly cold and
he shivered inside his topcoat. California spoiled you
for the rest of the country, he thought. Mounds of
snow framed both sides of the cab stand. At one side
of the hotel entrance, a snow-encrusted Salvation
Army Santa Claus rang his bell, keeping his back
resolutely to the chill wind that knifed down the
broad street.

"Merry Christmas, sir," the doorman said. Doohan
automatically dropped a few coins in his outstretched
hand and walked over to the cab stand. The twenty-
fourth, he thought: Peace on Earth and all that rot.
He shivered again; maybe he would find the Christmas spirit back in the Bay Area where quick-freez-
ing didn't threaten his lungs with every breath he
took.

He caught a cab to the British embassy and settled
back in the plastic seat. At the embassy itself, he
gave his name to the young man at the reception
desk. The man spoke quietly into his intercom and
then directed Doohan to a small reception room. The
room was unoccupied. Doohan settled himself in a
severe Chippendale chair, glanced casually through
an old copy of *The Tattler* from a nearby table, and
waited. It wasn't more than five minutes before another
door opened and a man informally dressed in brown
slacks and a corduroy sport coat entered. He had a
slightly pocked face and a magnificently large red
nose; Doohan guessed him to be about forty.

"Dr. Doohan?" He held out his hand. "Fenris, Brigadier Hugh Fenris; I'm the ambassador's aide. He's asked me to have a chat with you."

Fenris seemed friendly, relentlessly cheerful, a well-polished wall between Doohan and the ambassador.

"I thought I was to see the ambassador," Doohan said, somewhat uncertainly.

"My dear Doctor, Sir Dudley would be delighted to see you if he could, but with the season being what it is and with the social affairs in the capital . . . at this time of year, the American capital is by far the busiest of them all." Fenris' eyes probed Doohan, weighing and assessing him.

Doohan shook his head. "I'm sure the ambassador is busy, but I have to speak with him. You know my credentials?"

There was the faintest chill in the brigadier's voice. "Of course, we've checked them out quite thoroughly. You're a doctor with WHO and you're currently engaged in plague research on the West Coast." There was a hint of a challenge in the cold eyes. "The ambassador asked me to brief him on our conversation later in the day."

Doohan stood up. "My plane leaves early in the afternoon," he said thinly. "What I have to say can only be said to the ambassador. It's a matter of grave national security. I'm sure he'll be criticized later that he didn't hear it."

He started for the door and Fenris suddenly said, "Wait a minute, old chap. You think I'm putting you off, and I am, but the ambassador really is busy and the number of people who claim they have to see him is staggering. Can't you at least give me a clue as to what you want to see him about?"

Doohan turned, hesitated, then said: "I've been working with the Americans on the Veterans' Disease in San Francisco. What I have to say concerns that."

Fenris thoughtfully rubbed his nose. "Why don't you wait here a moment and I'll talk to the ambassador?"

He was back in five minutes and motioned for

Doohan to follow him. They walked up a flight of stairs to the second floor rear. Doohan was ushered into a large, paneled room dominated by a huge mahogany desk, strikingly bare except for a blotter and several brass ornaments including a rotating calendar and an obsidian-handled paper knife. Later, Doohan would remember little of the man behind the desk except that he had white hair, was thin to the point of emaciation, and had huge, bony hands covered with liver spots. The hands seemed to have a life of their own and constantly toyed with the paper knife.

After the introductions, the ambassador stared at him for a long moment, then said, "Brigadier Fenris tells me you have something of importance you wish to discuss, Doctor." His voice was heavy and surprisingly full of life.

Doohan glanced briefly at Fenris, who was leaning against a nearby bookcase, his eyes and nose giving him the appearance of a hawk about to swoop down.

"You've read about the outbreak of what the Americans are calling the 'Veterans' Disease' in San Francisco?"

The ambassador nodded. "We've been following that with some interest," he admitted. "Our own National Health Services have been alerted against the possibility of its being imported."

Doohan licked his lips nervously. "I've been working with them for the past two weeks. My office was in their Department of Health and when the outbreak occurred, I offered my services. The military came in about three days after the start of the outbreak." He hesitated. "There was good reason why they came in. It's not a natural outbreak. In point of fact, there's reason to believe it's a field test of a new biological agent by some unknown agency."

The ambassador turned to his aide. "Fenris?"

"MI-5 reached the same conclusion several days ago," Fenris said. "As I understand it, despite published reports, there have been no survivors."

The ambassador nodded at Doohan. "Please continue."

Doohan filled them in: Hanson's actions, including his own expulsion from the operation, and French's findings to date. He concluded with an account of his visit to Espinosa the day before.

"And Dr. Espinosa suggested a smaller country might be able to broach the matter on the floor of the General Assembly—provided you could supply proof?"

Doohan nodded. "That's correct sir."

"Can you?"

"Yes, sir," Doohan said quietly.

The ambassador leaned forward slightly. "Doctor, why the UN? I would have thought you might have come here first. As a British subject, you *do* have certain commitments to the Crown and by extension, even to the Americans who, after all, are our allies, at least when they choose to remind us of it."

The conversation wasn't going in the direction Doohan had intended. He stiffened slightly. "I thought the implications of the outbreak concerned everybody," he said shortly, "not just certain countries. To a disease, national borders are invisible."

The ambassador nodded imperturbably. "That's consistent with your WHO background. But we're not exactly discussing the smallpox virus." He glanced at Fenris again. "Any corroboration from any of the other intelligence services?"

"I've had some discussion with our French and Israeli counterparts since the start of the outbreak. They agree that it's not a natural one."

Doohan interrupted. "You have an intelligence operation in the United States?"

The ambassador raised an eyebrow. "Of course. It's not expected that the interest of allies will run parallel all the time. The Americans are well aware of it; the CIA has had its operation in England for years now. But we're not here to discuss the ethics of gentlemen reading other gentlemen's mail, as an American Secretary of War once put it. Brigadier, any idea who might be behind all of this?"

"The double-dyed villain? I should discount the Soviets immediately. We're on top of their major technological achievements and we've had our share of defectors who would have heard of something. Besides, I don't think they're that mad."

"The installations might be quite small," Doohan interrupted.

Fenris nodded. "Nothing of the size or complexity of a nuclear reclamation plant. Nor nearly as expensive. I'd opt for one of the smaller nations. Your Dr. Espinosa is quite right in that respect. Research in recombinant DNA is relatively inexpensive, and we've consistently heard rumors that one country or another has built a facility. So far they've been impossible to check; as you imply, they could be well hidden. I might vote for the Angolans or the Ugandans or the Algerians, perhaps even the Cubans—I don't imagine they relish living under Soviet guarantees that might be withdrawn depending on how warm *détente* becomes. Even some of our South American friends might be prospects."

"The important thing, Doctor," the ambassador said, "is that you've identified the field tests of such a weapon and you alone apparently have isolated the particular agent. The Americans will undoubtedly do the same eventually, and they will also undoubtedly cover it up. They may decide to tell us—some day—but in the meantime, as a country we're in a uniquely vulnerable position. We can hardly depend on the Americans for what they may or may not dole out in the future. Being a client nation is a study in uncertainty, Doctor." He leaned back in his chair and suddenly fixed Doohan with a cold stare. "I think, as a British subject, you have certain obligations, Doctor."

Doohan got to his feet. "This concerns everybody," he said thickly. "I don't think it's moral to fence with it for any sort of national advantage."

"You're assuming we'd act immorally if we had the knowledge, Doctor."

"It's a matter for the UN," Doohan said. "I thought that when I met with Dr. Espinosa; I still think that."

The ambassador spread his skeletal hands. "Then why did you come to see us? I'll tell you why, Doctor. It's because, despite what you say, you really have no faith in the United Nations. And probably rightly so. I can tell you exactly what will happen. Every member country will be properly upset by the charges and all will claim innocence. Any strong action that's suggested will be hamstrung—and not necessarily by the larger powers. There are many smaller countries that would consider bacteriological warfare a most inviting investment. It's cheap, easy, and deadly. I wouldn't grant many of them with the foresight to see the logical outcome. Getting the matter to the floor in the first place would be a major problem, and so would avoiding a lengthy and recriminatory debate that would end in deadlock."

"And if I bring everything to you?" Doohan asked.

"We could at least develop a defense. Our share of the world—and *your* share, Dr. Doohan—might be safe. At least for a little while." He hesitated. "In the meantime, you're in a particularly critical position." Pause. "And a dangerous one."

Fenris now stepped forward and leaned his knuckles on the table. "Would you be willing to collaborate with some of our people on the West Coast? Please note that I'm asking if you're willing; I'm not implying this is your duty."

Doohan considered the idea for a moment. "I would have some reservations," he said at last.

"Of course," Fenris said soothingly. "And we would respect you for them."

"I'll send out a complete report to Whitehall by Queen's Messenger in the evening bag," the ambassador said. "We'll keep you informed of the decisions made." He glanced up at Doohan again. "Will you do it?"

"For Queen and country?" Doohan said sarcastically.

Fenris looked relieved. "There have been worse motivations."

"What do you want from me?"

"As much as you can find out. A sample of the virus. And information on who developed it."

Doohan hesitated. "All right."

Fenris was brisk now. "Our man in San Francisco is Anthony Strout; he's with the British Trade Commission there. He'll contact you and take it from there. We'll try and check out your man Guitterez. We have our contacts at the Pentagon, and since he's presumably a veteran, we should be able to find out a great deal."

The ambassador pushed back his chair. "Will you excuse me? Another appointment. Delighted to have met you, Doctor." He left and Fenris filled Doohan in on the sketchy details of the San Francisco office.

As Doohan was leaving, Fenris cleared his throat. "Dr. Doohan?" Doohan turned. "I suspect this interview hasn't been completely to your satisfaction. But please remember that the stakes are very high. I wish I could say that it's a decent world out there and that it's possible for everybody to act decently in it. But that's a wish, not a fact."

"You've asked me to become a British agent," Doohan said.

"To help your native country, Doctor."

"It's a role I'm not exactly comfortable with."

Fenris' smile was wintry. "I'm sure you'll do your best."

On the walk outside, Doohan waved for a cab and wondered if he had made a mistake. Why would the British act any differently than the Americans? The rational basis for all countries was national self-interest. They'd find out what it was and add it to their arsenal—with variations. Merely another weapon for the holocaust to come.

He climbed into the cab that skidded to the curb and sank into the back seat. It would be good to talk it over with somebody. It would be good to bounce his ideas off of French and see what the fat biochemist thought of them.

It would even be good to have a cup of French's poisonous coffee again.

28

THE FLIGHT BACK to San Francisco was interminably dull, and the two martinis that Doohan had didn't help at all. He was more and more convinced that he had made a mistake, one that might be irrevocable. Granted that he was first and foremost a British subject and his knowledge conceivably bore directly on the security of the United Kingdom . . . but that was jingoism, he thought. The fact remained that any country would want the virus as a weapon for their arsenal, and they would want it without anybody else knowing about it. He tried to sleep, then ordered another martini but beyond a certain alcoholic numbness, sleep wouldn't come.

It was dusk when they landed and they were held on the ground for almost twenty minutes by traffic. After deplaning, Doohan tried to call French from a phone in the lounge, but there was no answer at home; he got a busy signal from the phone at the laboratory. There was a crush of holiday travelers around the baggage carousels and it was half an hour before he could claim his luggage. He almost had to fight his way to the second level of the garage where he had parked his Chevelle.

Once on the freeway, he felt better, though still tired. He dropped his baggage at his apartment and considered for a moment going directly to bed, then decided against it. It was Christmas Eve. He wondered what Suzanne was doing to celebrate it and he picked up the phone to call her. But it was French whom he really wanted to see, French whom he wanted to talk to and maybe share a cup of holiday cheer with. He hung up and dialed again; the line was busy. He recalled French's comment that he frequently knocked the phone off the cradle in his office.

Doohan made up his mind. He'd drive over, and if French wasn't there, he would go to Oleg's for a late dinner and bury himself in the atmosphere of students and young professors. Berkeley had little connection to the real world and every now and then he appreciated it.

It was nearly eight o'clock when he pulled up in front of French's laboratory. The building was dark except for a few lights on the top floors, French's among them. The area itself seemed strangely quiet. It was Christmas Eve in a college town, he reminded himself, when almost all of the students were home for the holidays. He noted trees in the windows of some of the surrounding houses; from somewhere came the lonely sound of Christmas carols, but there was little street traffic. Remembering Washington, he thanked Providence for no ice, no snow, no gutters filled with freezing slush or window ledges overlaid with snow-covered soot.

The door was open and he pushed through. There was no sign of the floor guard but he hadn't expected one on Christmas Eve; there probably wasn't a night watchman on duty either. He pressed the button for the elevator and waited, then pressed it again. He waited another minute, then gave up. Apparently the elevator was out of order. He walked up the stairs to French's office and knocked twice. No answer. The door was ajar and he edged it open. The lights were on but the office was empty. The phone was still on the hook. Something must be wrong at the switchboard, Doohan thought. French was probably in the lab.

The lab door was closed. Doohan reached out to grab the knob, then suddenly backed off. The wood around the knob was scratched; splinters were sticking out. Somebody had forced it. He pushed the door open cautiously.

It wasn't immediately obvious that anything was

wrong. The benches were still there and the stools were in position; then he realized that the skyline of glassware that decorated the far workbenches was gone. A quick glance now showed him that whoever had broken into the lab had done a thorough job.

The Plexiglas of the incubators and the glove boxes was shattered as if by a sledgehammer; eggshells and yolk and albumin made a slimy mess on the floor. Whatever French had been culturing in the eggs was now lost. The lab microscopes and spectrophotometers were smashed and bent and when Doohan walked over to take a closer look, he found himself walking on a sea of shattered Pyrex.

French . . . Jesus Christ, what had happened to Paul? If they had cornered him in the lab or the animal room . . .

He dashed out into the hall and raced down to the animal room. The door was ajar and he knew before he entered what he would find inside. Beyond the door was a slaughterhouse. The cages had been dumped on the floor; the far corner of the room was coated with drying blood and stacked high with the bloody carcasses of the experimental animals. He forced himself to move closer, ignoring the stench.

Someone had systematically gone through the cages; they had removed the animals, slit their throats with a razor, and dumped the bleeding bodies in the corner. Monkeys, ferrets, guinea pigs, white mice . . . at least two hundred laboratory animals had met the same bloody fate. Even the five white rabbits in their polyethylene and Plexiglas hutch in the corner had been killed, their red-splattered bodies still lying in the container.

It must have taken an hour, Doohan thought, to slaughter all the animals in the room this methodically.

He closed the door and leaned gainst it for a moment. Somebody other than himself had known that French had isolated the agent; somebody other than himself had known that French had inoculated the animals. Hanson? But Hanson would hardly have destroyed the laboratory. . . .

My God, the virus . . .

Doohan ran back down the hall, bursting into the big laboratory. He ignored the sticky squish of eggs beneath his feet and yanked at the latch on the massive oak door of the cold room. He tugged the door open and flicked on the overhead light. It was obvious that someone had gone through the room, but everything still seemed essentially in order. There were the ranks of sealed ampoules of various biological materials, many of them dried samples from the Veterans' Disease sampling program. They didn't seem to have been disturbed.

There were other racks of ampoules, and he paused a moment trying to remember the coding that French had used on the virus ampoules. Then it came back to him: V8430MF. He started searching through the racks again. They were toward the back, two sealed ampoules of an off-white dried powder. What had they thought it would look like? he wondered.

There was no sign of the mayonnaise bottle, though he remembered French placing it back on the shelf.

And where was French? he suddenly thought. He hadn't been in his office. . . . Thank God, he must have been home when the lab was burglarized. But French wouldn't have missed a day in the lab, not at this point, and the police and Hanson must know about it by now. . . .

Then he remembered. The stiffness of the carcasses in the animal room, the splotches of blood that were now a dried brown. The carnage was twenty-four hours old; he must be the first person to find it. If the police or Hanson had been notified the rooms would have been sealed. And French would have . . .

French.

He turned slowly. There was a thread of light under the second door leading into the subzero chamber. He walked slowly over and pulled at the door hasp. It swung back on squeaking cold hinges and a wave of frigid air rolled out at him. Inside, a familiar figure huddled over the workbench.

"Paul?"

Doohan heard a sound behind him and whirled.

type in a lab smock who had apparently been working late on another floor. He wasn't the only one to ignore the holiday. "I thought I heard somebody down here—looks like a cyclone hit this laboratory." Sudden suspicion chilled her voice. "Who are you? And what's . . ."

Doohan turned his back on her and walked into the room. He touched the stiff figure in the chair; the chair began to swing slowly around. For an instant French's dead eyes stared up at him, his hair and brows white masses of ice. The chair continued to turn, the ruin that was the back of French's head slowly swinging into view.

Behind him, the woman in the lab smock started to scream.

29

WHOEVER DESTROYED THE lab had done a thorough job, Hanson thought. The animal room and the animals in it had personally upset him even more than the main lab. He had raised hamsters as a kid. There was no way Humpty Dumpty was going to be put back together again. Atlanta might—probably would—duplicate whatever leads French had stumbled upon but there was no telling when.

He took one last look around the animal room, then wrinkled his nose and walked back to the main laboratory. He was frustrated and angry and frightened. He hadn't anticipated that French would work on Christmas Eve. There had been no guard, and the night watchman had apparently taken off that evening. The murderers had had all the time they needed. Now French was dead and Laval a suicide. . . . If it had been suicide, he reminded himself.

In the main lab, the medical examiners had left and the latent print people were just finishing up. They wouldn't find much; he was sure of that.

"Major Hanson?"

The voice disconcerted him for a moment; it was almost an octave too high for the body. The effect was comic until he glanced at the man's face; the eyes beneath the heavy brows were completely humorless. The man was around forty, dressed in a rumpled brown suit and holding a pad of paper and a pencil. Hanson shook his head. "There'll be no press—"

"I'm Detective Jessup," the man said dryly. "I understand Dr. French worked for you?"

"Not really. He was with the State Department of

Health, assigned to screening samples from the Veterans' Disease program."

"But you were in charge of the operation; so essentially he was working for you," Jessup insisted. "That is correct, isn't it?"

It was a civilian investigation, Hanson thought. His rank didn't mean much here. He was suddenly aware that it was two o'clock Christmas morning and how achingly tired he was. "That's essentially correct."

Jessup's gesture swept the room with his hand. "Any idea who might have done this?"

"No idea at all."

Jessup put away the pencil and paper. "Major, you understand that this is murder. It's a civilian investigation and we'll need some specific answers. I'll have to know exactly what Dr. French was doing and who was working for him and his relationship to you." His voice was quiet, almost a high-pitched whisper.

"I'm not at liberty to answer all your questions," Hanson replied, tight-lipped. "I've already notified Army Intelligence and the DOD section of the CIA."

Jessup sighed. "Then I guess I'll have to talk to them. You'll be in town, Major?"

Hanson nodded; the atmosphere between them became more relaxed. "Any fingerprints? Anything to go on?"

Jessup nodded. "A lot of fingerprints. They'll probably turn out to be Dr. French's and those of his assistants. Some footprints in the gunk on the floor, but unless they're pretty unusual, they won't be of much help."

Two white-coated ambulance attendants were coming from the cold room at the rear of the lab carrying a blanket-covered stretcher. They stopped by Jessup and he raised the corner of the blanket that covered the body beneath. French's frozen face stared up at Hanson, the eyeballs silvery with frost, ice crystals still clustering in his eyebrows and hair.

"I understand he was well liked," Jessup said quietly.

"I didn't know him very well," Hanson murmured.

He should have, he thought to himself. French had a reputation for being a teddy bear of a man; he would have found out far more from friendship than he ever would have as an employer. He had looked upon French strictly as a cog in the operation. In the long run, it had been a mistake.

"How was he killed?"

"Judging from the mess, probably a .357 magnum slug. It would have been much worse, except he was hit point-blank; the round was still at muzzle velocity without too much wobble. There are powder burns around the back of the head." Hanson looked at him quizzically and Jessup said, "Execution. Apparently he was first shot twice in the upper body, then shot in the head. He was killed out here, then carried into the cold room." Jessup covered the face again with the now damp blanket and the attendants disappeared out the door.

"You said Dr. Doohan found the body?"

"That's right. Englishman; friend of French. You know him?"

Hanson felt grim. "Yes, I know him. Where is he now?"

"He's in French's office, giving a statement." Jessup read the look on Hanson's face. "Forget it. Outside of finding the body, he doesn't have anything to do with this."

"I want to talk to him when you're through," Hanson said grimly.

Jessup shrugged. "If he wants to talk with you. We're not detaining him. He came in on the evening flight from Washington; we checked it. It would have taken twelve hours or more to have frozen French that completely in the cold room. Doohan's movements in D.C. have been confirmed; he was definitely out of town when French was killed."

A young man carrying a leather briefcase stepped out of French's office. "I'm finished with Dr. Doohan, Frank. You want to talk with him?"

Jessup shook his head. He glanced at Hanson, his expression poker-faced. "Be my guest, Major."

Doohan was sitting in a battered folding chair by the window, drinking coffee and staring out at the night. Hanson took a chair from near the wall and reversed it, straddling it so he could lean his chin and hands on the backrest. "I'm sorry about Dr. French." Doohan glanced at him, nodded, and went back to staring out the window. "I understand you found the body."

"I called the police department," Doohan said quietly. "I didn't know your number."

"It was Christmas Eve," Hanson said. "You had just come in from Washington. What made you come over here?"

"He was my friend. I thought it would be nice to have a Christmas Eve drink."

"Why not his home?" Hanson persisted. "Why here?"

Doohan exploded then. "Because he wasn't *at* home! There was only one other place he would have been and that was here!"

"You must have phoned first," Hanson said calmly.

"The line was busy; so I assumed he was here."

"If you had waited, the operator would have told you the line was out of order."

"Would she now? Maybe I was anxious to see him."

"What about?"

"None of your bloody business."

He could bully him, Hanson thought. But in Doohan's present frame of mind, it wasn't going to do much good. "It's two in the morning, Doctor. We're both tired."

"Two o'clock," Doohan murmured. He glanced around. "Merry Christmas, Major."

There was a knock on the door and Roberts slipped into the room. Hanson nodded to him to sit down. Doohan turned, stared for a moment, then turned back.

"There's no sign of any reports or lab books among French's papers," Hanson persisted quietly. "Do you have any idea what might have happened to them?"

Doohan took the time to light his pipe. "Of course. The men who murdered him must have taken them."

"Do you have any idea why he was murdered? Why they ruined his laboratory?"

"You would know the answer to that, Major. He was working for you; he wasn't working for me."

Doohan was pushing him, Hanson thought. He was upset by French's death but that wasn't the answer. He really didn't give a damn what Hanson thought or knew.

"Dr. French succeeded in culturing the virus, didn't he?"

Doohan abruptly laughed. "A virus? So you've decided it wasn't a toxin or nickel carbonyl or even a nice safe little bacterium? My God, man, what made you think of a virus?"

Hanson stood up and walked over to the coffeepot. "Mind if I have a cup?"

"Why ask me?" Then reluctantly: "It's at least a day old; it's pretty strong."

He was calming down a little, Hanson thought. Doohan didn't like him but at least part of his anger had been because of French's murder. "I know Dr. French was your friend. He was murdered apparently because of what he was working on. I'm anxious to find his murderers too, you know—and it would help if I knew the lab tests he was running."

"And you think I know?"

"Don't you?"

Doohan kneaded the bridge of his nose a moment. "Yes, he cultured the virus. He was working on a complete report for you and Miltrait. He probably would have turned it in on Monday."

"There's no sign of the report around."

Doohan shrugged. "I don't know where it is."

"But you knew what the contents would have been?"

Doohan turned. "Does it matter? I wouldn't tell you anyway."

Hanson lost his temper then. "Doctor, you're playing a goddamned dangerous game—or hasn't tonight convinced you of that? If you have any plans to conceal data that Dr. French developed and release it later to WHO, let me remind you that we have stiff laws about espionage in this country. I can hold you, if necessary."

"On what charge?" Doohan challenged. "You can't prove I know a damn thing."

"We can come up with a charge."

Doohan looked at him contemptuously. "Then go ahead."

Losing his temper had been a mistake, Hanson thought. And something about Doohan had changed. There was something more determined, more positive about the man. As if he had finally taken Hanson's measure and decided he had nothing to fear. Hanson felt tired and moody; he wasn't thinking very well, he realized. Then he wondered: Was Doohan really what he seemed? Or had he fingered French in the first place, then shown up to make sure the job had been done right?

It was two in the morning and he was being paranoid. "I think you know what French knew," he said. And then in a moment of prescience: "And I think that someday you'll tell me. In the meantime, I'm concerned about your safety. After what happened to Dr. French, I wouldn't want anything to happen to you."

"Does that mean I'm free to go?"

Hanson nodded and Doohan stalked out the door. After he had left, Hanson turned to Roberts and said: "Twenty-four-hour surveillance on Doohan, starting tomorrow morning. And get Gorshin and his men over to this lab."

Roberts raised an eyebrow. "Right now?"

Hanson sighed. "Yes, Lieutenant, right now."

Roberts disappeared and Hanson sank back in deep thought. Doohan said French had cultured the virus, but where the hell was it? In the mess of drying goop on the floor? Doohan wasn't going to tell him; maybe Doohan didn't know. Well, now it was a job for Gorshin and his troops. They'd have to go over the lab with a microscope; maybe they could find one unsmashed egg, something that had escaped complete destruction, to give them a clue.

He emptied his cold coffee in the office sink and walked to the window. On one of the lawns down Walnut, somebody had decorated a pine tree with what seemed like a hundred blue lights and a ton of plastic snow. The tree trembled in the wind that had suddenly arisen.

Ice blue, Hanson thought. A cheerless kind of tree for Christmas, but then Christmas was rapidly becoming a very cheerless season this year.

And a Merry Christmas to you, too, Tiny Tim, he thought.

30

DOOHAN STOOD IN the hallway for a moment, waiting for his heart to stop racing. It had been a rugged time with Jessup; it was even more difficult fencing with Hanson rather than simply telling him off and walking out. Neither of them had thought of doing the one thing he had feared the most: to search him. He had simply stuck the two ampoules of dried virus in his shirt pocket next to his felt-tipped pen. Neither one had noticed.

All he wanted to do now was to go home and go to bed and forget the horror. He had seen enough of death to realize how little resemblance there was between the friend you knew in life and the body from which life had fled. There was nothing of the larger-than-life, compassionate man he had known as Paul French left in the frozen body in the cold room. The essence was gone and what remained was the equivalent of a child's sketch, only vaguely reminiscent of the man himself.

But the heavy sense of loss was there, the sense of an empty spot in his life once filled by French. The energy, the arguments, the office coffee and the late dinners, the puns and the compassion . . . The kindest thing you could say about anybody was that there was no malice in them, and certainly there had been none in French . . .

"Dr. Doohan?"

The voice was tentative, slightly charged with emotion. Doohan turned. The boy in the hallway was perhaps seventeen, tall and just vaguely chubby with a broad, good-natured face that was the echo of an

older one. The resemblance was striking, even without the similarity of the voice. He was clutching a
photograph under his arm and Doohan knew that it
was the portrait of the boy and his father and mother
that used to sit on French's desk. He shook the boy's
outstretched hand. "I'm glad to meet you, Isaac." Then
turning to the policeman at the boy's side: "I can drive
him home; it won't be out of my way."

"All right with you, son?"

Isaac nodded dully. "It's all right." He and Doohan
started walking down the stairs. He was silent for a
moment, then said: "I got home from a skiing trip and
the detectives were waiting for me. They wanted me
to come down to identify . . . to identify . . ." He
couldn't finish. Doohan didn't try to help; he squeezed
the boy's shoulder.

They drove in silence to French's home. Doohan
parked, cut the engine and waited. The boy had been
dry-eyed all the way home; it had to come now.

Isaac was staring out the windshield; he didn't
make a move to get out of the car. "Dad . . . never hurt
anyone," he blurted. And then: "God *damn* it!" He
broke then and buried his head in Doohan's shoulder,
fighting desperately to regain control. Doohan held
him roughly until the spasms slowed, then said quietly: "Well, aren't you going to invite me in for coffee?"

Isaac fumbled for his handkerchief and blew, hard.
"Sure, come on." He seemed vastly relieved that he
didn't have to go into the house alone. In the kitchen,
he measured out the coffee for the coffeemaking machine. "We've got some steaks in the freezer—I could
defrost them in the radar oven and then broil them
up."

All he really wanted was to go home, Doohan
thought, but by the time they finished eating, it would
be close to morning. It would be easier then for Isaac
to face the emptiness of the house. "If you've got a
spare steak, Isaac, I'll eat it; I've never turned one
down yet."

"The freezer's in the garage; I'll be right back."

The boy disappeared out the connecting door and
Doohan sat down in the breakfast nook to wait. Mem-

ories of French kept crowding into his mind and he tried to blot them out; he didn't want to turn maudlin. Personal friendships aside, he had two allies against Hanson and now one of them was gone. Something tickled his mind when he thought about Hanson then. A possibility bubbled up, lingered, then vanished.

What the devil was keeping Isaac? "Isaac?" He got up from his chair with a rush and burst into the garage. Iasac was squatting by a large cardboard box, looking puzzled. "Dr. Doohan, this wasn't here before."

The cardboard box was about two feet on a side and had been hastily sealed with brown paper tape. Isaac was holding a five-by-eight file card that had apparently been taped to the box. Doohan recognized the handwriting as French's. The card read: "Isaac, call Dr. Doohan and give him this box. Don't let anybody else have it. Dad." Scribbled beneath was a P.S.: "Merry Christmas—for all the years to come."

Doohan knelt down and began to strip the brown tape from the box. From inside, there came the sounds of scurrying and scratching. He felt a sudden surge of excitement. He quickly pulled off the rest of the tape and opened the box. Inside was a wire animal cage, crowded with hamsters. From the odor, they had been there a while.

He reached in and pulled out the cage. Another file card was woven between the wires. "Calvin: These are the inoculated ones. By now, you know why I took the chance."

How French had gotten them out of the lab, he'd probably never know, Doohan thought. Presumably, he couldn't leave the building himself; so he'd sent them out with somebody. Probably Celia; she worked late at night far more often then did Anderson. He must have guessed that they had come after him, that they'd let Celia go. Why hadn't he asked her to call the police once she was out? Maybe he was afraid she'd panic then and not take the animals at all. . . .

But he had other problems now. He couldn't leave the hamsters with Isaac; whoever had killed French would come looking. The logical thing was to board them with Woodruff, his assistant in the rat program.

He put the cage back in the box and closed the flaps. "I'm going to have to take a rain check on that steak, Isaac. I've got to get these hamsters to a friend—right now." Isaac looked disappointed. "I'll call you later," Doohan promised. "Maybe we can both go out for Christmas dinner."

"I'll probably be eating at my aunt's," Isaac said, obviously feeling betrayed. Then, with a flash of his father's curiosity: "Are they really that important?"

Doohan nodded and clapped Isaac on the shoulder. "I wouldn't be passing up a steak if they weren't, laddie."

He left Isaac standing in the doorway and stowed the box in the trunk of his car. As he pulled away from the curb, he felt like shouting in triumph. He had the dried culture and he also had the animals that had been inoculated. And Hanson didn't know he had either one.

French would have appreciated that, he thought.

31

THE BIG, OLIVE-SKINNED *man is angry, far angrier than the young man has ever seen him before. It's a cold anger that shows itself in his eyes, in the frozen cast of his features and in the precise way in which he snaps out his words. The younger man has been subjected to cold anger before but then, he reflects with a slight chill, the most he could lose was his job. He stares out the window at the night brilliance of the Golden Gate Bridge, waiting for the older man to finish with the report.*

How few cars there are on the bridge at this hour, he thinks wistfully. Everyone else is at home with his family this Christmas Eve. He wishes he were too, but things have gone disastrously wrong and he knows he'll be up to all hours trying to pick up the pieces.

"I thought I made it clear there was to be no violence," the big man says in a voice of ice.

"The men made a mistake," the younger man says hesitantly. "They thought he was a guard—"

"A guard?" the older man interrupts. "In a lab smock? I thought I told you not to give me that crap!" He hits the table with his fist and some of the contents of his martini glass slosh out onto the polished top. "They could have questioned him if they'd kept him alive." He picks up a mayonnaise jar from the table, unscrews the cap and sniffs at the thick, milky substance inside. "A dime's worth of laboratory hand cream and a penny's worth of perfume."

"They didn't know," the younger man insists. "They were instructed not to open it."

"You can commend them on how well they follow

instructions," the older man says sardonically. "I don't suppose there was any vial conveniently marked 'virus culture.'"

"The jar was all they found," the younger man says stiffly.

"And the hamsters?"

"I interrogated both of the men carefully; there were none present in the animal room."

"Any indications that there ever were?"

"I think it's reasonable to assume there were."

"An assumption," the older man sneers. "You don't win wars with assumptions." His hands are working now and the younger man knows it's time to put a stop to this.

"The girl might be able to tell us."

The older man suddenly stops his pacing. "What girl?"

"The laboratory assistant. She left just before the men went in. They thought it wiser to let her go than to involve her."

"Did she take anything with her?"

The younger man hesitates. "A box," he says at last. And then: "They had to let her go: they didn't dare split up. French could have handled one. And the box could have been a Christmas present."

The older man, surprisingly, seems to calm down and the younger man suddenly realizes why. There is, at least, a lead. "I don't suppose you know where she lives or where she was going?"

"She was going home for the holidays. To Dayton." Pause. "We know the address." He smiles slightly. "I think she might be willing to answer some questions —if they're phrased right."

The older man is calmer now, calculating. "That leaves one more lead."

"One more lead?"

"Our British friend who found the body. He was the first on the scene. If something's missing from the lab, then it's possible he has it."

"I'm not so sure—"

"Be sure," the older man interrupts. "They told each

other everything. Now we'll have to get him to tell us. Everything."

"I suggested once before—"

"What you were going to suggest wouldn't have given us any answers at all. But for once you followed orders, which means he's still available to us. Think about that." The older man broods for a moment behind his bar, a hulking figure in his floral-patterned, short-sleeved shirt. "It's been all bad news so far. And there's more, isn't there?"

"It's Ramon. He mourns for his wife."

The older man starts to make a martini. He pointedly doesn't offer one to the younger man this time. "It's not unusual that he should mourn."

"He mourns too much," the younger man says. "He's becoming despondent and—"

"—and dangerous?" The older man walks over to the huge picture window that frames the lights of the city beyond. "So many lights," he muses. "Millions of them. You never notice the few that burn out each night."

The younger man is suddenly alert. "He's one of us."

"The highest decorations in a war are usually those awarded posthumously," the older man says quietly.

The younger man is now sweating. "We may be going too far. The others—"

"We can't afford to risk everything on Ramon's emotions," the older man says curtly. And then, almost as an afterthought: "You know, you're very valuable to me."

Comforting, the younger man thinks coldly. "And the girl?"

"Do you want her to tell somebody else what she tells us? I'm more interested in the omelet than the eggs, and so are you. So are all of us."

Two assignments in the same night, the younger man thinks. And then, sweating once again: He's misjudged the older man. Badly. "What about Hanson?"

The older man swirls the drink in his glass, unworried. "What about Hanson?" he asks.

32

It was a few minutes after six and the first hint of dawn painted the eastern skies as Doohan took the South San Francisco turnoff to Woodruff's house. He could imagine Alex's reaction at being awakened so early on Christmas morning, but it would have been adding insult to injury to call even earlier to say he was coming.

Woodruff lived on a quiet residential street in a brown-shingled house; the concrete, garagelike structure behind it was Woodruff's animal laboratory. Doohan rang the doorbell and listened to the complaining sound of voices within. The door finally opened and Woodruff's wife, Heather, wearing a quilted print robe and looking very sleepy, peered out at him.

"Calvin," she yawned, "what are you doing here this time of night?"

"Believe it or not, it's morning," Doohan said.

"Oh, I believe it; the kids have been up for hours." She pushed open the screen door and waved him in. "They can hardly wait to open their presents. Come on in and have some coffee; Alex is in the kitchen."

She left them alone in the kitchen. Doohan gulped down half a cup of boiling hot coffee, then said: "Alex, I don't have much time but I've brought something I want you to keep for me. Could you open up the lab?"

Woodruff rubbed at his eyes. "That important, old buddy?" Doohan nodded. Woodruff followed him out to the car where Doohan rescued the cardboard box from the trunk. Inside the lab, he placed the box on a workbench and pulled out the animal cage. Woodruff stared. "What the hell are they?"

"The hamsters from Paul French's lab."

Woodruff woke up enough to look serious. "Yeah, I heard about him on the radio, poor guy. What have the beasties got to do with it?"

For a moment Doohan wondered whether he should tell Woodruff the full story, then decided against it. He wasn't asking Woodruff to do anything illegal, merely to house the hamsters for a while. "French and I were running tests. But French's lab is now destroyed and the police are swarming over it. I couldn't leave the hamsters there."

"Nothing I can catch from them, is there?"

Doohan remembered the double exposure necessary and shook his head. "I rather doubt it."

"Clean the cages, feed them and water them, and I assume you'll look in on your pets every now and then. The Woodruff boarding kennels." He was bending over the cage, poking at the sleepy hamster inside. He suddenly reached in and pulled one out. It was a female and obviously gravid. "Your Dr. French wasn't quite as careful as he should have been."

"Blame it on a sloppy lab assistant." He hesitated, then said, "I wouldn't broadcast it around that you were keeping these."

Woodruff grimaced. "Look, Cal, it's either safe or it's not safe. It's not just me; there's Heather and the kids."

"For a week, it's safe," Doohan said. "Just let me know if anything happens to them."

"Some of them don't look too healthy now," Woodruff said dubiously.

"Don't contact me directly if anything comes up," Doohan said. He scribbled a number on a piece of paper. "This is Dr. Synge's phone number; she's a good friend of mine. I'll call in regularly, but in case of emergency, leave the message with her. Don't bother her with any of the details; just tell her you want me to call you."

Woodruff held the slip of paper between his thumb and forefinger, still uncertain. "It sounds pretty cloak-and-dagger, Calvin. You sure everything is kosher?"

Whatever Woodruff knew could only hurt him, Doohan thought. "If you want to back out, Alex, just say so. I can probably find another place."

Woodruff suddenly grinned, folded the paper and put it in his wallet. "Ever since medical school, you've had all the fun. I guess I should get in on an adventure or two myself." His face grew somber. "Just let me know if anything heavy's about to come down. I can take care of myself; it's the family."

Doohan drove slowly back to San Francisco, his eyes blurry from lack of sleep. French had been killed by somebody looking for the sample of the virus. They hadn't found it; so they had to be suspicious of him. He was French's confidante and he had been first on the scene after the murder. They would assume that he not only knew too much, but that he also had the culture.

The missing hamsters would be a problem too. French had kept a record of the laboratory animals and probably both the murderers and Hanson had taken an inventory by now. They'd be looking for the animals but there would be no reason at all for them to think of Woodruff and his animal lab. Sadly, there was no way he could have been more open with Woodruff; too many people knew too much already.

One thing Hanson had probably been right about: He, Doohan, had to be target number one.

He blinked a few times, trying to keep his tired eyes open. Then there was the blast of an automobile horn behind him, and he jerked awake just in time to avoid running up an embankment. He finally pulled up in front of his old Victorian apartment house, did a sloppy job of parking, then got out and fumbled for the keys to the front door. It was still early in the morning and the streets were deserted. There wouldn't be anybody moving until noon, he thought. It wasn't only Christmas Day, it was Sunday as well.

He was just going into the house when he spotted a green Impala slowly pass in front of the house. He wasn't sure but he dimly recalled one like it in the lane next to him at a spotlight a few blocks back.

His imagination, he thought. But once upstairs, he moved quickly to one side of the front window and glanced out. The Impala had parked across the street and a few doors down. Whoever was at the wheel was making no move to get out.

Who? he wondered with a thin chill. One of the men who had killed French? It was daylight but with the lack of either car or foot traffic, it might as well be night. Had it been like this with French? he wondered. Did they break in unexpectedly, or had they somehow isolated him as he sat in the darkness of his office, waiting?

Or was it Hanson's man in the car?

And then the thought that had bubbled into his mind once before came back. Hanson had wanted the culture as badly as anybody he knew. He must have known that French was getting close, might even have guessed that French had actually cultured the virus. Once done, would he have seized the culture and eliminated French so that nobody else could find out what it was or that they had succeeded in culturing it?

He grimaced to himself. He was getting paranoid. Much as he personally despised Hanson, it was difficult to conceive of the man as a murderer or that it would be government policy. The thought subsided and he discarded it. Almost.

He automatically felt at his pocket for the reassuring presence of the two ampoules, watched through the window a moment longer, then shrugged off the feeling of fear. He made himself a light breakfast of wheat toast and coffee with a small orange juice on the side. He had considered a kipper but more and more his breakfast habits were becoming Americanized.

After breakfast, he checked the window again out of curiosity. The Impala was still there but now the man in the driver's seat was talking to another man leaning against the side of the car. It was a little after eight in the morning and the streets were still empty. Doohan suddenly found himself wishing he had rented a more modern apartment with some kind of security guard or locked doors that required a card-key to activate the lock.

Well, he wasn't going to be a sitting duck, he thought. He went to the closet and dug out his Beretta and a carton of shells from the bottom of his suitcase. He loaded the gun at the kitchen table, then went back to the living room and stretched out on the couch to wait. . . .

He woke up around noon, feeling uncomfortable and sweaty; the gun was lying on the floor where he had dropped it. He looked at it foolishly, knuckled his eyes and walked over to the windows again. The Impala was gone.

Doohan was in the middle of a shower when he heard the phone ring. He cursed and stalked naked across the kitchen floor to the phone. On the other end of the line, a crisp voice said: "Dr. Doohan? Tony Strout. Can you meet me at the corner of Post and Powell in an hour—precisely at three?"

"How will I know you?" Doohan asked.

"You won't; I'll know you. I have your picture—it was snapped at the embassy. Park in the Union Square garage. The streets are deserted and your shadow will give you plenty of breathing space. You do have a shadow, right? Thought so." Strout didn't bother saying good-by; there was only a click.

Doohan had several more cups of coffee to help kill the thirty minutes, then walked down to the street and got into his car. He hadn't gone a hundred feet when the green Impala pulled around the corner. He drove slowly, watching the rear-view mirror. There wasn't any doubt that he was being followed.

He circled Union Square, entering the underground parking lot at the Geary Street entrance. He parked on the third level and took the elevator to the main floor, then walked west to the northeast corner of the St. Francis Hotel on Post and Powell. It was five of three. Even in the heart of San Francisco, there were still few people on the sidewalk. He looked up and down the street; there was no sign of the Impala.

At precisely three o'clock a yellow Ventura pulled

to the curb. The driver leaned out, opened the door and said: "Dr. Doohan?"

It was smooth, Doohan thought. He could have been a tourist meeting a relative by prearrangement. He got in and the driver pulled quickly away, turning right on Powell and a block later right on Geary. They took Gough to Market, crossed and then turned off on McCoppin, a short street lost in a maze of block-long one-way streets. They parked behind an ancient Vega with scaling black paint.

The driver and the passenger in the Vega got out and ran toward them. Doohan's own driver said crisply, "Follow me," and they switched to the Vega. They sat for a few minutes after the Ventura had disappeared into traffic and then they pulled out.

The driver smiled. "That final change should throw them off, if they've phoned in a description to the police." He turned and thrust out his hand. "Sorry about the drill, Dr. Doohan. I'm Tony Strout. It's good to have you aboard."

Doohan managed a smile and shook hands. He made a mental note to ask Strout later why he had been so sure it was Hanson's men tailing him.

33

"WE'RE GOING TO a small restaurant I know," Strout said. "I need a touch of something and it's a good place to talk."

Doohan split his time between watching the houses roll by and stealing an occasional glance at Strout, who was making a running commentary on the district they were driving through. "They call this the Haight-Ashbury, the former womb of the hippie movement— the Summer of Love, and all that rot. It hit bottom in '68—they were averaging one murder per square block—but it's quite nice now. San Francisco Quaint: freaks, boutiques, and antiques." They parked in front of a natural-foods restaurant. "I hope you don't mind carrot cake and herbal tea; I've grown quite addicted to the stuff myself. And it's not likely that anybody will spot us."

Once they were out of the car, Doohan saw that Strout was much taller than he had imagined, six-two and lanky, narrow of shoulder and slightly wide of beam. His hands were unusually large with knobby wrists; his broad face had a ruddy cast and was topped with short, sandy hair. He seemed like an awkward man, thoroughly innocuous and inoffensive, a bookstore clerk or a department store clothing salesman. Not at all what you might expect an intelligence agent to be.

The restaurant was furnished with a collection of odd-sized tables of different styles and from different eras; most of the chairs were cane-bottomed. Innumerable pots of ferns were suspended from the ceiling in macrame holders and Doohan had to dodge several as they made their way to the table. Nevertheless, the place was immaculate.

Strout picked a table in the back, near what was obviously a rear entrance. He made himself at ease in one of the chairs and glanced quickly around. His eyes didn't miss much, Doohan thought, either in the restaurant or on the street outside. "There really hasn't been much on your Dr. French so far," he said quietly. "The body was discovered too late for the news last night and also too late for the Sunday papers. Care to fill me in?"

Again, Doohan wondered if he had made a mistake. He had come this far, he decided, and he might as well be completely open. Strout interrupted occasionally to ask a question but otherwise was quiet throughout. Doohan thought he noted a glint of admiration when he told Strout about walking out with the two ampoules of culture.

"What about the hamsters?"

"I've got those too."

"In your apartment?" It was very good acting, Doohan thought, but the surprise was feigned.

"Not hardly."

Strout was blunt. "What do you intend to do with them?"

Doohan fenced. "What would you suggest I do with them?"

"Turn them over to us, of course," He took another mouthful of carrot cake. "But that's not what you intend, is it?"

"Mr. Strout," Doohan said slowly, "it's my belief that to use disease as a weapon is the most immoral thing in the world. I think most people look upon it as that; God knows enough covenants have been signed against its use. I think that waging biological warfare has to be a covert sort of thing; when it's no longer covert, I think the pressure against its use would be too great. I don't want the United States to hide the fact that there is BW research going on. Neither do I want to contribute such a weapon to the British arsenal."

Strout lit a cigarette and spoke around it in a low

voice. "All right, laddie buck; what the hell do you want to do?"

"I want to make sure everybody knows about it," Doohan said vehemently. "The Americans, the British, the Germans, the Russians—everybody. And I can produce the proof."

"And you think that once everybody knows, the outcry against its use will be so great, it will be stopped."

"That's right."

"You haven't considered the thought that you might just cause a panic?"

"I think I will cause a panic," Doohan said slowly. "That's probably what it will take. A panic—when everybody realizes that disease doesn't recognize national borders, that it's not just one country that's involved."

"I admire your idealism," Strout said.

"What would you do?" Doohan asked curiously.

"I suppose we'd put our people to work on an antidote. It would be a valuable thing to have in case of attack."

"And the Americans?"

"We'd share it with our allies in case of attack, naturally."

"But not the culture initially?"

Strout looked surprised. "With the Americans? One shares a defense. Defenses are intrinsically static. An offensive weapon, on the other hand, may be used unilaterally. And I can't quite see ourselves doing that. But the Americans? Come on, old boy, Vietnam is just a few years back."

"I could cite examples from our own history," Doohan said dryly. "The only difference between us and the Americans is that they're a bit more inept at power politics. But then, we've had more practice at it."

"Lately, the Americans could teach us a good deal about power politics." Strout wiped his mouth, leaned back and stared at Doohan for a long moment. "Forgive me, Doctor, but there's something of the bleeding heart in your decision. Your approach—which will tell nobody anything they haven't already suspected—is hardly going to stop men from manufacturing microbes and viruses to wipe out other men." He took a sip of his tea and carefully added another teaspoon of honey to it. "I get the impression you don't want to help us but you expect us to help you."

"You don't think it would be a help to know who originated the virus, who ran the test?"

Curtly: "All right. I've discussed the problem with our French and Israeli friends and they have no information. Whoever is behind the operation has been extraordinarily careful. Our normal sources are a complete blank."

"What about Guitterez and Melrose Foods?"

"Fenris has been checking him out in Washington; we should have something." Strout reached in his pocket and dropped a key chain with several keys on the table. "In the meantime, we have to assume that you're a prime target for our unknown assassins. We also have to assume that at this particular point in time, if the Americans find you, they'll take you into protective custody."

He shoved the key chain at Doohan, who took it and looked at the keys suspiciously. "What are these?"

"The Yale keys are to the lock of an apartment whose address you'll find on the tag attached to the key chain. The other keys are to the ignition and trunk of the Vega outside. You'll find toilet articles, a change of clothing and money in the trunk."

Doohan licked his lips. "I don't see why all this is necessary."

Strout leaned forward, his voice intense. "Dr. Doohan, you are in more physical danger than you realize. Your enemies know you have that culture and they want it. Unless you follow this drill, I give them three days before they find both it and you. The best we can do to help is to try and extend that time. The apartment is one of several safe houses we keep in the Bay Area. You have a new identity—shave that mustache, by the way—and we've removed you from close surveillance. Provided you don't do anything foolish, you should be able to remain under cover."

Strout motioned for the bill, paid it and got up from

the table. "We'll be in touch." He paused and then said, "This is no job for amateurs, Doctor. I would be a whole lot happier if you would simply turn over the culture and the animals and allow us to get you out of the country immediately. You really haven't thought it through, you know. You open up your mouth and you'll tell everybody the one bit of information that really *is* important."

Doohan felt angry. "And just what the devil is that?"

"Think about it, Doctor," Strout said, and then he was gone.

It was Christmas Day, Doohan thought ironically. He watched the tiny knots of people gather in front of the churches or disappear into the restaurants. He was now a non-person, cut off from the few friends he had and certainly from the people with whom he used to work. He had a tenuous connection with Espinosa in Washington and a similar one with Alex Woodruff. Perhaps later in the day, he'd try and contact Suzanne, but even there he hesitated. He didn't want to endanger her.

He checked the address on the key chain and drove across town to Noe Valley, not too far from the restaurant where he had once interviewed Miller. That seemed like an age ago. The house at the corner of Noe and Twentieth was a brown, cedar-shingled home built, like most of the others in the block, immediately after the earthquake. There was a lower unit, obviously remodeled from what had once been a garage. The key let him into the slightly musty atmosphere of a house that had been closed up for a long time.

It was pleasant enough, though nothing fancy. A kitchenette with a small wooden bar opened off the living room. Directly opposite the entrance was a bedroom furnished with a maple bed and dresser. French doors opened from this onto a patio holding a number of plants in redwood pots. It was pretty much an anonymous neighborhood from what he had seen driving up. You could ignore your neighbors if you wished, and they would certainly ignore you.

He opened the suitcase on the bed. Two suits, four wash-and-wear shirts, some underwear, and a toilet kit. A flat leather wallet that contained three hundred dollars, two hundred of it in twenties. In addition, there were two gas credit cards, a driver's license made out to Carl Dobbs—they'd been smart enough to keep the same initials—and an identification card declaring that Carl Dobbs was a field representative for Victoria Laboratory Consultants, Ltd. There were a small number of business cards from the same company which, according to the small script at the bottom, was a "contractor for fine laboratory and precision equipment."

There was milk in the refrigerator, along with lunch meat and bread. He poured himself a glass of milk, made himself a sandwich and ate standing over the sink. He was settled in—as settled as he was going to be. He wanted desperately to take a nap, but there was one thing that had to be done first.

He roamed the apartment once more. Pleasant but utilitarian. Good enough for—how long had Strout said? Three or four days? All the comforts of home: a stove, a refrigerator, a phone and answering machine. . . . Of course, there would be an answering machine. He inspected it out of curiosity. A standard machine, battery-operated, with a small opening in back for the batteries. A sudden thought occurred to him. He pushed down the latch that held the lid over the batteries. There was just room enough to one side of the battery container. He took the ampoules from his pocket, wrapped them in toilet tissue and put them next to the batteries.

Afterward, he went into the bedroom and lay down on the bed, turning the clock-radio down low. There had been a light layer of dust over everything, which meant the house hadn't been used in a long time. He wondered what sort of trouble the last occupant had been in. . . .

It would have been easy to turn the culture over to Strout, he thought. He would be out of it then and he could return to Wales, a young, little-known country doctor who had had more than his share of adventures. He could devote the rest of his life to black lung disease, fractures, and birthing babies.

He had started to doze off, but the memory of Strout kept returning. He wondered idly what Strout would have done if the British agent had known that he, Doohan, had been carrying the culture on him. . . .

What he had done so far was exactly what they had wanted him to do, he thought sleepily. Return to San Francisco, locate the ampoules of culture . . . and then deliver them to Strout. Once back in the city, he would have to realize his life was in danger, that it was only a matter of time before somebody tracked him down and took the culture from him. Maybe the real question was who did he want to have it? The Americans? The British, who could at least lay claim to a certain national loyalty? Espinosa and the World Health Organization who would then bring it up in the United Nations—maybe?

But did he really want that? Strout had said something before he left. That if Doohan talked, he would give away the one bit of knowledge that was really important.

Of course. It was like the secret of the Manhattan Project. The real secret was not how a Bomb was made but that a Bomb *could* be made.

With that bit of knowledge, it had only been a matter of time before a dozen nations had made their own.

Like the Bomb, the secret of the virus was not how it was made but that it had been made at all.

34

IT WAS MONDAY, the day after Christmas, and Celia Kovacs decided to go downtown to see what specials the Dayton stores might be featuring. It was the first time in three years that she had been in Dayton during the winter and the weather was hard to take. She had often toyed with the idea of moving back home and finding laboratory work; this time she knew it was impossible, that she couldn't stand the climate.

She bundled up until she could hardly move and still the wind seemed to cut right through her. The thermometer on the porch read 35° and the ice on the sidewalk was turning to slush; she shivered at the thought of what it must be like when it was zero. She made up her mind to come back in mid-afternoon, before the falling temperatures froze the slush into ruts of ice.

She caught a bus downtown and wandered leisurely from store to store, stopping once in a drugstore to buy a picture postcard of the city to send Professor French. She'd probably be back before he ever got it, but he'd appreciate the thought. . . . Odd, how the merchandise varied so much in the Dayton stores from that in the Bay Area. The Christmas displays were coming down, but there still seemed a preponderance of coats and mufflers and gloves. The first signs of the white sales were appearing. She almost bought a towel set when she realized she could probably get the same thing back home at Macy's and she wouldn't have to carry it with her.

She didn't notice the man until she had sat down in the drugstore sandwich shop for a Coke and a tuna salad. She chose a booth by the window so she could look out and think—for the umpteenth time since she had been home—how lucky she was that she didn't live there any more. The snow was turning to black slush; every now and then a bus or a truck outside would pass close to the curb and spray the window with a light coating of muck. She had forgotten how dirty the city was, she thought, then realized that during the wintertime, all cities east of the Rockies were dirty.

The man was standing across the street; she realized suddenly that he was looking straight at her. She might not have noticed him at all except that he was unusually good-looking and he didn't seem to be dressed for the weather. A worsted suit and a light London Fog topcoat; no heavy galoshes or muffler. Just a slender, handsome man, this side of thirty, lightly dressed and staring at her while she ate her tuna salad sandwich in the drugstore window.

And he looked familiar.

She stared for a moment, then was afraid he might notice and buried her face in her Coke. Where had she seen him? Then, with a slight thrill, she remembered. It had been in one of the department stores. He had passed her on one of the escalators and flashed her a faint smile. At least, now that she thought of it, it seemed that he had. She had thought at first that she knew him . . . but no, that was quite impossible. She had probably reminded him of somebody he knew.

She was suddenly a little frightened. She was no raving beauty—reasonably pretty, she reassured herself—but why was he following her? She giggled to herself. Get her! Whoever he was, he was too well dressed to be a mugger and he certainly didn't look like a rapist—however they looked. Besides, for God's sake, she was sitting in the middle of downtown Dayton.

She forgot him, paid her bill, and headed for another store two blocks away. As she walked, she realized with some alarm that she was being followed. He was at a newsstand, hiding his face in a magazine as she strolled by. Later she saw him loitering by a shop window as she wandered past, pretending to look at the display inside. She wasn't the sort that men picked up, she thought bitterly, though God knew there were some pretty strange men around. She had the oddest feeling about him then; it seemed as if she weren't being followed so much as she was being . . . stalked.

She tried again to forget him and this time made a conscious effort to shake him, just in case. When she left the store, loaded with packages, she ignored the bus and hailed a cab. It was still midafternoon when she arrived home and nobody else was back yet. Her father wouldn't get home until six; her mother was spending the day at school catching up on paperwork, even though classes had been dismissed until after New Year's. She wouldn't be home until five.

She stacked her packages on the dining room table and went into the kitchen to make some tea. That damn man, she thought. She had come home for a rest and she resented being upset by him. She rummaged around in the kitchen and found a small tin of Christmas cookies, then poured hot water in a cup and dropped in a tea bag. It was getting cold outside, but she felt comfortable in the warm kitchen.

She was sipping the tea when the doorbell rang. The short, balding man on the front steps said formally: "Miss Celia Kovacs?"

She knew without asking that it was something official, and she could feel her heart skip a beat. "Yes?" Her voice was uncertain.

"I'm Detective Sergeant Willows." He flashed an ID at her and she caught a glimpse of a name and a small color photograph and the words "Dayton Police Department." His voice was official but sympathetic. "I'm sorry, Miss Kovacs, but your father's been in an auto accident."

Her hands flew to her throat. "How bad?"

"He was driving home from work," Willows said. "He's at St. Francis; the doctors believe he'll pull through, but they think you might like to be there— just in case."

It had been such a fine Christmas, she thought chaotically. "Just a minute; wait until I get my coat." She was almost out the door when she remembered the tea kettle on the stove and ran back to turn it off. "What about my mother?"

"She'll meet us at the hospital."

She didn't remember any St. Francis; maybe he meant St. Elizabeth's. Or maybe it was a new hospital. She climbed into the dark green Malibu, Willows following close behind her. She didn't get a good look at the driver.

As the car pulled away from the curb she said, "Can you tell me anything more?"

"We see a lot of this at Christmas," Willows said sympathetically. "Some high school kid, drinking too much, went through a red light."

She huddled in the back seat, suddenly missing the West Coast more than ever. She hadn't wanted to come home at this time of year, but her mother had practically insisted; it had been so long since she had been home for the holidays. It was getting dark now and the houses on either side of the street seemed so cheery and warm as they passed. She should be home, drinking tea in the kitchen and waiting for her mother to start supper. Warmed-up turkey and dressing . . .

She had been staring out the window, but something inside the car kept catching her eye. Police cars in Dayton were blue with white tops, she thought, but of course they were plainclothesmen and they wouldn't be driving an ordinary police car. When she got in the car, the driver had been looking the other way. She had glanced at him and also noticed the rear-view mirror. The back of the mirror, oddly enough, was painted yellow. She twisted around in her seat. There was a decal on the left side of the back rear window.

"This is a rental car," she said.

Willows slid over in the seat until he sat next to her, his arm around her shoulder. "There's nothing to get upset about," he said casually.

She shrank away from his arm. "I want to go home," she said in a small thin voice. She started to fill her lungs to scream when Willows suddenly clamped his hand over her mouth.

The driver now turned around. It was the same good-looking young man who had followed her downtown. He smiled at her, but it was a mechanical smile with no friendliness in it at all. "Take it easy, Miss Kovacs," he said quietly. "We just want to ask you some questions, that's all. Just some questions."

35

DOOHAN AWAKENED, and for a moment he lay in bed, wondering where he was. Light flooded through the thin-curtained doors that looked out on the patio; he could hear children playing next door. He rolled over to check his watch laying on the bed table. Nine o'clock. He had overslept, but he still felt the weight of fatigue from staying awake most of the previous night. And there had been the emotional shocks . . .

The trip to Washington to see Espinosa and then the embassy, finding French dead, the meeting with Strout . . . He shivered and staggered into the bathroom. He ran his tongue around the inside of his mouth, then soaked a washcloth in cold water and rubbed it over his face. Calvin Doohan, he thought, inspecting his stubbled face in the mirror. One thoroughly frightened Calvin Doohan and one not at his best . . . no, he had to amend that now. Not Calvin Doohan at all. A Carl Dobbs. Not a very Scottish-sounding name, but it would do. It would have to do, for at least a few days.

Carl Dobbs, a foreign agent in a not very friendly foreign land.

He soaped his face and started to shave. He had reached his upper lip and was removing the mustache as Strout suggested when the phone rang. He nicked the very edge of his lip. Damn, the worst kind of cut; it'd be hell to stop the bleeding. . . .

The phone was on the wall between the kitchen and the dining room. He picked it up, hesitated, then said, "Yes?"

"This is Tony Strout, Mr. Dobbs. Do you own a

camera?" Strout didn't wait for a reply. "No matter, you do now. And you need some film for it. Buy two rolls of Polacolor II and a set of flash cubes at the camera store on Castro Street between eighteenth and nineteenth. At ten o'clock. I'll meet you there. Don't be late, please."

Doohan finished dressing. He realized he'd have to eat out and buy groceries later. He had breakfast at the same cafe at which he had interviewed Miller—a lifetime ago, it now seemed—then walked up the block to the camera store. The sign on the outside read COULET'S CAMERA SUPPLIES. There was a young kid of perhaps nineteen behind the counter as well as an older clerk, a wiry, saturnine man in his late forties.

He ordered the film and the older man checked the racks of film supplies behind him, then said casually, "We're out of stock—could you come in back a moment?"

The room in back was raw-looking, lighted by a hanging green-shaded drop fixture and a goose-necked lamp on a linoleum-topped desk. The walls were stacked with boxes of camera supplies and in one corner were several four-drawer filing cabinets; papers were piled on top and stuck out of the drawers at random. Doohan had a hunch, however, that Coulet could lay his hands on whatever he wanted in a second. In the center of the room, directly beneath the hanging light, stood a small table with several folding chairs around it.

Strout was sitting at one of them, leafing through an old photography magazine. He glanced up when they entered. "We're running you around, aren't we, Doctor? Sorry about that. I'd like you to meet George Coulet, an old friend."

Coulet now turned, bowed slightly, and pumped Doohan's hand. "Glad to meet you, Doctor." Doohan couldn't place the accent but it definitely wasn't British. It sounded as if there were some French somewhere in his background.

Strout motioned both of them over to the table. "Welcome to general headquarters—this week. Its solid advantage is that it's a place unlikely to attract attention, and it's also convenient to your apartment." He looked at Doohan sharply. "Your friend, Guitterez. Between our own people and those of George's organization, we've assembled some rather interesting data."

"George's organization?" Doohan said stupidly.

"We collaborate quite frequently with the British these days," Coulet said quietly. He waved his hand around the room. "We don't exactly open up offices saying who we are, but then, neither do the Americans."

Strout continued. "George's country maintains an organization in Vietnam and Korea plus an embassy in Cuba; they've filled in several gaps in Guitterez's record." There were no papers on the table, Doohan realized, and guessed that both Strout and Coulet had committed all the information to memory. "His full name is Ramon Eduardo Philippe Guitterez, born in Puerto Rico in July of 1922. His family moved to Cuba while he was still a boy and returned just before World War II. He enlisted in the Army at the start of the war and served with distinction in the European Theater of Operations; he came out of it a commissioned officer. He stayed in the Army after the war was over, and in 1950 requested a transfer to the Army Chemical Corps."

Coulet cleared his throat and took up the recital now. "He served in Korea from 1950 to 1952 with the Second Chemical Mortar Battalion, transferring in late 1950 to the 691st Smoke Generator Company." He paused a moment, anxious to impress on Doohan just how important the next information was. "The 691st was the company the North Koreans accused of dispersing bacteriological agents as smoke aerosols. Guitterez and two other officers signed BW warfare confessions, but Guitterez apparently held out. All three of them were repatriated in 1954. The two officers with Guitterez were court-martialed and dishonorably discharged. Guitterez stayed on in the service until 1971 when he resigned and took his thirty-year pension."

Strout stretched out his long legs, watching Doohan

intently. "It doesn't stop there. From his repatriation until 1969, Guitterez was stationed first at Camp Detrick, the Army's Bacteriological Warfare Research Center, and later at Dugway Proving Grounds in Utah—that's the Chemical Corps installation where all the goats were accidentally killed by nerve gas in the sixties." He paused. "In 1974, he came into a fair sum of money, source unknown."

"How can you be so sure of that?" Doohan asked.

"Courtesy of the Internal Revenue Service—simply a matter of asking the right questions of the right people and giving them the right reasons."

Coulet was drumming his fingers on the table top, listening with one ear to the flow of customers in and out of his store just beyond the partition. "We've developed some other information recently that's even more interesting. Guitterez visited Mexico City on an Argentine passport in 1971. There he got a Cuban visa and spent three months in Cuba. He apparently got into some trouble with the authorities, was held incommunicado for four weeks and then suddenly released, and returned to Mexico by the Cuban authorities."

It was coming at him too fast, Doohan thought. And then: He had expected a plot; now he was being told the details of one and still finding it hard to believe.

"You may recall," Strout interrupted laconically, "that this was during the period of the so-called 'killer flu' that swept Cuba."

"You're implying something," Doohan said bluntly.

"'Imply' is the wrong word," Strout apologized. "I think it probable that Guitterez may have been involved in some American plot against Cuba and then, under duress of imprisonment, defected." He spread his hands. "Another possibility is that the American apparatus in Cuba somehow got him out."

"The timing's wrong," Doohan objected. "The Americans discontinued all offensive bacteriological warfare research in 1969."

"That was research, Doctor. The United States didn't destroy the last of its biological weapons until 1973, after signing a pact with the Russians. But it doesn't matter. Maybe Guitterez wasn't working for the Americans. He had a lot of valuable knowledge; perhaps he was free lance, available to the highest bidder. The Castro government certainly has more enemies than just the United States." He glanced at his watch, then back at Doohan. "There's something we haven't talked about and that's how close your Major Hanson and his men are to culturing the agent."

"I have no idea how close they might be," Doohan said, glancing sideways at Coulet. "I suppose it's a matter of time." His glance stayed with Coulet.

"You can trust George," Strout said reassuringly. "At this particular point in time, we're all in this together. You know that the CDC has been phased out and what's left of Hanson's apparatus is moving across the Bay tomorrow? I believe a Dr. Synge is in charge of the move—from what I understand, a very attractive lady. A friend of yours?"

How much did Strout know that was of a personal nature, Doohan wondered, and how had he found out? "We're friends," he admitted cautiously.

"There's somebody else involved, a Dr. Thomas Gorshin. Do you know him, too?"

Doohan shook his head. "Only by reputation; he came in with Hanson. He's a university professor from back East."

Strout nodded. "To be specific, a molecular biologist; he's written several papers on DNA analytical techniques. Does that suggest anything to you?"

"It suggests what I've already told the ambassador's office in Washington," Doohan said curtly. "That the agent is an artificially tailored one."

Strout looked concerned. "Is there any way that Gorshin could culture the agent from what was left in the lab?"

Doohan hesitated a moment too long. "You've asked me that before. I said it was probably a matter of time."

Strout stared at him shrewdly. "You can't dissemble worth a damn, Doctor. I think if they succeed in culturing it, they're going to have to be lucky, aren't they? They'd have to know what Dr. French knew—and what I think you know. Only you haven't told them and you aren't going to tell us." He laughed. "You're in a double bind, Doctor. You won't help them culture it, which means you have the only sample of it. And as long as you have the only sample, your life is in jeopardy. If they do culture it, then your sample really isn't that valuable any more." Strout thought for a moment, then made up his mind. "I think we should know just how far along they are. And I think perhaps you might be able to find out through your friend, Dr. Synge."

"You want me to pump her for information?"

Strout feigned astonishment. "You didn't consider that on your own? But your life may depend on it, Doctor, and she's your best pipeline. The difficulty is that you're working against time. You have to know what they do as soon as they do it."

The phone rang and Strout answered it. He spoke in monosyllables for a moment, then hung up and turned back to Doohan. "To sum it up, Doctor, the test of the virus was enormously successful. The question is: How soon after the field test comes full-scale usage? That's why you're so important to us, and so important to Hanson. Except for whoever was behind the test, you're the only one with a sample of the culture. If something happens to you, then the culture is lost and we—and the Americans and every other country with the sole exception of our unknown enemy—become vulnerable to attack. If you believe in humanity as much as you profess, then I should think you would turn it over to us."

Doohan hesitated. "I've told you how I feel," he said at last.

"Then at least make arrangements for us to get it if something happens to you."

There was a lot of merit in what Strout was saying, Doohan thought. "I'll see Suzanne and try to find out what she knows. If the Americans have cultured the virus . . . then we'll talk about my own sample."

Strout nodded. "That leaves our man Guitterez and his plant in Hayward. I think tomorrow would be a bloody good time to pay him a visit."

Doohan stared his surprise. Strout half-smiled. "Doctor, you came to us for aid, both in keeping you alive and in finding out who made your virus. As you say, it affects the people of the world—and we happen to be some of those people. We're partners, now. We were from the moment you opened your mouth at the embassy. You couldn't very well expect it to be any different. Mr. Guitterez apparently knows a great deal about your virus. We intend to find out what he knows and it's not a case of having to ask your permission. For all I know, perhaps *he* has samples."

Strout was right, Doohan thought. He couldn't have expected anything else. "I'll go with you."

Strout raised an eyebrow. "I think not, Doctor. It could be dangerous and you're the one we can least afford to lose."

"Would you recognize what you're looking for?" Doohan asked.

Strout hesitated, then sighed. "All right—I'll meet you at your apartment at nine."

Doohan walked back to his apartment, his mind whirling. Guitterez was the link to the spreading of the Veterans' Disease; he had used Laval as a pawn and provided the culture-contaminated mayonnaise. The question now was: Who was he working for? Or with? They couldn't walk up to Guitterez and ask for his cooperation. Strout must know that. What on earth did he hope to accomplish?

He let himself into his apartment, dropped his coat on the bed, and walked into the bathroom. He got three paces past the door when he stopped, a silent alarm ringing in his head. Something was wrong. He retraced his steps into the bedroom and looked around. It took him a moment to figure out what it was. The suitcase he had stowed under the bed was now standing against the bedroom wall.

Now that he knew what he was looking for, there were a dozen tiny signs. A dresser drawer not quite closed, a picture hanging a little differently so that a slightly lighter area of the wall was exposed. In the bathroom, the porcelain cover on the watercloset was slightly off its seating.

Doohan stared for a moment, then thought: My God . . . He rushed out into the living room. The answering machine was in a different position on the table. He quickly turned the machine over and opened the battery compartment. The ampoules were still there, nesting to one side of the battery pack. Whoever had searched the apartment hadn't thought of opening the machine.

He grew angry then. It had to have been Strout. No one else would have known of his new apartment this soon. And even the offer of the apartment was, at least in part, a setup. They knew the apartment inside out; they must have known in advance every logical hiding place, which was why they could have gone through the apartment so quickly. The call that Strout had received at the camera shop was probably an all-clear signal.

Odd, they couldn't have known what they were looking for, either. He could have left the ampoules in plain sight and they might have gone right over them. The fact that they were deliberately hidden was what would have given them away. Nevertheless, he didn't dare leave them in the apartment any longer. If Strout searched it again, or if Hanson did, or if French's murderers did, next time they might be more fortunate.

He walked back to the bathroom, wrapped the two ampoules in several tissues from a Kleenex box and bound them with Band-Aids. Then he put the ampoules in the inside pocket of his coat. He'd have to find another hiding place. . . .

He glanced around the apartment again and this time he had a different thought, an unsettling one. At the moment, at least, he was dependent for his very life on Anthony Strout.

And Strout was sloppy.

36

It was late afternoon when Doohan left the Bay Bridge and took the freeway north to Berkeley and Emeryville. Hanson's main move from Laguna Honda was scheduled for tomorrow but the switchboard at the hospital had told him Suzanne was already over at Endo-Syn. When the operator kept asking who he was, he hung up. A call to Endo-Syn hadn't been any more satisfying. Sorry, the phones to the CDC section weren't installed yet; the holidays had held up work. Dr. Synge would have to be paged. Who was calling, please? He couldn't give his right name, he thought, and Suzanne had never heard of Carl Dobbs. And the lines could be tapped . . .

But he had to see her that night, he thought; time was running out on a number of fronts. He had to know what Hanson was doing . . . and he had to find a hiding place for the ampoules.

A final call to Laguna Honda established that Hanson himself was still there so there was little chance of running into *him* at Endo-Syn.

It was risky; he had no idea what security might be like at Endo-Syn. But the tissue-wrapped ampoules were a dead weight in his pocket. Some time today he would have to find another hiding place, and the choices had rapidly been narrowing down to one. He could rent a safe-deposit box, but that included the signing of forms and the inevitable problem of what to do with the key itself. And it was still the first place a government man might think of looking. Besides, he wanted the ampoules available at all hours, not just during banking hours, depending on the situation in which he found himself. He could leave them at Isaac's house, but that would be placing Isaac in jeopardy and he had already done that, however remotely, with Woodruff. Chances were good that French's house would be paid a visit in any event. . . .

Which left the one person he felt he could trust, who stood completely divorced from the system in which she was working. Suzanne. She was, of course, condemned in Hanson's eyes as well as Strout's because of her friendship with him.

But both of them were aware that he knew that, that to leave the ampoules with Suzanne would strike him as the riskiest thing he could possibly do.

It was, therefore, the most logical. They would never check the one thing they had convinced themselves he wouldn't do. . . .

Endo-Syn was in the southern part of Emeryville, hugging the shore line of the Bay, an enormous complex of four buildings enclosed by cyclone fencing. He parked in the large lot before the two-story Administration Building, topped by a large neon sign spelling out: ENDO-SYN, DIVISION OF BLAKE PHARMACEUTICALS, INC. He cut the engine and felt in his wallet for the Carl Dobbs identification. The photograph wasn't bad—they had retouched out his former mustache—and he had no doubt it would pass muster. How closely they might inspect it, he didn't know. No guards were visible, but there had to be some. . . .

While he was watching, a bus pulled up before the building and a number of men, all in business suits, climbed out. All of them were carrying attaché cases and wearing small enameled pins in their lapels. If memory served, the pin was a model of the tetracycline molecule, the Endo-Syn trademark. Detailmen on a tour of the plant, he decided—the ubiquitous salesmen who waited patiently in a physician's outer office to tout the latest miracle concoction from their laboratories and just incidentally drop a few dozen physician's samples behind. They were a godsend to doctors who worked in the ghettoes and could dispense the free samples.

On impulse, Doohan grabbed his own briefcase and walked over to mingle with the group.

The reception hall of the Endo-Syn was two stories high, with a large circular reception desk where guests were expected to sign in with one of the three uniformed girls who manned it. The walls were covered with massive abstract-impressionist canvases that had obviously been painted specifically for the lobby. Below them were color photographs illustrating different phases of the manufacturing end of the Endo-Syn operation.

Doohan walked up to the girl on his left and shoved his card at her. "Dr. Suzanne Synge, please."

The smile turned on as if he had flicked a switch. "Just a moment, sir." A quick consultation with a bound volume before her and a moment of confusion. "I'm sorry, sir, I don't have a listing for her."

"She's a part of the CDC team that will be moving in tomorrow. I understand she moved over as part of an advance team."

The smile returned. "Major Hanson's research group, that would be Building B, the P-3 facility."

"Could you dial her for me?"

Once again the smile wilted. "The phones won't be connected until tomorrow, sir. I can have her paged, if it's absolutely necessary." Doohan sensed it would be a mistake to insist it was necessary and said, "Thanks anyway, I'll return tomorrow." He retrieved his business card, but the girl didn't seem to notice.

He idly inspected the bank of photo murals on the wall and edged into the group of detailmen again. Company guides were dividing them into sections and Doohan walked over to the closest one and tried his best to look like an enthusiastic Endo-Syn salesman. Nobody seemed to notice him, and a moment later a white-coated youngster had taken the group in tow, making a few introductory remarks about Endo-Syn, and then shepherding them through a rear door into the plant proper.

Once inside, the group was ushered down white, immaculately clean halls lined with large plate-glass windows. On the other side, rotary pelleting machines were turning out, according to their guide, hundreds of tablets per minute of everything from sulfa drugs to birth-control pills. Here, too, there were stretches where the walls were lined with color photographs illustrating Endo-Syn's continuing screening program for antibiotics.

Doohan looked for a chance to break away from the group and see if he could find Suzanne's new office. Once he almost succeeded, but was collared by the stern-faced guide who expressed an official disapproval of "stragglers" and then guided the group into a fermentation building. Here, the guide explained, were massive fermentation vats, constantly aerated, that produced deep fermentation penicillin and tetracycline as well as fermented materials that were further modified to produce such hormones as testosterone and cortisone.

At the entrance to the P-3 facility, the guide brought the tour to an abrupt halt. "This is our high-containment facility—can you hear me back there? It's entered through an airlock and all our workers must wear disposable coveralls. The blowers on top of the building maintain a negative pressure within the facility so that no airborne contaminants can leak out. Upon leaving, all personnel must shed their coveralls, shower with a disinfectant, and expose themselves for one minute to a bank of ultra-violet lights."

They passed by the doors to the P-3 facility to an enclosed ramp that bridged the street and led to another building. They had passed by a bank of offices and Doohan noticed a sign painter stenciling a new name on a glass door. He fell behind and waited a moment for the tour group to round a corner. "Do you know where Dr. Synge's office is?"

The painter smudged an "s," said "Damn!" and glanced up. "Let's see—all the new personnel coming in . . . Synge. Synge—third door on the left." He pointed down the hall.

Doohan knocked once at the door, then pushed it open. Suzanne was sitting behind a desk, studying a

page of figures on a clipboard. She glanced up, her
eyes widening. "Good God, Calvin, what are you doing here?"

He gestured down the corridor. "I came in with a
tour group." Pause. "I wanted to see you." He *did*
want to see her, he thought; he wanted to see her just
about more than anything he had ever wanted. "I was
going to call you Christmas Eve. In case you didn't
have anything planned, I thought you and I and
French . . ." He let it trail off.

She looked away for a moment. "Why don't you call
me this evening? Now you better leave before somebody sees you."

"You don't look glad to see me."

The gray eyes glanced at him intently. "You know
better than that." She hesitated. "Hanson has the police looking for you—or did you know that?"

He should have expected it. "And if they find me
here, you're compromised."

"I'd certainly be no good to you then."

"I better catch up with the tour group." He paused
at the door. "What time tonight?"

"Suppertime." She lowered her voice. "It was a lousy
Christmas without you, Calvin."

He caught up with the tour group, explained apologetically to the put-out tour guide how he had gotten
lost, and ten minutes later they were back in the reception area. The guide started to collect badges and
Doohan casually slipped away to look at the photographs on the near wall and work his way toward the
exit doors. The guide had gotten into an argument
with a detailman from Lincoln, Nebraska, who had
lost his badge, and Doohan guessed he wouldn't be
missed at all. The guide would collect badges and
take a head count and that would be that.

Out in the driveway, he turned and looked at the
sprawling complex of buildings. Back in the city, the
CDC was winding up its work. Their staffs were de-
parting and the whole military staff that Hanson had
brought in would disappear with almost the same
effectiveness tomorrow. The move to Endo-Syn, he
realized, was a masterpiece of public relations. Han-

son and his group would continue their quiet investigation, but the operation would quickly fade from the consciousness of San Francisco reporters. Who cared, really, what happened across the Bay? With typical San Francisco chauvinism, the press would shift its attention to other matters.

His hand touched the bulge of the ampoules in his coat pocket. All at once, they seemed to weigh pounds.

37

Doohan wasn't sure whether Hanson's men would be watching Suzanne's apartment. If Hanson thought she was *that* closely connected with him, he probably wouldn't have taken her along to Endo-Syn. In any event, Hanson couldn't have an inexhaustible supply of security men to watch everybody. . . .

The chances were that she wasn't being watched; it was a risk he had to take. He had to get rid of the ampoules and soon.

Because he had promised to make dinner that night, he stopped at the supermarket to pick up some chicken breasts, a variety of salad lettuces, and a container of yogurt. Fruit and cheese for desert, and two bottles of Mondavi's Chenin Blanc, enough to . . .

Seduce her? He smiled to himself. There was no need of that. There had been invitation in her voice and certainly he was excited at the prospect of seeing her again. The possibility of sex was involved, but she had far more appeal to him than just that. He was attracted by her almost studied independence, and yet she had a vulnerable side. She held herself in reserve —an easy thing to understand in view of her collapsing marriage—but every once in a while, she seemed to drop her defenses and he could sense an uncertainty beneath, an uncertainty that sought for someone to rely upon. He knew she liked him, that indeed it went further than that, that behind her reserve, there was something there for him beyond sex.

When she answered the door, he said, "Take me to the kitchen before I drop all this."

She turned to lead him down the hall. It was a

typical San Francisco railroad flat with the kitchen at the far bend of a long hallway and the bedrooms and living room opening off of it. "I didn't expect you to buy out half of Safeway."

"You've never tasted my cooking."

"That almost sounds like a threat."

He dumped the groceries on the table and automatically pulled her closer for a kiss. She was dressed in startling contrast to the old-fashioned kitchen. She was wearing a white silk dress embroidered with tiny peacocks, cut plain and long in the Chinese style which quietly accented her figure. Her hair was cut short and she wore small, blue-enameled earrings. He hadn't realized her ears were pierced until now. It was a shock to compare her in his mind's eye as she looked now and as she had looked when he had first met her.

"We've only been away a few days," she said, teasing him at the intensity of his kiss. He moved away, almost hurt, and said, "What'd you do for Christmas?"

She busied herself setting the table and taking down the necessary glasses from the cupboard. "What do lonely people usually do on Christmas? I went out to eat, saw a film, came home and watched television. I tried calling; you weren't home."

That was the day he had seen Strout and been taken to the safe house, he thought.

She turned to face him then. "You aren't living there any more, are you?"

He had started to sauté the chicken breasts while she put away the rest of the groceries. "No, I don't," he said briefly. He didn't offer to tell her where he was staying now and she didn't ask. What she didn't know, Hanson could never force her to tell, he thought.

"You bought yogurt," she suddenly said, accusingly.

"It's for a brandy cream sauce, only I substitute yogurt."

She made a face. "I hate yogurt."

"Cream will do, then. Got any?"

"In the fridge. Care for a drink?"

"One cube, lots of scotch."

He opened the refrigerator and paused in dismay.

The vegetable crisper held lettuce that had almost liquefied, it was so old. The shelves themselves were crammed with half-opened cans sealed with plastic wrap and innumerable plastic refrigerator containers filled with bits and dabs of leftovers.

She was suddenly standing by his side with the glass of scotch. "In answer to your unasked question," she said tartly, "neatness in the kitchen has never been one of my virtues. I wasn't born holding a silver frying pan in my hand."

"I didn't say a word," he murmured. He found a carton of half-and-half on the top shelf and decided it would do. He dumped the dishes of leftovers and wilted produce that were beyond saving and washed out the crisper.

"You'll make somebody a great husband," Suzanne said. He almost thought he read contempt in her voice, and then she noticed the look on his face and said, "Don't be so sensitive."

It was toward the end of dinner that she said, "I'm sorry about Paul; I know what good friends you were."

Doohan nodded; there was nothing to say. "Has Hanson talked much about Paul, or myself?" He could feel himself slipping into a black mood.

"He doesn't like you, which should come as no surprise. He's convinced that Paul cultured a virus and that's why he was killed. But they never found his notes." She looked at him expectantly. Again he nodded without saying anything. "The lab log shows that the twelve hamsters are missing." He didn't reply to that either; he had known that Hanson would have to check the log sooner or later.

Suzanne suddenly pushed her plate away, her eyes bitter. "What the hell is going on, Calvin? Hanson and his toady, Gorshin, don't tell me anything; you won't tell me anything. All I know is that it's military and secret and people are being murdered because of it." She paused, challenging him. "Well, do I move to Australia now or later?"

"It wouldn't do much good," Doohan said laconically, angry that the mood of the meal had been broken. Then he realized what he was going to do later and softened. "Hanson interrogated me after French's murder. Yes, Paul cultured the virus. He wanted to finish a complete report for the CDC. But he didn't trust Hanson; he felt that Hanson had used him when Hanson released the nickel-carbonyl theory." He poured himself a glass of wine and leaned back in his chair. "What's important is whether or not Hanson and Gorshin have cultured the virus."

She shook her head. "Not to my knowledge, but I'm not so sure they'd tell me in any event." She looked up at him. "I think Hanson is convinced you have a sample of the viral agent."

He could feel the ampoules burning a hole in his jacket pocket. "I can't help what Hanson thinks."

"He probably thinks you have the hamsters as well."

"They're in a small cage in my bathroom," he said sarcastically.

She played with a piece of chicken on her plate. "You know where they are," she said cautiously.

"Does it matter where they are?"

"You know a lot," she said.

"Why the sudden interest in how much I know?"

She flared up again. "Because I give a damn about you! Because what you know and what you have is dangerous and people will kill you for it! It's completely a military operation; you know that. That's why the move to Endo-Syn. It's out of public sight, it's out of mind. Security can be tighter and Endo-Syn's done government work in the past." She started cleaning off the table. "What about the military interest?" she asked. "You know the answer to that, too, don't you?"

He was suddenly standing up, gripping her shoulders. "The Veterans' Disease was the clandestine test of a new biological warfare weapon. The government's thought that right from the start; that's why Hanson was assigned."

"That's what you think, too?"

"That's what I think, too."

She shook out of his hands and went back to cleaning up. "That's hard to believe—really. Of all the countries in the world the United States is probably the best equipped to handle such an attack. It has the biggest medical system, the biggest and best drug industry . . ."

She was quiet for a long moment, then said, "You would be out of it if you turned everything over to Hanson, wouldn't you?"

"You're assuming that I have everything," he evaded. "If I did, I think I would take it all to Espinosa at the World Health Organization. It's one world, whether you like it or not. When you work with disease, you appreciate that more than most people."

"When I asked," she said quietly, "I was thinking of you. Hanson will do a lot to get hold of your information. And whoever's behind it will do even more to keep it from him."

"Which is probably why I shouldn't tell you much," he said gently. "What you don't know can't hurt you."

She glanced at him contemptuously. "Are you kidding? It's not the knowledge that I have, Calvin; it's the knowledge they'll assume I have."

They cleaned up the kitchen in silence and stacked the dishes in the dishwasher. Once he touched her lightly on the shoulder and she glanced up at him; there was something in her eyes that he couldn't interpret. "Is something wrong?"

Briefly. "Yes. I'm worried about you."

"I can take care of myself."

The brief look of concern flashed across her face again. "Like a small boy in a lion's cage."

Later, they went to bed and lay together without speaking. He held her gently in his arms and she buried her face in his shoulder. She had never before been so quiet or so passive. They hadn't undressed yet, and for once he felt no great hunger or passion. He touched her lightly and she moved slowly but easily toward him. He held her for a moment and thought, my God, I'm falling in love with her.

She was sleeping lightly now, and Doohan stared at the shadows on the ceiling cast by the reading lamp in the living room. Something had been bothering him for days, he thought; an anger had slowly been growing within him. He was tired of being manipulated by Hanson, he was tired of being manipulated by Strout, he was tired of sitting around waiting for the ax to fall from parties unknown.

With or without Strout, he'd look into the matter of Guitterez. And then he'd check once again into why Dr. Roy French had been collecting blood for the blood bank. From what Paul had to say, his brother Roy was anything but an altruist. Why the change? And it was time to check back with Woodruff and see how the hamsters were coming along. And God help them all if they turned out as he suspected. . . .

He jerked awake in near darkness, the curtains ruffling slightly in the breeze from the partially open window. He was faintly chilled and his arm felt numb where Suzanne's head had cut off circulation. He gently disengaged his arm and glanced at his watch. It was four in the morning. He turned to look at Suzanne's quiet face. She looked very peaceful and very exotic in the shadowy light from the reading lamp. For a moment he thought of Lilith, and then wondered why that reference. The soul within was absent and all he could see was a blank innocence. . . .

He slipped quietly out of bed, gently drew a coverlet over Suzanne and walked out into the living room to find his coat. He took the glass ampoules out of his coat pocket and considered them for a long moment. But there could be no changing of plans; there was no alternative that was as practical.

He walked into the kitchen, closing the door after him so the light wouldn't show, and quietly opened the refrigerator door. Odd, he thought, the precise plan had occurred to him hours before when he was preparing dinner. He took the yogurt container over to the sink and opened it, then stripped the tissue from the two ampoules and thrust them deep into the yogurt until they sank from sight.

He returned the carton of yogurt to the bottom shelf, masking it with containers of jam and mustard and salad dressing. There was no doubt it would be safe. Suzanne never cleaned the refrigerator; for the next week or so, she'd probably never run across the yogurt and she certainly wouldn't use it if she found it. Even if somebody searched the apartment, the chances of their finding the ampoules would be vanishingly remote.

He turned to leave and then hesitated at the kitchen door. To a certain extent, he was fooling himself. For no other reason than that she knew him, Suzanne was in danger. But there was no helping that now. Whether or not he hid the vials there would make no difference. If Suzanne were to be damned, it would be because she had been friendly with him in the first place.

And he had no choice, not really. He couldn't keep the ampoules in his apartment and he couldn't carry them with him.

Besides, if what was at stake was more important than his life, it was equally true that it was almost more important than Suzanne's.

But somehow the thought didn't make him feel any better.

38

"Look in the glove compartment," Strout said.

Doohan pressed the button and the door fell open, banging his knee. He rummaged around in the interior and pulled out a tan leather holster holding a Smith and Wesson .32 with a mottled brown plastic grip, its side scored like a rasp. "Put it on," Strout commanded. "It's a shoulder-loop holster."

"You don't think Mr. Guitterez will be glad to see us?"

"Hardly. At the very least, I don't think he'll be cooperative. We may have to persuade him." He swung onto the Hayward turnoff from the Nimitz Freeway. "It's also for protection. I have no idea what we may run into. It's best to be prepared."

Strout was calling the shots, Doohan thought. It apparently wouldn't have made much difference if he had come along or not.

"Do you have any plans for what we'll do when we get there?"

Strout shrugged. "Play it by ear."

Melrose Foods was in the industrial part of town, a collection of warehouses and loading docks and small factories made of concrete block and corrugated aluminum siding. A few had rusting railroad tracks threading past the docks, long since converted to truck use. The Melrose Foods plant was relatively small, a sprawling warehouse and a smaller and newer brick structure. They pulled up in one of the executive parking spaces and a workman on the docks yelled, "Hey, you can't park there. Company cars only."

Strout rolled down the window. "We're looking for Guitterez."

The workman hopped off the docks and strolled over. Wiry, white-haired, in his late fifties. He had probably worked for Melrose since it had opened, Doohan thought. The man spat on the ground and leaned on the car to get a good look inside. "Well, you won't find Ramon; he didn't come in today."

"Who are you?" Strout asked.

"Foreman. When Ramon or his partner aren't around, I'm in charge. There's an office manager inside, but hell, he don't know nothing."

Doohan fumbled for one of his cards and passed it over. The foreman took it, read it carefully and grew a shade more deferential. He rubbed his chin and finally reached a decision. "Ramon's been home almost all last week. He's been taking a lot of time off since his wife died. Doesn't even come in at night to work now."

"He worked a lot at night?"

"In the formula lab. He worked up all the formulas we use; doubled our billing since he took it over."

"When was that?" Strout asked.

"About a year and a half ago." The foreman was suddenly suspicious. "He doesn't owe you fellows money, does he?"

Strout shook his head. "We're just trying to trace a lost shipment. It's very important. Do you have his address?"

The foreman gave them a searching look, then shrugged. "You fellows look all right to me; besides, it's in the phone book." He took out a small address book, thumbed through the pages, and read them the street number. "Don't tell Ramon I sent you. Like I said, he's pretty cut up about his wife."

It was Doohan who asked, "How did she die?"

"Doctors said pneumonia. It really came on strong: Took her in less'n three days."

The Guitterez house was in a middle-class neighborhood of redwood board and lathe construction with shake roofs, each house almost the twin of its neighbor. The one thing that set Guitterez's house apart from the others was the towering palms in the front yard, contrasting with the houses on either side, which favored Monterey pines or silk oaks. The driveway was a shining new blacktop, suggesting that it had been recently resurfaced.

Strout parked; they walked up the sidewalk and Doohan pressed the bell. After five minutes, he tried again. "Don't bother," Strout said, pointing. Beneath a bush to one side of the door were two daily papers and the Sunday edition, thoroughly soaked by the sprinklers. "Our distraught friend has apparently left town."

"I'm not so sure," Doohan said. He peered in through the living room window but there was no sign of life. He circled the house while Strout waited out front. In the kitchen, dishes were piled in the sink and an open loaf of bread lay on the counter; two slices next to it had dried sufficiently to curl. Through the bedroom window, he could see a rumpled, unmade bed.

He passed the garage on the way back to join Strout and noticed that the overhead door was slightly ajar. He grabbed the handle, tugged at it and the door rolled up. Inside was a '75 Olds Cutlass. The man behind the wheel was slumped over and Doohan guessed that he was dead.

"Strout!" The agent came running and they opened the car door. The man inside was small, rather obese, and would have had an olive complexion if it hadn't been for the discoloration from carbon monoxide poisoning. Doohan glanced at the dash. The ignition key was turned on but the lights were dead. He touched the body. From the looseness of the muscles, Doohan knew he had been dead longer than twenty-four hours. Rigor mortis had come and gone.

Doohan glanced quickly around the garage and then back at the body in the front seat. He could feel a chill at the back of his neck. "The foreman said he had been depressed about his wife."

Strout had been watching over his shoulder. "I'm afraid that's what we're supposed to think, old man. But it wasn't suicide, it was murder."

"How can you be so sure?"

"It's set up," Strout said slowly, "to look as though Guitterez drove in, probably drunk, closed the door with his radio-transmitter, then passed out with the motor running and died of carbon monoxide poisoning. The autopsy will probably find a heavy percentage of alcohol in his bloodstream."

"So what makes it murder?"

Strout felt alongside the body and pulled out a small rounded plastic box with a single button. He pointed at the ceiling. "The door's radio-actuated. The overhead chain runs in a continuous loop that engages a lever that opens the door. Watch." He pressed the button and from somewhere overhead a motor began to turn. The chain went through a full cycle but the door remained opened. "The door's disengaged from the motorized chain; somebody had to close it manually. There's a button on the wall by the steps over there but my guess is that it's too far from the garage door for you to press it and still get out before the door closes. Somebody probably doped up poor Guitterez, drove him in here, then disengaged the door from the automatic closing chain and shut it manually from outside."

"You're quite a detective," Doohan murmured.

"It goes with the territory," Strout said quietly. "Though the fact that Guitterez was murdered comes as no surprise. Now let's get out of here before some nosy neighbor calls the police."

"Not yet," Doohan objected. "Come inside and close the garage door."

Once the door was closed, Doohan turned on the overhead lights and looked around. There was an oil-stained toolbox in the corner, along with a few garden tools. He rummaged around, found a crowbar, and set the pry between the door to the house and the jam just above the lock.

"What the hell are you doing?" Strout asked.

Doohan pushed. On the second attempt, the flimsy

paneled door bowed and popped outwards as the latch pulled out of the frame. "Dead men sometimes do tell tales."

The kitchen was separated by a breakfast bar from the inevitable California family room, furnished with a rattan sofa and a chair in a bright floral print and a large console color television set. On the wall above the set was a series of framed photographs. In many Doohan saw a smiling Guitterez with his arm around the same plump, jovial-looking woman. They formed a series in time, he thought; both Guitterez and his wife had put on weight through the years and Guitterez had gradually grown bald. Several of the photos showed a younger, leaner Guitterez in army uniform. One showed him with the stripes of a Technician Fifth Class while another showed him wearing the bars of either a first or second lieutenant.

The living room was a repeat of the family room, crowded with brightly upholstered overstuffed chairs and sofa. Here again there were photographs of Guitterez and his wife on the walls or in frames standing on the end tables. The couple in the standard pose in front of the Arc de Triomphe; leaning against a highway sign that read FIFTY MILES TO PALM SPRINGS; in ski togs at Aspen.

It was always the same basic photograph: Guitterez with his arm around his wife and both of them looking at each other with obvious affection.

Strout studied the photographs for a moment. "They certainly didn't hate each other, did they?"

A den opened off the living room, and Doohan walked in and sat at the desk. Pushed against the wall was a large stack of Christmas cards and he quickly thumbed through them. The only name he recognized was that of Laval.

He quickly riffled through the drawers, then pulled open the deep file drawer on the left. Inside were a number of manila file folders, all of them carefully labeled. He leafed curiously through them, noting that most were completely trivial. There was even a folder for grocery receipts.

He was about to close it when right in front, he

noted two folders labeled "VAW" and "ELKS." The VAW folder contained a receipt for a "special formula" mayonnaise from Melrose Foods, signed by Laval. Included was a copy of the convention program, a receipt for hotel reservations for two, two torn banquet tickets and a "thank you" note from the local VAW commander for helping set up the convention. The ELKs' file was similar.

But there had been no record of their attending the Elks' convention, Doohan thought. He looked quickly through the few sheets of paper, which included a note from the local Lodge Convention Chairman thanking Guitterez for helping procure the hotel reservations and inviting him to look in on the convention. Everything would be open but the organizational meetings.

So that was it, Doohan thought. Guitterez hadn't been a member but he had helped with the arrangements, probably because he was a personal friend of the chairman—or because he had been assigned to do it as part of his role in the plot. Doohan turned the page, paused, then picked up the remaining items and held them under the desk lamp. Strout crowded closer. "Two tickets to the banquet," Doohan said quietly. "He and his wife attended both banquets."

Strout frowned. "It doesn't make sense. She died; he didn't."

"Maybe he didn't eat salad," Doohan said slowly. "But he allowed his wife to do so, a woman to whom he was obviously devoted."

"Perhaps he wasn't as devoted to her now as he once was. Maybe it was an easy way to get rid of her."

Doohan shook his head. "You're reaching. The foreman said he was broken up about her death. And everything we've seen here indicates they were close. I think the answer is more obvious. He wasn't aware of the sensitizing effects of the first exposure."

"But Guitterez was at the heart of the plot," Strout objected. "You're telling me that he didn't know two exposures would kill?"

"That's exactly what I'm telling you."

Strout sat down, confused. "You mean they never intended the damned virus to kill anybody in the first place?"

"That's right," Doohan said. "They all handled it with relative impunity—Roy French, who collected the blood from the conventions; Cedric Laval, who served up the salads with the mayonnaise on them, and Ramon Guitterez, who had provided the virus-laden mayonnaise to begin with. None of them really knew what they were dealing with."

The plotters, Doohan mused. Roy French, who had suddenly suffered a personality change of some kind eighteen months before. "Pops" Laval, who had been able to spend an amazing amount of money on his childlike wife. And Ramon Guitterez, who had bought Melrose Foods—again, eighteen months before.

Who had they been working for? Which foreign country?

"Dr. French died of the disease but you don't know for sure he was a . . . plotter," Strout said.

Forgive me, Paul, Doohan thought to himself. "I'd bet on it. He died because he ran afoul of the occupational hazards of collecting the virus-laden blood twice."

"None of what you're saying explains why Ramon Guitterez was murdered."

"Of course it does. The man had inadvertently killed his own wife, a woman he loved above all else. He must have been close to the breaking point, probably ready to go to the authorities and confess. He was probably killed to shut him up."

"And Laval?"

" 'Pops' Laval wouldn't have hurt a fly," Doohan said with disgust. "His wife said he was depressed— and why shouldn't he be? He must have known he was partially responsible for the deaths of dozens of people. The police found him without a mark on him. My guess is that it was suicide from remorse."

Doohan got up from the desk. "The fact is, all of

them were probably as shocked as anybody else at the outbreak of the Veterans' Disease."

Strout didn't move. "Doctor," he said quietly, "if they didn't intend the virus to kill, just what did they intend it to do?"

39

"WHEN YOU WERE assigned to me," Hanson said angrily, "they assured me you knew your business."

Roberts looked uncomfortable. "There's no way you can guard against all contingencies."

"As a security man, you're supposed to be a professional," Hanson said in a silken voice. "Doohan is not a professional. Your men followed him downtown and then he gave them the slip. For an amateur he's doing rather well."

"We staked out his car and his apartment; he's never returned to either."

"He just dropped into thin air," Hanson said sarcastically.

"He probably had help," Roberts suggested cautiously. "We know he visited the British embassy in Washington."

"And made some kind of alliance with them?"

"He's a British national. And we know the British have an organization in this country."

"Put a man on Dr. Synge's apartment. Chances are good that he'll show up there sooner or later. If he does—" Hanson broke off, an idea occurring to him.

It was Gorshin who spoke next. "You consider Dr. Doohan a threat to national security?"

"Of course." He didn't much like Gorshin, a feeling that hadn't changed at all in the two weeks he had known him. A cold, flabby, fat man who hid his disdain for lesser intellects behind his thick glasses. Hanson would have bet that Gorshin didn't consider ten people on the planet his intellectual equal.

"You think, perhaps, he could be an observer for the enemy as well as for WHO?"

The "enemy," Hanson thought. How concrete, how definite it sounded when it was spoken. And how vague it was in reality. What enemy? Who?

"Doohan is dangerous not for what he might say; he's dangerous for what he can prove."

Gorshin took off his glasses to polish them. The change was startling; without them he seemed oddly defenseless, almost avuncular. "I'm not sure I follow you."

"We don't know who the 'enemy' is," Hanson explained patiently. "I don't think that Doohan does either. But if he publicizes that this was a BW warfare test—and proves it—then every country in the world will have to consider the possibility that any epidemic that comes along has been planned with malice aforethought. Countries are like individuals; most of them are paranoid. There are more than a hundred and fifty nations in the world, which is the same as saying there are a hundred and fifty potential enemies out there. That kind of situation could escalate to a different kind of warfare very quickly."

"Just for the record," Roberts said, "when we find Doohan, you want us to pick him up?"

"No," Hanson said quickly, making up his mind. "I don't. I want him watched very carefully. The people who developed the virus in the first place will also be looking for Doohan. I want to find Doohan first. He leaned back in his chair and tapped his pencil on the desk. "And then I want him left out there as bait."

Gorshin looked uneasy. "Dr. Doohan said that Dr. French had cultured the virus, which means it must have been some place in his laboratory."

Hanson nodded, wondering what the fat man was driving at. "That's right."

"We can assume that Dr. French's murderers were looking for it," Gorshin continued. He had a classroom style of talking that annoyed Hanson even more. "From the completeness of the destruction of the laboratory, we can assume they never found it—or they didn't find it until the very last."

"There's the matter of time," Hanson said, still wondering what Gorshin was driving at. "There were thousands of bottles in that laboratory; they didn't have the time to inspect each one."

"I've had the time," Gorshin said dryly. "There was no container of culture in Dr. French's laboratory. If the murderers didn't find it, then the most logical suspect would be the man who first found the body."

"We interrogated Doohan," Hanson said. "He wasn't carrying anything with him."

Gorshin blinked at him through his thick glasses and asked quietly, "Was he searched? The virus could have been kept in a very small ampoule. There are several places on the human body where he could have hidden it."

"No, he wasn't searched," Hanson said heavily.

Gorshin nodded, looking oddly like a bullfrog behind his glasses. "Dr. French was quite friendly with Dr. Doohan. I believe Dr. Doohan knew everything that Dr. French was doing. He knew he cultured the virus, and I think he knew how the virus was cultured."

"You're suggesting?"

"I think it would be a mistake to let Dr. Doohan run free once we locate him. I think we ought to pick him up immediately. If we hesitate, we risk losing both the culture and his knowledge."

Hanson cursed quietly to himself. Gorshin was trying to back him into a corner where whatever decision he made stood a good chance of being the wrong one. "Your reasoning has only one flaw in it, Doctor. Doohan didn't create the virus and he wasn't responsible for its dissemination. He's an annoyance, not a villain." Gorshin looked slightly discomfited and Hanson felt oddly pleased. "In the meantime, what do you think your chances are of isolating the virus?"

Gorshin was once again remote and impregnable. "I've developed some analytical techniques that should give us an answer directly from the tissue samples we have. Unfortunately, the disease has burned itself out—there are no victims left with whom we can work; the mortality rate has been a hundred per cent."

The man always used double-talk, Hanson thought, wishing he'd had a background in biology. "I hope you're more successful than the CDC has been."

Gorshin stood up to leave. "The CDC?" His tone of voice suggested his opinion of the CDC. "They're hamstrung by routine. I'm sure we can bring a fresh approach to the problem."

He lumbered out and Hanson stared after him. "The members of the priesthood—they're insufferable," he murmured.

"They claim he's a brilliant man," Roberts said.

"I'm sure he'd be the first to agree with that opinion." Hanson opened a file on his desk. "I'll be going East for two days. I want you to find Doohan by the time I get back."

Roberts looked unhappy once more. "We'll do our best."

"About the murder of French—any leads?"

Roberts shook his head. "None. The police picked up Anderson; he hadn't been in the laboratory since that afternoon. That evening he spent at a beer party. That's been confirmed by a dozen people, including the girl he spent the night with."

"It's too bad Kovacs—"

"We haven't contacted her yet," Roberts interrupted. "I think she'll be the more productive of the two."

Hanson stared grimly at Roberts and tapped his fingers slowly on the desk. "When's the last time you talked with the local police or your FBI contacts?"

Roberts flushed. "I haven't had time to get to them this morning; I was going to do so right after this meeting."

Hanson took a yellow teletype sheet from the file folder and slid it across the desk. "Celia Kovacs' body was found in the trunk of a rented car in Dayton, Ohio, this morning. There was no evidence of rape. No leads. A neighbor reports she left the house in midafternoon with a man, apparently voluntarily."

Roberts took the sheet and read it. When he glanced up at Hanson, he looked whipped. "We didn't get to her soon enough," he said. "We don't have enough men."

There was no point in chewing out Roberts again, Hanson thought; it could become a lifetime occupation. "Do better with our good doctor. He's had help; I want to know who helped him. And leave him out there. If anybody tries to jump him, get them. Do so even if you have to sacrifice Doohan. They're the ones we really want."

"We'll be picking up Doohan eventually, right?"

"That's a problem?"

Roberts wet his lips. "What do we do once we have him? We can hardly let him go; we can't let him babble to the world."

"You have an idea," Hanson said sarcastically.

"We could hold him under general sedation in a controlled hospital."

"Forever?" Roberts was driving at something and Hanson was curious what it was. "You have another suggestion?"

Roberts was defiant now. "I think we could probably hold him as long as we wished. But there's another way—"

"Which is?"

"In Nam we called it 'termination with extreme prejudice.'"

Hanson shuffled the papers back into the file folder. He was afraid to look up for fear Roberts would read his face. His voice was brittle. "Just find Doohan and then do exactly as I've told you. Any deviation from my orders will have to come from a higher source than me."

"Time's running out," Roberts said. He sounded almost cheerful about it.

After he had left, Hanson stared at the door and wondered what the Army was coming to. "Terminate with extreme prejudice." Had the world changed that much or had it always been like that? he wondered. And to think there was a time he had liked the murderous little fool.

But Roberts was right about one thing.

Time *was* running out.

40

BACK IN HIS apartment, Doohan dropped his coat on the living room sofa and made the rounds of the small traps he had planted before leaving: a match balanced on the hinge of the bedroom door, a tiny strip of paper leaning against the bottom of the kitchen door, a couple of toothpicks on the tops of windows. None of them had been disturbed.

He walked back into the living room and sank into the easy chair, fumbling for the tobacco pouch in his pocket. It was then he noticed the white signal flag on the phone message machine. He rewound the tape. Only one message, and it had to have been from Suzanne.

When he played it back, a tinny replica of Woodruff's voice came from the speaker. "Calvin, I got your number from your lady friend. It's about your pregnant hamsters." Even with the poor fidelity of the machine, he could sense the excitement in Woodruff's voice. "They've aborted, damnedest thing I've ever seen. You've got to see for your—" The thirty-second message time was up and Woodruff was cut off.

Doohan played the tape back once more. He had been planning to call Woodruff about the hamsters anyway. But they weren't even at half-term; the births weren't due for days yet. He had been expecting something, but spontaneous abortions hadn't been among the possibilities. He dialed Woodruff's number and the operator's voice came on after half a dozen rings. *Sorry, the number you have dialed is temporarily out of order.* . . . He'd drive out to South San Francisco and see for himself what had made Woodruff so excited, he thought. It wasn't like Alex . . . and there was no telling when the phone line would be working.

It was getting dark when Doohan took the cut-off to Woodruff's house. Half a mile away, he could smell the sweet-sour odor of burned wood and smoldering charcoal. Then he took a left turn and could see the smudge of smoke and the tangle of hoses that crossed the street. A police car was parked at the intersection, blocking traffic. In the middle of the block was a hook-and-ladder and a pumper and the chief's red car. A hundred yards ahead, Woodruff's house and the laboratory behind it were smoking ruins of scorched wood and blackened cinder block. The flames were out and several firemen were poking through the ruins with their pulldown hooks.

Doohan felt sick. *Oh, my God . . .* He parked and ran toward the house. A policeman caught his arm as he passed the patrol car. "What's the hurry, mister?"

Doohan shook him off. "I'm a friend of the family. . . ." He thought he heard the policeman say, "Poor bastard," and then he was working his way through the cluster of fifty spectators lining the edge of the lawn and watching the firemen comb through the embers. Off to one side, nearer the house, was a small knot of people including the fire chief, several children, and a woman in a bathrobe. Heather and the kids. For the moment, at least, Doohan couldn't bring himself to go over to see them.

The fire chief left the group to go back to his car and Doohan intercepted him. "I'm a friend of the family—how are they? How's Alex?" It was going to be Alex, he thought, agonized. It had to be.

"Didn't catch the name . . . Doohan? Doctor, huh? They could use one." He pumped Doohan's hand once. "Goodman, Dan Goodman. Oldest boy's in the hospital, third-degree burns and smoke inhalation. Tried to get his father out." He took off his helmet and ran his fingers through thinning hair, glancing back at the family. "What the hell do you tell them, anyway? I'm not a priest . . ."

"To get his father out?" Doohan repeated stupidly.

"He was working in the lab." There was a sudden question in Goodman's eyes. "Could you identify the body for us? His wife did, but we could use corroboration. The boys are too young to see this."

Doohan followed him over to a tarpaulin-covered heap on the ground. "How did it start?"

"Arson; you could smell the kerosene. The family had been waiting dinner for him for about half an hour when they caught the stink of the smoke. The lab went up first and then the house caught. Lucky they got out."

"How come Alex didn't?"

"Murder—see for yourself." He nodded at a near-by rookie who knelt down and whipped aside the canvas. "Hold it up more so the man can get a good look." Doohan bent closer. The smell was different now, the sweetish odor of burned flesh mixed with that of charcoal. Goodman pointed at the figure's back. "You can see the remains of the electrical wiring where they bound him hand and foot; I assume he was gagged as well. The family claimed they heard somebody drive up around four o'clock; they didn't think anything of it. Whoever it was went right to the lab. They assumed it was somebody on business; that's why they waited so long before calling him for supper. By then, it was too late."

Doohan stood up and the fire chief looked at him sharply. "Woodruff?"

"It'll take a dental chart to be positive, but I'm pretty sure. Even . . . like that."

Goodman unbuttoned his slicker and took a notebook from his shirt pocket. "I'll need your full name and address for the police."

Doohan hesitated, then shrugged and gave his right name and the address of his old apartment. He'd be gone before they started checking it, if they ever did. "All right to talk to the family?"

Goodman glanced over at the little group still huddled under a eucalyptus tree on the lawn. "They're not taking it too well; the gawkers aren't helping any. But I imagine they'd be kind of glad to talk to you."

Doohan walked over. Heather was dry-eyed but she looked in shock; the two small boys clung to her bathrobe and were still crying. "We never heard a thing over the intercom, Calvin," Heather mused, her eyes looking at something just past him. "I was frying up a chicken and I had even made a cake and we never heard a thing . . . just the sound of the car driving up. An hour later we smelled smoke and Ralph went out to see what was wrong." She was twisting her handkerchief, desperately ·fighting for composure. "They took Ralph to the hospital; bad smoke inhalation."

She turned to look at the smoldering heap of cinder blocks that had been the laboratory. "Before the ambulance took him away, Ralph said his father was already dead." Her voice had started to fade away. "That was a blessing. They asked me to identify him and I'd hate to think he died . . . like that."

She turned back to Doohan, her eyes coming to a slow focus on his face. "Why would anybody want him dead, Calvin? He said he was working on something secret for you, but it couldn't have been that, could it? You wouldn't have asked him to risk his life, would you?" She was talking in a flat monotone, her empty eyes pinning him so he couldn't make excuses and walk away. "You were always good friends, Calvin. I can't imagine you'd put his life in danger." She shook her head. There was no change in the inflection of her voice. "I couldn't ever forgive you if I thought you had."

Doohan looked down at her, feeling the sweat start to run under his collar. "I don't know who did it, Heather. But I'll do my damnedest to find out."

He turned to walk away then, feeling her eyes following him, questioning his innocence. He wasn't sure how they had found Woodruff but it probably hadn't been too difficult. They could have followed him on his first visit or just knowing that Woodruff was connected with him in the rat survey, if they guessed he had the hamsters, they might also have guessed that he had taken them to Woodruff's for safekeeping. It would have been a logical deduction.

When he had asked for Woodruff's help, he had signed his friend's death warrant.

Doohan jammed his hands in his pockets and walked slowly around the smoldering ruins of the laboratory. He'd do his penance later, he thought bleakly. All the rest of his life . . .

He forced his mind back to Woodruff's phone call. What had excited Alex so much about the hamsters aborting? What did he think Doohan should see for himself? Whatever it was, there was no chance now; the hamsters were so much charcoal along with Woodruff's notes. And Woodruff himself wouldn't be answering any questions.

He was at the back of the building now, watching the firemen still poking around in the debris, separating smoldering pieces of wood and spraying any suspicion of a tiny blaze. The loading dock had survived far better than the building proper and Doohan guessed the wind had blown the flames away from it. A fireman was dragging a hose along the length of it when he stumbled and knocked a plastic garbage can off the dock. The lid fell off and the can rolled toward Doohan, spilling its contents as it rolled.

He stopped it with his foot and set it upright, then suddenly hesitated. There was a gleam of black plastic on top and he glanced at it, then picked it up. The black plastic backing from a Polaroid photograph, the part you peeled off after you had waited the required sixty seconds. A black-and-white shot with the plastic backing carrying the picture in negative. Doohan gave it a fast inspection, then quickly searched the contents of the can and along the ground for any more backing strips.

He found nine backing strips in all, the negative picture showing dimly in the dusk. He carefully put them in his pocket. Nobody was watching and probably nobody would care, he thought.

Nobody except Hanson and Espinosa and Strout and the people who had murdered French and Woodruff.

He thought for a moment of going back to say good-by to Heather and the kids and then decided against it. The accusation in her eyes had been more than he could take. He walked back to his car and once inside, turned on the dome light and pulled the backing strips from his pocket. The photographs themselves had undoubtedly been destroyed in the fire, but he was sure he could make new positives from the negative backing strips.

Doohan held them up to the light, tilting them so he could get the best view possible. Even in the dim light of the car, he could make out mid-term animal embryos floating in some liquid-filled containers. Probably the tops of Petri dishes.

Who was it who said that ontogeny recapitulates phylogeny? he thought with growing excitement. Depending on the stage of development, all mammalian embryos resembled each other to a more or less greater degree. But these looked like nothing he had ever seen before.

Each and every one of them was monstrously deformed.

41

It took Doohan nearly an hour to find a commercial photographer on Polk who was open and who had any idea what he wanted. In the shop, the man took the backing strips, looked at them critically, and said, "Can't guarantee you a thing. Same size prints? Come back Friday; I might have something for you then."

Doohan didn't move. "I'd like them in an hour—less if you can possibly do it."

The photographer looked disgusted. "Why do I get all the whackos? Not a chance, mister; nobody—"

Doohan pulled fifty dollars from his wallet and laid the bills on the counter. "A set of eight-by-ten glossies by Friday; same size prints in an hour or less?"

The man took the money tentatively. "It'll take at least an hour, and I can't guarantee results. This isn't the sort of thing we do every day. Wait next door at the coffee shop."

In the restaurant, Doohan ordered coffee and sat in a rear booth, out of sight of the street itself. Woodruff was gone, he thought grimly, but there was little he could do about that now. A sense of guilt that he would carry the rest of his life and maybe some day the chance of exacting retribution . . .

But in an hour he would pick up the final bit of proof and then he would have to decide just what he was going to do with it. Espinosa? The British? Turn it over to everybody at once? But that meant Espinosa again. And for all its faults, the UN was the forum in which the United States first accused the Russians of shipping missiles to Cuba. . . .

An hour and three cups of coffee later he went back to the photographer's shop. The clerk shrugged when he pushed over the envelope of prints. "That's the best I could do. Better than that you'd have to take them to Polaroid itself."

Doohan opened the package and fanned out the photos quickly in the light. The edges of the Petri lids showed and he estimated the range in size of the hamster fetuses from one centimeter to as much as three, none of them really close to full term. Each had aborted because of a variety of malformations . . . failure of the brain vesicles to close, lack of bilateral fusion, organs external to the body . . .

"Pretty ugly set of photographs," the clerk said tentatively. "Something medical?"

"I'm a doctor," Doohan said shortly. He discarded the envelope and slipped the pictures into his wallet. "Thanks a lot."

He could sense the clerk staring after him as he left. "Yeah, sure, come again, Doc. Always glad to help the profession."

Doohan ate supper farther up on Polk, and it was well after ten when he returned to his apartment on Noe Street. He parked the car in the driveway, then stood in the recessed doorway and fumbled for his key in the dark. Something was ticking in the back of his mind, but he ignored it; he was dead tired and whatever it was, he'd think about it in the morning.

He opened the door and walked in, closing the door behind him. His hand was on the light switch when he suddenly remembered what he should have recalled outside. He had left the outside light on earlier that evening. It could have burned out, but chances were he had a . . .

Visitor.

He reached for the gun in his shoulder holster, then cursed silently to himself. He had left it in the top bureau drawer just before leaving for Woodruff's. He quickly moved to one side of the door now, his breathing shallow and his ears straining to catch any possible sound.

Nothing.

He edged toward the bedroom and then he heard it: the faint creak of a complaining floor board in the kitchen as somebody shifted his weight. He went into an automatic crouch, staring at the kitchen window outlined by the light from a street lamp.

Another creak from the kitchen floor, this time slightly nearer the door to the living room. He still had a chance, Doohan thought, but that depended on how long his guest had been there. If he had been there only a short time, the gun might still be in the bureau. He sidled toward the bedroom door, carefully feeling in front of him for any obstacles. He was crouching low now to avoid silhouetting himself against the French doors that opened out on the small courtyard garden. His muscles were complaining; he hadn't frog-walked since his days in the Army.

Then it was his floor's turn to creak.

Instantly, a figure was outlined against the dim rectangle of the kitchen window. Doohan had an impression of a raised arm, and then there was a flash of fire and a hissing *thupp!* as something slammed into the wall behind him. He flattened to the floor and rolled toward the bedroom door. Silencers, he thought inanely. It would be rigged afterward to make it look as though he had interrupted a burglary.

The shadow had moved into the living room now; Doohan could make it out as his eyes adjusted. There was another *thupp!* and he realized he couldn't make it to the bedroom. He scrambled for safety behind the living room sofa. Somewhere he could hear a window shatter.

He was trapped, he thought sickly. He couldn't get to the bedroom and he couldn't make it back to the front door and the relative safety of the street. He felt around in the darkness for something he could use as a club. A dozen feet away, he could hear the quiet breathing of his would-be assassin as the man crept closer.

Suddenly the whole room erupted in confusion.

The back door exploded inward and there were the sounds of somebody running across the kitchen floor. Then the glass in the front door was smashed in and a moment later the door flew open violently as another figure plunged in. The intruder was caught in the middle; rapid fire blazed from all three silencers, small flashes of flame from both the kitchen and the front door.

The man in the middle was running back toward the kitchen now, firing as he went. He ran into a low end table, knocked it over, and stumbled for a moment, then was framed for a second in the kitchen doorway. There were two silent *thupps!* and the figure exploded backward into the kitchen, slamming into the gas stove and sliding to the floor. It didn't move.

"Dead hit," a voice said casually. The living room lights came on and Tony Strout was looking down at Doohan behind the sofa. "You all right, Doctor?. Nothing hurt aside from your dignity?" He put out his hand and helped Doohan to his feet.

"That was good timing," Doohan said, his voice shaky.

Strout shook his head. "Actually, it was very bad timing. A few minutes later and I'm afraid that would have been you scattered all over your kitchen floor." He raised his voice. "Mark, see if any of the neighbors are up and about—we don't want the police showing up." He turned back to Doohan. "I doubt that anybody will get excited. It's the time of year for firecrackers and in this part of town, there are always lovers' quarrels. I don't think anybody will raise a fuss."

"You got here fast," Doohan said.

"Mark and I take turns watching you. I was just coming here to relieve him. Lucky for you—one man alone might not have been so fortunate."

Mark, a small, almost wizened man who looked like a London cab driver, came back in. "Nobody seems disturbed. I think there's a police show on the telly; that would have been cover enough."

"Very good." Strout nodded toward the kitchen.

"Get *him* out of here—rear door and to the car. He's a drunken friend, if you run into anybody."

Doohan watched, almost hypnotized, as Mark went into the kitchen and grabbed the corpse under the arms, opened the door and dragged him through it, closing the door after him.

Strout stood up. "I think you ought to take inventory, Doctor. I don't know how long he was here and I suspect he did more than merely wait for you to show."

Strout was right. The bedroom had been thoroughly ransacked, the drawers thrown up and what little clothing there was strewn about. Even the tubes of toothpaste and shaving cream had been slit open. Doohan noted that with a sinking feeling. They knew what they were looking for now.

The cushions on the living room sofa and the easy chair had been cut open; and in the kitchen, the entire contents of the refrigerator had ended in the sink. Oddly, the intruder couldn't have been there long; the ice cubes that clogged the drain had only partially melted.

Mark came back in and Strout nodded toward the front door. "Why don't you wait in the car, Mark? I'd like to talk to Dr. Doohan alone for a moment." After he had left, Strout walked into the kitchen and put on a kettle of water. "Tea? Better than a tranquilizer to soothe the shattered nerves."

Doohan nodded and Strout came back and spread out on the sofa. Unlike the first time he had met Strout, Doohan thought, the man looked very big— and very tough.

"You've been watching me ever since I moved in here?"

"Courtesy of Her Majesty's Government—and one or two others. My God, man, you don't think we're going to let you run around free, do you? You wouldn't last twenty-four hours out there alone."

There was the whistle of the tea kettle and Strout went back to the kitchen to pour two cups. Once back on the sofa, he studied Doohan for a long moment, then said quietly: "Let's be serious, Doctor. If you stay in the United States, you're going to be murdered. You were lucky—and so were we. None of us might be so lucky the next time." He hesitated. "I know they got your friend Woodruff."

Doohan was suddenly suspicious. "How'd you know that?"

"The wonders of communication; I heard it on the car radio."

"Killing me won't help them recover the culture."

Strout looked thoughtful. "That may be so. But then again, we don't know what kind of time schedule they're playing with. After a certain time, recovery of the culture becomes academic. You've hidden it, and presumably you're the only one who can find it. It may be enough simply to remove you and let the culture stay hidden." He smiled slightly. "Not a pleasant thought, but it would accomplish exactly the same end."

Strout tasted his tea and went back to the kitchen for the sugar bowl. "There are other alternatives. If Hanson finds out where you are, you'll be picked up immediately—and I don't think that you would see the light of day again. You would grow to a very ripe old age—under continuous government surveillance. I doubt that there would be any time when they would consider it safe to let you go. This is, perhaps the freest of all countries, Doctor; but it's happened to others."

"You're about to make a recommendation."

Strout nodded. "Of course. The same one I've always made. Over the river and through the woods to Canada you go. We can get you out without any trouble. Entering and leaving the United States is like walking through an open door; half a million wetbacks do it every year."

Mark came back in and without saying a word stripped off a length of paper toweling and sopped up the large bloodstain on the kitchen floor, following the first cleaning with a thorough wiping with wet towels.

"But I can't leave until I give you the culture," Doohan said.

Strout's eyes narrowed. "In your eyes, Doctor, I suppose I rate as a British agent. In my own, I'm a patriot. Your bit of the culture could save my country—and incidentally yours—some time in the future. Frankly, I think you owe it to us—and to the rest of the world —to see that your friends don't succeed."

"Give me time to think about it," Doohan said slowly. He was tired now. He was willing to agree, but something was wrong and he wanted time to think. "Give me twenty-four hours."

Strout stood up. "Don't think too long, Doctor. There's a limit to how much we can do for you. And if you should be killed, then only one power will have this information. The power that developed the agent originally. The same power that murdered friend French and burned another friend of yours to death. You should be able to add up the score, Doctor: *We* saved your life. I should think that would count for something."

Then Strout was gone and Doohan leaned back on the couch, exhausted. Something was wrong, he thought slowly. Something had been wrong from the moment he had walked in the front door and had noticed that the vestibule light was out. Silly mistake for a man to make who had intended to surprise him. . . .

And why the cat and mouse game in the dark? Why hadn't his assailant simply turned on the light and potted him? In fact, since his eyes had adjusted to the gloom long before Doohan's, why had he been so inept with his pistol? Why had he waited?

He got up and walked toward the front door and the section of the wall he had crouched by when he had first been shot at. There was a hole in the wall all right, a good six feet from where he had been crouching. But they wouldn't have sent that rotten a shot.

Back in the kitchen, he inspected the floor where Mark had cleaned up after the body. There was no trace of the bright stain that had spread out over the kitchen linoleum. Then he knew what had been wrong with the image of Mark cleaning up the stain.

There had been a measurable amount of time before Mark had removed the body and gotten around to wiping up the blood. The edges of the pool should have started to clot and it would have taken some scrubbing.

He glanced into the kitchen trash can. There was no sign of the toweling that Mark had used; he had taken it with him. He hesitated a moment longer, then opened the back door and used a flashlight to light the steps leading down to the back walk. The man had bled badly in the kitchen. Why hadn't he continued to bleed on the walk outside? Doohan flashed the light a little farther ahead to where the walk ended in a strip of mud that led to the back gate.

Two sets of footprints going out, two coming back. The ground had been soft from an early evening drizzle and he could make out the prints clearly. The two sets coming back. The first made by the would-be assassin when he had first come in; the second made by Mark when he was returning after dumping the body in the automobile.

But what about the two sets going out? Mark and the assassin, who had been curiously ambulatory for a "corpse."

He walked back into the apartment, slamming the door behind him. It had been great theater, he thought. Strout had been wonderfully convincing. Time was running out on Doohan, his life was in danger, and he, Strout, good fellow that he was, had saved Doohan's life . . . "It must count for something." That was what Strout had said. It had been an elaborate scenario, staged especially for his benefit.

Strout must be under a great deal of pressure, he thought. What would he do the next time around if Doohan remained unconvinced and uncooperative? There wasn't any doubt in the world that his life was in danger. Paradoxically, that put even more strain on Strout to get the culture from Doohan. He wouldn't wait longer than a day more, and then he'd apply more positive pressure of his own. And Strout, he was reasonably sure, could be quite brutal, if he had to.

He glanced around. Safe house? he thought. Not

very. He was going to have to leave, and when he considered it, he finally made up his mind.

He had the photographs. He'd pick up the culture from Suzanne's apartment and catch the earliest possible flight to Washington to see Espinosa.

42

THE CORPORAL SAID, "General Varger's been expecting you, sir." She was an exceptionally pretty girl, Hanson noted. At another time, he might even have been interested enough to ask her name. . . .

Varger was much as Hanson had remembered him: a big, bluff man in a carefully tailored uniform that artfully hid his developing paunch, red hair that was now turning pinkish and gray, a flushed complexion that indicated too much good living and probably a high-blood-pressure problem, and blue eyes that always seemed remarkably opaque. The best poker face in the Army, Hanson thought, though now Varger seemed genuinely glad to see him, even coming around from his desk to shake hands. "Great to see you, Larry. How was the trip?" A firm handclasp and a clap on the shoulder.

"Too damn long, and too many things hanging fire back in 'Frisco. I want to catch an early plane back if that's possible."

"Don't let the natives hear you call it ' 'Frisco'—and don't worry; we'll probably break by noon." Varger scooped up a pile of papers from his desk and thrust them into a red manila folder. In the corridor he said, "You haven't been to Gravelly Point in—how long, Larry? Five years? We've expanded the planning and Intelligence operations considerably—got some top men out of the Pentagon and down here in Virginia where they can get some work done for a change."

At the end of a satellite corridor, Varger stopped before a door above which a red light glowed. Under it, a sign read: SECURITY AREA: DO NOT ENTER WHEN

LIGHT IS ON. A white-helmeted MP braced to attention when Varger approached, inspected the badge attached to his lapel, and then looked at Hanson's visitor's badge. "Go right in, sirs," he said, standing to one side.

The somewhat Spartan conference room was dominated by an oblong walnut table at which ten men were now seated. At the far end was a large projection screen, while from the middle of the table a slide-type assembly jutted up about six inches. Hanson guessed that during ordinary conferences, it would be recessed within the table itself. A uniformed sergeant sat opposite the console, a box of magnetic wafers before him. Two of the men at the table were in business suits, the rest in uniform. One general, one lieutenant, and the rest full colonels, Hanson noted.

No one called attention when they entered nor did Varger choose the seat at the head of the table. Instead, he led Hanson to the two vacant chairs on the left side, keeping up a running whispered commentary on those present. A Colonel Kolfacks, G-2 Intelligence Chief from Varger's office, Colonel Bercovitch, security specialist with the Joint Chiefs, a civilian named Camden from ARPA—the Advanced Research Projects Agency, a Colonel Markston ...

It was Bercovitch who walked to the head of the table to assume command of the meeting. Hanson was mildly surprised: no formal introductions. He glanced around the table again. There were only himself, Varger, and one other officer who wore the lapel insignia of crossed retorts over the enameled benzene ring that indicated they were from the Chemical Corps. He guessed most of the other officers were from the different military intelligence branches, and the civilians were probably CIA and FBI.

Bercovitch was a chunky man in his early thirties, with heavy brows and watery blue eyes. He assumed the head of the table with a casual nonchalance, and Hanson wondered how many other meetings he had chaired. "Major Hanson, to save time, we've reduced certain portions of your report to magnetic records. We'll now briefly review the situation in San Francisco. At the end of the presentation, please tell us if we have the complete picture, or if there have been any errors in assumption or fact."

Bercovitch nodded at the sergeant who dimmed the room-lights and started inserting wafers into the console, each of which projected a graph or display on the screen. Unusual security to use wafer records, Hanson thought. It was impossible to recover the image without a special scrambler pattern to punch into the console, and the wafers themselves could be easily erased with a single magnetic impulse. No problems of shredding and burning, no chance of accidental compromise . . .

It took half an hour for Bercovitch to cover the essential data on the infection and mortality pattern and to review the CDC sampling operations and the extensive work that had failed to develop a culture. When he finished, he said simply: "Colonel Kolfacks will give us the Intelligence summary."

Colonel Kolfacks was equally assured at the head of the table. "To put this into perspective, we've received a number of unevaluated reports from our own people and from the CIA on biological warfare research throughout the world. Our own work and that of our major allies have been officially restricted to research on defensive measures since 1969. We have reason to believe this restriction has not been strictly adhered to by either the British or the French, but their work has been devoted primarily to conventional agents, as has almost all the BW research in Third World countries."

Most of the people at the table looked faintly bored, and Hanson guessed that they had heard all of the information before. Oddly, in some areas, he was probably the least informed of any of them.

Kolfacks took a quick drink of water from the pitcher in front of him and continued. "The U.S.S.R. has officially ended all BW warfare research, but in fact is working in the area of recombinant DNA, principally on typhus and glanders. We have no clear picture of the level of research in the People's Republic of China, particularly since the recent political instability. The Cuban effort has been largely devoted to agents that attack livestock and grains, though there's some evidence they've recently become interested in respiratory bacteria. Generally, we know of no country which has developed a sophisticated technique for tailoring pathogenic viruses."

Camden, one of the men in civilian dress, asked: "What about the so-called Smolensk strain?"

Kolfacks shook his head. "A natural outbreak. The Soviets moved quickly to isolate all victims and so far as we know there's been no recurrence."

"Could it have been a test situation, similar to the one we now face?" Varger asked.

"It's . . . possible. There have been a number of new strains appearing in the past three years. It's difficult to determine if they're of natural or artificial origin. We now have the problem of increased air travel spreading previously unidentified strains and a number of these tend to mutate when they're introduced into a new population."

"But it's possible they could be of artificial origin?" Varger insisted.

Kolfacks considered it for a moment, then finally said: "General, I suppose anything is possible." He sounded slightly sardonic.

Hanson was starting to feel uncomfortable. He could sense the others around the table watching him, weighing him. They were familiar with everything that had gone before, he thought; they were waiting for his report.

Bercovitch took over at the head of the table again. "I think the conclusions are rather obvious. Direct assaults on nations are now largely suicidal or far too costly. But it's now possible for an enemy to wage a silent and subtle war, to sap the social and commercial vitality of a nation without an attack being obvious. A series of influenza epidemics spread over a decade could have a serious effect on a nation's gross national product. Such a protracted attack could be just as serious in the long run as a more obvious virulent disease that would invite counterattack by the affected nation." He glanced at Hanson for the first time. "A fact we may have to reconsider in connection with Major Hanson's report."

He glanced at his watch. "I think I'll throw this open to general discussion. Major Hanson, correct me if I'm wrong, but so far your unit has been unable to culture the San Francisco agent?"

Hanson cleared his throat nervously. "One of our consultants did; unfortunately, he was murdered and any culture he might have developed, destroyed. We have reason to believe a sample of the culture, however, may be in the hands of a foreign national."

Bercovitch nodded. "The Dr. Doohan you mention in your report. Colonel Markston, what do you have on Doohan?"

Markston rose. "Everybody here has read the history on Doohan that I've passed around. We have no hard information that this history has been fabricated; if it's a cover, it's a damned good one."

Bercovitch turned back to Hanson. "I assume you've had no luck in finding Doohan?"

Hanson could feel himself begin to sweat. "Not so far, though I think it's a matter of time."

"Almost everything is a matter of time," Bercovitch murmured.

"I think it's obvious he had outside help in going underground," Hanson continued. "Probably from a foreign intelligence apparatus operating in the United States. It's unlikely he could have disappeared so easily without professional help. Unless, of course, he's a sophisticated agent himself and his history is an elaborate cover."

"Markston?"

"I don't think so. In fact, I'd say not a chance."

"Continue, Major."

"There is at least one other foreign agency operating in San Francisco besides the one that may be helping Doohan." He had their full attention now. "Whoever they are, they murdered French and one of his assistants, and we believe they murdered Guitterez. If they succeed in locating Doohan, they'll undoubtedly kill him as well."

"This agency you mention," Bercovitch cut in. "The

same agency that developed the virus? In your opinion?"

"Of course."

It was Markston's turn now. "And if you locate Doohan, you'll pick him up immediately?"

Hanson shook his head. "I had thought of following his actions very closely but leaving him out there as bait."

Markston nodded. "Good idea."

"The viral agent," Hanson said slowly. "It's not the standard influenza type; there are double-exposure aspects to it. And we're not sure that the plotters who handled it were aware of that; in fact, several of them may have died because of their carelessness. The implication is that since they were unaware of the double-exposure aspects, there may have been a different purpose for the agent than to start an influenza-type epidemic."

It was Bercovitch who said easily, "I rather doubt that; the influenza strains are too easy to work with and actually too difficult to combat. I think you'll find the so-called 'double-exposure' aspects have a perfectly natural explanation."

"Your Guitterez," a colonel said. "Cuban?"

Hanson nodded. "Guitterez had a Cuban background, but he was a staunch Miami anti-Castro Cuban."

The colonel looked unconvinced. "That could be a cover. I'd look into that further, if I were you."

They'd start jumping him now, Hanson thought, sweating. Now the questions would start coming about his failures. . . .

But they never did.

He had an hour to kill before his plane left, and Hanson sat in the bar at Dulles Airport and soothed his nerves with straight shots of scotch. He had an intense feeling of failure that he couldn't shake. Damn it, he *had* failed—and failed badly. French had actually cultured the virus but had then been murdered; Doohan had vanished; and several of the conspirators had been murdered. . . .

And what had he actually found out?

He stared unseeing at a 727 taxiing down the runway. After the meeting he had complained to Varger about Gorshin and been assured once again that Gorshin was one of the country's top molecular biologists. In short, he would not be replaced.

There was something in that thought and he toyed with it a moment, then gave it up. His head was getting mushy. But considering what was at stake and the small size of his own investigation . . . something was oddly out of proportion.

He ordered another scotch and thought back to the meeting again. It should have been a grilling, a heavy session with himself constantly on the defensive. He had failed, but nobody had called him on it. And he knew damned well that General Varger and at least some of the colonels should have been after his scalp.

He had been in the Army too long to have expected it to be any different.

43

DOOHAN LEFT THE kitchen light burning and then went into the darkened living room and looked out at the street. It hadn't taken him too long to figure out which parked car Strout's man was in. At first he feared there might be two men in the car, but after watching for half an hour, he had decided there was only one. It had been a difficult equation at first. There was no way he could leave with his guardian out there; the logical action was to decoy him away from the house. That was obviously impossible, which left the next most logical action.

Decoy him within the house.

He glanced at his watch, left the window, and walked into the bedroom. His suitcase was already packed. He picked it up off the bed and placed it by the rear door in the kitchen. Then he sat down at the kitchen table with the collection of small aspirin and cough-medicine bottles he had found in the bathroom. The rest of his supplies consisted of a box of match-books—nearly forty of them—and a razor blade. He quickly slit the head from each match. When he had enough, he tamped the matchheads into one of the bottles and then stuffed in toilet-paper wadding un-til the bottle was so full he had difficulty screwing on the top. After half an hour, he had four matchhead-filled bottles.

The metal wastebasket from the living room was next. He filled it with rags and paper toweling, then soaked the contents with cooking oil, finally placing his four matchhead bottles on top. Back in the living room, he positioned the wastebasket in front of the large picture window and dropped a match in the basket. He slipped over to another window and held a damp handkerchief to his face as clouds of black smoke boiled from the wastebasket. Out in the street, Strout's man suddenly noticed the smoke. He got out of his car, obviously confused as to what to do next.

At that moment, one of the bottles stuffed with matches exploded. In the living room, it sounded like a shotgun and Doohan guessed it sounded the same outside. The man by the car started running toward the house.

Doohan raced back to the kitchen and opened the rear door. Another bottle exploded. An acrid, sickening smoke was filling the kitchen as he grabbed up his suitcase and slipped out onto the back stairs. The man was pounding at the front door now and shouting his name. A third bottle exploded and the pounding changed to a battering. Strout's man was trying to kick the front door down.

In the distance, Doohan thought he could hear the sound of fire engines. He ran down the back stairs to the path that led to the sidewalk. Behind him, dense clouds of smoke were pouring from a shattered living room window. Neighbors had begun to turn on their lights to see what was happening.

He threw his suitcase in the back seat of his car and eased behind the wheel. It was parked pointing downhill toward Market Street; he released the brake and turned the steering wheel to start it on the downgrade. He was a block from the house before he started the motor and turned on the lights.

Behind him, the fire engines had drawn up in front of his house. He smiled to himself. Strout's man must have broken into the house just before the fireman got there; now let him explain exactly what he was doing there and just whom he had been trying to "save."

It was going to be a game of hare and hounds now, he thought—with three sets of hounds: Hanson, Strout, and the people who had created the virus. The latter had killed French, Woodruff, Guitterez, and Kovacs, and they certainly wouldn't hesitate to kill him. The ampoules of the virus and the photographs in his wallet were all that remained to implicate them. . . .

He was sick of it, he thought suddenly. He wasn't a secret agent by nature or trade, and he was tired of being confronted by decisions he really didn't know how to make. He could turn the ampoules and the photos over to Strout or Hanson and he would be out of it then. But their superiors would see to it that the information about the ampoules remained secret. If they had their way, only they and the nation that had developed the virus would ever know it existed. And someday, inevitably, it would be used.

The easiest way out was the best way out. Dump it all in Espinosa's lap. Pick up the vials from Suzanne's and catch the first plane to Washington. Maybe Espinosa would, in the long run, be powerless; perhaps he himself was being naïve. But he wanted to get out, and badly. He had spent most of his professional life as a doctor and he wanted to go back to being one.

It was close to eleven as he pulled into a service station with a telephone booth against the building wall. He dialed Suzanne's number; there was no answer, though the phone rang a dozen times. He hesitated in indecision. He couldn't stay in the city any longer; he had to leave that night. Which meant he had to retrieve the ampoules now. She would be back soon; perhaps she had merely gone out for a late dinner or movie.

And then the thought came: If she had, then with whom?

It took him twenty minutes to drive to Suzanne's apartment house. Once in the foyer, he buzzed Suzanne's apartment. There was no answer, but he really hadn't expected one; there had been no lights on in the apartment. He tried several of the other apartments. One of them finally buzzed back and he pushed through the door.

"Who is it?" A young girl's voice sounded from the stairwell. She was probably expecting a boyfriend, he thought.

"Sorry—pressed yours by mistake."

A pleasant, "That's all right," and the slight slam of a closing door. No further questions. Doohan waited a moment; apparently no one else was bothering to answer the buzzer. He went up to Suzanne's apartment, grateful that she had wanted to enjoy the real flavor of the city and had rented in an older building rather than one with all the modern guard devices.

The door was old, the lock was ancient. A moment to spring the lock and then he was inside. "Suzanne?" There was no answer. There was no indication that she had left in a hurry, however. Her clothes were in the bedroom closet, her toilet articles in the usual tangle on the bathroom floor. Out for the night, he thought again.

And once more, more acutely: With whom?

He went into the kitchen and opened the refrigerator. He fished the two ampoules from the yogurt, then washed the outside and replaced the container in the refrigerator behind some stalks of wilting celery. He had just finished washing the ampoules off in the sink when he heard the slam of a car door in the street below. It was a subliminal sound at first and then he froze.

He hurried to the window and looked. The man walking across the street looked familiar. One of Hanson's men, he thought. Suzanne's apartment faced the street, and, like an idiot, he had turned on the lights when he had walked in. The man was on stake-out; he must have known about what time Suzanne was due back but Doohan had shown up early.

Damn it, what time *would* she be back? And who with?

No time for jealousy, he thought grimly. He could get out of the apartment but he wasn't going to get far. He had broken in while she wasn't there; there wouldn't be any doubt what he was there for, and it was either flush the ampoules down the drain, with the resultant risk to the population that *that* implied, or get rid of them somehow.

He ran to the desk in the living room, ignoring the door buzzer. Maybe two minutes, not much longer than that. He rummaged through the drawers and found a mailing box with checks from a Los Angeles bank. The return address was Suzanne Pahlevi at a Bel-Air address. Well, he thought, she *had* said her husband was wealthy. He dumped the checks back in the drawer and crumpled some stationery to cushion the ampoules. He placed them in the box, cramming some more paper to insure a tight fit, then sealed the box with Scotch tape. Finally, he shoved it in the mailing envelope with the same return address on its label. He taped a strip of blank paper over the bottom part of the label and quickly wrote in Espinosa's address. There were only two stamps in the stamp box in the upper drawer, but they would have to do. He wrote FIRST CLASS on the label and shoved the envelope in his pocket.

The doorbell had been buzzing for the last thirty seconds and now abruptly stopped. His tail has gotten in, he thought, and walked over to one side of the door. He could hear two men coming up the steps, taking them two at a time but still trying to be quiet about it. A knock on the door. "Miss Synge?" Doohan hefted a table lamp in his right hand and waited. When they came in, they'd be coming in a hurry.

The door burst open then, and Doohan swung the lamp at the first head in and blocked the other with his shoulder on the way out. He heard a squeaked "God *damn!*" and one was down and the other doubled up, at least for the moment. Doohan plunged down the stairs and out through the foyer. He raced down the sidewalk, faintly slick from the evening fog. He fumbled out his car keys and climbed in, hastily turning on the ignition and starting the engine.

It grumbled a few times and wouldn't turn over. The dampness; wet plugs, he thought, and tried again. This time he smelled gasoline and realized he had flooded the engine . . .

He jumped out and started sprinting, his footsteps echoing up the block. A mistake, he thought; he should just walk. It was a foggy night and all he needed was to turn a corner and he would be lost. . . .

He slowed to a jog and then he heard a door slam several hundred yards behind him. A moment later there was a soft *spang!* and concrete exploded from near his feet. He started running again, heading for the corner. San Francisco, he thought, cursing the city under his breath. There were no alleys he could duck into; there were no gaps between the houses where he could lose himself.

The footsteps behind him were drawing closer. He dashed for the end of the block. There was a mailbox just out of sight around the corner; he had to get to it and drop in his package before they saw him. He was running scared now; then he was at the corner and had pulled the package out of his pocket. He stumbled near the mailbox and the package shot from his hand to land on a storm grating. It teetered on the grating a second and he dove for it, barely catching a corner of the flap before it could slip through.

A moment later, he had slid it into the box and heard the soft thud as it landed on other mail below.

The steps behind him were closer now. He started running down the side street, slipping on the pavement once and scrambling for his footing. He was still out of sight of his pursuers, but as he looked around the street he realized with despair that there was no place to hide.

He sensed the car following him before it drew up to the curb. The door opened, and a slightly accented voice said, "Hop in, Dr. Doohan—hurry." Doohan quickly climbed in the back seat, his chest heaving. He could hear the footsteps on the sidewalk hit the corner and slow as Hanson's men looked for him; then the car had picked up speed and turned the corner. He realized with relief that he was free.

He had mailed the ampoules, he thought. There was no way Strout could get them from him now; so there was little to fear from him. He caught his breath and said, "I'm sorry if I've proved difficult, Tony; better you than Hanson, I guess."

Then Doohan realized with a sudden shock that he had miscalculated for the final time. There were two men in the car besides the driver.

They weren't Hanson's men.

And they weren't Strout's.

He jerked toward the door, reaching for the handle; but before he could grab it, something very hard struck him behind the ear and he sank into a painful darkness.

44

DOOHAN WAS AWARE of his head jerking back and forth; it was minutes before he realized that someone was slapping him hard, first on the left side of the face and then on the right. He coughed, and then somebody was holding his head up by the hair; he sensed the acrid fumes of ammonia burning the mucous membranes of his nose.

"That's enough of the smelling salts," somebody said distantly.

Another voice said, "Did you have to hit him so hard?"

He tentatively opened his eyes, then immediately squinted. Two photo flood lamps were pointed directly at him. He shielded his eyes with a hand and narrowed his eyes to slits. Directly behind the flood lamps was a bulky shape slouched in a chair of some kind and clutching what appeared to be a small glass. A thin figure stood to the right of the sitting man, while on the left stood a massive figure almost as wide as he was tall. A very fat man or a very muscular one, he couldn't tell which. When the man moved slightly, Doohan saw a thin glint of light around his eyes and guessed that he was wearing glasses. Doohan tried to take a step forward and then realized that two men, one on each side, were holding him. Somebody had taken off his coat and rolled up his shirt sleeves.

Despite the shadows, he could tell that the room was huge. His eyes were adjusting now and beyond the sitting figure he could see a solid sweep of glass window and through it the distant lights of the city.

To the right and closer, he saw small moving lights bobbing up and down and realized they must be the mast lights of boats in the bay. He was in a house on a hill overlooking the Golden Gate Bridge. Sausalito or Tiburon, he thought, but where?

"How are you feeling now?" the sitting figure asked. The voice was deep and very sure of itself, the voice of a man accustomed to giving orders.

Doohan licked his cracked lips. The slight movement made the whole side of his face hurt. "I can't believe you really care."

"Strangely enough, I really do, Doctor. I'm very concerned about your well-being at this moment."

Doohan's mental fuziness was slowly disappearing. There had been a threat in the man's voice. "Your every wish is for my comfort, I'm sure," he said sarcastically.

"They are," the man said simply. "Would you like a drink?" He held out his glass.

"Water," Doohan said inanely.

The man nodded at somebody and a moment later somebody was holding a glass to his mouth. He drank it all, but something was jarring his memory now. Damn, the smell of ammonia was still clogging his nostrils. . . .

"No scotch to go with it?" the sitting man asked regretfully. "I had understood you were a scotch drinker. Too bad. I pride myself on my martinis; I go to a great deal of trouble to import the proper gin. Have you ever tasted *habhel* gin?"

It was Mad Hatter conversation, Doohan thought. They were going to spend the whole night discussing amenities.

"We're wasting time," the standing figure said.

"I'll decide when we're wasting time," the sitting man replied quietly, a wire edge to his voice. "Dr. Doohan." An almost regretful pause. "You've caused us a great deal of trouble. About a matter that doesn't really concern you."

"It concerns a great deal of people," Doohan said, wanting to be angry and too weak to put the strength in his voice.

"The thing that really matters is that you're a trouble-maker."

"You have a bloody vicious way of handling those who give you trouble," Doohan said. To his own ears, it sounded like a whine.

"There's nothing personal in it," the sitting man said quietly. "I'm not a sadist, Doctor; I derive no pleasure from the sufferings of other people. But there *is* such a thing as the greater good."

The allusion escaped Doohan, but he was suddenly very tired of the studied politeness. "Go to hell," he said weakly.

"Doctor." There was a harder note in the voice this time. "You have a sample of the culture. We want it back."

"I don't know anything about a culture."

"I'll be patient, Doctor—for now. We're aware of Dr. French's success and we know that he left the culture in a place where you could find it. We now want to know what you did with it."

"I turned it over to Major Hanson," Doohan said.

The sitting man didn't say anything. Suddenly the figure on Doohan's right bent Doohan's arm up behind his back and started twisting. "Stop that!" the sitting man said. The pressure let up immediately. "Forgive me, Doctor—for the lack of subtlety, if nothing else. Blindfold him, please."

The man to Doohan's left pulled his head back and the guard on the right placed heavy gauze pads over his eyes, then strapped them in place with adhesive tape. Doohan could feel the hair on the back of his head twist and pull as the man yanked the adhesive strips tight.

"You could tell us now, Doctor," the sitting man said, "and save us all a lot of time and trouble. You'll tell us before the night is out in any event."

Doohan repeated, "Go to hell!" He was suddenly yanked around and forced to walk in front of his guards. He sensed he was in a hall; the flooring was hard and somewhat slick as if he were walking over tile or marble. Then somebody opened a door in front of him and he was thrust into a small room; his shoes rang on tile again and the close walls threw back an echo. He was suddenly forced to his knees; he thrust out a hand to keep from falling forward. He touched a smooth, rounded, curved surface and then a void beyond. A sunken tub, he thought. He was in a bathroom, a fairly large one from the echoes and from the fact that two other men were in there with him.

The door swung open again and he heard the sound of a small leather case being dropped on the tile surface. The further sounds of buckles and straps being undone, and finally a moment of silence. "Hold him up, please." A soft, accented voice, with no sense of warmth to it. The man who spoke was fairly close to him, and Doohan could feel the presence of bulk and smell the sweetish odor of perspiration. The fat man from the living room, he thought.

"Are you familiar with the action of apomorphine, Doctor? This is a variation of it from my own research but much more effective." The voice had a factual, almost schoolroom tone to it. "In this form, I've never been able to find a use for it, but I suspect it would come in handy as an anti-personnel spray in warfare. Much more humane than bullets or gas." A pudgy hand gripped his right arm and Doohan jerked away. A moment later, it had been twisted behind him and he almost cried out in pain.

The pudgy hand returned with a swab of cotton dipped in alcohol and rubbed the upper part of his arm. Almost immediately he felt cold metal against the bare skin and heard a soft *chuff*. He recognized the sound all too well—the noise made by a helium capsule vaccine jetgun. He had used them extensively in the smallpox program. The serum, or whatever it was, had been driven by a fine pressurized spray directly into the skin.

"It shouldn't take but a moment, Doctor," the fat man said.

Nobody else said a word; Doohan was conscious only of the fat man's body odor and the heavy sound of breathing. His own, he decided after a moment.

Then he began to feel queasy, such as one might after a long bus ride or a half hour on the choppy waters of the Bay. At first it was a faint nausea, and then it gradually built. He could sense a sour taste growing in his mouth and throat. Now there were tremblings in the smooth muscles of his stomach, followed by small convulsions.

"No point in fighting it, Doctor," the fat man said sympathetically.

He was going to be sick, Doohan thought with some amazement. Waves of nausea began to wash over him. He tried to breathe deeply, to beat back the dizziness. Then he began to gag.

"Hold his head over the tub—quickly."

A hand pushed his head forward just in time. The next instant he was bent double, his chin pressed tight against the cold porcelain surface of the tub's edge, vomiting over the side.

He heaved repeatedly for several minutes and then sank to the floor, weak with the effort. His eyes were watering under the bandages and his throat burned with the acid from his stomach. His mouth tasted of puke. The cold tile of the floor felt momentarily soothing; then he could feel the sense of uneasiness again and another spasm seized him. This time the vomiting was longer and more violent. He was throwing up very few solid particles; he was losing primarily liquid. He now understood the sitting man's generosity with the glass of water.

"All you have to do, Doctor, is tell us what we want to know. The antidote works very quickly—in something less than two minutes, actually. You could have supper with us and share our eggplant parmigiana." There was no attempt to hide the sadism in the voice this time.

Doohan began to vomit again. He was having the dry heaves now; there was nothing left to come up but green bile. He finally fell back on the tile, exhausted.

Somebody yanked at his hair to lift up his head and a damp cloth was run over his face. Then he was turned over and a glass of water was poured down his throat. The damp cloth was paradise; the drink of water much less so.

"We don't want you to suffer too much—at first,"

the fat man said. His voice turned accusatory. "What did you do with the culture, Doctor?"

"I don't have it," he whispered.

"Doctor, you're a medical man; you know the limits." The voice managed to be cajoling and reprimanding at the same time. "Your degree of dehydration will gradually become severe. And the damage to your stomach lining might be irreparable."

"You can—" he began to whisper.

Cold, commanding. "Hold his arm."

Doohan could feel the man's body pressing against him as he was hauled to a half-sitting position. A soft, obese man with a protruding, jellylike stomach. The brief caress of cold metal against his arm and once again the soft *chuff*. He crawled to the edge of the tub as he felt the waves of nausea ripple upward.

"Like a lemming heading for the sea," the fat man said. "I can keep this up all night. Can you?"

Doohan clawed at the edge of the tub, his body wracked with convulsions. At one point he inhaled at the wrong moment and started choking on his own vomit.

"Watch him," the fat man said, sounding bored. "Let me know when he wants to tell us something." The door opened again, Doohan could hear two sets of footsteps shuffle out, and then the door slammed shut. They had left only one guard behind, he thought, but they may as well have left an army. There was the flick of a lighter and then the smell of cigarette smoke.

"Want a drag?" The guard blew a cloud of smoke at his head and Doohan started heaving again. The guard laughed quietly. Then there was silence and finally the sound of magazine pages being turned. The guard was bored, Doohan thought, but then, how fascinating was it to watch somebody vomit? He leaned lower into the tub, keeping his breathing shallow so the stench wouldn't bring on another round of vomiting. He held his head with his hands, quietly forcing the bandage up over his eyes with his thumbs. Finally he could see underneath it. He was staring down into a green porcelain tub, its side running with vomit and phlegm. He groaned and rolled back slightly, turning his head so he could see the shoes of the man sitting on the commode.

His stomach felt uneasy again, and then the convulsions started in. What came up this time was a pinkish bile, the first signs of capillary bleeding. He was literally tearing his stomach lining apart, he thought. The gagging ebbed, and he realized the periods of relaxation were becoming longer. That would change when the fat man returned to give him another shot, but in the meantime he was alone with only one guard.

He lifted his head. On the other side of the tub was a large picture window. There were the dark shapes of trees just beyond, and small ragged hills, and then the ocean.

"No sight-seeing," the guard said, suddenly realizing what he was doing. "How the hell did you work the bandage up anyway?" Doohan could hear the guard walk over. He saw a close-up of a pair of brown, wing-tipped shoes, badly scuffed. The man bent over and grabbed him by the hair, to haul him off the floor.

Doohan jerked away, more by automatic reflex than by design, and the guard stepped forward to get a better grip. One foot suddenly slipped on the wet lip of the tub and he was off-balance. Doohan whipped his body around with all the strength he had and hit the guard behind the knees. The man's legs buckled and he fell forward, swearing. At the last moment, he pistoned his legs against the side of the tub to keep from falling into the vomit below.

There was the sudden sound of shattering glass and a scream and Doohan could feel cold air against his face. He sat up and worked the blindfold the rest of the way off his head, wincing as the adhesive tape tore out tufts of hair. For a moment he did nothing but sit on the floor, smelling the stink from the tub and letting his eyes adjust to the sudden brilliance reflecting from the enameled walls of the room.

He had to get out, he thought next. On the other side of the tub, most of the window had disappeared, leaving sharp shards sticking out from the frame.

Christ, I'm sick; I can't do it. . . . He staggered to his feet and lifted the porcelain lid off the water closet. For a moment he wasn't sure he had the strength. He cradled the lid in his arms, then took a long step to straddle the tub and started smashing out the daggers of glass with the porcelain top.

He had cleaned most of the shards out of the bottom of the frame when he heard footsteps in the hall. He turned just as the door opened.

Framed in the opening was an immensely fat man, his eyes blinking in surprise behind his glasses. They stared at each other in shock for a moment. Then the fat man yelled at somebody behind him and waddled forward, clutching at Doohan. Doohan let the lid drop out the window. The fat man leaned over the tub and grabbed his arm. Doohan half-turned and grabbed the fat man's hand, then slowly leaned out the window. The fat man scrambled for purchase on the bathroom floor, but it was too slippery and the rigid fixtures were too far away to grab onto.

Doohan let go just as the fat man tumbled into the slime at the bottom of the tub. He wavered for a moment on the sill, listening to the fat man making gagging sounds, and then he heard people running down the hallway.

Got to get away, he thought, starting to feel sick again. *Got to get away . . .* He sat down on the sill, then turned and hung on the ledge for a moment with his hands. He heard people enter the bathroom and automatically let go. He dropped about two feet onto a broad wooden beam, part of the cantilever system that supported the house. Another beam slanted up to meet it; quickly he wrapped his arms around it and began to inch downward. Splinters bit into his fingers and he felt a sliver rip some skin from his bare left arm. That was all right, he thought. The cold air and the pain worked against the nausea.

Above him, he could sense light from the bathroom window and hear the babble of voices. But he was beneath the house now; there was no way they could see him. Then he suddenly froze. The damned vomiting was coming on again. He hung onto the beam and had the dry heaves in silence. Then he felt his hold loosen. He was too weak. A brief moment of falling, and he was lying in the soft dirt underneath the house. From above him came the sounds of doors slamming and cars starting. If they caught him now, he would be a dead man.

He half-crawled, half-stumbled into a mass of shrubbery near the house. There was no sign of the man who had tumbled out the window—probably bleeding his life away, Doohan thought with satisfaction. He worked his way as quietly as he could through the underbrush, always toward the bay. There was a road that ran along the waterfront and back to San Francisco. He would have to find a washroom to get cleaned up, pack another shirt and coat and then call Espinosa to tell him he was coming to Washington.

He suddenly remembered something and felt for his hip pocket. His wallet was still safely wedged in. They had given him a quick search, but it was obvious that he couldn't have hidden the culture there and they had missed the photographs.

He was at the bottom of the slope now. Several hundred yards above him he could hear the thrashing of bodies in the underbrush and see the beams of flashlights. He pulled himself erect holding onto a scrub pine while the feeling of nausea swept over him again. He retched, letting some pink drool dribble down his shirt front. It was all downhill now and he stumbled forward.

Suddenly he was walking on something hard and when he looked down, he saw that the ground had turned black. Macadam. He was standing on the edge of a road. He glanced up at the overhead lights. Not a road. A freeway.

A car was coming and he waved both hands at it. It roared past, the horn blaring. He took off his shirt and waved it at the next one which also passed him. There were no cars for a while and he walked along the pavement, trailing his shirt behind him. He was bone tired and starting to fight what he guessed would be the last wave of nausea. If they followed him now, he thought, he would be done for. He was too tired to resist and he didn't particularly give a damn anyway.

There was the sound of another car. He turned to face the headlights some hundreds of yards away and waved his shirt half-heartedly. Then the nausea seized him once again and he sank to his knees, vomiting a blood-flecked drool on the blacktop.

The car pulled over on the shoulder and then two men were racing toward him. It wasn't until one reached down to help him to his feet that he realized they were in uniform.

Through a thickening haze, he heard one of the highway patrolmen say, "Oh, Christ, another drunk."

45

DOOHAN SPENT A sleepless, uncomfortable night in the Sausalito station drunk tank, his wrists still smarting from the handcuffs the patrolmen had used. In spite of their repeated questions, he refused to tell them where he had left his car. They released him the next morning, returning his keys and wallet and warning him that the next time there would be a stiff fine.

He caught a bus into San Francisco and took a taxi to the Miyako Hotel. Five minutes later he had stripped and was soaking in a hot tub in the Japanese baths. He paid one of the women attendants to take his clothes to a nearby laundry. When he finally finished soaking, they were laid out for him in the dressing room, clean-smelling and stain-free.

In the early afternoon, he made flight arrangements to Washington and then called Espinosa to warn him what he would be receiving in the mail the next day, and to let him know he'd be arriving early that evening. When Doohan hung up, he stayed in the phone booth for a moment with his hand on the receiver. He still didn't know who had created the viral culture in the first place, or who had murdered French and Woodruff and Guitterez. Or who had wanted him to vomit his insides out. What would have happened if he had told them what he had done with the ampoules, he wondered. An overdose of the drug so he would have died of internal bleeding? Nausea was as much a psychological weapon as a physical one, he thought; it had the advantage of making you *want* to die. And then he had to throttle the thought; just thinking about it brought back the tremors in his stomach.

His hand holding the receiver was white and he forced his fingers to unclench. There was nothing more he could do. He wasn't a private detective or a secret agent or even a man with a mission, not any more. What was the difference between a hero and a coward—their perception of reality? He was just a country doctor and God, how he wanted to get back to doctoring . . .

Doohan stepped out of the booth and glanced at his watch. There were three hours to kill before flight time and before—in all probability—leaving San Francisco forever. It would be nice to be able to lift the phone and say good-by to Anna Goldstein. It would be even nicer if he could see Suzanne.

By now she was probably being watched by both Hanson and Strout and whoever had kidnapped him the night before. Besides, he wasn't too sure she'd be glad to see him. Hanson's men must have searched her apartment by now and probably interrogated her for most of the night.

He could call her, he thought, and stepped back inside the booth to dial. It rang three times and then a man's voice said, "Hello?" One of Hanson's men, Doohan thought.

Doohan hung up. And then for no good reason at all except he wanted to say good-by to someone, he thought of the first friend he had made in town.

Benoit.

It had been nagging him for days and now the thought finally surfaced like a bubble of gas in a swamp: Why had Benoit died of the Veterans' Disease? Because he had known Roy French? Had he been the one fluke, the one person who had been capable of being infected? No, Doohan thought, that was reaching for it.

What had been Benoit's connection?

Laval, Roy French, Guitterez . . . he knew their involvement, the parts they played. But what about Benoit? He had never talked much about himself, Doohan had never known what Benoit had done the years before, what he had worked at, who he had worked with.

But one person might know. Benoit's sister. She should be at the house, packing up the last of her brother's possessions and putting the house up for sale. He had the time; he could pay a courtesy call. . . .

And it would be very satisfying to discover that there was no connection, that Benoit's death had been coincidental, that his first friend in San Francisco had been just what he had always appeared to be—a retired doctor, living alone, who out of his own generosity of spirit had taken an interest in one Calvin Doohan and his life . . .

The cab dropped Doohan off at the top of the hill where Market turned into Portola. It was a clear day and Doohan could see almost all of the city. He stared at it for a long moment but there was no feeling of great affection for it, no sense of regret that he was leaving.

He turned back to the house. Benoit's sister had obviously come and gone. There was a "For Sale" sign in one of the empty windows and the flowers in the pots on the steps had long since withered and died. She hadn't wasted much time cleaning out the house and turning it over to the real estate agents.

There was a gas station on the corner; he'd call another cab and go out to the airport. He turned to go, then hesitated and tried the door. It wasn't locked. He walked up the stairs to the living area. The windows were all closed; the air was dry and musty with the flat smell of houses for rent. The rooms had been thoroughly stripped; the furniture had been moved out, the carpets taken up. All that was left were a few scraps of papers lying on the floor and, in a corner, an empty box holding a burned-out light bulb.

He let a sense of nostalgia creep over him as he roamed the house. He paused a moment in the library to stare at the fireplace where he and Benoit had talked about the morass that was Bangladesh and where world politics were going. Benoit's views had been extreme, but then the old man was entitled to them and certainly his mind had been sharply honed.

And above all else, Benoit had been a friend when he had known no one else in town. Doohan laughed quietly to himself. Benoit had always let Doohan do most of the talking. There's nothing interesting about an old man, he used to say. And then, almost apologetically: I'm not very good at sharing my memories. A quiet, hawk-faced, sharp old man. He hadn't died in a nice way, but then few people do.

Doohan walked over to the huge picture windows overlooking the Bay and the city and slid open the glass doors to let in some air. He stood in the doorway for a moment, the chill air hitting his face, then glanced at his watch. He'd have to be leaving soon.

But the feeling wouldn't go away. . . .

Benoit hadn't been an innocent.

Shades of a past friendship and I go blind, Doohan thought. *I can be bought like anybody else, only the currency is different. A little human kindness for me when I'm lonely and I can ignore a plot to kill millions.*

What had been Benoit's connection? he wondered.

He shivered and closed the doors. Paranoia. Hanson had never mentioned Benoit; Strout had never mentioned Benoit. There was no connection at all outside of Roy French, and who knew what that connection was? He took a last-minute tour of the house, telling himself that he was just touching all bases, as the Americans would say, then admitted he was actually looking for something but he wasn't sure what. In any event, he was a few days too late. There was nothing left but the scraps of papers on the floor, an old photograph dangling from a single thumbtack on the corkboard in the library, and the cardboard box with the burned-out light bulb.

He started down the stairs to the front door, paused, and walked back to the library. He had seen the photograph on the corkboard a dozen times but had never taken a good look at it. He took it off the board and over to the window where the light was better, then felt his breath catch.

Fort Detrick, 1962—the photographer had been kind enough to write it on the back. In the photo, Roy French and Laval and Guitterez, all much younger and thinner, smiled at the camera. Slightly forward and to one side, Dr. Hugh Benoit stood with his hand on the shoulder of a fat man whose head was turned and whose features had been partially cropped by the edge of the photograph. Doohan couldn't make out the face.

But there was no mistaking Benoit's sharp nose and pencil-thin mustache, black then. Smiling. Joking. Comfortable with his comrades. Civilian clothes, not military. How had he met them? As a civilian contractor of some kind? Perhaps as a consultant or a doctor on temporary assignment? What had they seen in each other? And who had they sold out to? To what other country had they betrayed their own?

The self-conscious smiles in the photograph. The slight physical separation, with the chiefs in front and the Indians in back. They must have been on assignment to Benoit for some sort of secret project. Then years later, after they were all out and established in civilian life, Benoit had contacted them once again. It hadn't been in the role of friend or confidant or ex-service chum.

Hugh Benoit had been their employer.

There was something else that occurred to Doohan then. Benoit had been engaged in a monstrous plot, and it must have taken an enormous amount of time. But he had always had time for Doohan; he had always had. time for a game of GO and a long talk about what it had been like to eradicate smallpox in Bangladesh. A hundred conversations flashed through his mind then, and a hundred recollections of Benoit's intelligent, probing, persistent questions. What had it been like to control a plague?

He had always wondered what Benoit had seen in him, why the old man had taken the time.

Now he knew.

46

THE SUN WAS bright but a chill wind was blowing in from the ocean, pushing shreds of fog across the top of Mount Sutro as Doohan closed Benoit's door. He had half-turned his back to the wind and didn't see them at first.

"Hello, Doctor," Hanson said.

Hanson and Roberts and two uniformed police officers were standing at the curb. Hanson, Doohan thought, never looked more military, but he should have had an army at his back. Hanson's government car and the patrol car were parked a hundred yards away; he couldn't have seen them from the windows.

"How did you know?"

"The housewife's early warning system; the woman next door called the police when she saw you go in. I had asked them to let me know if anybody came around."

"You got here pretty fast."

Hanson's smile was without humor. "You've been here almost an hour." He walked over, the others trailing. "The State Department has given me permission to pick you up."

"*Persona non grata?*"

Hanson nodded. "That's right. The U.S. marshals will meet us at Endo-Syn."

Doohan hesitated, shivering in the wind and staring at the little group for a moment. He had had his own suspicions about Hanson but something wasn't making any sense now. It didn't matter; there was no possibility of getting away. "All right," he said quietly. "Let's go."

Hanson glanced at him sharply and Doohan decided his reaction wasn't what Hanson had expected. What Hanson didn't realize was how little fight was left in him. The police officers quickly searched him for weapons and turned his wallet over to Hanson. Doohan held his breath but Hanson wasn't interested in his family photographs—or the others carefully inserted beneath. The important thing was that there obviously were no ampoules hidden in the wallet. Hanson flipped through it once and handed it back. They walked up to the car which Roberts was driving and Hanson opened the door. "In the back," he ordered as Roberts stepped to the pavement.

Doohan got in and Roberts squeezed in beside him. Roberts' coat was open and Doohan glimpsed a shoulder-holstered weapon. Odd, he thought. Hanson had once said there would come a time when he would tell him everything he knew. He was right; there would be no holding back this time. He looked through the window at Hanson talking to the police officers, and then one of them shoved a clipboard at him to sign. The transfer of the prisoner, Doohan thought.

They rode in silence back to Emeryville, Roberts never taking his eyes off Doohan. Something glittered in Roberts' expression and Doohan hoped desperately that they didn't hit a bump—if they did, Roberts might well use it as an excuse to blow a hole in him big enough to drive a truck through.

Guards patrolled the gates at Endo-Syn now and Hanson had to show identification to get through. There were more guards in the lobby and on the various floors. They had tightened up a lot, Doohan thought; but from their ages and the way they acted, they were Endo-Syn guards and not MPs in mufti. And they looked much tougher than the average rent-a-cop.

His topcoat and suitcase, the ones he had left in the car when he had gone to Suzanne's apartment, were in Hanson's office. "We found your car this morning," Hanson said. "We waited to see which one was left behind when everybody else had gone to work.

You can take the suitcase with you when we ship you out."

Doohan sat down in front of Hanson's desk and waited. Hanson signaled Roberts to leave and the young lieutenant went out the door reluctantly, turning to cast a veiled look at Doohan. When he had left, Doohan said casually: "He doesn't much care for me, does he?"

"Neither do I," Hanson said dryly.

Doohan stared at Hanson for a long moment. "The marshals really aren't going to show up, are they?"

"They might," Hanson said. "But not right now. Perhaps not at all." He looked as though he were doing something he didn't want to do and for a moment, things started to shift in Doohan's mind. He was surer now that he had made a misjudgment. "We can lose you, Doctor. We can lose you for years. Do you understand what I'm saying?"

"I do," Doohan said. "I'm not so sure *you* do."

"Co-operate and I'll turn you over to the U.S. marshals; they'll escort you to the airport and you'll be on your way back to England. That is, I'll turn you over to the marshals when and if I find you." He paused. "I may never find you."

Doohan sprawled back in his chair. He had been right. "Why don't you just ask me what you want to know?"

"Where did you go last night?"

"I didn't go; I was taken." Doohan described at length the events of the evening.

"Did you have any idea where you were?"

"Some place in Sausalito—I'm not sure where."

Hanson looked disturbed. "You can give us a full description later; it shouldn't be hard to find." Hesitated. "I assume they got the culture."

"No. I had mailed it before then."

"You *what?*"

"I mailed it to a friend. I can have him turn part of it over to you, if you want it."

Hanson tapped his pencil on his desk. "That's very generous, though I can guess to whom you sent it; you don't have that many friends. I can have Espinosa's mail intercepted."

Doohan glanced at his watch. "Washington's closed for the night and it will be delivered in the morning. My guess is you'll have to go through channels and it will be too late by then."

Hanson's face reddened. "How did French culture it?"

"The virus requires a trace of vanadium to grow. Paul used ten to fifty parts per million; you'll have to experiment." He looked at Hanson quizzically. "You understand that's why the virus was non-infective. It couldn't grow without vanadium."

"The vanadium was the secret that Paul didn't tell us?"

"He was murdered before he could."

A moment's silence. Then: "Who's been helping you?"

Doohan wondered if he owed Strout any loyalty at all. "I won't tell you that."

Hanson looked bored. "You don't have to. You went to the British embassy while you were in Washington. Let's assume their apparatus here has been giving you aid and assistance." His expression suddenly changed to one of suspicion. "You're being very co-operative. Why?"

Doohan leaned forward. "Who suggested sending the nickel-soaked tissue specimens to French?"

"It was necessary to mislead the public."

Doohan felt as though he was closing in for the kill. "Somebody advised you on that, didn't they? The public, yes—but why mislead Paul French?"

Hanson's smile was wintry. "We didn't mislead him very far, did we? But you're not answering my question."

Doohan realized that Hanson knew he was fencing, but he had to build him up a little more. "What type of viral weapon are we dealing with, Major?"

"You know what type it is." Hanson had started to sweat. "It's an influenza. They're easy to work with and they're dangerous."

"That's all the government believes it is? That it's simply a version of an influenza strain? There's no significance to the double-exposure aspects?"

Hanson's face was glistening. "There are some doubts about that."

Doohan stared his disbelief. "Who told you that? There aren't any doubts at all, Major. You know that."

Hanson's voice was hard. "We have our experts. And you still haven't answered my question."

"How much of a threat do you think the virus is, Major?"

Hanson was staring at him like a bird at a snake. "The most serious we've ever faced."

"You didn't know whether I had the culture on me or not when I was in Benoit's house," Doohan said. "Yet to handle that most serious threat, you show up with your head of security and two policemen. A simple murderer would have had a dozen waiting for him. For a terrorist group, your government would have mobilized a hundred men. For me—four. What kind of authority do you really have, Major? What's your total manpower? Less than what you started with? Ever since you came here, you've been bled of men and authority—"

"Answer my question!" Hanson exploded.

"Why am I co-operating?" Doohan repeated slowly. "Partly because you're being set up, Major. And you know it but you won't admit it."

Hanson's face froze. "And the motive?"

"When things went wrong, they needed an investigation as a cover, but not a very good investigation. So they hamstrung you from the start. And then French got close and it was necessary to keep you from discovering what the virus really was. You're an honorable man, Major. They knew you would have done something about it."

It was so quiet in the room, Doohan could hear the major breathing.

"I suppose you know what the virus actually is?"

Doohan nodded. "Yes."

A tic had developed in Hanson's left cheek. "I'm waiting."

"The double-exposure aspects," Doohan said slowly. "They exist. You know that. But Roy French didn't commit suicide, and Ramon Guitterez didn't deliberately kill his own wife, whom he loved dearly, by allowing her to be exposed twice. The double-exposure aspects came as a complete surprise to the conspirators; they had no idea of the double-exposure danger."

"You built up a case for the double-exposure feature," Hanson said. "If that wasn't the purpose of the virus, then it remains an influenza variant, as I've said."

Doohan took out his wallet and spread the positive prints of the Polaroid backing sheets across the table top. "The double-exposure was an unexpected byproduct. This is what the virus was meant to do."

Hanson stared at the photographs without comment, then took out a magnifying glass from a desk drawer for a closer look. "They're fetuses."

"The hamsters," Doohan said. "Paul French had inoculated a dozen pregnant hamsters with the culture. The virus is linked with a DNA fragment that causes the fetus to become a monster, resulting in early abortions. Once the DNA fragment has been incorporated within the body cells, including the sperm cells . . . no pregnancy will ever come to term."

Hanson kneaded the bridge of his nose. "And as a weapon?"

"You spread the virus among the enemy in whatever pattern you wish; you can be selective, as they were with the veterans. Spread it among the farmers or the blue-collar workers or the intellectual class. In a matter of months, or years, depending on when you spread the agent, the birth rate falls. The population dwindles and ages. Within a limited number of generations, the original country simply disappears. Its cities will empty, its farmlands will lie fallow. All you have to have is patience—and you win the war."

"It doesn't make sense," Hanson objected. "When our birth rate showed signs of dropping to zero, we would know we'd been attacked; we'd find out who did it and launch a counterattack."

"You weren't listening," Doohan said, tired. "It's not a disease; it doesn't spread by infection. It can be done slowly; you'll probably think it was due to more effective birth-control methods. It will be years before you recognize the situation you're in and by that time, it will be too late."

Hanson waved a hand at the photographs. "Of course we would know. These monsters . . ."

"Those were hamsters, Major, and they aborted very late in term. But in human beings a lot of pregnancies end in spontaneous abortions very early in term. That month the menstrual flow is just a little heavier. I suspect the virus just helps nature along a little. Early enough—and I am sure the virus is designed to be effective early on—the fetus would be too small for the malformations to be even noticed."

"The final solution," Hanson said quietly, still staring at the photographs. "Sans gas chambers, mass murders, firing squads or any kind of major war."

Doohan pulled another photograph from his pocket and put it on the table, flattening out the folds. It was the photograph that had been on Benoit's corkboard. "The plotters. Taken at Ford Detrick in 1962." His forefinger traveled over the cracked emulsion, pointing out the faces. "Roy French; he supervised the collection of the blood to test the effectiveness of the virus. Cedric Laval, the *garde-manger,* the salad chef who made sure the virus-laced mayonnaise was fed to the veterans. Ramon Guitterez, who supplied the special mayonnaise to begin with . . ."

Hanson studied the faces. "Who did they work for?"

Doohan's finger traveled half an inch. "This man Dr. Hugh Benoit."

Hanson looked up. "You knew him, didn't you?"

"Apparently not very well," Doohan said bitterly. "He befriended me when I first came to town. I was, after all, an expert in plague control. I think he toyed with the idea of enlisting me."

"And who was he working for?"

Doohan shrugged. "I have no idea."

"And this man?" Hanson pointed at the fat man on whose shoulder Benoit was resting a friendly hand.

Another shrug. "I don't know."

Hanson sagged back in his chair. "I've been a patsy," he said quietly.

A rigid man, Doohan thought with sympathy. Despite his own denials, a man who followed orders. A man who could be relied upon. "They sold out their own country. And to do it, they sold you as well."

"It must have been risky," Hanson mused. "Bringing in the culture from overseas."

Doohan slowly shook his head. Hanson still hadn't guessed. "Too risky. So they made it right in this country. They needed a manufacturing base with P-3 facilities. And they found one—right here at Endo-Syn. That was the beauty of it. Everything was hidden where it was least likely to be found: in plain sight. Benoit was a consultant; he probably touted them on it."

There was a knock on the door and Hanson snapped, "Come in!" It opened and framed in the doorway was an enormous fat man, his eyes blinking behind his Coke-bottle lenses, his bulk filling the entrance. Doohan's jaw dropped. The man glanced at him but Doohan guessed that even with glasses, the fat man's eyesight was so bad that recognition was probably a measurable number of seconds. And then he'd have to be up close. . . .

Close enough to give injections, Doohan thought. There was no doubt it was the same man who had given him the shots the night before. And there was no doubt it was the same man in the photograph. Unlike the others, the years had neither added to nor thinned that gross body.

"I'm sorry for intruding," Dr. Thomas Gorshin said.

47

FOR JUST A moment, time was frozen. Neither Doohan nor Hanson said anything. Gorshin glanced nervously from one to the other, the words dying in his throat. He took a tentative step further into the room; the thick neck swiveled and watery eyes blinked at Doohan for a second.

Then Gorshin, with a speed surprising for his bulk, backed out of the office and slammed the door behind him.

"The fat man," Doohan said stupidly.

Hanson jiggled the phone on his desk. "Where the hell is Roberts? The bastard's never around when you need him!" He tried once more, then came around his desk belting on a holster and a .45. "Gorshin has an office near the P-3 area; he'll be dangerous now that we've found him out."

In the outer office, Hanson paused just long enough to snarl at his startled secretary: "Get hold of Murphy and Steed and tell them to meet us at Gorshin's office; they're probably playing cards in the ready room. And keep trying to get Roberts. He's got to be around somewhere."

Doohan lagged behind and Hanson turned to him, his expression bitter. His voice held a manic note. "You want to see the end of the story, don't you, Doctor? Find out who's been pulling my strings? Maybe Gorshin can tell us both."

Hanson plunged down the corridor, Doohan running to keep up with him. They took an elevator two floors up and raced down the hall. At the end, a company guard seated at a desk looked up in surprise as Hanson and Doohan ran up.

"Did Dr. Gorshin come this way?"

The guard nodded and Hanson pushed through the door.

"Major! You have to sign—"

"Shove it!" Hanson growled.

Gorshin's door was locked. Hanson kicked it open without hesitation. Inside, the fat man was just putting down the phone. In the large ashtray on his desk, the remains of several crumpled pieces of paper still smoldered. Doohan glanced quickly around the room. On the far wall, various charts showed a succession of chemical reactions. All of them, he noted, centered around a basic DNA fragment.

Gorshin sat behind his desk like a fat Buddha, blinking furiously as he tried to catch all their movements. "Before you threaten me," he said nervously, "you should realize I have no intention of answering any questions."

Hanson cocked the pistol and pointed it at Gorshin's head. "I'm prepared to argue the point. If you can't answer my questions, then who can? And I'm not going to wait long for the answers."

Gorshin wet his lips. "With Dr. Benoit dead, I'm probably the only one who can."

"Benoit was a traitor," Doohan cut in angrily.

The thick lenses turned in his direction. "On the contrary, Dr. Benoit was a great patriot."

"The viewpoint undoubtedly varies," Hanson said sarcastically. "Depending on which country you owe your allegiance to." He stepped closer to Gorshin. "You used me," he said, his voice an inch away from murder. "You and the others."

Gorshin didn't react. Doohan couldn't tell whether he was frightened witless or had passed beyond it to an area of unfeeling calm. "We had no choice," Gorshin said. Then nervously: "What do you want?"

"I think what I want is something I never got," Hanson said slowly. "I want a tour of the plant—the important part. And I want a complete explanation. A complete one, Doctor, or I'll splatter your brains all over the catwalks."

Gorshin hesitated, then nodded at Doohan. "And him? Shouldn't the guards hold him?"

Hanson shook his head. "He goes with us."

Gorshin reluctantly got up from the desk and Hanson waved him toward the door with his gun, then holstered it. "You, first, Doctor. And if there's any difficulty, please remember that you'll die a fraction of a second before I do."

"You won't understand all the explanations," Gorshin said.

"I'll try."

Doohan followed them out, suddenly wondering why the two MPs hadn't arrived yet. Neither, he thought, had Roberts; and instinct told him that following Gorshin any place without their own men along would be risky.

At the doorway to the manufacturing section, Gorshin signed in for them. In the anteroom, they put on white paper coveralls and filter masks. A sign on the door to the inner corridor read: YELLOW AREA. COVERALLS REQUIRED. MASKS OPTIONAL.

They went in and found themselves on a catwalk in the completely self-contained world that was the primary P-3 facility. On one side of the walk, Doohan could see large revolving fermentation vats, each of them two stories high, and a huge stainless steel continuous centrifuge. On the other side were overhead solvent vats with the warnings CAUTION! FLAMMABLE! stenciled on their sides. He guessed that the solvents were used to precipitate whatever compounds were being generated in the fermentation vats.

He looked further down the walk and realized he was standing in the middle of a production line for manufacturing bulk pharmaceuticals.

"This is where you make it?" Hanson asked.

Gorshin nodded. "Yes, the Benoit Factor is manufactured here in these vats."

Doohan stared. "The Benoit Factor?"

Something close to awe crept into Gorshin's voice. "Dr. Benoit created it and he was justifiably proud of it. Originally, it was a rather obscure virus that attacked chlorella—algae. Its basic structure is very similar to that of the Tobacco Mosaic Virus. He had great plans for it as a carrier of genetic material." Gorshin's voice acquired a subtle glow. "We could tailor the human race so that good characteristics could be added and harmful ones deleted. Hereditary diseases could be eliminated forever, perhaps the genes for intelligence or courage or obedience could be added."

What was it Espinosa had once said? Doohan thought. *It begins with the do-gooders and it ends with the exterminators.*

Hanson waved at the dozen or so workers in white coveralls moving among the fermentation vats. "Do they know what they're working on?"

Gorshin shrugged. "Hardly."

"They couldn't guess?"

"It's not that unusual a procedure. Besides, they're workers; they just follow directions."

Gorshin stopped to talk to one of the nearby technicians and Hanson pulled Doohan back. "Stay close by me. Roberts hasn't shown up and neither have Murphy or Steed."

"Trouble?"

"Look up above—don't stare."

He should have noticed them immediately, Doohan thought. At the corners of the huge, three-story-high room were small towers. Behind the glass in each of them he could see a uniformed guard. Company guards again, not military personnel.

Gorshin had stopped before one of the fermentation vats. "We keep a culture of Benoit Factor A—the precursor to the final agent—in continuous growth in the tanks. As I implied, we grow it in chlorella, monitoring the level of the virus. At a certain point, we filter off the algae, rupture the cells, and extract the virus. Then we modify it to the final strain we want; the virus molecule is very easy to modify, just the last three units of the DNA chain."

The glass-walled P-3 enclosure itself was entered through an airlock, the inner door opening with a small sob of air. There were filtered air intakes in the ceiling, and Doohan could hear the mammoth exhaust fans laboring behind them. The fans maintained a small negative air pressure in the enclosure so that in the event of accident, no viral material would escape into the main building. He guessed the final air supply went through one-micron filters and several fluid sterilizing baths.

Gorshin walked over to a glass wall separating the enclosure area from the culture area, reached through a diaphragm in the wall, and took out a container from the rack on the other side. He held up the bottle and swirled the silver-flecked liquid inside. "The Benoît B Factor, ready for the final steps. We split the double helix of the virus after removing its protein coat, and then insert the DNA fragment." He glanced at Doohan. "Did you know there's a naturally occurring abortive agent found in most animals? It's a hormone, but we've isolated the DNA molecule that causes it to be made in the body. That's the one we mate with the Benoît Factor. And finally, of course, we make the virus dependent on vanadium."

"How many people know the whole process?" Hanson asked.

There was a palpable aura of power about Gorshin now. If he were a thinner man, Doohan thought, he could have played Moses on the Mount. "Now that Dr. Benoît is dead, I'm afraid I'm the only one." He kept glancing back into the main laboratory room and Doohan followed his gaze. The outer room seemed oddly deserted. "I rather doubt that any of my colleagues could reproduce the heart of the work—good minds, but simply not of the caliber required."

"And I imagine you've taken precautions," Hanson said wryly.

Gorshin allowed himself a small smile. "I took those precautions just before you broke into my office."

Gorshin was watching the main laboratory room again and Doohan felt his skin begin to crawl. The man was waiting for something.

"What are those men doing over there?" Doohan asked suddenly. He pointed toward the far end of the lab.

"They're probably getting ready to leave," Gorshin mumbled. "It's time for the shift change." He looked toward where Doohan was pointing, the disappointment heavy in his voice. Hanson looked too, then glanced sharply at Doohan. There was nobody there. At that distance, Gorshin could probably distinguish only light and shadow. They were clearing out the main lab, Doohan thought; that was what Gorshin was waiting for. And then the sharpshooters in the turrets could pick them off when they left.

"I think I better check on Roberts," Hanson said quietly. Before Gorshin could say anything, he had slipped back out the airlock. Doohan watched him cycle the outer door and step cautiously out, then immediately jerk back in. At the same time, a small castle of glass tubing on a table nearby Hanson suddenly shattered and collapsed. It was too late, Doohan thought. The lab had been cleared.

He sensed something behind him and turned to see Gorshin fumbling in his pocket. Doohan grabbed for the arm. Gorshin was stronger than he had guessed, far stronger. Gorshin slowly pulled his arm out and levered it toward Doohan, his hand clutching a small automatic. Doohan abruptly let go and buried his fist in the massive stomach. Gorshin grunted but didn't seem to feel it. Doohan dodged and grabbed at the arm again; a moment more and Gorshin would be able to fire. The fat man's eyes were blazing now, his face tense with concentration.

There was a small low cart directly behind Gorshin, the kind used to trundle in supplies. Doohan suddenly put his shoulder down and rammed the fat man. Gorshin stumbled backward and hit the cart. He fell sprawling as the gun skittered across the floor.

"All right, freeze!" Hanson was back in the enclosure, blood welling from a shoulder wound. He pointed at Gorshin. "You. Get up. We'll all three leave at the same time. They won't dare fire at you, Doctor."

Gorshin went white. He licked his lips. "You're wrong; I'm not in charge—"

"Out. You first." The three of them crowded through the airlock. The moment they were out, Doohan heard a *spang!* and more glass tubing collapsed in a pile of shards. Hanson pushed Gorshin ahead of him and ran toward a fermentation tank. Doohan raced after them. The three of them fell to the catwalk grating just behind the tank. Half a dozen shots had rattled the area around them, but Doohan didn't think they had hit anybody. Then he noticed the gouts of bright arterial blood soaking Hanson's coveralls, staining them a vivid red.

There was another shot from one of the guard towers and Gorshin tried to scramble away. Hanson grabbed him by one foot. A moment later he had Gorshin's head in an arm lock, the muzzle of his pistol pressed tight against it.

Doohan took out a pocket knife. "I can stop the bleeding." He started cutting away Hanson's clothing.

"You've been very good," Hanson said to the trembling Gorshin. "You've told me almost everything we want to know."

"Almost?" The lenses turned toward Hanson like miniature searchlights. "I swear I didn't leave anything out."

"The customer," Hanson said tightly. "You haven't told me who your customer is. You haven't told me who ordered the virus, who sponsored your research, who's paying you scum."

"I can't," Gorshin bleated.

Hanson's voice suddenly went dead of emotion. "I'll give you five to tell me," he said dully, "or I'll blow your brains out right here. And don't ask for pity—I have none for traitors."

Surprisingly, there was sudden strength in Gorshin's voice. "They'll give me a medal," he said defiantly. "They'll—"

"Who will?" Hanson asked. He tightened his arm still more and Gorshin started to make strangling sounds.

"The Department of Defense," Gorshin groaned, the words forced out of him. There was dead silence except for Gorshin gasping for air and Hanson's own ragged breathing. "We've been working under contract to ARPA, the Advanced Research Projects Agency."

There was another long moment of silence, and then Doohan heard Hanson whisper to himself: "So it *was* one of ours."

Gorshin started to babble in indignation. "You never guessed? There's no way a foreign power could have carried on a project of this magnitude right here!"

Doohan was almost finished with the tourniquet. He glanced up at Hanson who had nothing but anguish in his eyes. "You'll have to testify," Doohan said in a low voice. "Some day, in some court . . ."

Hanson closed his eyes. "I was only following orders," he whispered softly.

Doohan gave a final twist to the tourniquet. "I know," he muttered. There was nothing more to say. What Hanson needed now was a priest.

Gorshin tried to squirm away and Hanson gripped him tighter. His face was pale from loss of blood. "Where are you in the production run?" he suddenly asked Gorshin.

The fat man gulped for air. "We start mass-producing the Benoit B Strain on the next shift. We ran the test sample—"

Hanson interrupted, looking down at Doohan. "Leave the leg alone and get the hell out of here, Doohan. I'll try and cover for you, but you're going to have to run for it."

Doohan didn't move. "I can't leave—"

"Doohan, you fool, I took you along for insurance! You're the only one who's going to know! Get out of here! *Now!*"

Doohan started to run. Shots spattered around his legs. Then he heard two shots close by followed by the sudden feel of intense heat at his back. He half-turned. Hanson had fired at one of the massive solvent tanks. The tank was erupting in a shower of blue flames. An alcohol fire. The solvent cascaded down in flaming torrents and for a moment a huge fat man was outlined in flickering blue, screaming while he pulled at his burning coveralls. Doohan started back to try to get Hanson. Then he saw, sickly, that it was already too late.

The other solvent tanks were going now. He ran through the main lab exit door and was trapped in a corridor filled with running, screaming technicians. Somewhere a P.A. system was squawking: *"Containment breech! Emergency! Containment breech!"*

He made it across the bridge between the buildings and then was in the Endo-Syn lobby. He thought he saw Suzanne in the milling crowd, and then an ether tank erupted, the explosion jarring the entire building. He helped a crying secretary to her feet and they both ran out into the blessed open air. Behind him, flames leaped from the wing that held the shattered P-3 enclosure. Lesser explosions were throwing clouds of sparks into the sky.

What was it Hanson had said? he thought, dazed. He was the only one who knew. The conspirators were dead; the victims were dead; French and Woodruff and Celia had been murdered. And Hanson and Gorshin had died in the ruins of the P-3 enclosure. He still had the photographs and Espinosa would have the ampoules. But he suddenly wasn't sure that would count for much. There was only himself now.

And the plotters within the government.

48

Espinosa never got the ampoules.

Doohan went into hiding immediately after leaving the flaming building at Endo-Syn, reading later and with great satisfaction about the details of the fire and the rumors of a pending congressional investigation; the loss of life; the hints of secret research possibly involving recombinant DNA. The upper levels of the governmental bureaucracy were springing more news leaks than at any time since Watergate, he thought. But if you read between the lines, there were also indications that the investigation would be choked off, that the whole story was simply a seven-day wonder that would be relegated to the back pages on the eighth.

He was pretty sure that nobody except possibly Strout was concerned with his own whereabouts.

When he finally called Espinosa and the old man confirmed that the ampoules had never arrived, he reviewed his actions in Suzanne's apartment that night a dozen times. Finally he decided if Espinosa hadn't received the ampoules, the package had either been intercepted, lost in the mails—or returned to sender for lack of sufficient postage. He stewed about it and then recalled that the box of checks had originally been mailed from Suzanne's home in Bel-Air. He hadn't scratched out the return address; if there hadn't been enough postage, the package would have been returned there.

Finally, he risked a call to Suzanne's apartment and found that the number had been disconnected. He made a blind call to the Public Health Department;

they told him she had packed and left for Southern California the day after the fire. He thought of calling her, then decided to fly down there instead. It was a slim possibility, but it was worth checking out.

And he wanted to see her very badly.

Saturday morning, he caught a PSA flight out of San Francisco for Los Angeles. Half an hour after arrival, his cab was winding its way past the grillwork fences of the estates of Bel-Air.

"Here we are, mister. Want me to wait?"

Doohan fished some loose bills out of his wallet. "I don't think so. I'll call for a cab later."

The house was large and opulent, even by Bel-Air standards. The section he could see through the trees was field stone and rough-sawed redwood stained a golden green. The rest of the house was lost among the trees, though he could see part of a Japanese garden with a small reflecting pool fed by a bamboo pipe. One end of the pool was bordered by black bamboo and a small stone lantern that was reflected in the water. It looked very calm and peaceful.

The tiled walkway leading to the huge, double-entrance doors was protected by cast-iron gates, decorated with brass medallions. Doohan pushed the button in the center of one of the medallions, noticing that a small intercom was hidden behind the other.

There was a long pause and he caught the sound of birds in the carefully sculptured trees and somewhere somebody splashing in a backyard pool. Finally a tiny voice said, "Yes, who is it?"

He hated himself for his instant reaction to her voice. "Dr. Calvin Doohan."

There was an even longer pause this time, and then the buzzer sounded. He pushed through the gate and walked up the tiled pathway to the house. He reached the large ebony doors just as the one on the right opened.

For a moment, he didn't recognize her. She was wearing royal-blue slacks that were obviously tailored and obviously expensive, along with a light-blue blouse that was little more than a halter, knotted at the waist. Her hair was now ash-blond; a top stylist must have worked on it for hours to tease it into the casual tresses that now framed her face. Her eyebrows had been formed and her make-up skillfully applied, her lips a dusty pink.

"Calvin, what a pleasant surprise!"

The voice was the same, he thought, but the eyes belonged to somebody else. They were the eyes of a stranger, polite with a hint of friendship but nothing more. There was no indication that she had ever lain naked with him, had ever run the gamut of passions with him on sweat-stained sheets, had ever let him bury himself within her body.

Strange. Those memories would have fit this woman better than the other. "I couldn't contact you right away," he said.

She laughed pleasantly and waved him in. "I shouldn't keep you standing there—come in, Calvin. It's really very good to see you." She took him by the hand and drew him inside, then let him kiss her politely on the cheek. There was a hint of perfume about her, an exotic scent that reminded him of . . . what?

The massive entry hall was two stories high, illuminated by the sunlight streaming through a stained-glass skylight. The wall to the left of the doors was filled with the largest Miro he had ever seen, easily six by eight feet. The floor was an intricate tile mosaic in earth colors.

He followed her into an equally massive living room that opened off the hall. The far glass wall looked out over a large yard dominated by a huge swimming pool. The pool and yard had been designed to look like a forest glen, with carefully placed rocks and water-hugging vegetation. Somebody was swimming naked in the pool, brown limbs flashing in the sun, and Doohan watched for a moment, then turned away.

It was overwhelming, he thought. The whole effect would have been stunning except that it constantly reminded you of how much it must have cost.

Suzanne was sitting in a recessed conversation pit facing the glass wall and patting the sofa as a sign for him to sit down next to her. He did; it was awkward. His right arm grazed hers and she absently stroked it, a near parody of the times she had run her fingertips lightly over the hairs of his arm when they were in bed.

"You left right after the fire," he said.

She shrugged and tossed her head slightly. She should let her hair grow, he thought absently; the gesture then would be spectacular. "There wasn't much sense in staying around. I had already been released from the CDC and assigned to the major. After Major Hanson . . . there wasn't anything left to do. So—poof!—here I am."

Her eyes were guileless, her face more and more a cruel reminder. He was waiting for her to ask how he had been, what had happened, that she had missed him.

She offered him a cigarette and said: "How was your flight?"

There was no sense in staying, he thought; it would be an exercise in masochism. She had once said that she had loved money, that she had been bought. She had claimed she hated it, but obviously the objection had been to the price and not to the act.

"It was fine," he said quietly. He stood up. "Has your mail arrived yet?"

She looked puzzled and slightly piqued and waved a hand at a credenza against the far wall. On top was a large silver dish piled high with letters. He spotted the brown envelope immediately.

"Why on earth do you ask?"

He glanced down at the carpet and looked almost apologetic. "I sent you something," he said simply. "I think that now, perhaps . . . it would be inappropriate."

That was it, he thought. His acknowledgement that, of course, it was all over, he understood that.

She picked up on the softness of his voice and lowered her own. "Of course, Calvin."

He picked the package out of the pile and dropped it into his pocket. All he wanted to do now was get out of there. He'd find a phone someplace and call a cab from outside.

In the entranceway she kissed him lightly on the

lips. There was no warmth, not the faintest sign of passion. "You're sweet, Calvin—I'll never forget you."

"Sorry to intrude, Suzanne," a man's resonant voice said. "I didn't know we had guests."

Doohan turned. The man looked and sounded oddly familiar, though he could have sworn he had never met him before. Physically massive, but the sense of power held in leash didn't come from the physique alone. He was somewhere between forty and fifty with heavy shoulders and thick arms. He was almost Doohan's height with a heavy chest that strained against the tailored sport shirt. His hair was jet black, touched with frost at the temples. His eyes were intense, the sort of eyes that most men would have difficulty meeting.

He walked as if he were a prince born to the purple, a king without a throne. An Alexander or a Caesar, born out of his time and place in history.

Suzanne took Doohan by the hand and led him back into the living room. "This is Dr. Calvin Doohan," she said casually. "We worked in the CDC together."

"I'm Arnold Pahlevi, Suzanne's husband," the man said, extending a stubby-fingered hand. The grip was just right, firm but not crushing. The clue to the man's character, Doohan thought. Just the right amount of pressure . . .

The sense of familiarity was even stronger now. "I've heard of you," Doohan said formally.

"Something pleasant, I hope. Would you like a drink?" Pahlevi stepped behind the huge bar at the right-hand side of the room. "Anything special?"

Doohan stared. "I was just leaving," he said slowly.

Pahlevi completely ignored him. "How about a martini?" He picked up a decanter from the shelf behind him. "You might enjoy this. It's *habhel* gin; something rare in these parts."

Doohan remained staring. He didn't say anything.

Pahlevi smiled. "That *was* a stupid giveaway, wasn't it? See his face, Suzanne? Dr. Doohan is just remembering that we've met before."

The house in Sausalito, Doohan thought. The big

man slouched in his chair, offering him a martini and then ordering Gorshin to administer the shots. Suzanne swept past him, walking toward the couch, and he had another shock. The exotic scent. At the time his nose had been almost anesthetized by the smelling salts, but he had still caught a wisp of the perfume then. It was Suzanne who had given him the glass of water.

Suzanne curled up on the couch, looking bored. "There are times when your sense of humor is too much even for me," she said blackly.

A door at the far end of the room opened and a young man came in. He was wearing a swimsuit and sandals and drying his hair with a beach towel. He finished and draped the towel casually over his shoulder. He glanced at Doohan, nodded and said, "Hello, Dr. Doohan." There was none of the hostility he had formerly shown Doohan. Like Suzanne, he was casually friendly.

Roberts, Doohan thought coldly. No wonder Murphy and Steed had never showed up when Hanson had called for them; no wonder Roberts couldn't be found. When they had broken into Gorshin's office, the fat man had just hung up the phone—from telling Roberts they were in trouble. And Gorshin had said he wasn't in charge, that he wasn't calling the shots. It must have been Roberts, as Pahlevi's right-hand man. And it must have been Roberts—

Pahlevi glanced at Roberts with affectionate contempt. "Put on some clothes, Mark, and make yourself useful. We could use some coffee." He watched the younger man leave, then turned back to Doohan. "Lieutenant Roberts has worked for me for some time now, ever since I was in the service myself. He isn't always the most effective agent, but he's loyal. That counts for a lot, loyalty."

The heart of the matter, Doohan thought, his mind frozen, the center of the web. Then he detected once again the faint aura of Suzanne's perfume and for a brief moment he felt faint, then sick and weak. It hadn't been Hanson. And it hadn't been Roberts.

"Come on, Doctor, don't just stand there looking

shocked. I can assure you that you can leave the same way you came in. In the meantime, let's have a drink. We might as well be civilized about this."

Doohan was having a heavy time of it. He turned to Suzanne and said almost wonderingly: "For a long time I thought it was Hanson, or possibly Roberts, but I never talked to either one of them. I talked to you, though. I spilled my guts to you almost every day. You set up Woodruff, didn't you? Only you knew that he had the test animals. And when he called to you to get my phone number, you probably pumped him as to what was happening, and once you knew, he was murdered. And French. He liked you; he talked to you, too. He probably told you enough so that you guessed he was getting close."

She stood up, her eyes blazing. "I don't have to listen to this!" Pahlevi walked over and put his arm around her waist possessively. "So your guest is upset; take it in stride." She fit very comfortably into Pahlevi's arm and Doohan suddenly realized that she loved Pahlevi, at least in any way that mattered to her. She had probably always loved Pahlevi, and he meant more than just money; he was also power and protection. That was what he so frequently sensed was wrong in his relationship with Suzanne—that she was still in love with her husband.

Pahlevi turned back to him. "Dr. Doohan, you've proved yourself remarkably resourceful. That's a valuable trait in our society. It's a trait that could prove very valuable to me."

"Dr. Benoit tried to recruit me once," Doohan said dryly.

"He showed good sense." Pahlevi shook his head. "Benoit. I'll miss the old bastard."

The key, Doohan thought. "You're one of the major stockholders in Endo-Syn?"

"Shut *up*, Arnold!" Suzanne hissed.

Pahlevi looked at her and shrugged. "Why? It's public record. And there'll be some kind of Mickey Mouse investigation. It'll come out then."

He turned to Doohan. "The sole stockholder, Doctor." An affectionate glance at Suzanne, still standing

in the crook of his arm. "I never share my holdings."
She remained wooden-faced and he added candidly:
"Except when there's something to be gained, of
course."

"Why?" Doohan asked in a strained voice. "Why
the slaughter in San Francisco—"

"You mean, why did I try and develop the final
weapon for my country?" Pahlevi leaned back and
chuckled. "God, you moralists. You're an endangered
species. You really think there's a difference between
whether a man dies from disease or from an atomic
bomb or from being hit by a truck. Come on, Doctor,
for once try living in the real world."

"That was a genocidal agent," Doohan said, shaking
his head. "You were plotting the deaths of whole pop-
ulations!"

Pahlevi sighed. "My good Doctor, I was plotting
nothing. I'm a businessman. ARPA of the Department
of Defense comes to me and says, 'Officially we've
abandoned all offensive BW research, but the rest of
the world is hard at it and we don't dare stop. Will
you help us?' What am I supposed to do? My company is heavily into recombinant DNA research; we
have the facilities to do the job. And if I don't take the
contracts, others will. Dr. Benoit was a consultant for
me. I knew he had the right connections from some
former work at Fort Detrick; so he put together the
rest of the team." He hesitated. "A politically agreeable
one, of course."

"When they investigate this, you'll have a lot to
answer for," Doohan said tightly.

"Do you really think so?" Pahlevi laughed. "The
work was and is financed from the Department of
Defense discretionary budget. Do you know how large
that budget is? Do you think that the people in the
DOD who made the decision without consulting the
President and the Chiefs of Staff will confess all? Or
that their congressional allies will let them down?
Bullshit, my dear Doctor. A few generals or civil service types will resign or retire—and they'll be taken
care of handsomely. The congressional inquiry will be
behind closed doors, and eventually they'll issue a re-

port that seems to say something and will then be lost somewhere between the Government Printing Office and the Library of Congress."

Roberts reappeared from the kitchen now, pushing a small cart carrying a silver coffee ewer and four cups and saucers of delicate, almost transparent china. Suzanne poured, her hands shaking only slightly as she handed Doohan his cup.

"So much for mass murder," Doohan said bitterly.

"Mass murder?" It was Pahlevi's turn to look angry. "How many precautions do you think we took? We tried that culture on animals. For God's sake, man, since some of us were overage and others didn't want children, we even tried it on ourselves. I did; Roberts did; Benoit and Roy French did; some of the others . . . and when we had to make a mass test, we made sure we tried it on people above childbearing age, the Elks and the veterans and their wives. What happened was an accident, Doctor, a goddamned accident! We had taken every precaution. Benoit, French, Guitterez—they were my friends. Ramon's wife was a delightful house guest. Do you think I would willingly condemn my friends to death?"

"You forget," Doohan said bitterly. "You *did* condemn Ramon Guitterez to death. And Paul French and Celia Kovacs and Alex Woodruff. And you would have killed me."

Pahlevi cracked his knuckles, the expression on his face unreadable. "We were at war, Doctor, and I had to hire my own mercenaries. So I didn't do a very good job; but that's not my line of business. And in a war, you have to expect casualties. I'm sorry about your friends; I'm sorry about my own. Ramon pushed me into it; he left me no choice."

"And Gorshin? And Hanson?"

"When the . . . accident . . . happened in 'Frisco, we knew there would be an investigation, that the CDC would certainly be there. So we arranged to have Hanson put in charge. He wasn't too bright; we thought we could control him. And we took no chances. Dr. Gorshin misled him; Roberts watched him and made sure he didn't do too much damage.

And I arranged to have Suzanne sent there as further insurance. You were a potential problem. . . ."

"Roberts had Hanson killed."

The lieutenant was standing by the window, seemingly oblivious to the conversation behind him.

"In the last analysis, Hanson killed himself."

"But Roberts would have."

Pahlevi sighed and shook his head. "Doctor, you're beginning to bore me—and I'm starting to wonder why I'm trying to justify myself to you. You worry about a few lives and yet the world revels in mass murders. What do you want us to do? Play the innocent when we know damned well the world's a jungle? Everybody's been developing biological agents —and they've been using them. Before Sadat kicked them out, the Russians were cultivating dengue fever in Egyptian laboratories. The Chinese are working on Lhasa fever in their African client states. And what do you think is behind the Russian program to mass-inoculate their population by aerosol agents in theaters and public places? Do you think the decline in the Chinese birth rate is a coincidence or is it something else? The CIA tried to spread African swine flu in Cuba and the Cubans planned to spread hoof and mouth disease in Texas. Or the Smolensk strain—was that ours, or one of the Red Chinese?"

He finished his cup of coffee and Roberts went to the kitchen, came back with a filled pot, poured some in Pahlevi's cup and then put the pot on the bar.

"We're under attack, Doctor. World War III started in 1969—and it's being fought today with the most subtle weapons imaginable. You think I sell myself for money; I think I'm a patriot. But what really matters, Doctor, is not what you think but what I think."

It was going to go on and on, Doohan thought. As Pahlevi said, there would be an investigation and that would die. A brief flurry in the papers, perhaps, and that would be it. The ploy with the UN would undoubtedly fail. The United States would veto any action and deny everything that had happened. What he needed was a confession. But there was nobody left alive to confess . . .

"Where's the washroom?" he suddenly asked.

Pahlevi pointed, smiling. "Roberts makes strong coffee; I have trouble handling it myself."

In the washroom, Doohan quickly opened the package and dropped the wrappings in the small basket under the sink. He took out the ampoules, snapped off the tops, and then placed them carefully back in his pocket. There was no touching Pahlevi, he thought. Human sympathy and compassion had long ago been replaced by ambition and rationalization. It didn't matter whether countries won or lost, the Pahlevis of the world would always win. The goal was power, and they rode piggyback on the hopes and fears of individuals and nations.

Back in the living room, he took his cup and walked over to the coffee pot on the bar. Nobody was watching; Pahlevi and Suzanne had strolled over to the picture window to watch some birds hop around a bird feeder in their artificial forest glen. Roberts was deep in a magazine. Doohan took the ampoules out of his pocket and dumped the contents into the coffee pot, swirling the pot slightly so the bluish crystals completely disappeared. He desperately hoped the culture had no taste. It probably didn't. Mayonnaise had disguised it once before, and the black coffee would cover the slightly yellow color given by the crystals.

Back in the conversation pit, he said: "Let me warm up everybody's cup." He was sweating and nervous and hoped to God that nobody noticed.

Pahlevi turned away from the window. "Let Roberts do it; that's his job."

Doohan handed the pot to Roberts who first filled Pahlevi's cup, Suzanne's, and then his own. Doohan had already filled his.

"What will you do, now that the agent's been destroyed?"

Pahlevi shrugged. "Win some, lose some, Doctor. There are other promising strains in one of our eastern laboratories. And, of course, there are other subcontractors." He grinned. "I'm not the only one, you may be sure."

"I remember reading of the Legionnaire flu in Philadelphia," Doohan said. "Was that one of yours?"

"No, but as I said, there are other contractors. Who knows?"

Doohan lifted his cup and drained it and watched Pahlevi do the same. He glanced at his watch. "I guess I better leave."

"I'll have Roberts call you a cab."

Suzanne stood up and said, "Let me freshen up a bit; I'll be right with you." Doohan watched her disappear into the same washroom he had just used and felt a brief pang of anxiety.

For a moment, Doohan and Pahlevi were alone in the entryway. Pahlevi looked at him with a touch of regret. "Everybody has a price, Doctor. You have one too, you know, though it isn't money. Suzanne told me of the feeling you get when you cure people; that's your sense of power. Greater than my own, I suspect. And if you consider the mere possession of power to be evil, then you're more of a sinner than most men." The friendliness disappeared now and Pahlevi wore a different mask, a frightening one. "You'll keep this information quiet, Doctor. We can still reach you if we have to."

"You bastard!"

The three of them turned. Suzanne had slammed out of the washroom, her hair disheveled and eyes blazing, holding the wrapping that Doohan had crumpled and dropped in the basket. "You mailed something to Espinosa and that's what was returned! What was it?"

They were staring at him now, Pahlevi with a surprised expression, Roberts ashen, Suzanne with a face made ugly by hatred.

"The ampoules," Doohan said quietly. "I had mailed them to Espinosa in Washington."

"Where are they?" she shrieked. "What did you do with them?"

Doohan held them out in his hand. Pahlevi took them, glanced at them, then let them fall from his hands to shatter on the tile. "Empty," he said in a flat voice. He looked at Doohan. "The coffee?"

Doohan nodded. "I drank it too."

"It doesn't matter for *you*," Suzanne said. "You hadn't been previously exposed." She started moaning. "You've killed us; my God, you've murdered us!"

Doohan shook his head. "You have a chance."

Pahlevi's face was unreadable. "How? There were no survivors in San Francisco."

"The CDC must have done a lot of work on it," Doohan said, suddenly very tired. "There might be something they could do—if they had more information. You could call them, tell them what you know. Gorshin is dead but the three of you must know a lot about the process."

Robert's face was red with fury. "You'll die before we will!" he raged.

Doohan glanced at him with contempt. "French told me a lot," he said. "I'll be passing that information along, too. Not only because it might help you—it will help a lot of people."

Roberts shuddered, then broke and collapsed in a chair. He started to cry.

"You've murdered us!" Suzanne screamed again, the tears streaking her make-up. She looked much older now. "There's no way they can make a vaccine in ten days; there's no way they can save us!"

"You don't know," Doohan said, starting for the door. "They might be able to do something." He opened one of the huge entrance doors, then turned. "There's hope," he added. "There's always hope."

In the living room, he could see Pahlevi dialing.

49

"You still have a few hours before your plane leaves," Espinosa said. "I imagine it will feel good to go back and have your own practice."

"Maybe." Doohan managed a smile. "They don't have smallpox in Scotland."

They sat in silence for a moment, then Espinosa said: "I suppose the one who interests me the most is Hanson. A rigid man, but an honorable one. 'Death before dishonor.' It sounds very trite until you see it actually carried out."

"I didn't understand him very well," Doohan said regretfully. "Not until the end."

It was late and only a few diners remained. Two waiters, impeccable in white ties, stood at the far end of the room surreptitiously watching them and waiting for them to leave so the room could close.

"And the vaccine?"

"I understand from Anna Goldstein that it's coming along. Perhaps in a few more months . . ." He seemed lost in thought for a moment. "I still remember Gorshin holding up the flask of Benoit Factor B. If any of it survived the fire—well, we may need that vaccine."

Espinosa hesitated. "It's too bad they couldn't have done the impossible."

"Pahlevi died with honor too, you know. He told everything he knew. I understand that Roberts . . . didn't go out so gracefully. At the end, he accused almost everybody."

"How's Suzanne doing?"

"With Pahlevi's death, she's enormously wealthy. She'll be able to buy anything she needs, everything she wants. I hope she provides for Roberts' widow." Pause. "You know, she expected to die, too. But Pahlevi had seen to it that she was never given a shot of the virus, she received a placebo. Maybe he had a premonition. Perhaps he loved her so much he didn't want to see her subjected to even a little bit of danger."

"And your feelings for her?" Espinosa asked quietly.

A look of pain fled across Doohan's face. "She was instrumental in the murders of Paul French and Alex Woodruff, though I can't prove that. How can I feel anything for her? I was lonely; I hadn't slept with a woman for . . . longer than you might think possible, Doctor. She was a tonic for my ego. Maybe she was more than that; maybe she wasn't. I'm not sure I'll ever know." He hesitated. "I saw her recently. She looked haunted."

Espinosa was thoughtful for a moment, then said: "Tell me something, Calvin: Why didn't you just turn the ampoules over to the CDC?"

"Pahlevi said there were other contractors and that he himself had other strains. People needed to know what was going on. And to really believe it, they had to have a confession. From somebody at the top."

"But you had two ampoules. You couldn't have saved one?"

Doohan shook his head. "I didn't know the dosage; I didn't know if there was a threshold level or not. If they didn't . . . start to come down with the disease, they would have thought I had been bluffing."

Espinosa poured the last of the wine into his glass. "You got your confession—and your investigation—all right. I see that General Varger has resigned and a number of high-ranking officers have chosen early retirement. Even the Secretary of Defense has submitted his resignation."

"I wonder if he was ever aware of the project?" Doohan mused.

Espinosa shook his head. "I doubt it. There are so many self-contained autonomous empires within the American bureaucracy. In a budget the size of the Defense budget, it would be very easy to hide a clandestine project." He sighed. "As you get older, Calvin, you get more philosophical. There is always a point in the history of nations where the stakes are so enormous that one group of men decides that only they know best, that their colleagues are feather-headed or, worse, traitors. So they go ahead on their own with the solution or plan of action they 'know' is right. It happened more than once in America at the start of the Civil War, when the states were choosing up sides. Abraham Lincoln was a man like that."

"Pahlevi said that World War III started in 1969," Doohan said. "Do you believe that?"

"I don't know, Calvin. Perhaps it did; perhaps it didn't. The historians will tell the next generation; we'll never know." He filled up Doohan's wine glass again. "Calvin, you're more than usually depressed. Why?"

Doohan looked uneasy. "Because there are times when I think Arnold Pahlevi may have been one of the greatest men in history, and I may be one of the biggest villains. Pahlevi had discovered the most humane way of fighting a war that there is. Nobody dies —except of natural causes. No bombs bursting in air, no cities wiped from the map in one fiery ball of flame, no gas chambers, no deaths running in the millions. Everybody lives their allotted span but that's it."

Espinosa dismissed it. "You said that Pahlevi had other strains under development in his East Coast laboratories. I rather doubt that they were of so humane a nature." He looked at Doohan with compassion. "Calvin, if that's what bothers you, I can't grant you absolution. Any more than you could have given it to Hanson. You'll have to judge yourself; you'll have to determine your own guilt, if any. If it's any help, I think what you did was right." He suddenly sounded somber. "I have my own nightmare."

Doohan looked up from the elaborate doodle he had started to draw on the tablecloth. "What's that?"

"Remember my talk at the medical center where I remarked about one life-form, humanity, declaring genocidal warfare against another, the smallpox virus, and eliminating it completely?"

Doohan nodded and Espinosa signaled for another bottle of wine. They sat silent while the waiter uncorked and poured it. When he had left, Espinosa swirled the dark red liquid in his glass and held it up to the light, finally taking a sip. He seemed lost in thought for a moment, then said: "You know, the shoe is on the other foot now. Some day one of our tiny creations will escape from its cage and shortly thereafter we'll have our final war, with humanity pitted against a horde of brainless, mindless microscopic enemies totally without feelings or remorse. And we will lose, Calvin."

He took another sip of wine and let it roll over his tongue. "Oh, it will take a while. The large population centers will be decimated first, then the more remote backwaters. But when it's over, there won't be anybody left alive to deliver a eulogy about the final days of the last human being on Tierra del Fuego." He smiled sadly. "I wonder if the rest of the world will miss us."

Doohan felt uncomfortable. "It doesn't have to be that way."

Espinosa stared thoughtfully into his glass. "No, I don't suppose it does."

But there was no conviction in his voice at all.

RELAX!
SIT DOWN
and Catch Up On Your Reading!

WHAT IF . . .

Fires, floods, air disasters, political intrigue. Events that could happen . . . and do in these exciting bestsellers. Guaranteed to keep you on the edge of your seat.

☐	12245	AIRPORT *Arthur Hailey*	$2.25
☐	10940	BLACK SUNDAY *Thomas Harris*	$2.25
☐	11708	JAWS 2 *Hank Searls*	$2.25
☐	12600	JAWS *Peter Benchley*	$2.50
☐	10888	RAISE THE TITANIC! *Clive Cussler*	$2.25
☐	11766	DELUGE *Richard Doyle*	$2.25
☐	11767	IMPERIAL 109 *Richard Doyle*	$2.50
☐	12679	RUNWAY ZERO-EIGHT *Arthur Hailey*	$2.25
☐	10048	SEVEN DAYS IN MAY *Knebel & Bailey*	$1.95
☐	11631	22 FIRES *Agel & Boe*	$1.95
☐	12520	ICEBERG *Clive Cussler*	$2.25
☐	12302	AVALANCHE *Robert Weverka*	$1.95
☐	12151	ICE! *Arnold Federbush*	$2.25

Buy them at your local bookstore or use this handy coupon for ordering:

Bantam Book Catalog

Here's your up-to-the-minute listing of over 1,400 titles by your favorite authors.

This illustrated, large format catalog gives a description of each title. For your convenience, it is divided into categories in fiction and non-fiction—gothics, science fiction, westerns, mysteries, cookbooks, mysticism and occult, biographies, history, family living, health, psychology, art.

So don't delay—take advantage of this special opportunity to increase your reading pleasure.

Just send us your name and address and 50¢ (to help defray postage and handling costs).